Black is for Beginnings

Laurie faria Stolarz

Adaptation by Barbara Randall Kesel
Artwork by Janina Görrissen

flux™
Woodbury, Minnesota

Also by Laurie Faria Stolarz

Blue is for Nightmares
White is for Magic
Silver is for Secrets
Red is for Remembrance

For Andrew Karre,
Janina Görrissen,
and the BifN fans

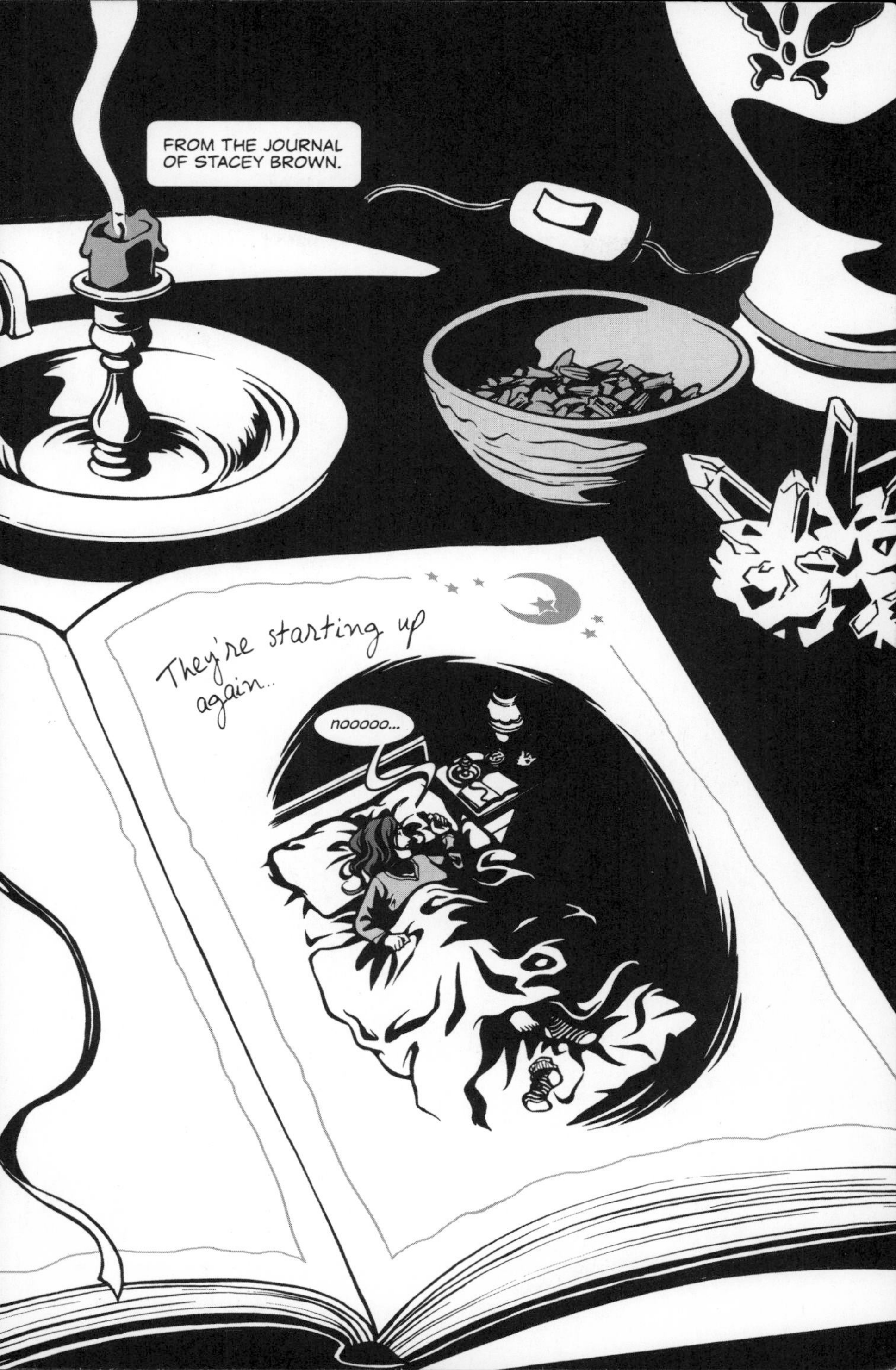
FROM THE JOURNAL OF STACEY BROWN.
They're starting up again...
nooooo...

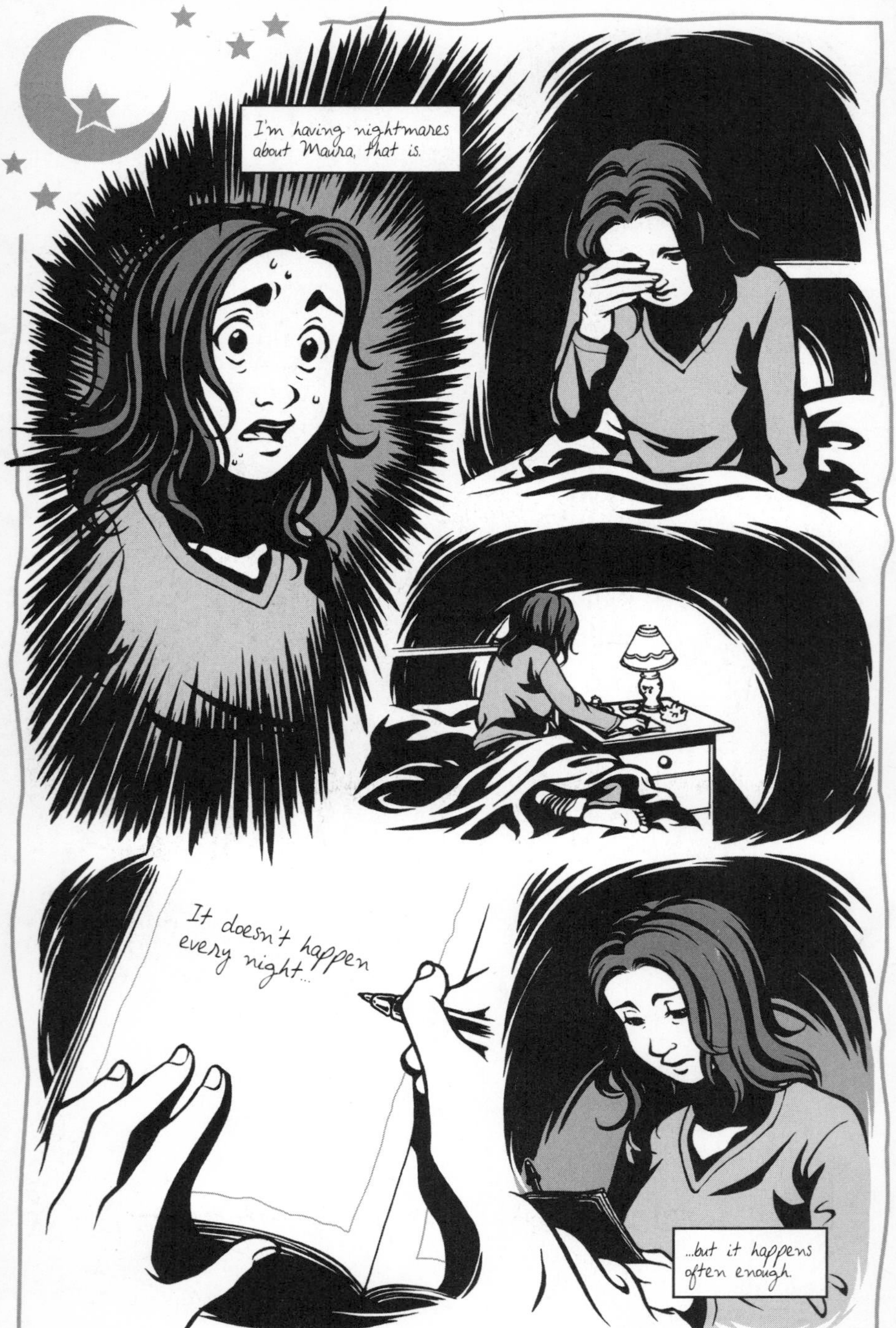
I'm having nightmares about Maura, that is.
It doesn't happen every night...
...but it happens often enough.

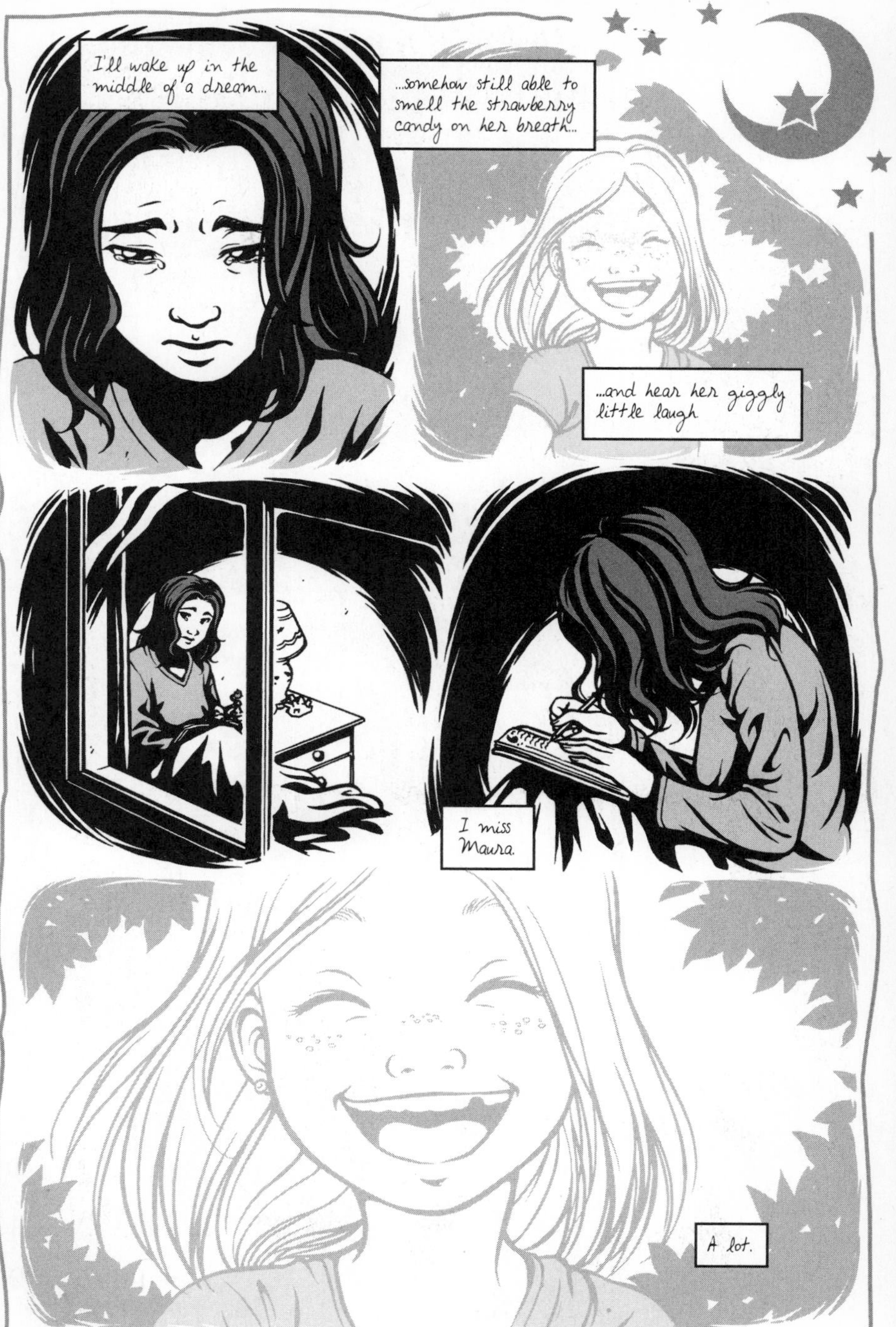
I'll wake up in the middle of a dream...
...somehow still able to smell the strawberry candy on her breath...
...and hear her giggly little laugh
I miss Maura.
A lot.

A Pouch Spell for Sweet Dreams

Ingredients:
Jasmine incense, 2 teaspoons of vanilla extract, the peel of one orange, a sprinkling of cinnamon, and a handful of dried lavender buds taken from the branches

Directions:
Combine ingredients inside a moon-bathed bowl and stir until well blended. Pour mixture into a plain cloth pouch and knot the opening. Hold the pouch and its contents toward the moon, and speak these words:

"May this magical pouch give me peace while I sleep. May my dreams be serene, and may it be bliss that I reap. Blessed be the way."

One week ago.
The thing is, even though the dreams I have about her scare me awake, I know they're not really nightmarish at all...
At least, not on the surface.
Two nights ago.
And no, I don't think I'm having these dreams because I still blame myself for what happened to her-
Almost six years ago now.
It's just that sometimes even the sweetest of memories can have a haunting effect-
Especially when they creep up in our sleep.
Two weeks ago.
And so, I do spells to try and counter the haunting effect of my nightmares.
Like my pouch spell for sweet dreams.
May this magical pouch give me peace...

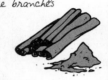

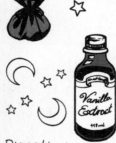

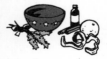

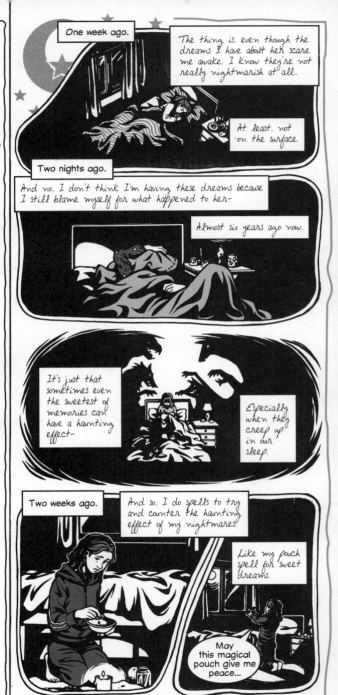

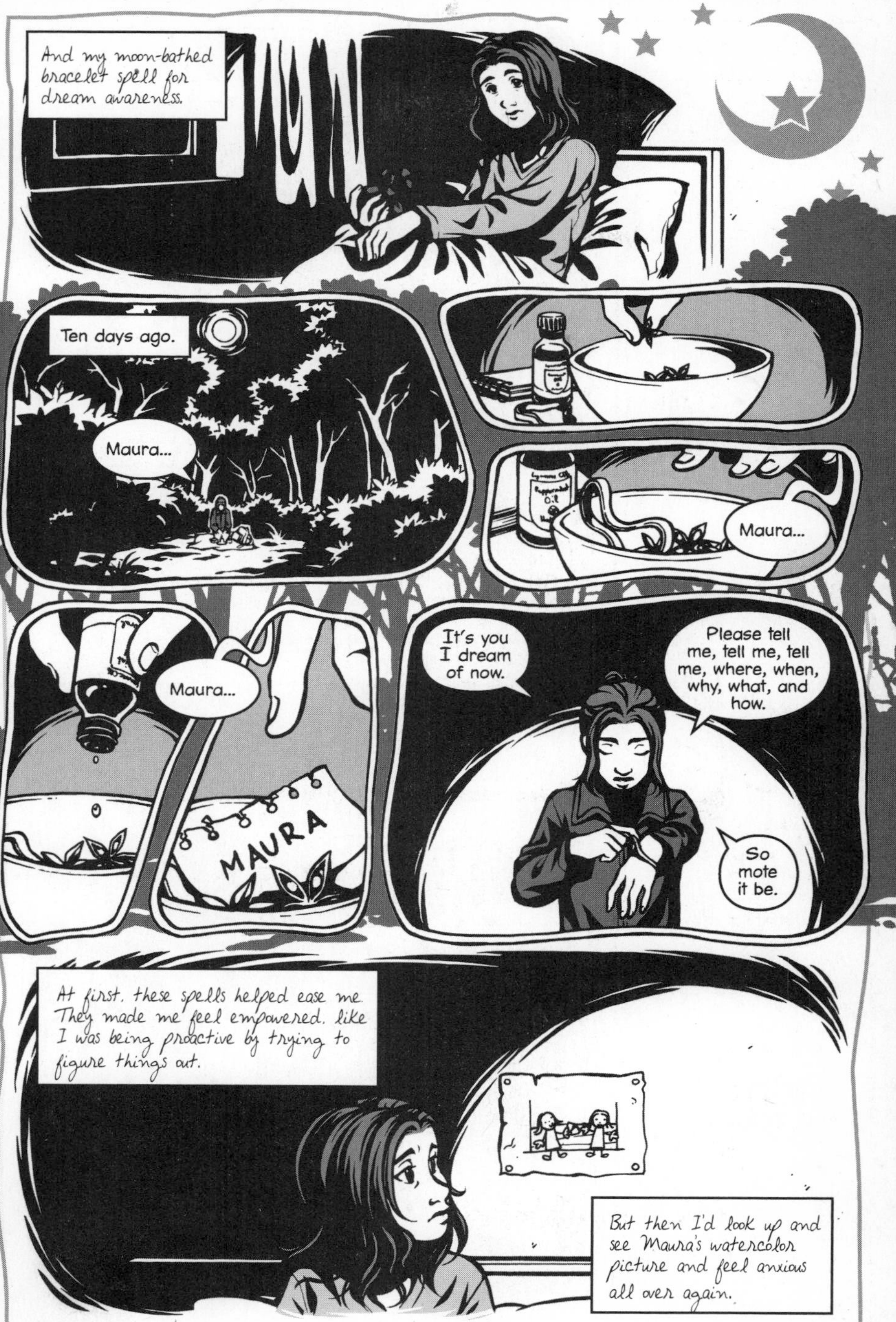

And my moon-bathed bracelet spell for dream awareness.
Ten days ago.
Maura...
Maura...
Maura...
MAURA
It's you I dream of now.
Please tell me, tell me, tell me, where, when, why, what, and how.
So mote it be.
At first, these spells helped ease me. They made me feel empowered, like I was being proactive by trying to figure things out.
But then I'd look up and see Maura's watercolor picture and feel anxious all over again.

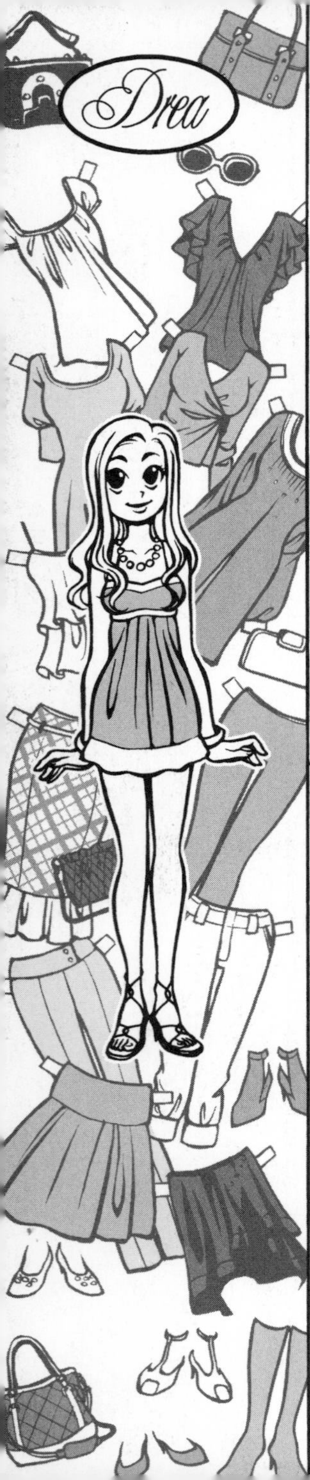
Drea

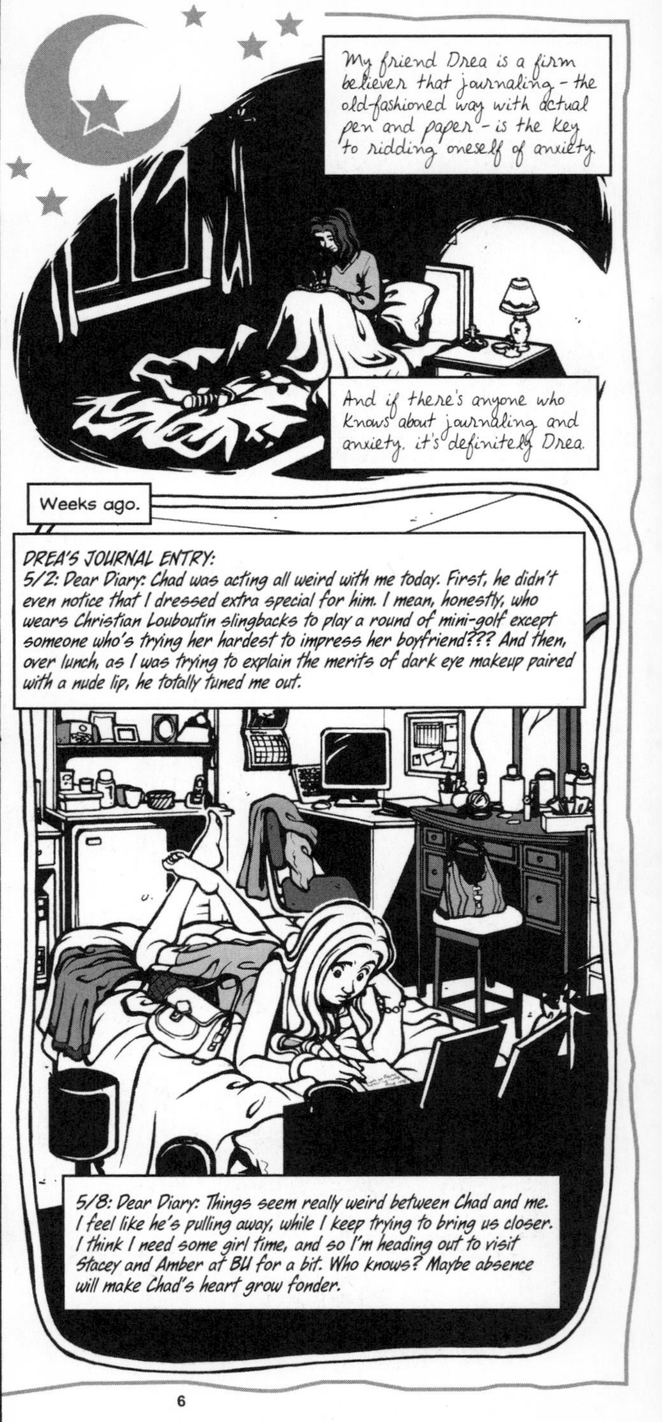
My friend Drea is a firm believer that journaling - the old-fashioned way with actual pen and paper - is the key to ridding oneself of anxiety.
And if there's anyone who knows about journaling and anxiety, it's definitely Drea.
Weeks ago.
DREA'S JOURNAL ENTRY:
5/2: Dear Diary: Chad was acting all weird with me today. First, he didn't even notice that I dressed extra special for him. I mean, honestly, who wears Christian Louboutin slingbacks to play a round of mini-golf except someone who's trying her hardest to impress her boyfriend??? And then, over lunch, as I was trying to explain the merits of dark eye makeup paired with a nude lip, he totally tuned me out.
5/8: Dear Diary: Things seem really weird between Chad and me. I feel like he's pulling away, while I keep trying to bring us closer. I think I need some girl time, and so I'm heading out to visit Stacey and Amber at BU for a bit. Who knows? Maybe absence will make Chad's heart grow fonder.

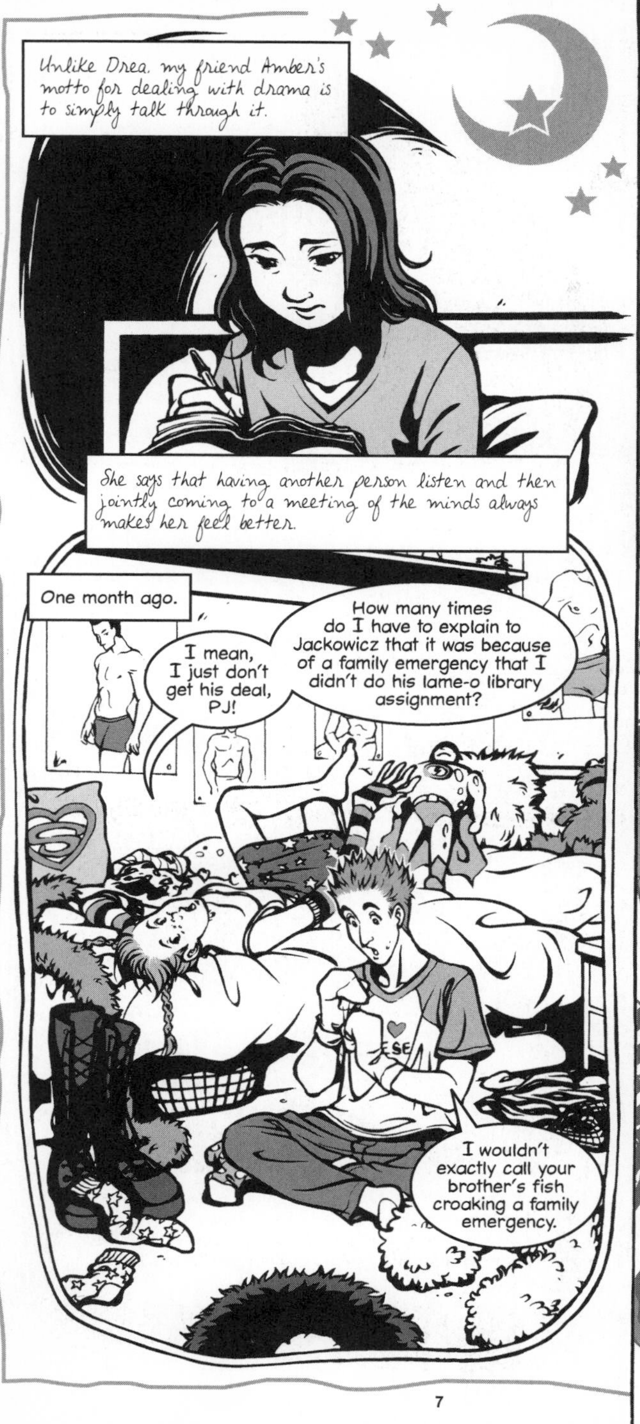

Unlike Drea, my friend Amber's motto for dealing with drama is to simply talk through it.
She says that having another person listen and then jointly coming to a meeting of the minds always makes her feel better.
One month ago.
I mean, I just don't get his deal, PJ!
How many times do I have to explain to Jackowicz that it was because of a family emergency that I didn't do his lame-o library assignment?
I wouldn't exactly call your brother's fish croaking a family emergency.

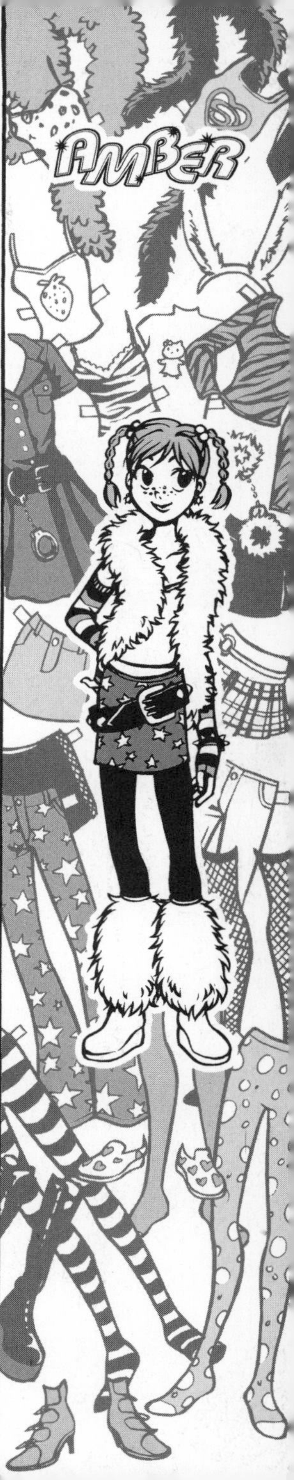

AMBER

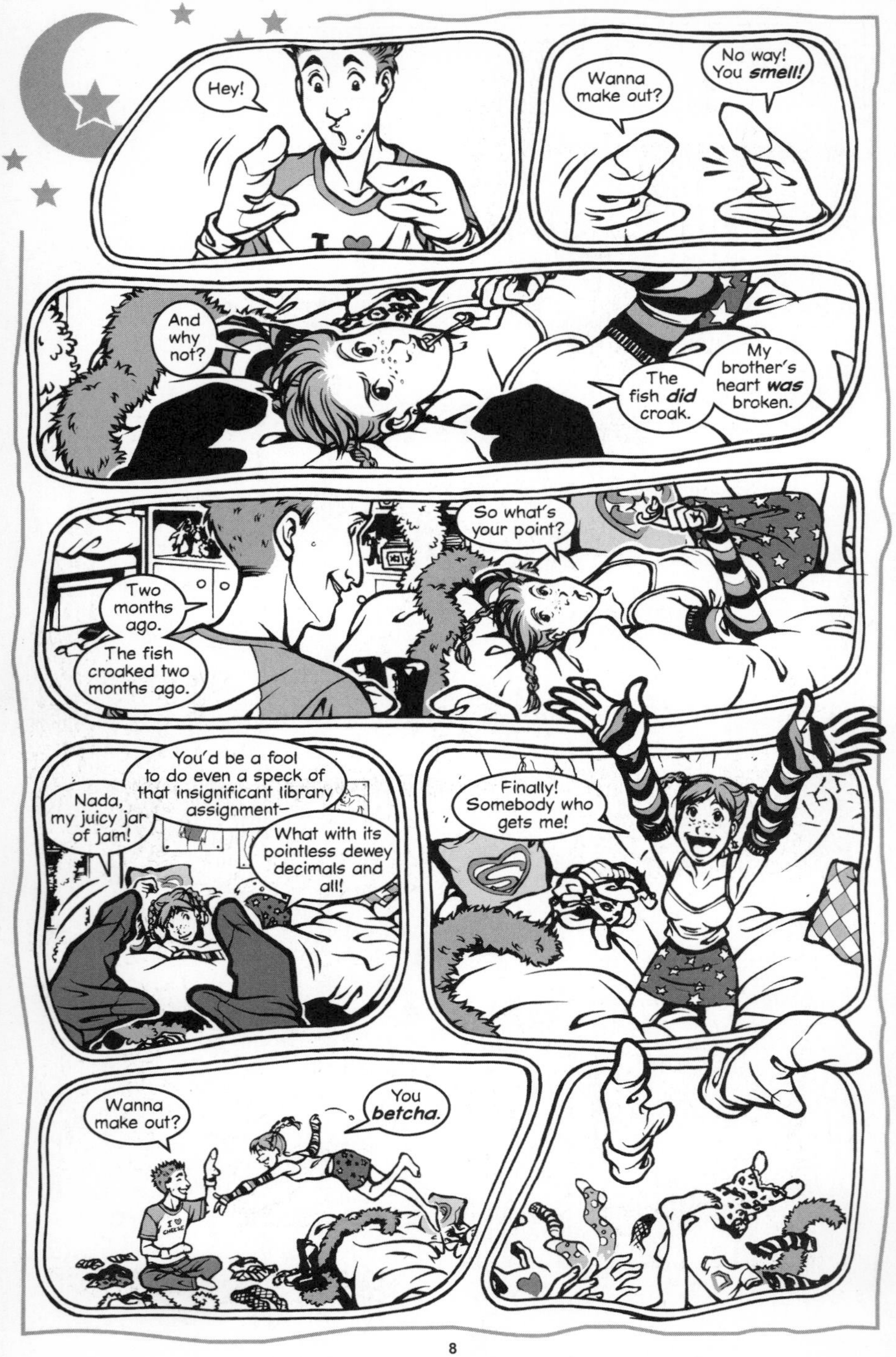
Hey!
Wanna make out?
No way! You **smell!**
And why not?
The fish **did** croak.
My brother's heart **was** broken.
So what's your point?
Two months ago.
The fish croaked two months ago.
Nada, my juicy jar of jam!
You'd be a fool to do even a speck of that insignificant library assignment–
What with its pointless dewey decimals and all!
Finally! Somebody who gets me!
Wanna make out?
You **betcha.**

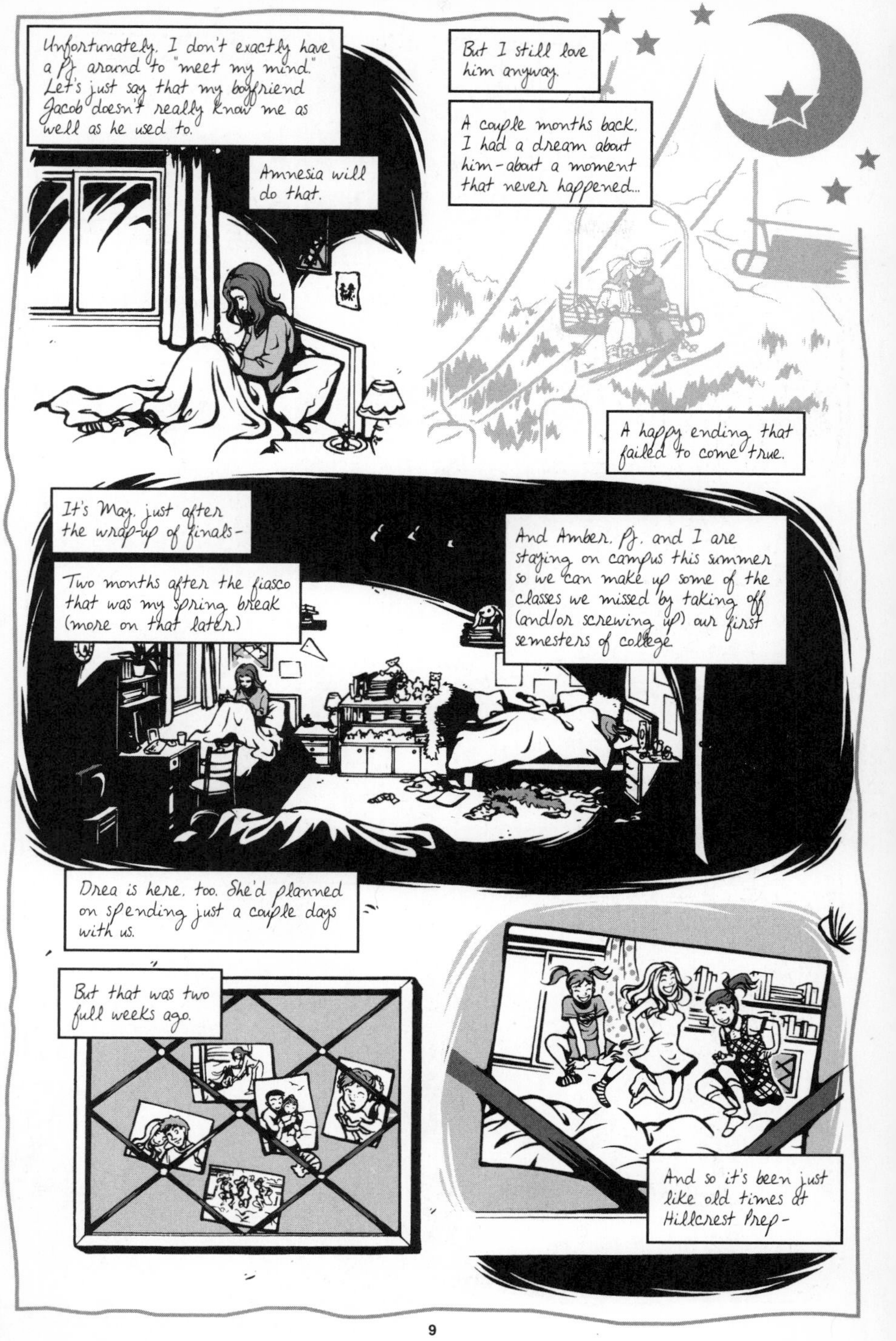
Unfortunately, I don't exactly have a PJ around to "meet my mind." Let's just say that my boyfriend Jacob doesn't really know me as well as he used to.
Amnesia will do that.
But I still love him anyway.
A couple months back, I had a dream about him-about a moment that never happened...
A happy ending that failed to come true.
It's May, just after the wrap-up of finals-
Two months after the fiasco that was my spring break (more on that later.)
And Amber, PJ, and I are staying on campus this summer so we can make up some of the classes we missed by taking off (and/or screwing up) our first semesters of college.
Drea is here, too. She'd planned on spending just a couple days with us.
But that was two full weeks ago.
And so it's been just like old times at Hillcrest Prep-

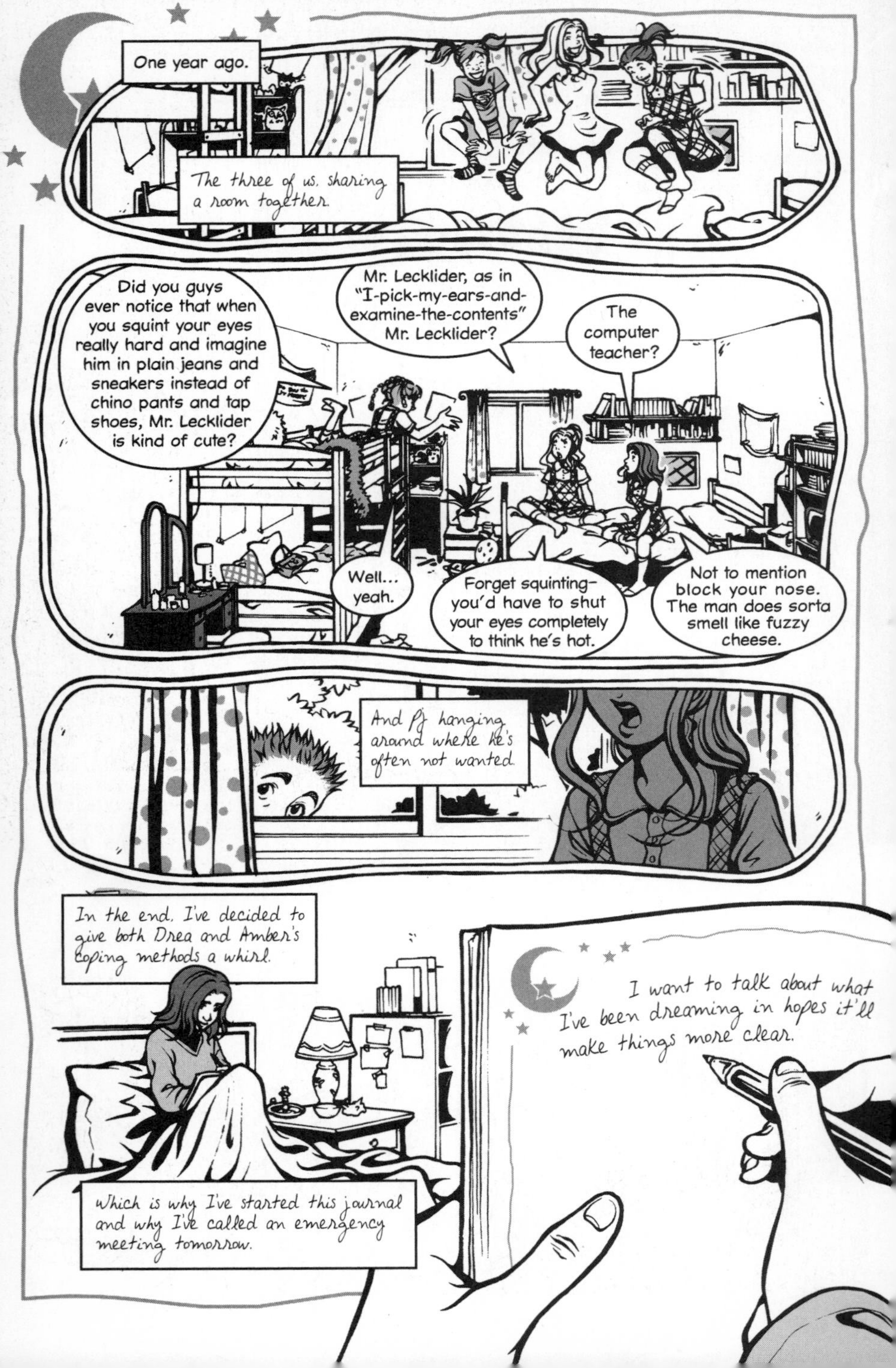
One year ago.
The three of us, sharing a room together.
Did you guys ever notice that when you squint your eyes really hard and imagine him in plain jeans and sneakers instead of chino pants and tap shoes, Mr. Lecklider is kind of cute?
Mr. Lecklider, as in "I-pick-my-ears-and-examine-the-contents" Mr. Lecklider?
The computer teacher?
Well... yeah.
Forget squinting–you'd have to shut your eyes completely to think he's hot.
Not to mention block your nose. The man does sorta smell like fuzzy cheese.
And PJ hanging around where he's often not wanted.
In the end, I've decided to give both Drea and Amber's coping methods a whirl.
I want to talk about what I've been dreaming in hopes it'll make things more clear.
Which is why I've started this journal and why I've called an emergency meeting tomorrow.

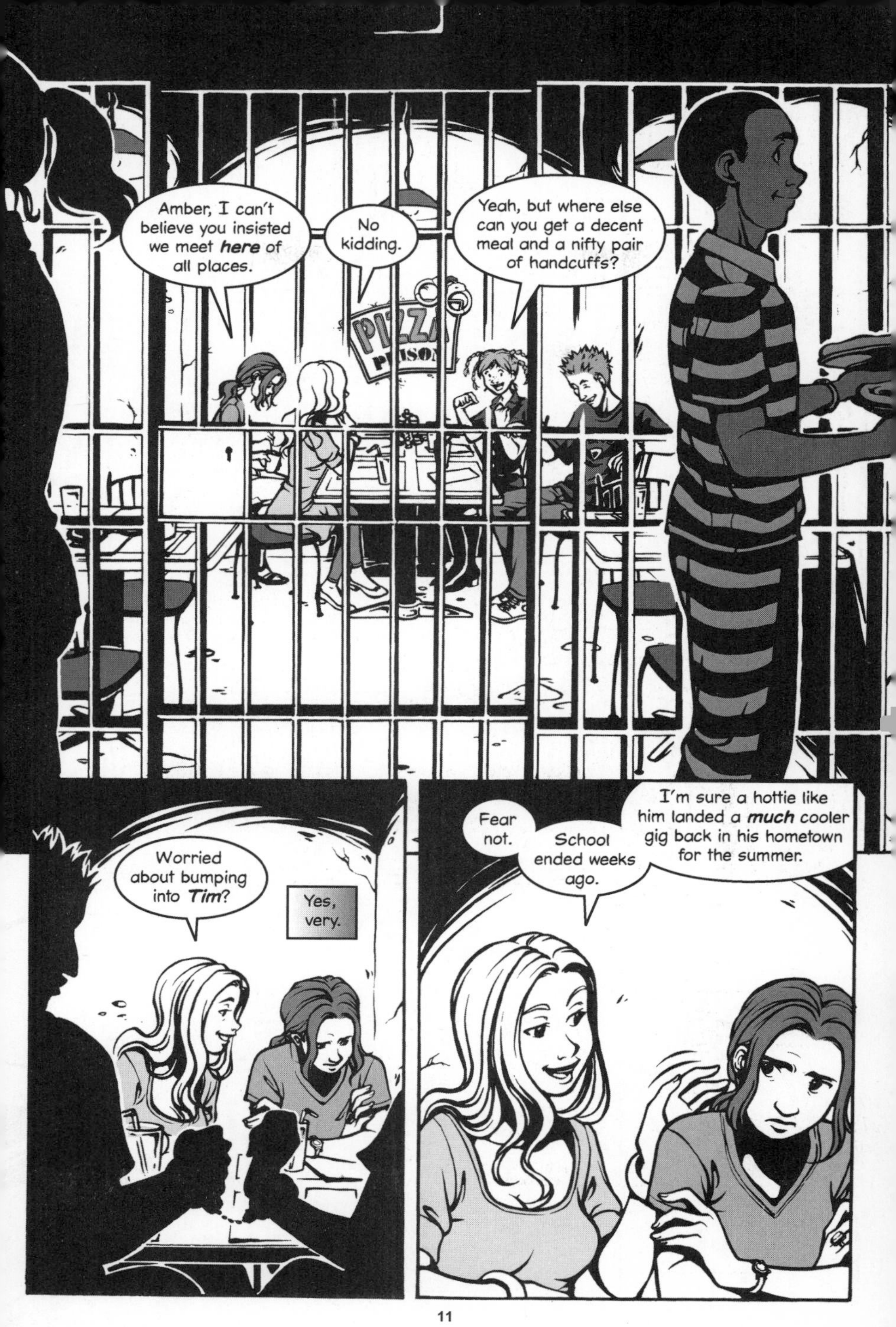
Amber, I can't believe you insisted we meet *here* of all places.
No kidding.
Yeah, but where else can you get a decent meal and a nifty pair of handcuffs?
PIZZA PRISON
Worried about bumping into *Tim*?
Yes, very.
Fear not.
School ended weeks ago.
I'm sure a hottie like him landed a *much* cooler gig back in his hometown for the summer.

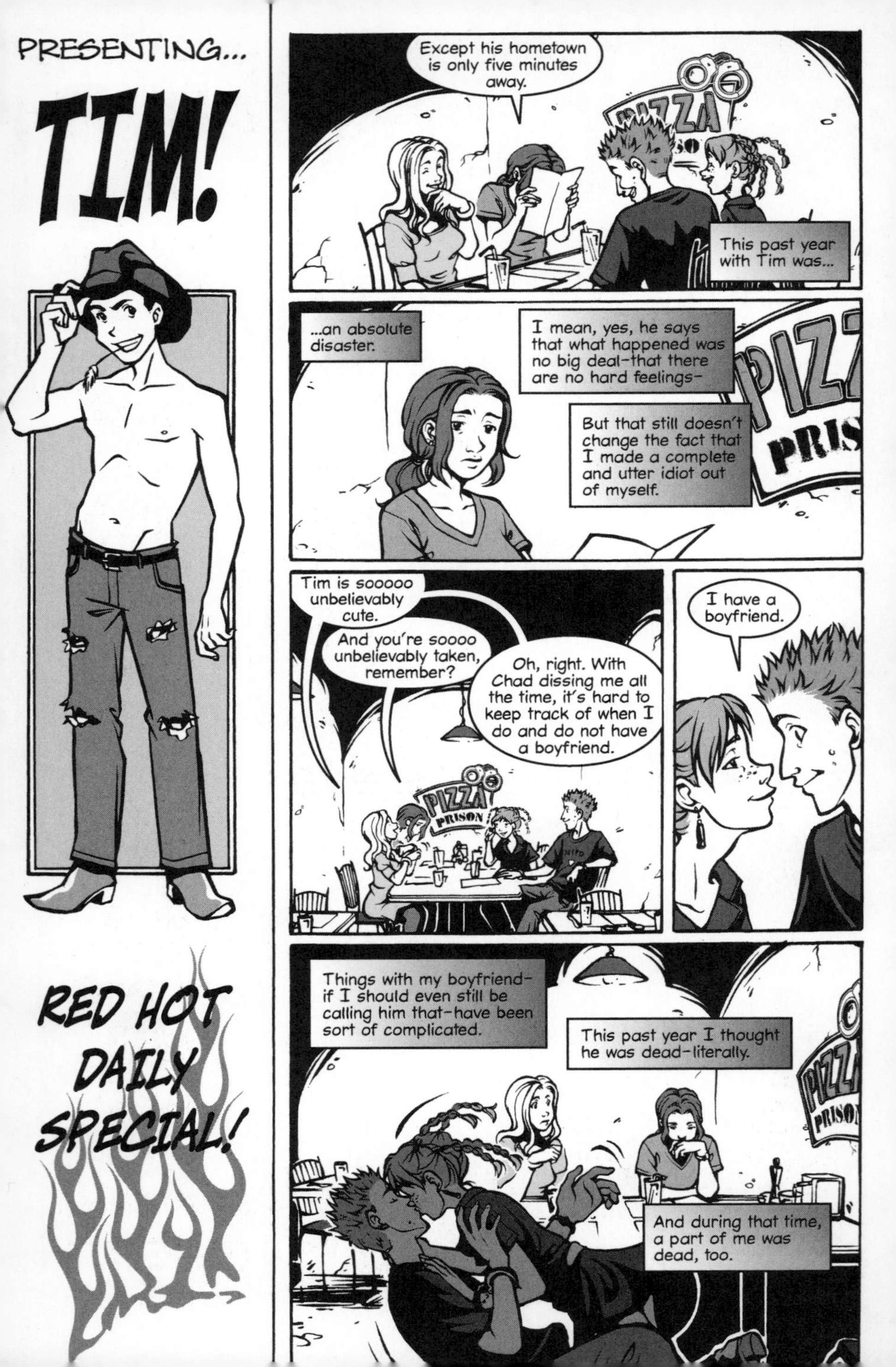
PRESENTING...
TIM!
RED HOT DAILY SPECIAL!
Except his hometown is only five minutes away.
PIZZA
This past year with Tim was...
...an absolute disaster.
I mean, yes, he says that what happened was no big deal—that there are no hard feelings—
But that still doesn't change the fact that I made a complete and utter idiot out of myself.
PIZZA PRIS
Tim is sooooo unbelievably cute.
And you're soooo unbelievably taken, remember?
Oh, right. With Chad dissing me all the time, it's hard to keep track of when I do and do not have a boyfriend.
PIZZA PRISON
I have a boyfriend.
Things with my boyfriend—if I should even still be calling him that—have been sort of complicated.
This past year I thought he was dead—literally.
And during that time, a part of me was dead, too.
PIZZA PRISON

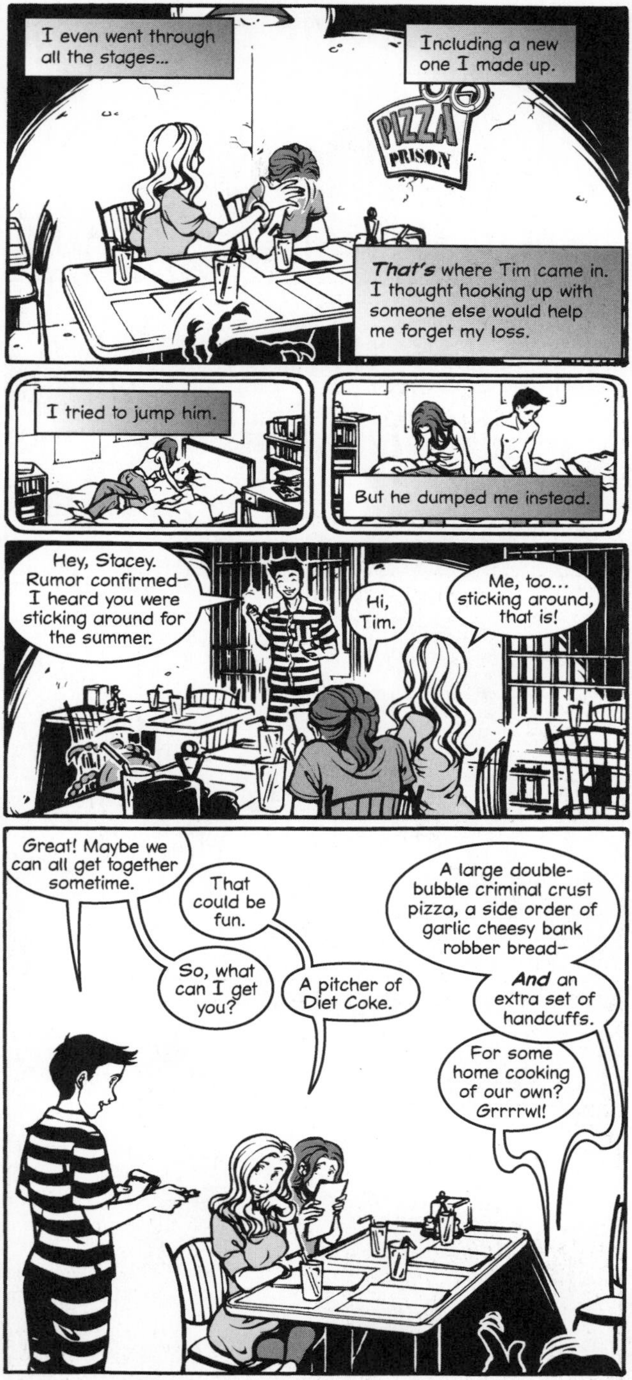
I even went through all the stages...
Including a new one I made up.
PIZZA PRISON
That's where Tim came in. I thought hooking up with someone else would help me forget my loss.
I tried to jump him.
But he dumped me instead.
Hey, Stacey. Rumor confirmed– I heard you were sticking around for the summer.
Hi, Tim.
Me, too... sticking around, that is!
Great! Maybe we can all get together sometime.
That could be fun.
So, what can I get you?
A pitcher of Diet Coke.
A large double-bubble criminal crust pizza, a side order of garlic cheesy bank robber bread–
And an extra set of handcuffs.
For some home cooking of our own? Grrrrwl!

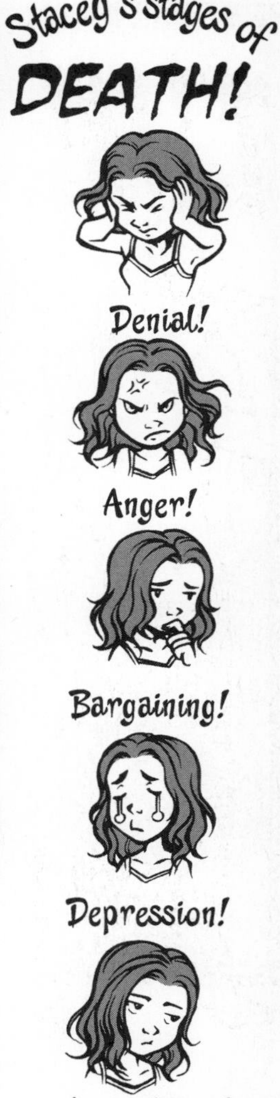
Stacey's stages of
DEATH!
Denial!
Anger!
Bargaining!
Depression!
Acceptance!
and introducing...
DESPERATE LUST!

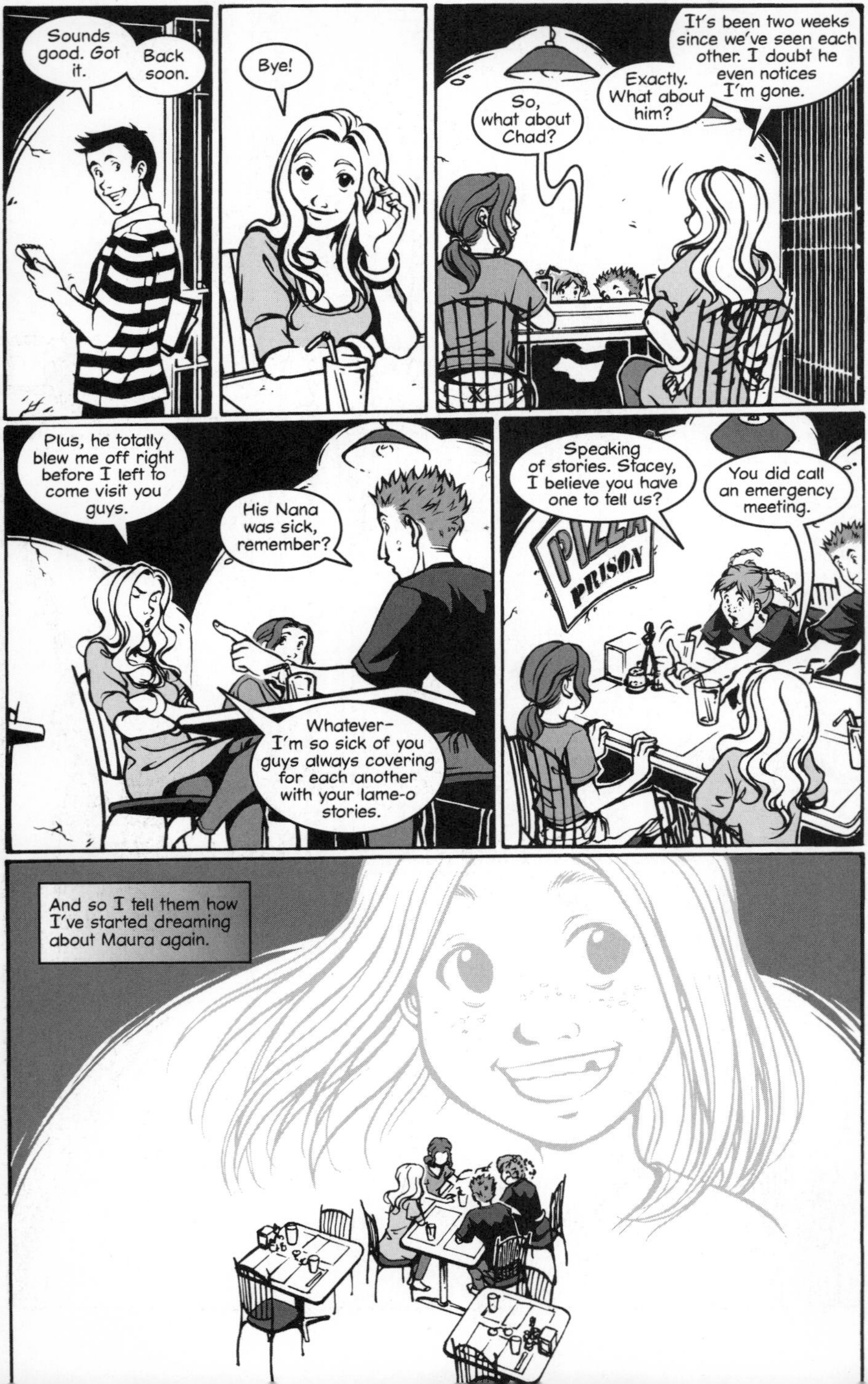
Sounds good. Got it.
Back soon.
Bye!
So, what about Chad?
Exactly. What about him?
It's been two weeks since we've seen each other. I doubt he even notices I'm gone.
Plus, he totally blew me off right before I left to come visit you guys.
His Nana was sick, remember?
Whatever– I'm so sick of you guys always covering for each another with your lame-o stories.
Speaking of stories. Stacey, I believe you have one to tell us?
You did call an emergency meeting.
PIZZA PRISON
And so I tell them how I've started dreaming about Maura again.

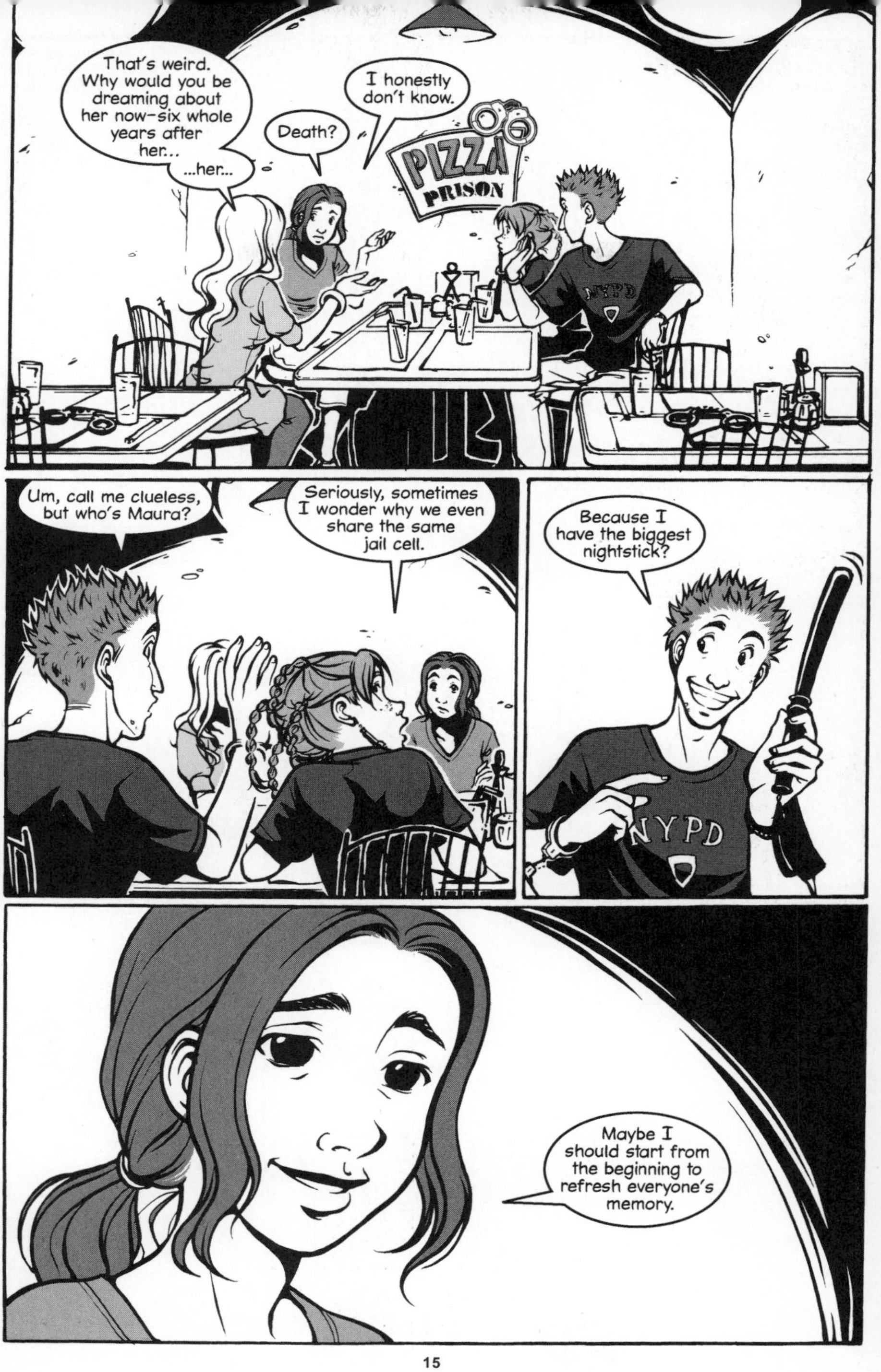
That's weird. Why would you be dreaming about her now–six whole years after her...
...her...
Death?
I honestly don't know.
PIZZA PRISON
NYPD
Um, call me clueless, but who's Maura?
Seriously, sometimes I wonder why we even share the same jail cell.
Because I have the biggest nightstick?
NYPD
Maybe I should start from the beginning to refresh everyone's memory.

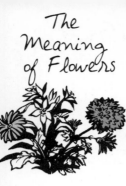

The Meaning of Flowers

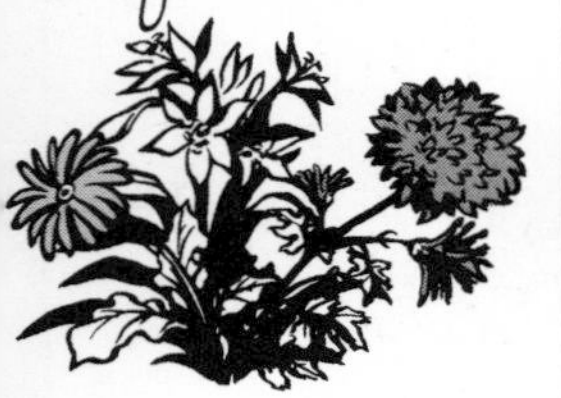

Lilies - Death

Chrysanthemums - Truth

Daisies - Purity

Roses - Love

Irises - Friendship

Lilacs - Openness

Violets - Deceit

Pansies - Thoughtfulness

Yarrows - Healing

Zinnias - Affection

Sweet Basil - Luck

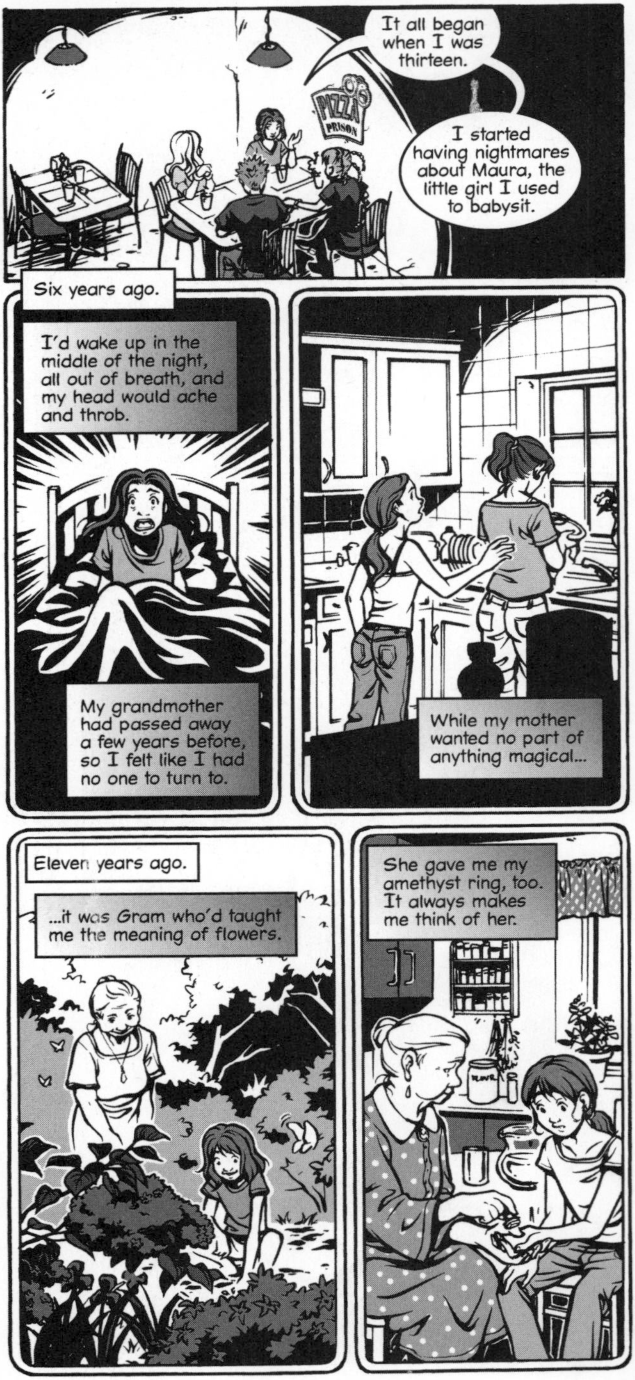
It all began when I was thirteen.
PIZZA PRISON
I started having nightmares about Maura, the little girl I used to babysit.
Six years ago.
I'd wake up in the middle of the night, all out of breath, and my head would ache and throb.
My grandmother had passed away a few years before, so I felt like I had no one to turn to.
While my mother wanted no part of anything magical...
Eleven years ago.
...it was Gram who'd taught me the meaning of flowers.
She gave me my amethyst ring, too. It always makes me think of her.

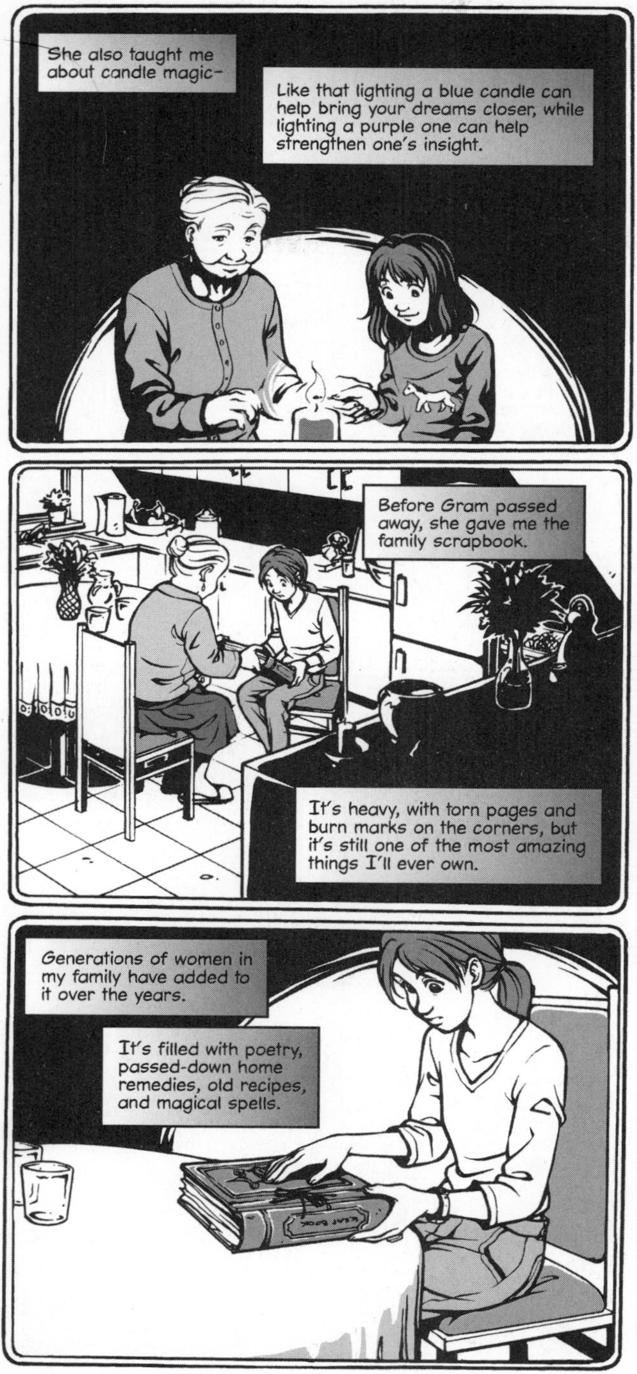
She also taught me about candle magic–
Like that lighting a blue candle can help bring your dreams closer, while lighting a purple one can help strengthen one's insight.
Before Gram passed away, she gave me the family scrapbook.
It's heavy, with torn pages and burn marks on the corners, but it's still one of the most amazing things I'll ever own.
Generations of women in my family have added to it over the years.
It's filled with poetry, passed-down home remedies, old recipes, and magical spells.

Candle magic

Red: strength, remembrance

Blue: dreams, nightmares

Black: new beginnings

Purple: spirit, insight

Orange: friendship

White: magic

Yellow: clarity

Brown: intuition

Pink: affection

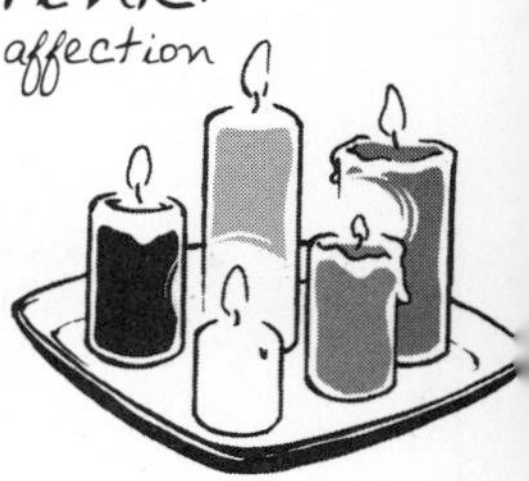

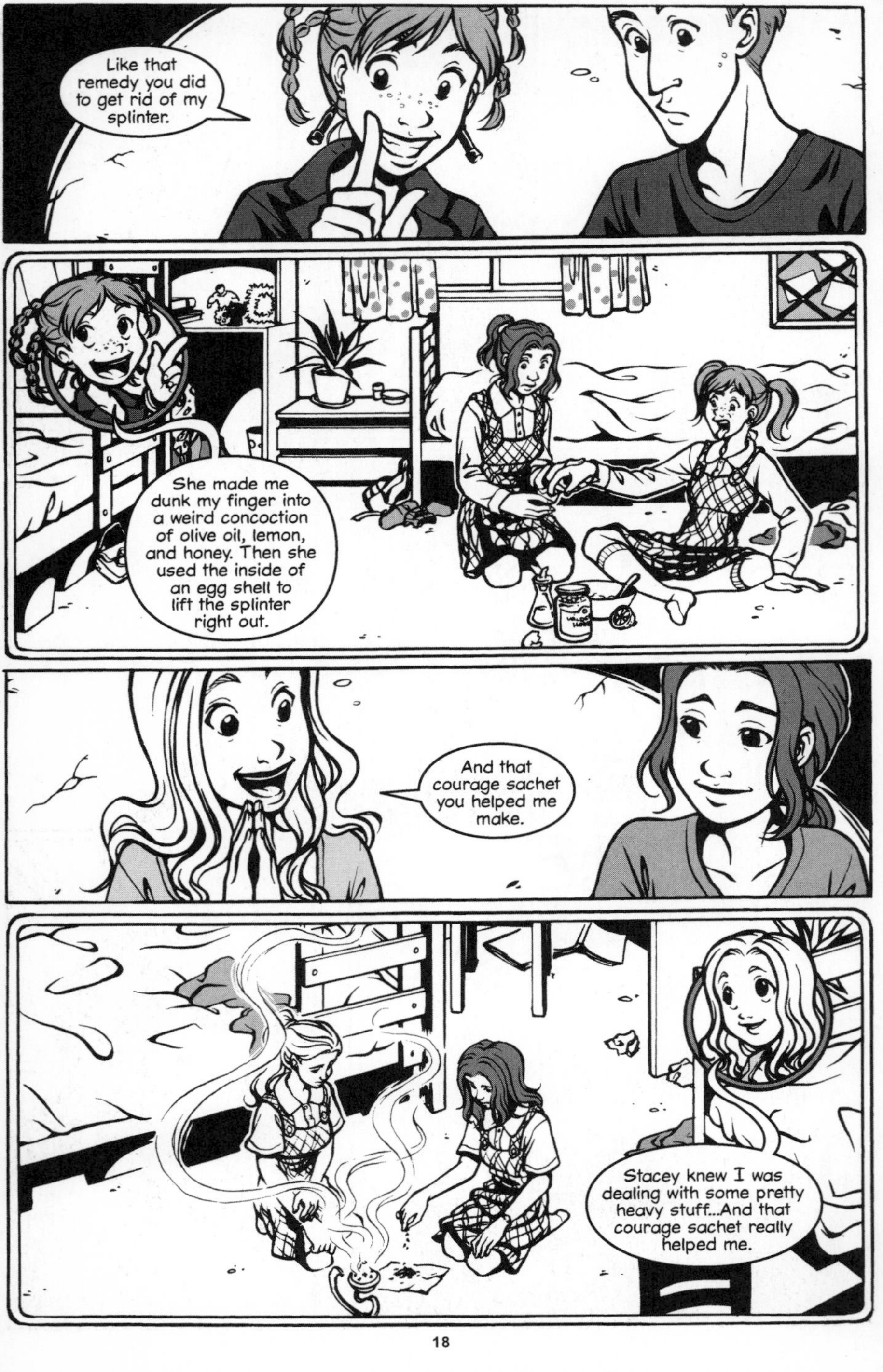
Like that remedy you did to get rid of my splinter.
She made me dunk my finger into a weird concoction of olive oil, lemon, and honey. Then she used the inside of an egg shell to lift the splinter right out.
And that courage sachet you helped me make.
Stacey knew I was dealing with some pretty heavy stuff...And that courage sachet really helped me.

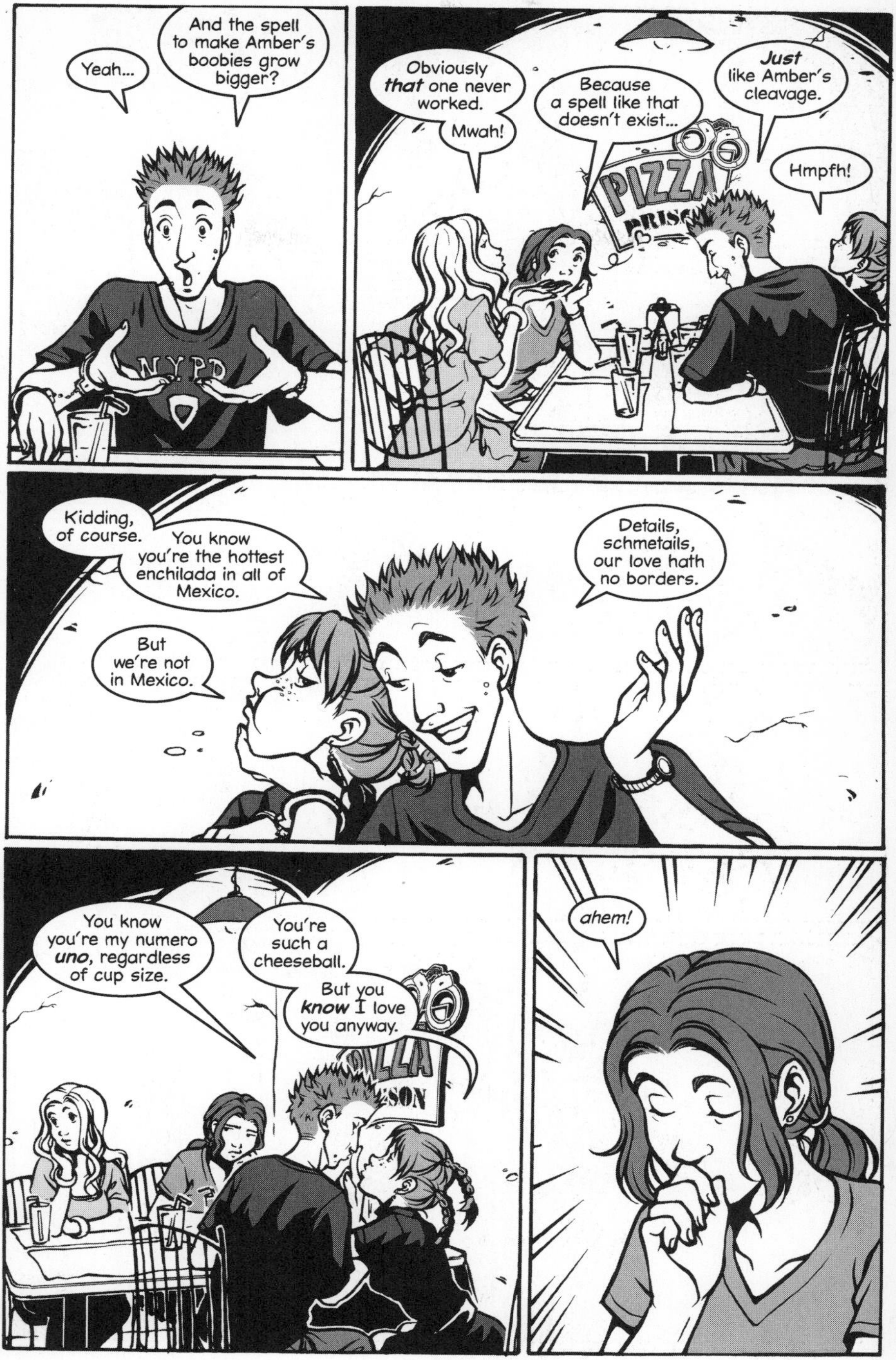
Yeah...
And the spell to make Amber's boobies grow bigger?
Obviously *that* one never worked.
Mwah!
Because a spell like that doesn't exist...
Just like Amber's cleavage.
Hmpfh!
PIZZA PRISON
Kidding, of course.
You know you're the hottest enchilada in all of Mexico.
Details, schmetails, our love hath no borders.
But we're not in Mexico.
You know you're my numero *uno*, regardless of cup size.
You're such a cheeseball.
But you *know* I love you anyway.
ahem!

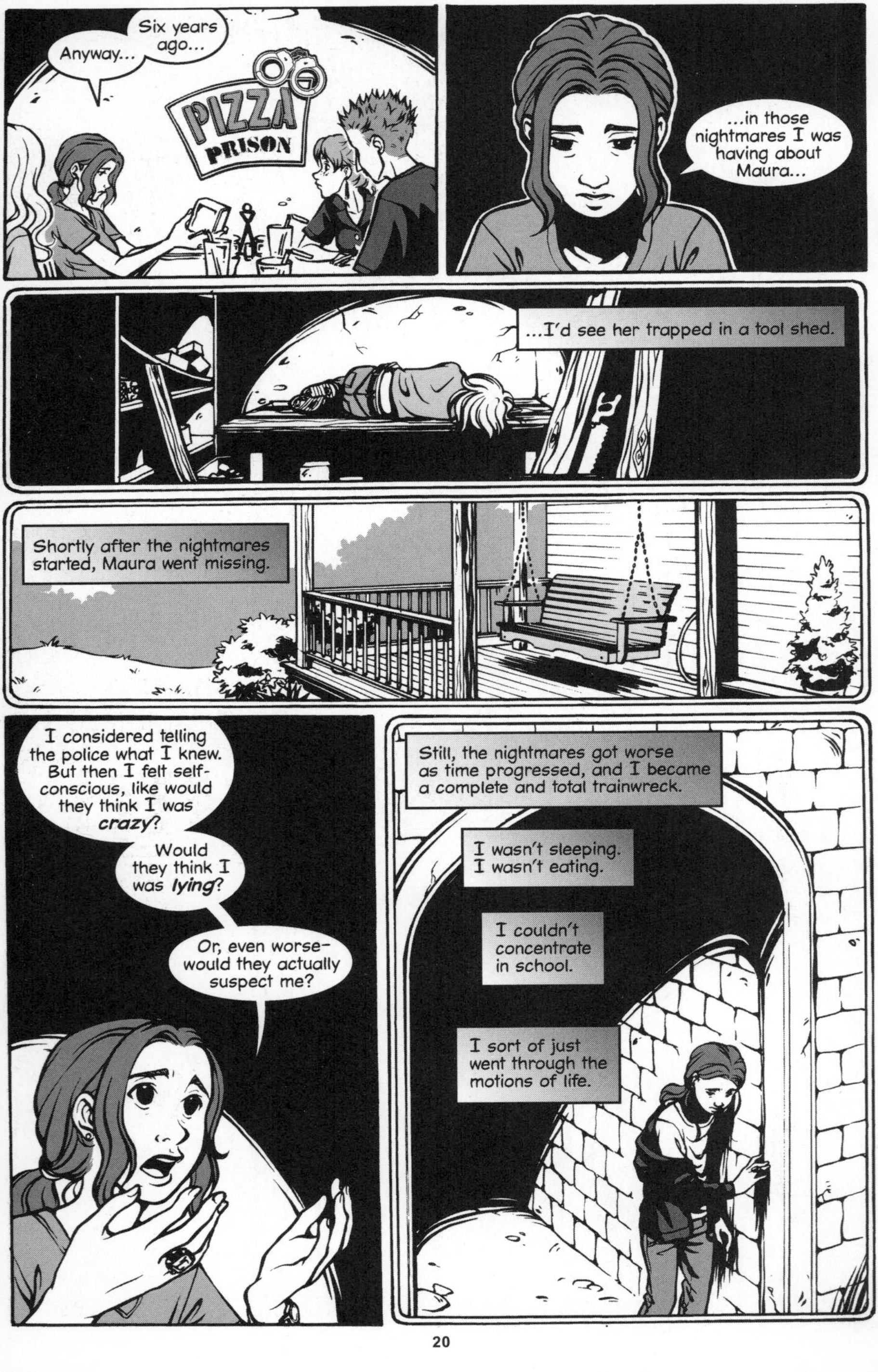
Anyway...
Six years ago...
PIZZA PRISON
...in those nightmares I was having about Maura...
...I'd see her trapped in a tool shed.
Shortly after the nightmares started, Maura went missing.
I considered telling the police what I knew. But then I felt self-conscious, like would they think I was crazy?
Would they think I was lying?
Or, even worse-would they actually suspect me?
Still, the nightmares got worse as time progressed, and I became a complete and total trainwreck.
I wasn't sleeping. I wasn't eating.
I couldn't concentrate in school.
I sort of just went through the motions of life.

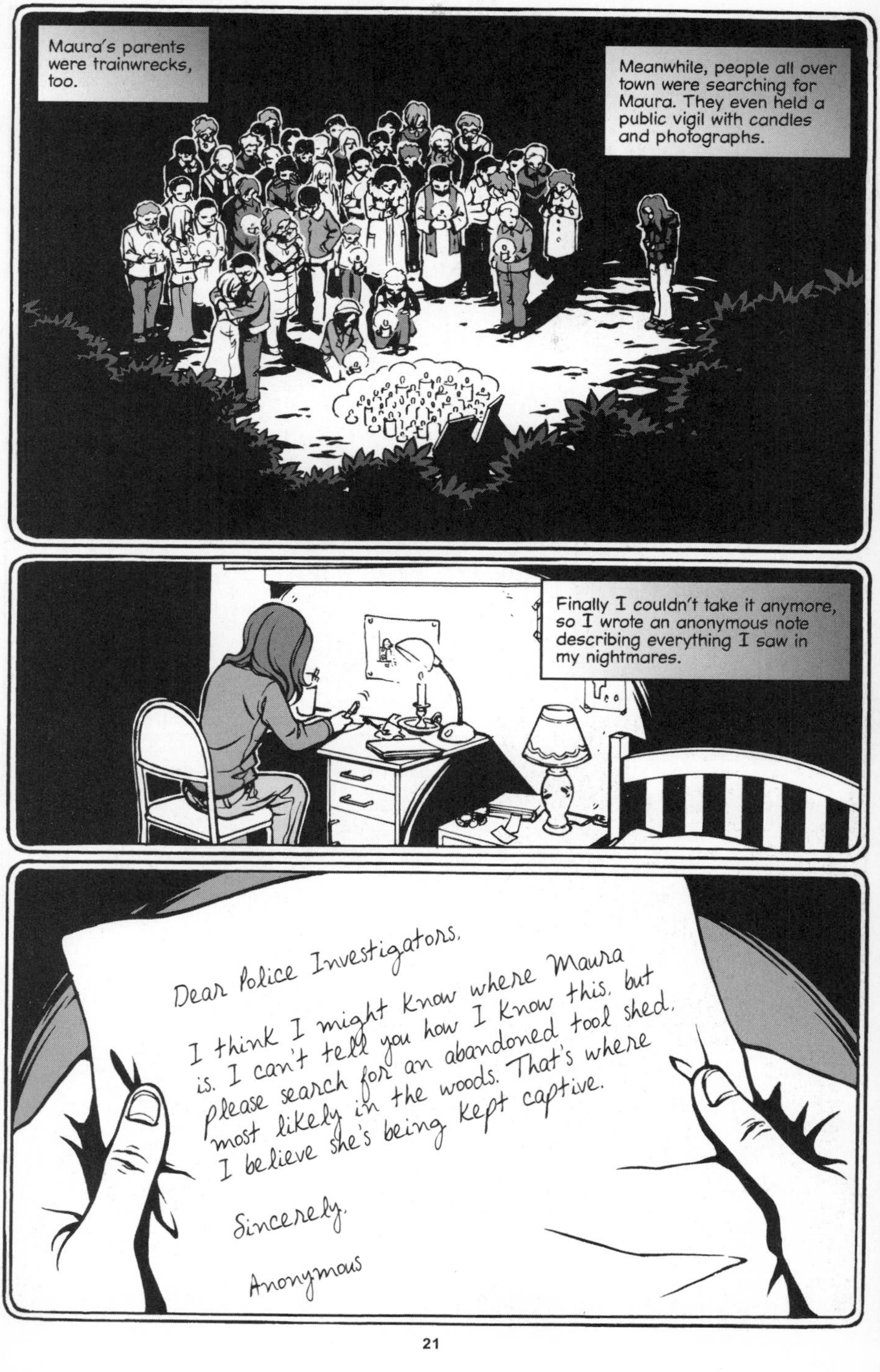
Maura's parents were trainwrecks, too.
Meanwhile, people all over town were searching for Maura. They even held a public vigil with candles and photographs.
Finally I couldn't take it anymore, so I wrote an anonymous note describing everything I saw in my nightmares.
Dear Police Investigators,
I think I might know where Maura is. I can't tell you how I know this, but please search for an abandoned tool shed, most likely in the woods. That's where I believe she's being kept captive.
Sincerely,
Anonymous

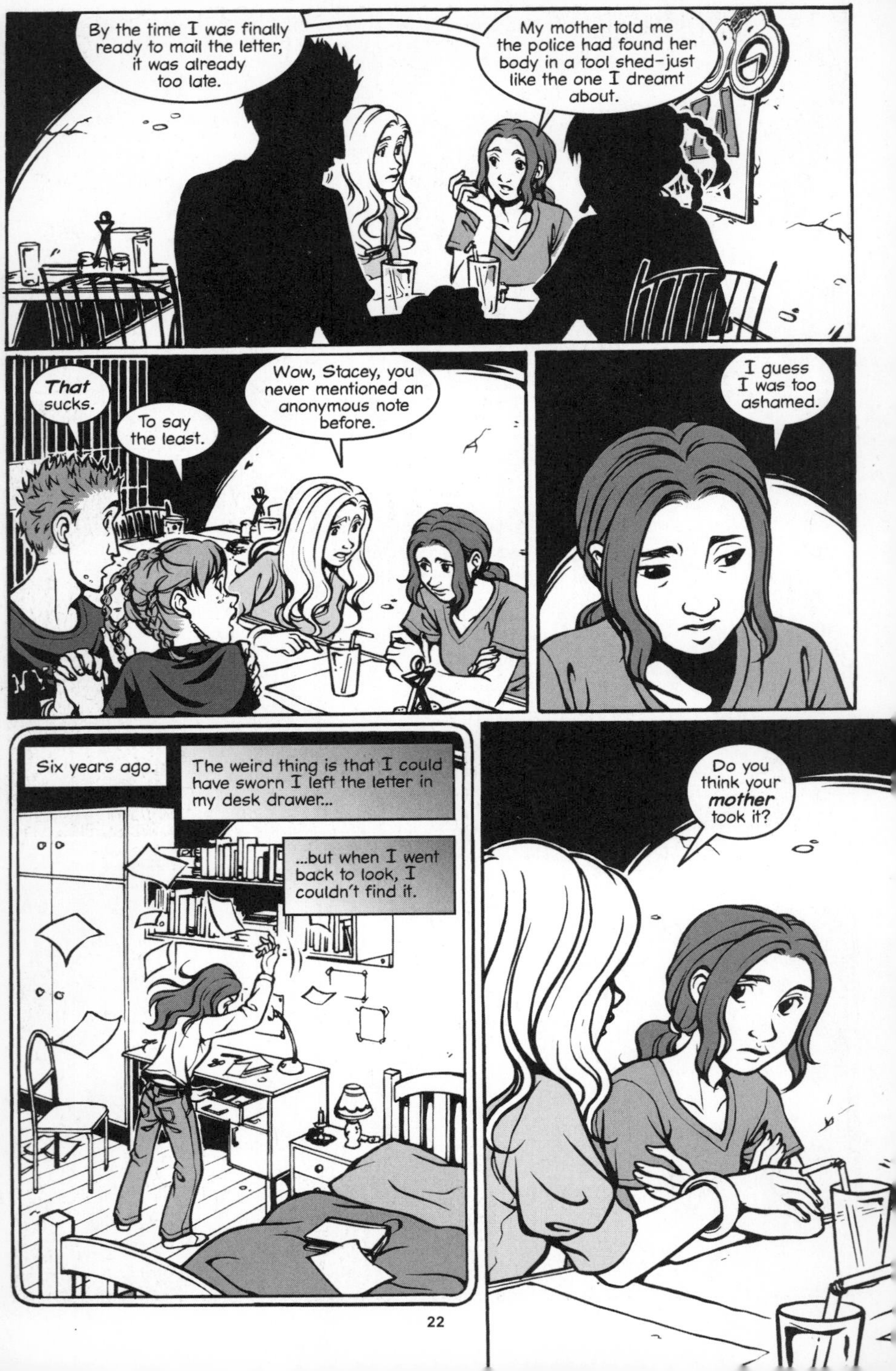

By the time I was finally ready to mail the letter, it was already too late.
My mother told me the police had found her body in a tool shed—just like the one I dreamt about.
That sucks.
To say the least.
Wow, Stacey, you never mentioned an anonymous note before.
I guess I was too ashamed.
Six years ago.
The weird thing is that I could have sworn I left the letter in my desk drawer...
...but when I went back to look, I couldn't find it.
Do you think your ***mother*** took it?

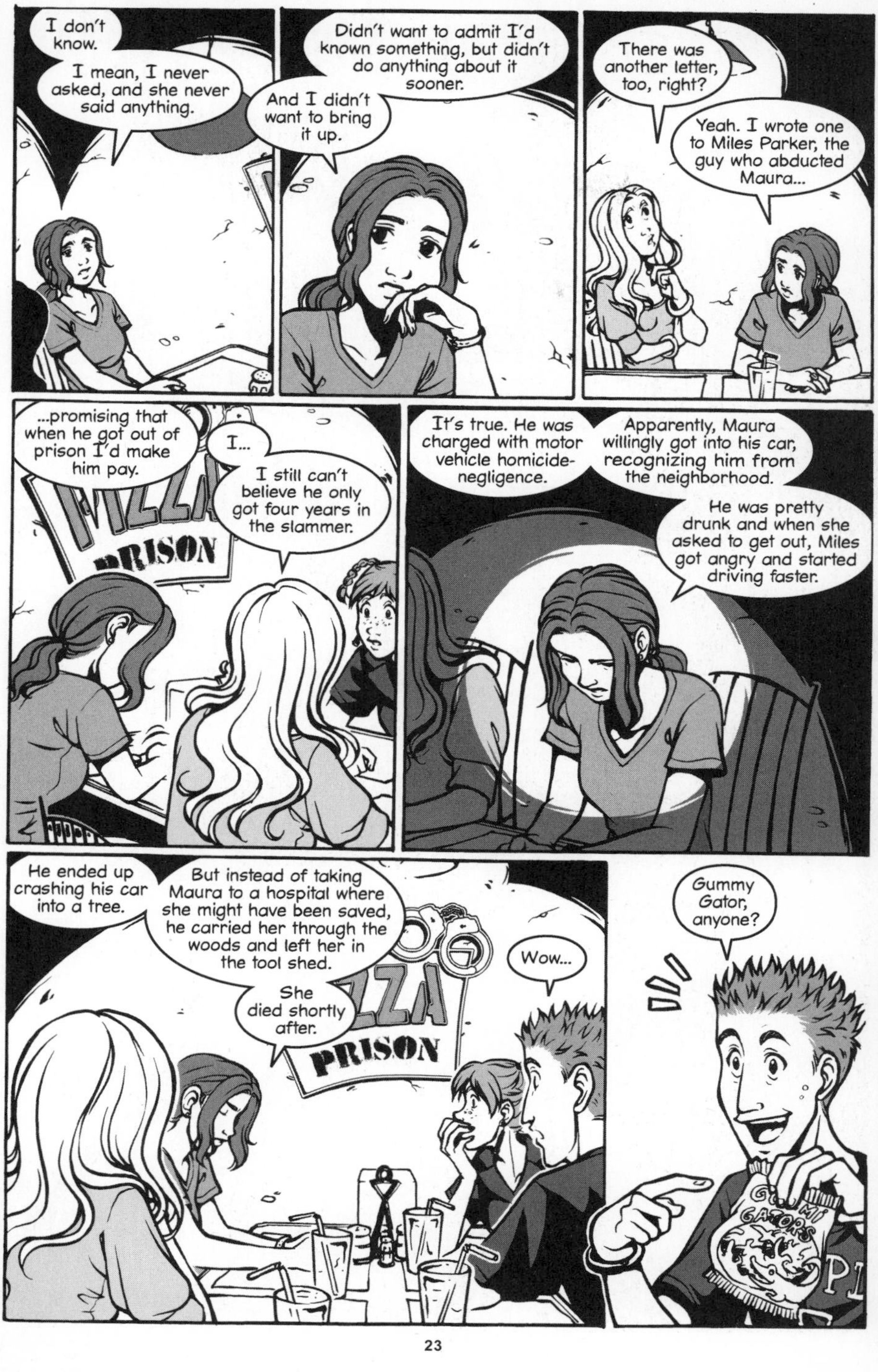
I don't know.
I mean, I never asked, and she never said anything.
Didn't want to admit I'd known something, but didn't do anything about it sooner.
And I didn't want to bring it up.
There was another letter, too, right?
Yeah. I wrote one to Miles Parker, the guy who abducted Maura...
...promising that when he got out of prison I'd make him pay.
PIZZA
PRISON
I...
I still can't believe he only got four years in the slammer.
It's true. He was charged with motor vehicle homicide-negligence.
Apparently, Maura willingly got into his car, recognizing him from the neighborhood.
He was pretty drunk and when she asked to get out, Miles got angry and started driving faster.
He ended up crashing his car into a tree.
But instead of taking Maura to a hospital where she might have been saved, he carried her through the woods and left her in the tool shed.
She died shortly after.
PRISON
Wow...
Gummy Gator, anyone?

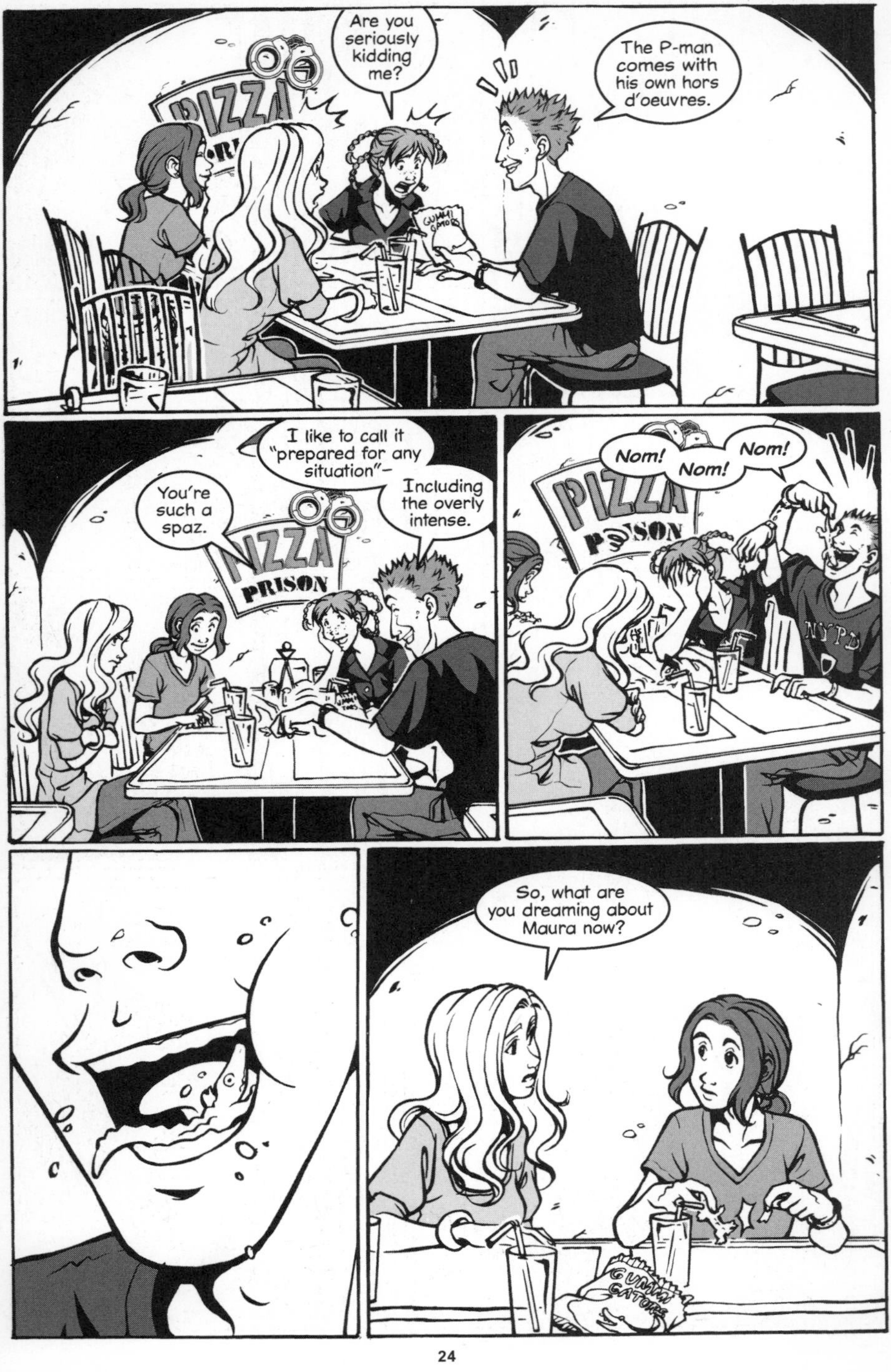
PIZZA
GUMMI GATORS
Are you seriously kidding me?
The P-man comes with his own hors d'oeuvres.
PIZZA PRISON
You're such a spaz.
I like to call it "prepared for any situation"–
Including the overly intense.
PIZZA PRISON
Nom!
Nom!
Nom!
NYPD
So, what are you dreaming about Maura now?
GUMMI GATORS

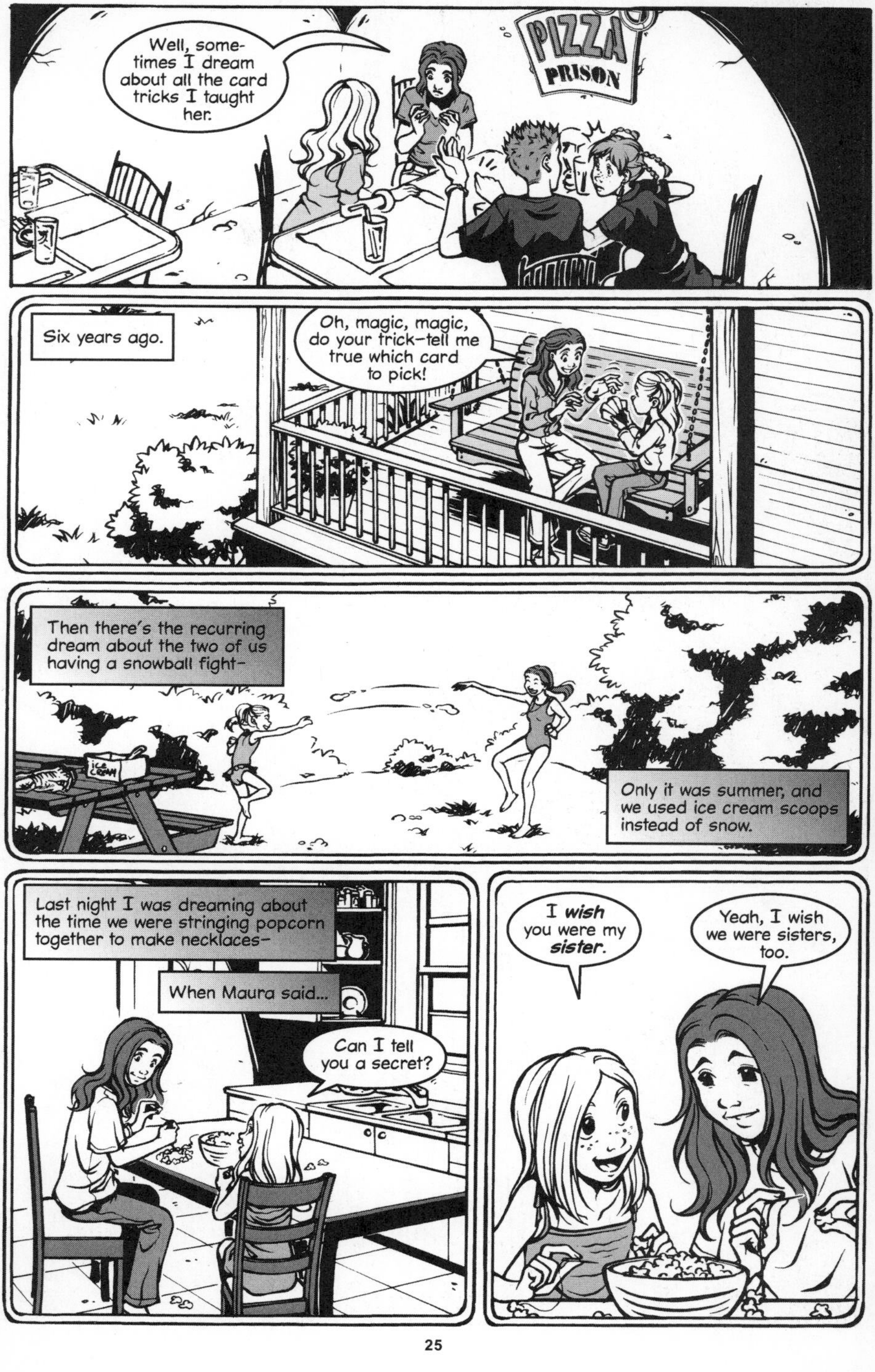
Well, some- times I dream about all the card tricks I taught her.
PIZZA PRISON
Six years ago.
Oh, magic, magic, do your trick—tell me true which card to pick!
Then there's the recurring dream about the two of us having a snowball fight—
ICE CREAM
Only it was summer, and we used ice cream scoops instead of snow.
Last night I was dreaming about the time we were stringing popcorn together to make necklaces—
When Maura said...
Can I tell you a secret?
I *wish* you were my *sister*.
Yeah, I wish we were sisters, too.

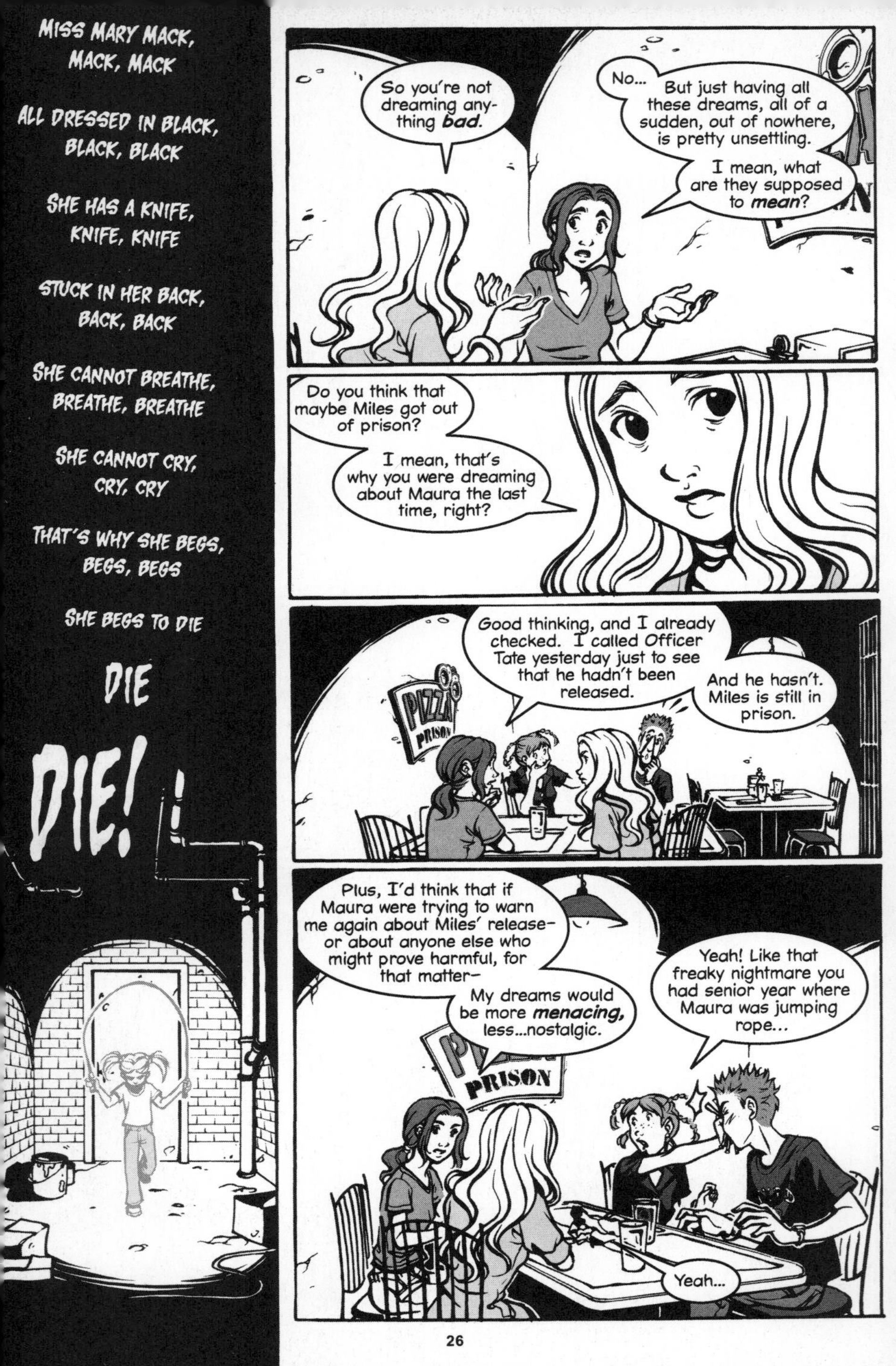
MISS MARY MACK, MACK, MACK
ALL DRESSED IN BLACK, BLACK, BLACK
SHE HAS A KNIFE, KNIFE, KNIFE
STUCK IN HER BACK, BACK, BACK
SHE CANNOT BREATHE, BREATHE, BREATHE
SHE CANNOT CRY, CRY, CRY
THAT'S WHY SHE BEGS, BEGS, BEGS
SHE BEGS TO DIE
DIE
DIE!
So you're not dreaming anything ***bad.***
No...
But just having all these dreams, all of a sudden, out of nowhere, is pretty unsettling.
I mean, what are they supposed to ***mean***?
Do you think that maybe Miles got out of prison?
I mean, that's why you were dreaming about Maura the last time, right?
Good thinking, and I already checked. I called Officer Tate yesterday just to see that he hadn't been released.
And he hasn't. Miles is still in prison.
PIZZA PRISON
Plus, I'd think that if Maura were trying to warn me again about Miles' release– or about anyone else who might prove harmful, for that matter–
My dreams would be more ***menacing,*** less...nostalgic.
Yeah! Like that freaky nightmare you had senior year where Maura was jumping rope...
PRISON
Yeah...

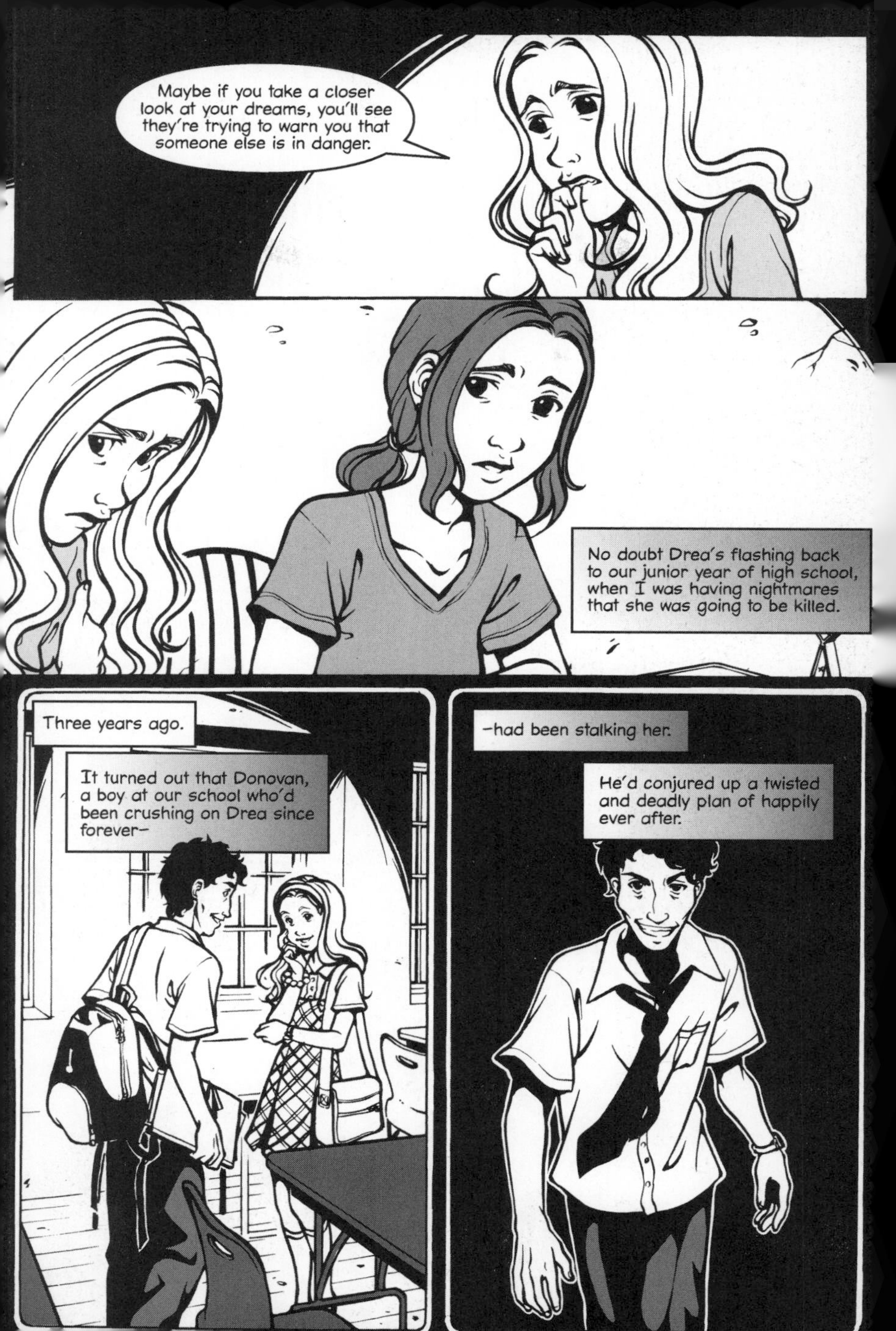
Maybe if you take a closer look at your dreams, you'll see they're trying to warn you that someone else is in danger.
No doubt Drea's flashing back to our junior year of high school, when I was having nightmares that she was going to be killed.
Three years ago.
It turned out that Donovan, a boy at our school who'd been crushing on Drea since forever–
–had been stalking her.
He'd conjured up a twisted and deadly plan of happily ever after.

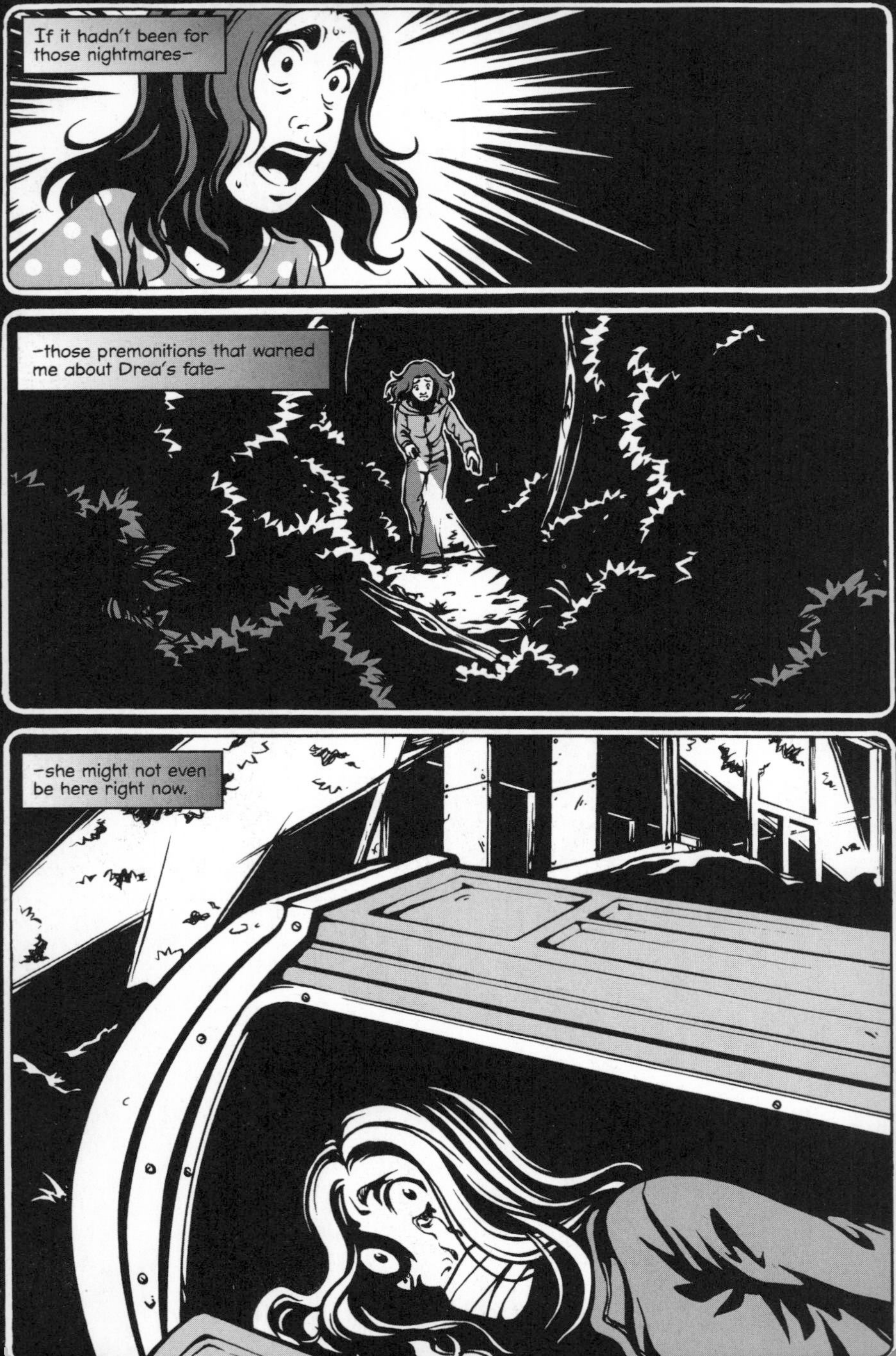
If it hadn't been for those nightmares–
–those premonitions that warned me about Drea's fate–
–she might not even be here right now.

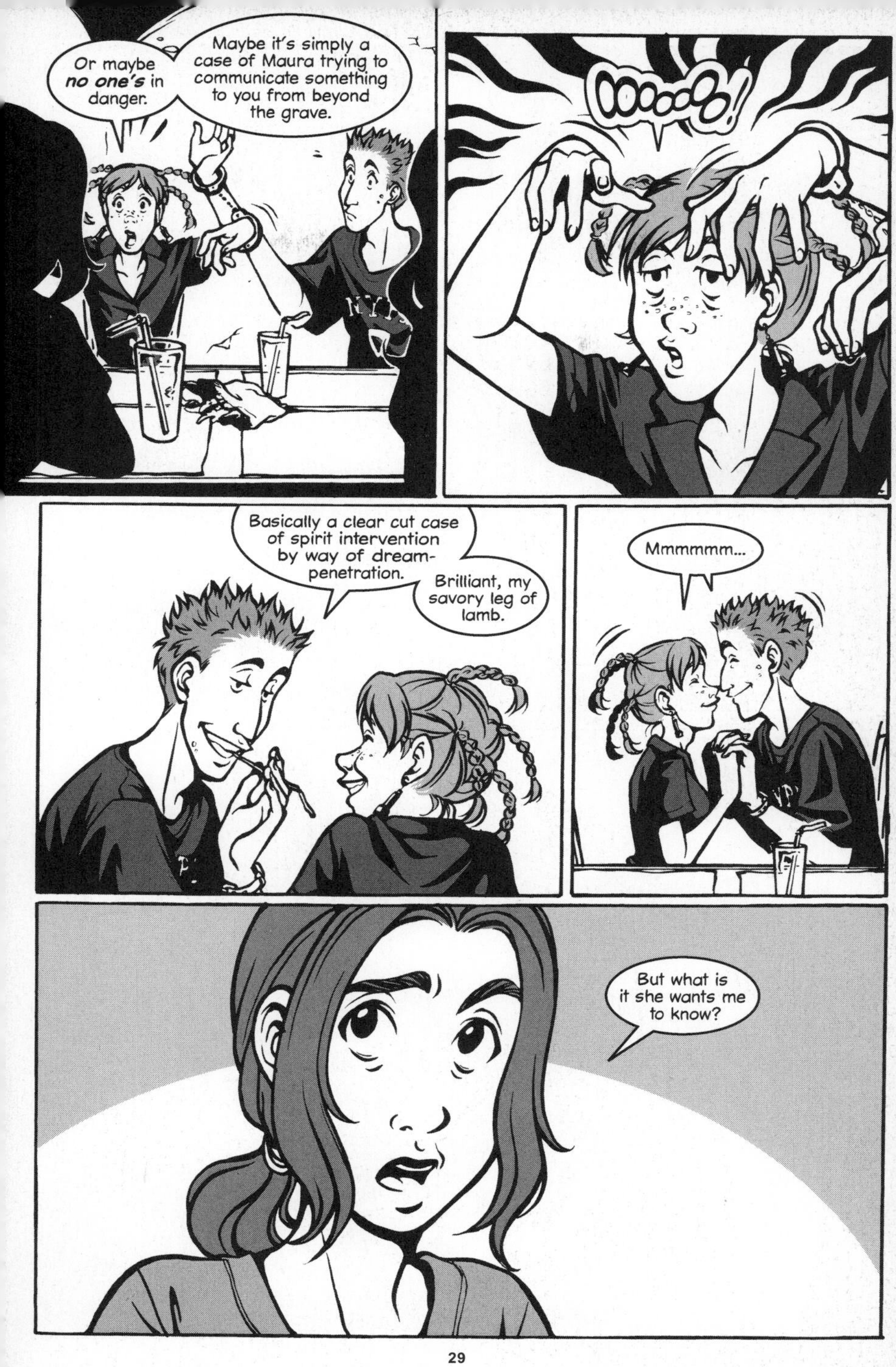

Or maybe *no one's* in danger.
Maybe it's simply a case of Maura trying to communicate something to you from beyond the grave.
OOOooOO!
Basically a clear cut case of spirit intervention by way of dream-penetration.
Brilliant, my savory leg of lamb.
Mmmmmm...
But what is it she wants me to know?

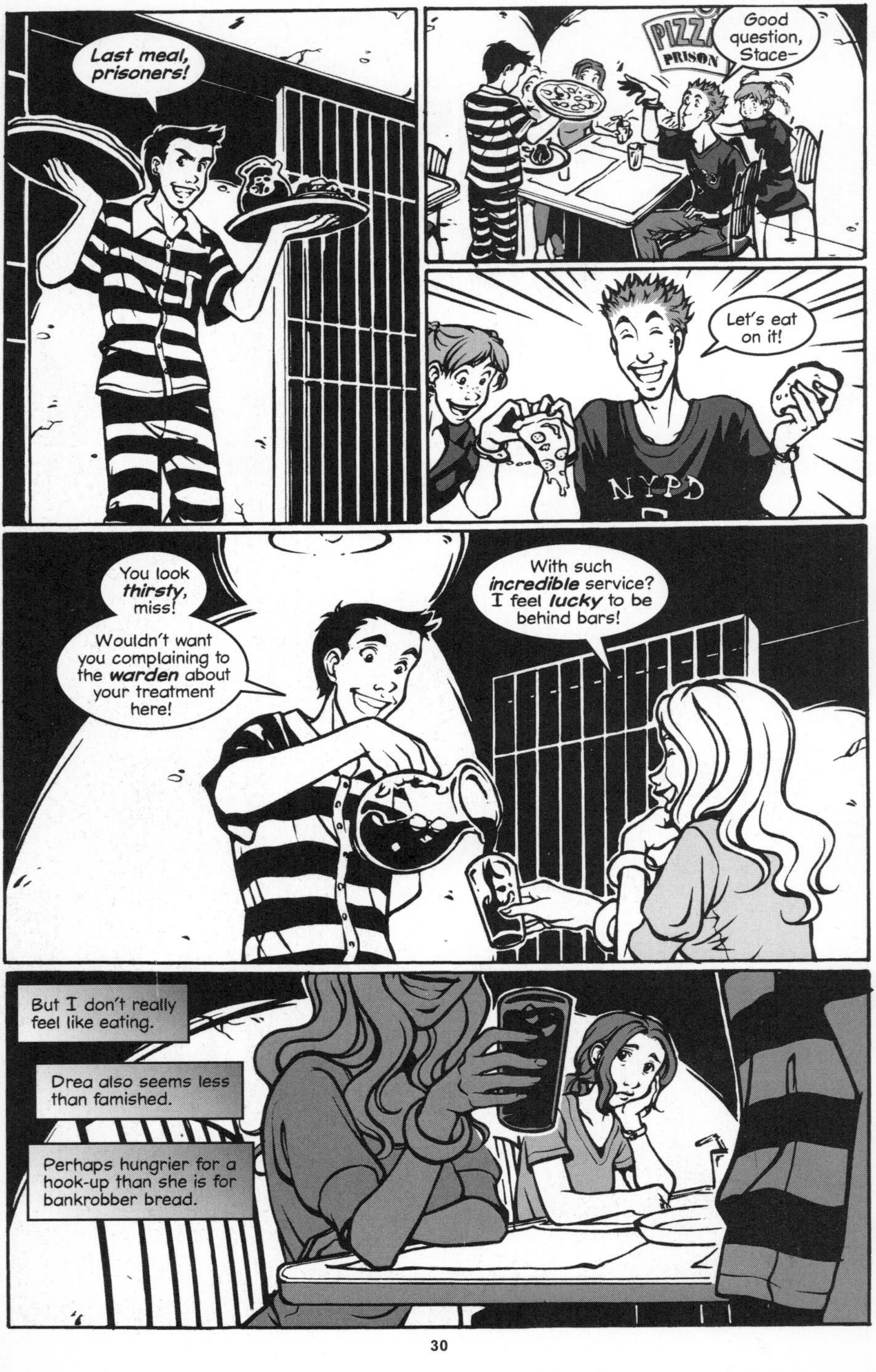

Last meal, prisoners!
PIZZA PRISON
Good question, Stace–
Let's eat on it!
NYPD
You look thirsty, miss!
Wouldn't want you complaining to the warden about your treatment here!
With such incredible service? I feel lucky to be behind bars!
But I don't really feel like eating.
Drea also seems less than famished.
Perhaps hungrier for a hook-up than she is for bankrobber bread.

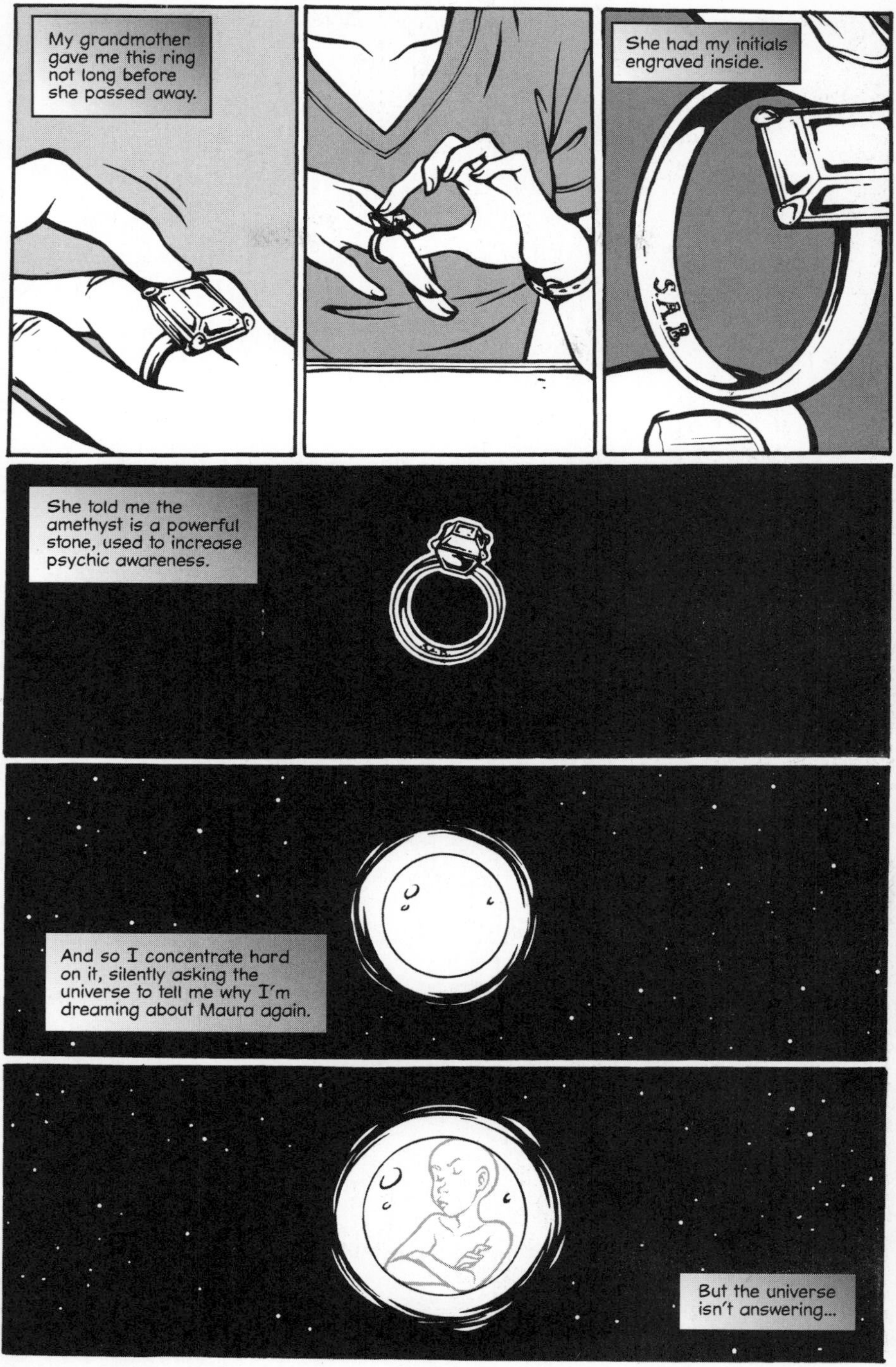
My grandmother gave me this ring not long before she passed away.
She had my initials engraved inside.
S.A.B.
She told me the amethyst is a powerful stone, used to increase psychic awareness.
And so I concentrate hard on it, silently asking the universe to tell me why I'm dreaming about Maura again.
But the universe isn't answering...

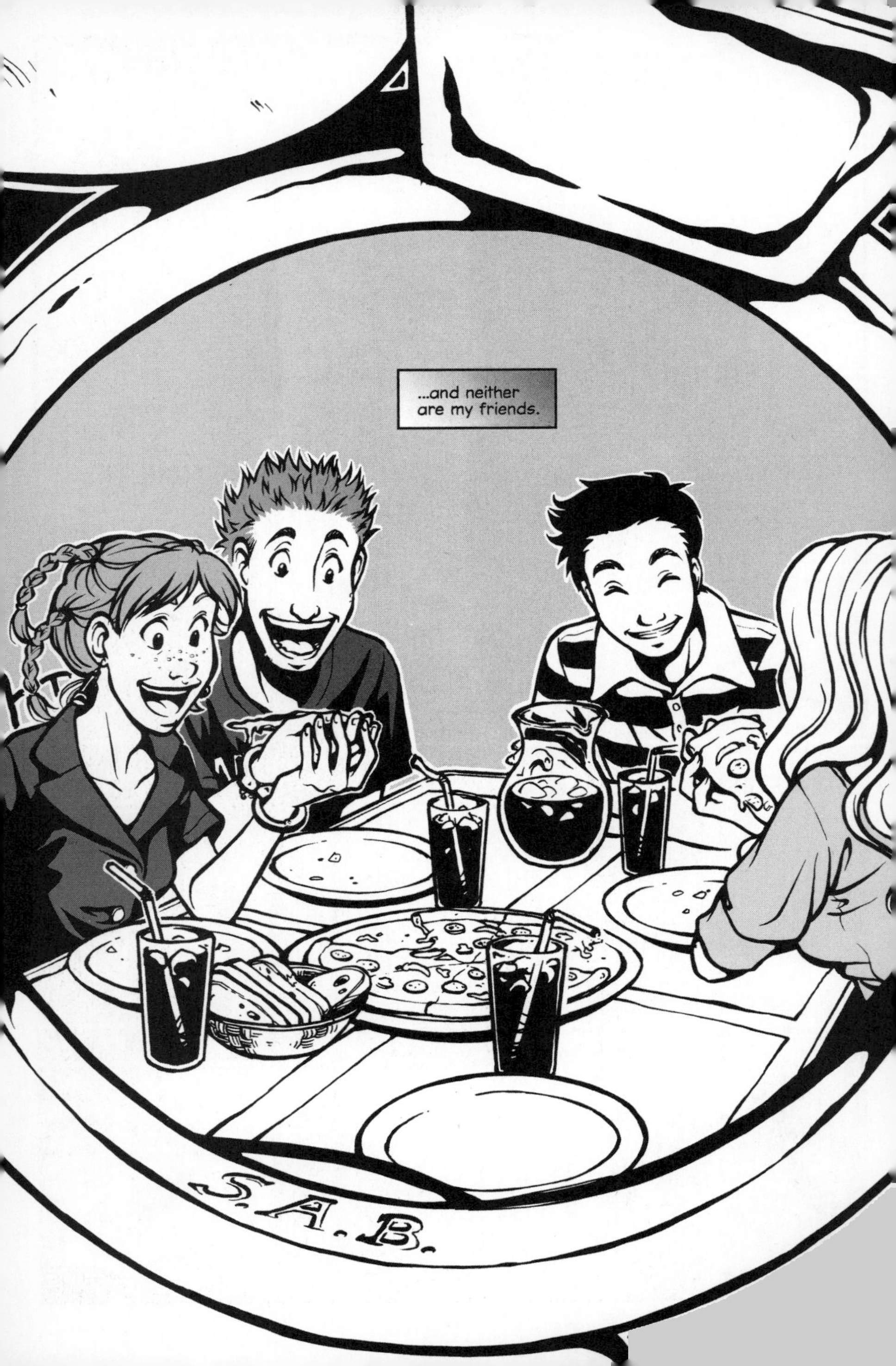

...and neither are my friends.
S.A.B.

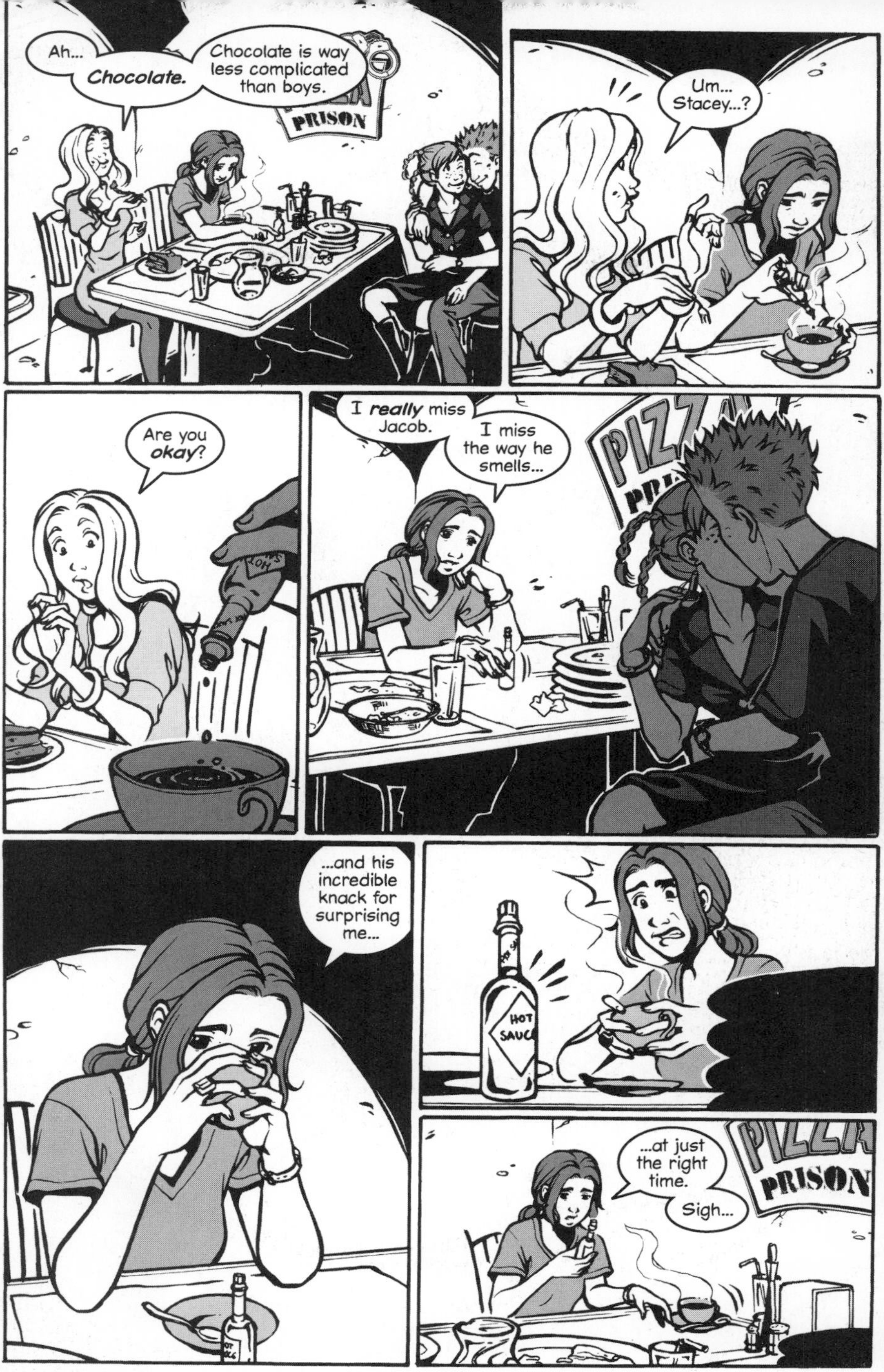
Ah...
Chocolate.
Chocolate is way less complicated than boys.
PRISON
Um... Stacey...?
Are you okay?
I really miss Jacob.
I miss the way he smells...
...and his incredible knack for surprising me...
...at just the right time.
Sigh...
PRISON

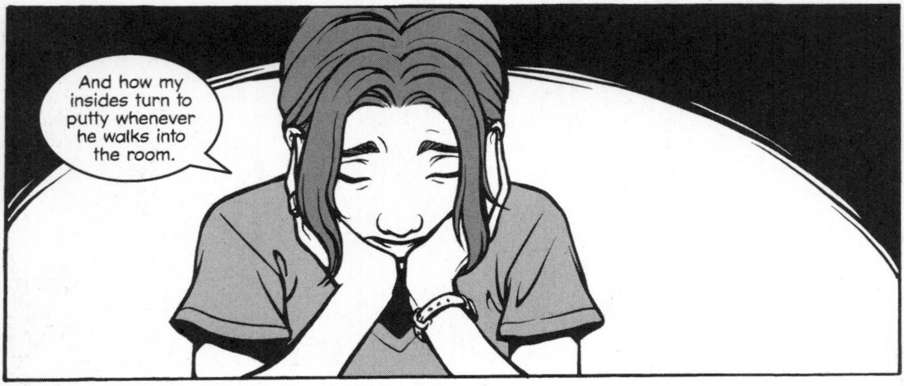
And how my insides turn to putty whenever he walks into the room.

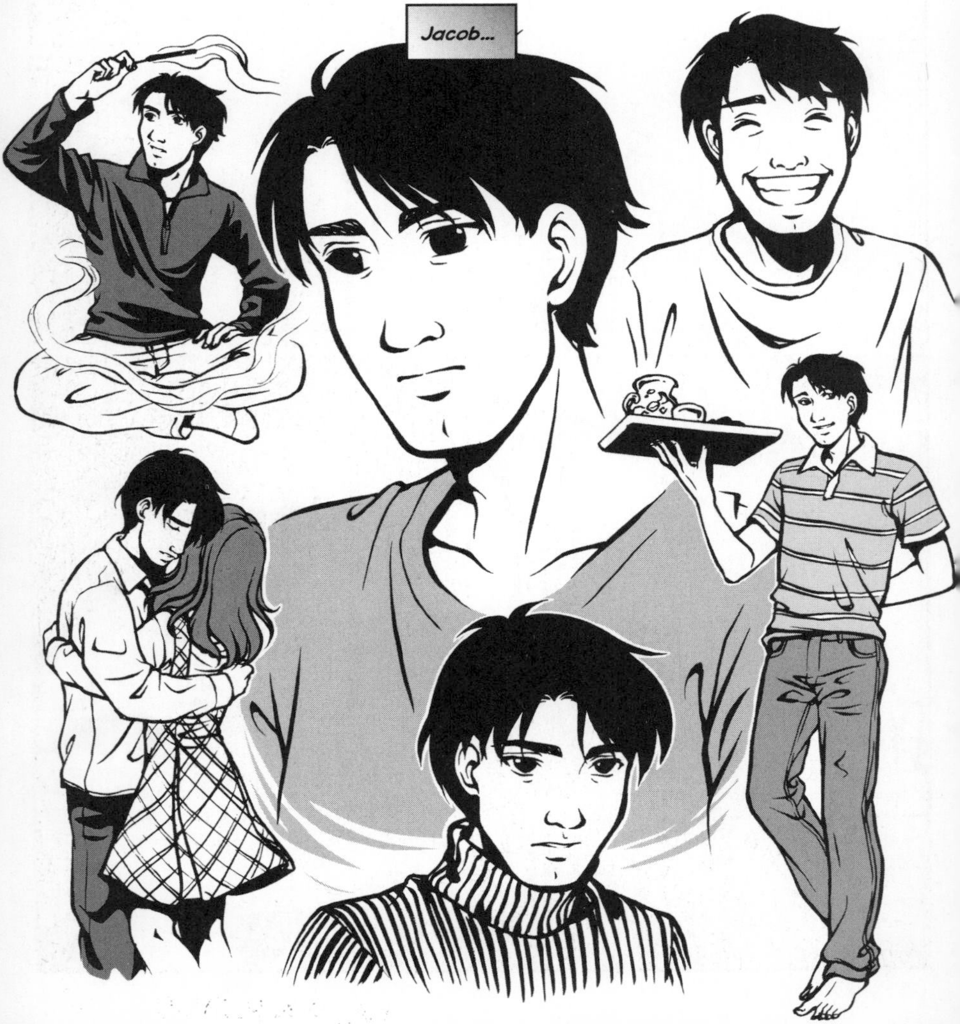
Jacob...

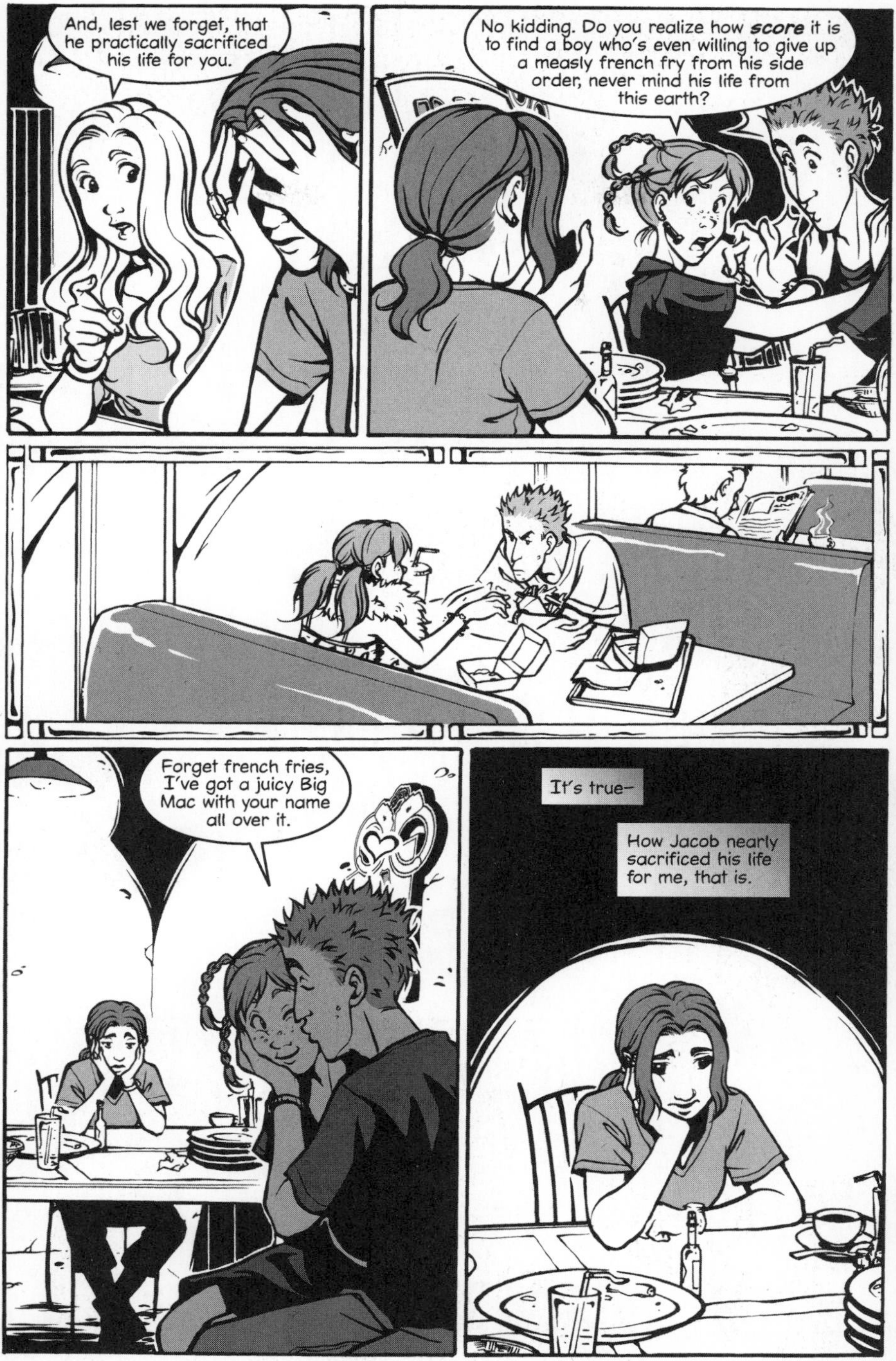
And, lest we forget, that he practically sacrificed his life for you.
No kidding. Do you realize how ***score*** it is to find a boy who's even willing to give up a measly french fry from his side order, never mind his life from this earth?
Forget french fries, I've got a juicy Big Mac with your name all over it.
It's true–
How Jacob nearly sacrificed his life for me, that is.

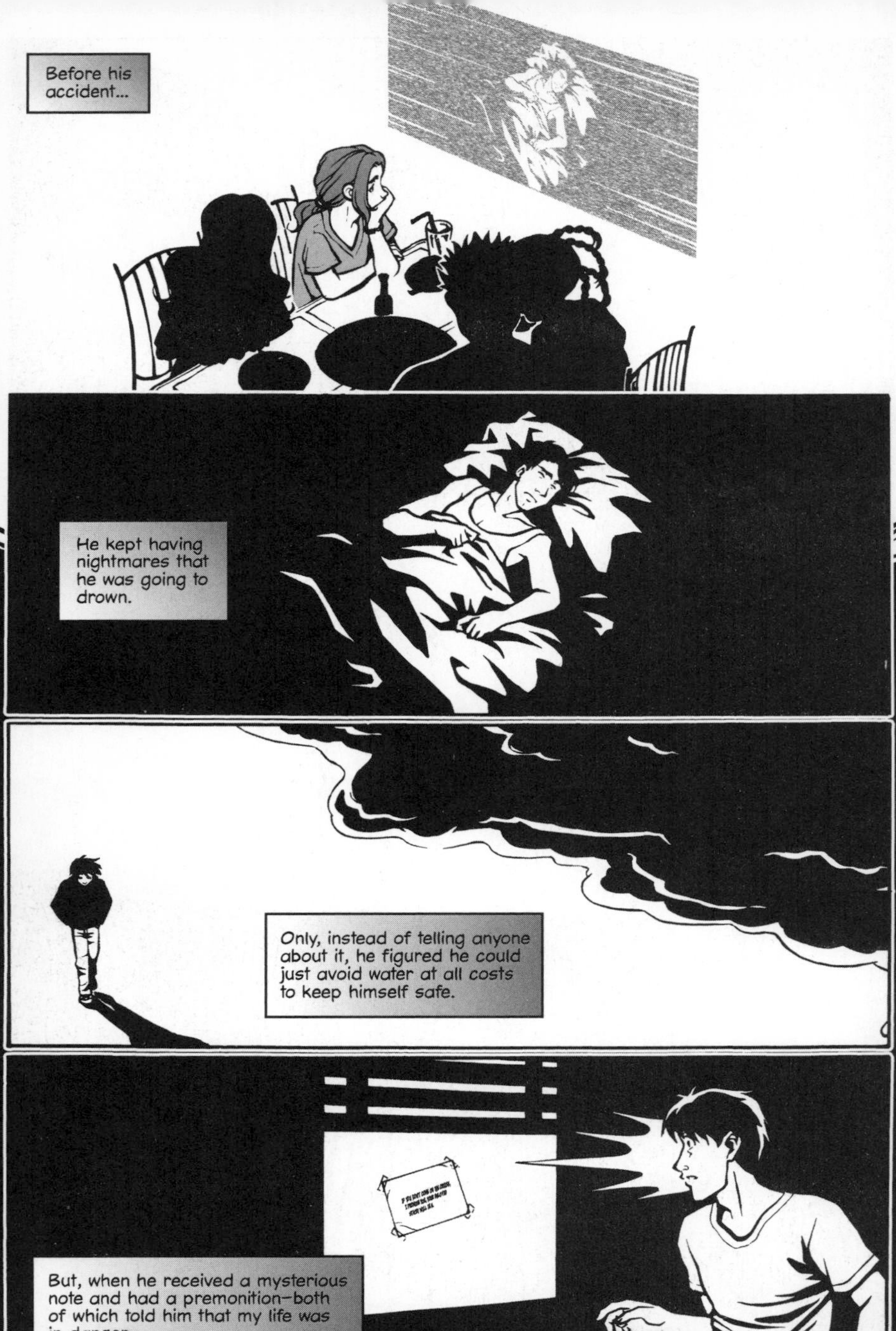
Before his accident...
He kept having nightmares that he was going to drown.
Only, instead of telling anyone about it, he figured he could just avoid water at all costs to keep himself safe.
But, when he received a mysterious note and had a premonition—both of which told him that my life was in danger—

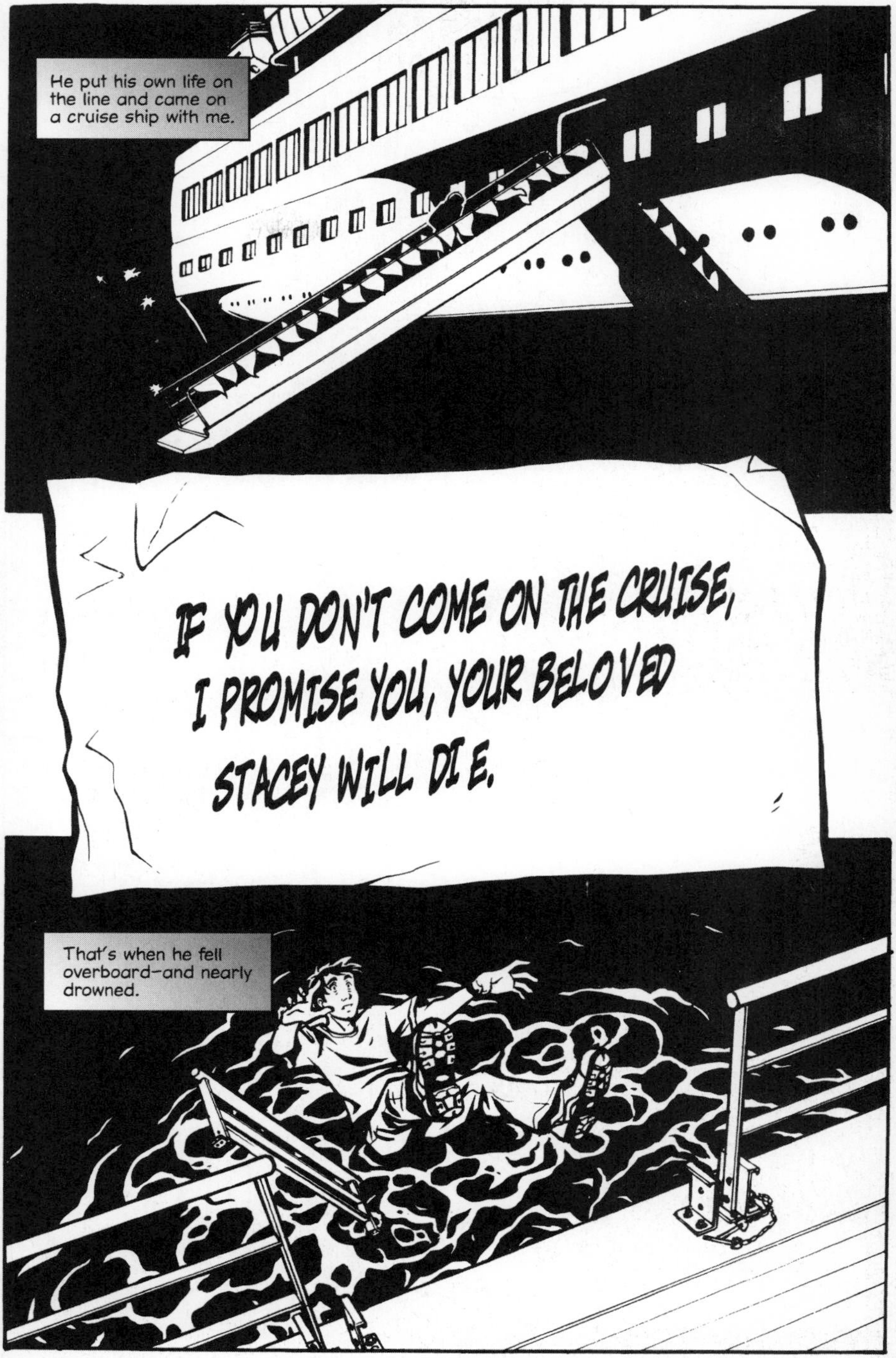
He put his own life on the line and came on a cruise ship with me.
IF YOU DON'T COME ON THE CRUISE, I PROMISE YOU, YOUR BELOVED STACEY WILL DI E.
That's when he fell overboard—and nearly drowned.

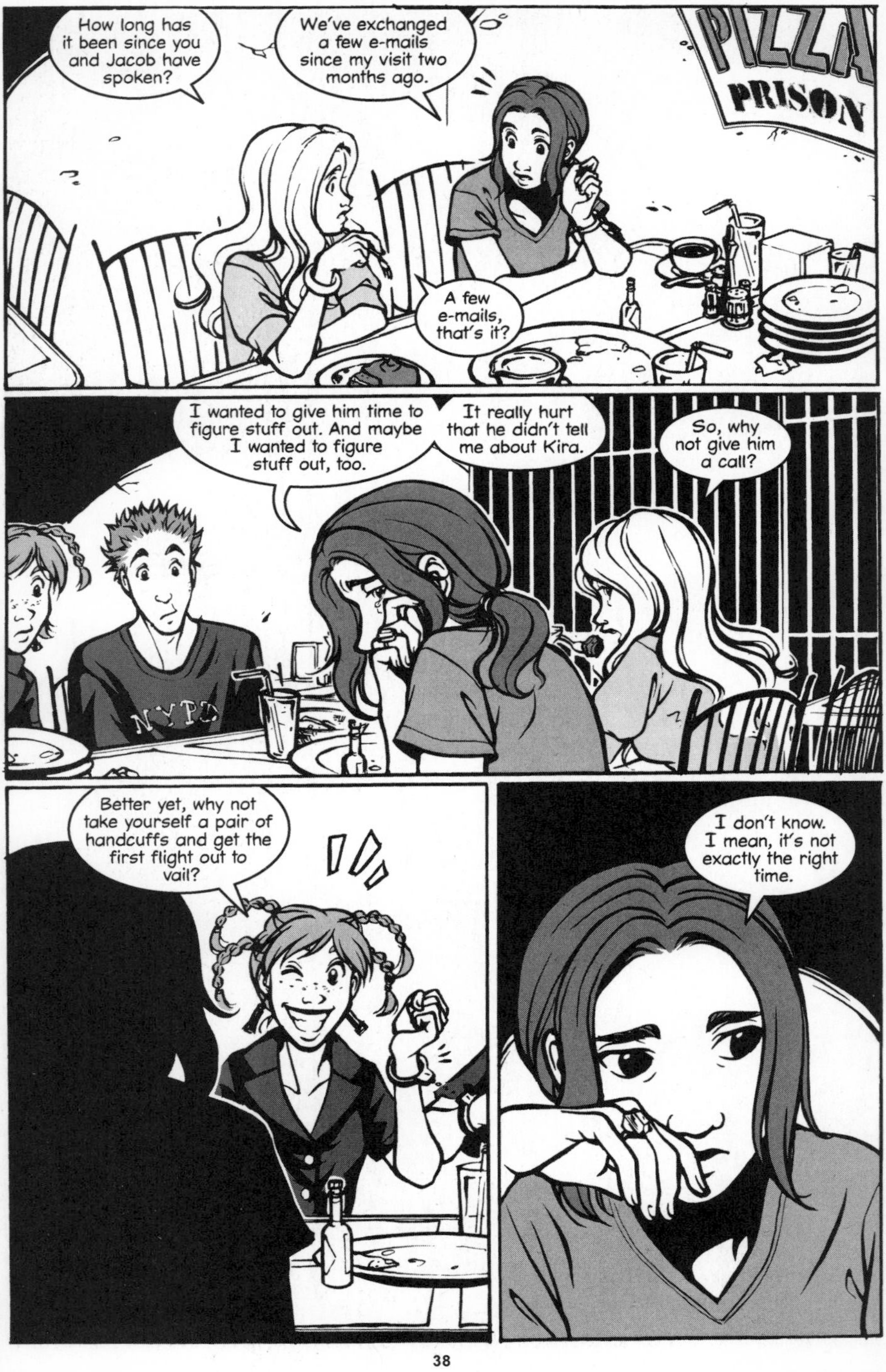
PIZZA
PRISON
How long has it been since you and Jacob have spoken?
We've exchanged a few e-mails since my visit two months ago.
A few e-mails, that's it?
I wanted to give him time to figure stuff out. And maybe I wanted to figure stuff out, too.
It really hurt that he didn't tell me about Kira.
So, why not give him a call?
NYPD
Better yet, why not take yourself a pair of handcuffs and get the first flight out to vail?
I don't know. I mean, it's not exactly the right time.

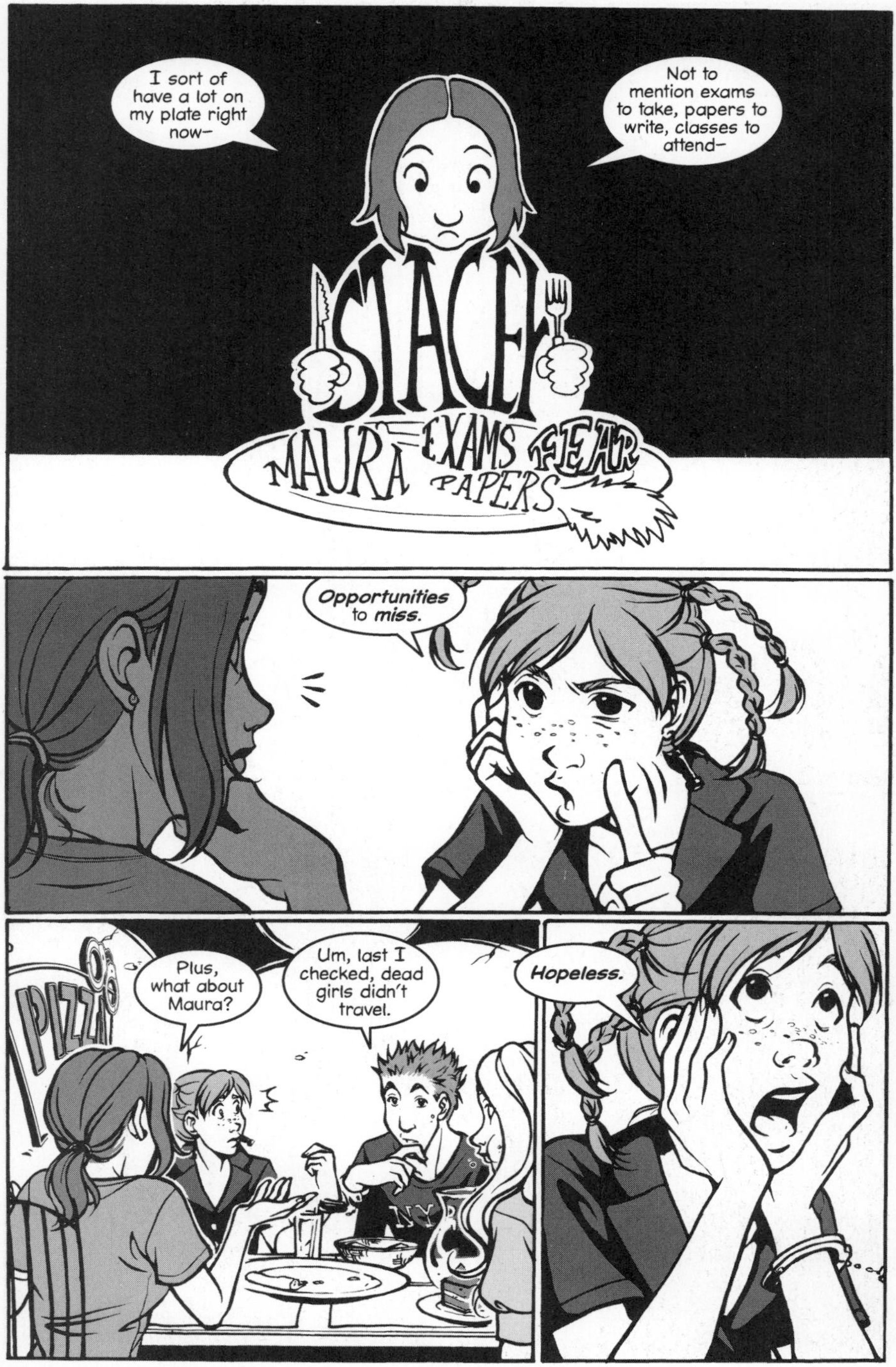
I sort of have a lot on my plate right now–
Not to mention exams to take, papers to write, classes to attend–
STACEY
MAURA
EXAMS
FEAR
PAPERS
Opportunities to miss.
PIZZA
Plus, what about Maura?
Um, last I checked, dead girls didn't travel.
NY
Hopeless.

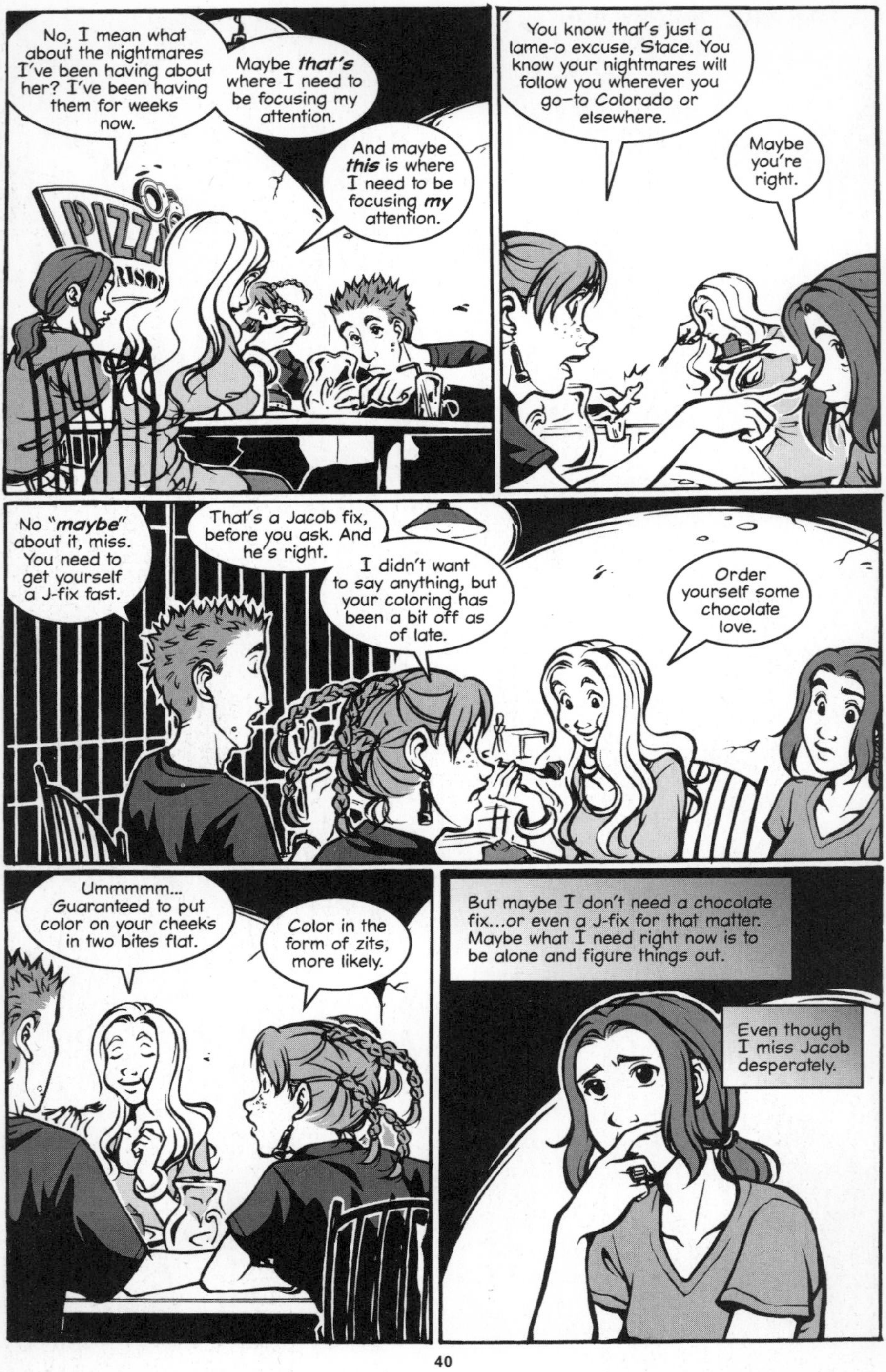
No, I mean what about the nightmares I've been having about her? I've been having them for weeks now.
Maybe ***that's*** where I need to be focusing my attention.
And maybe ***this*** is where I need to be focusing ***my*** attention.
PIZZA
PRISON
You know that's just a lame-o excuse, Stace. You know your nightmares will follow you wherever you go–to Colorado or elsewhere.
Maybe you're right.
No "***maybe***" about it, miss. You need to get yourself a J-fix fast.
That's a Jacob fix, before you ask. And he's right.
I didn't want to say anything, but your coloring has been a bit off as of late.
Order yourself some chocolate love.
Ummmmm... Guaranteed to put color on your cheeks in two bites flat.
Color in the form of zits, more likely.
But maybe I don't need a chocolate fix...or even a J-fix for that matter. Maybe what I need right now is to be alone and figure things out.
Even though I miss Jacob desperately.

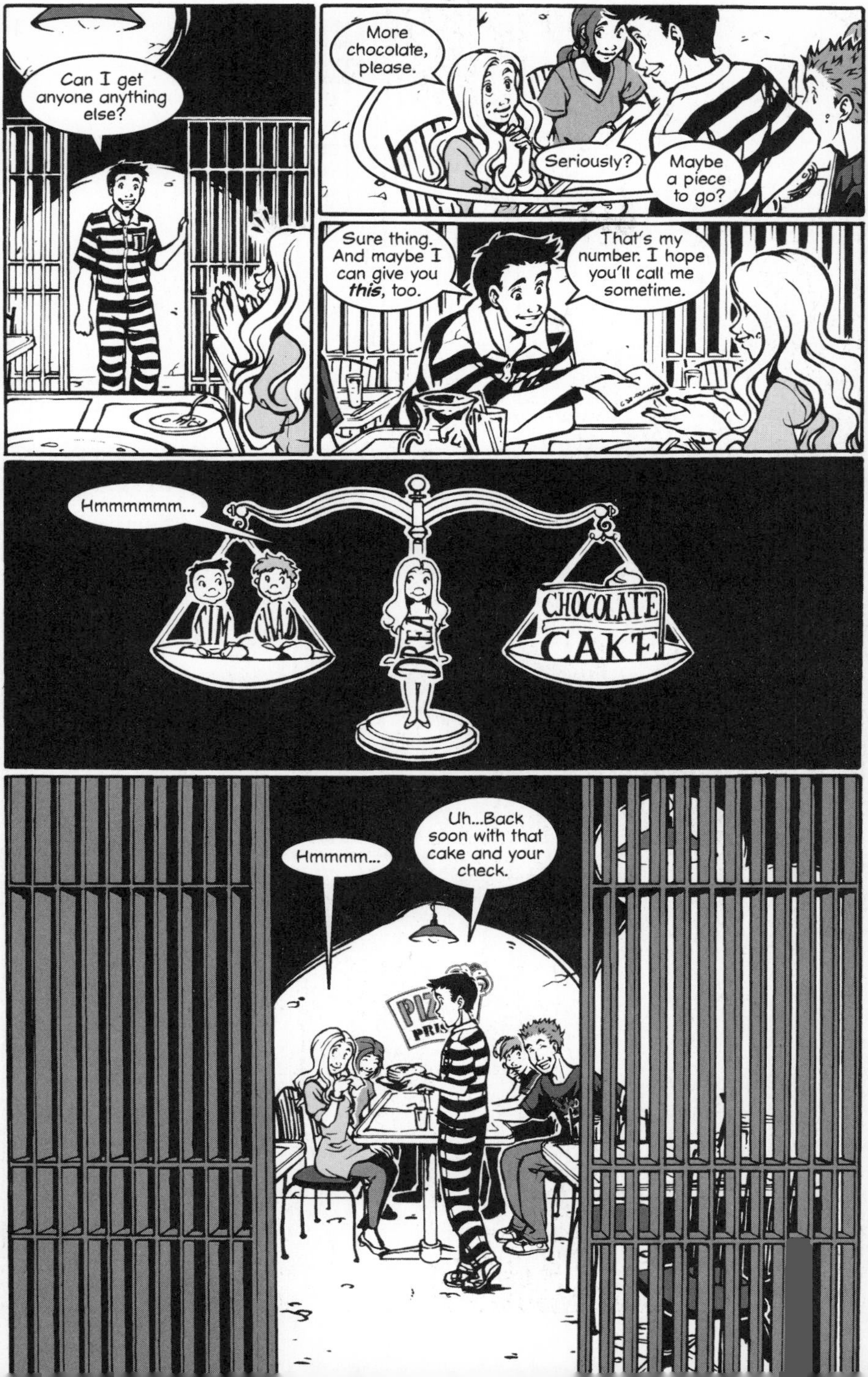

Can I get anyone anything else?
More chocolate, please.
Seriously?
Maybe a piece to go?
Sure thing. And maybe I can give you *this*, too.
That's my number. I hope you'll call me sometime.
Hmmmmmm...
CHOCOLATE CAKE
Hmmmm...
Uh...Back soon with that cake and your check.

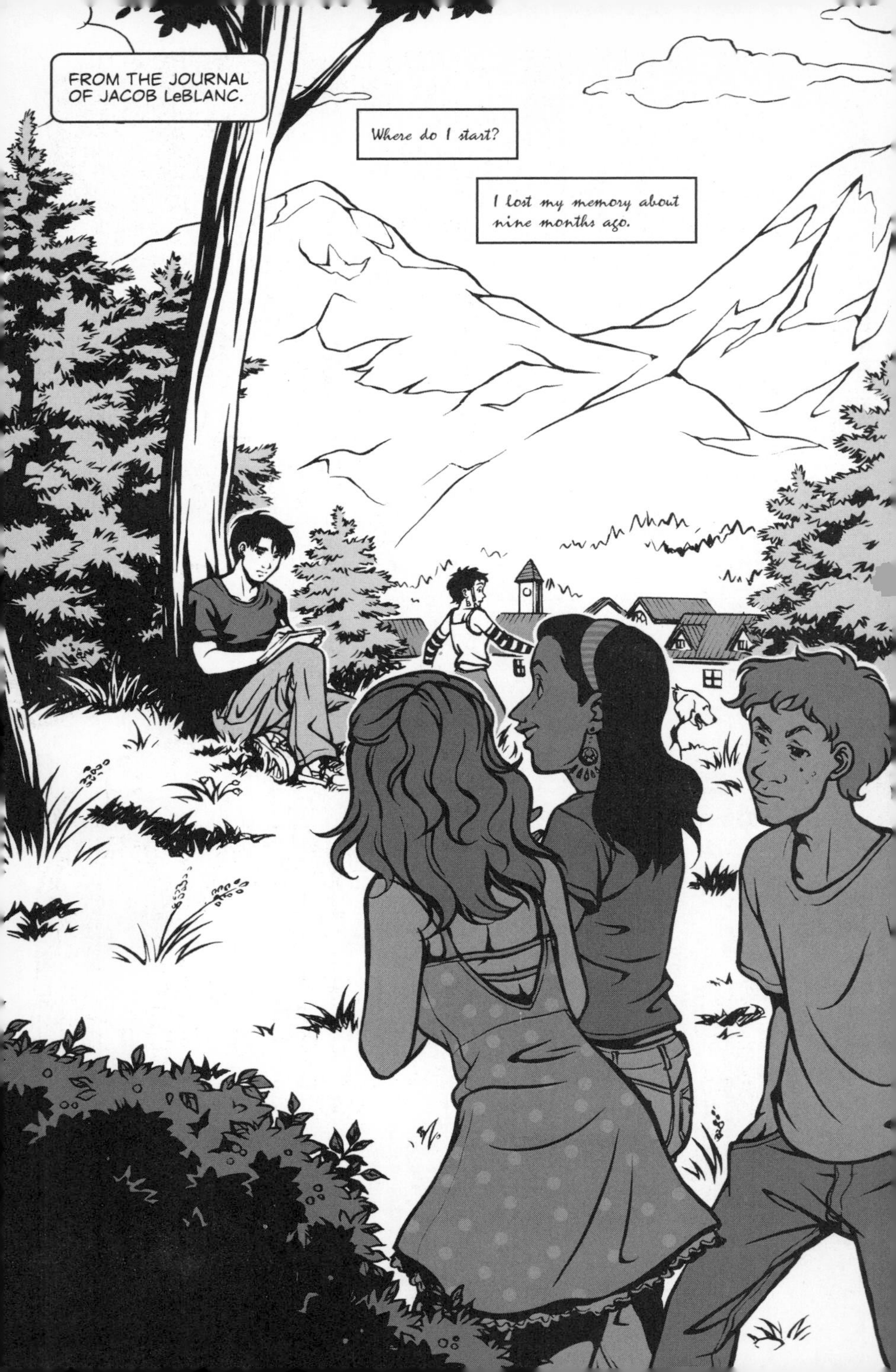
FROM THE JOURNAL OF JACOB LeBLANC.
Where do I start?
I lost my memory about nine months ago.

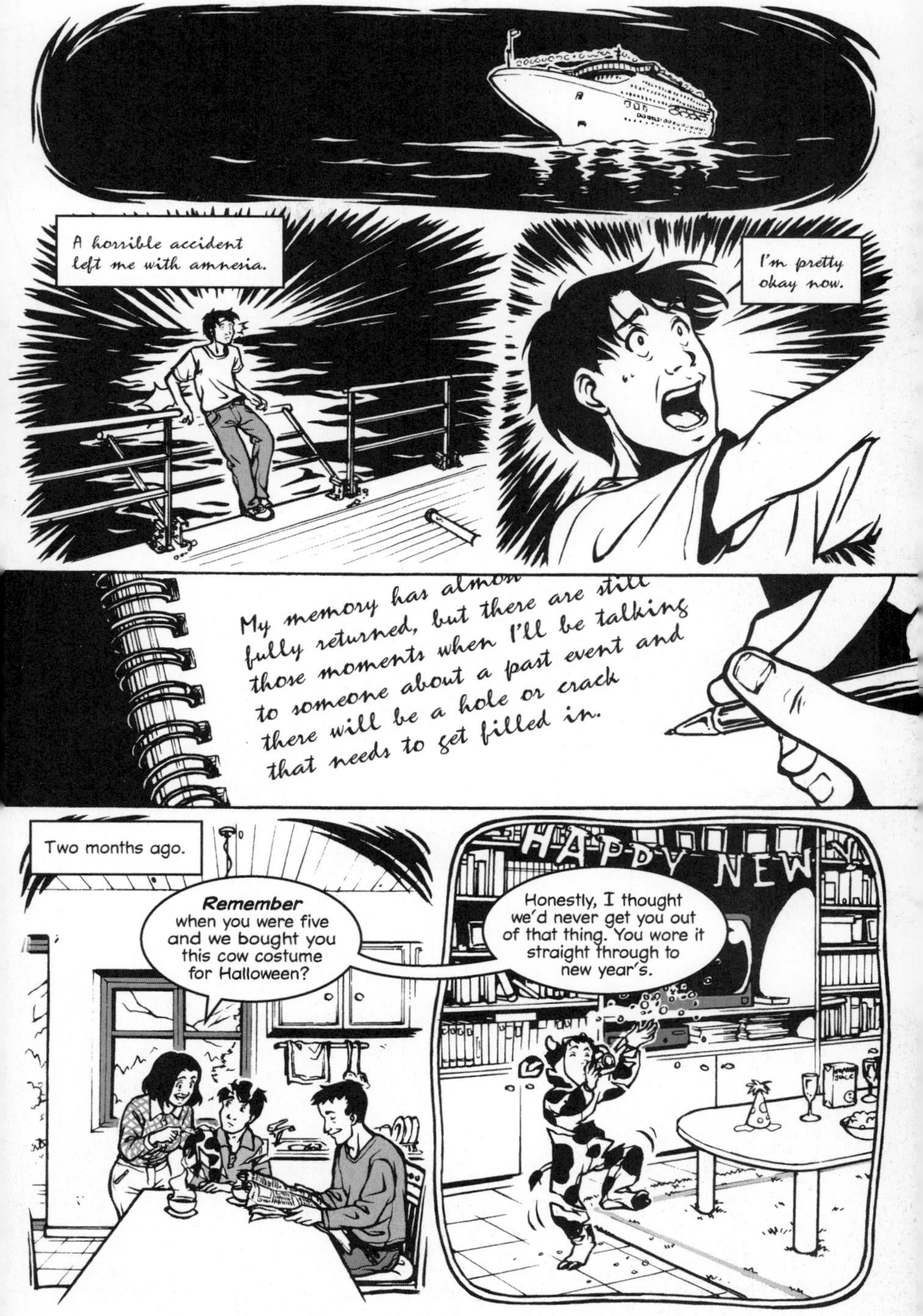
A horrible accident left me with amnesia.
I'm pretty okay now.
My memory has almost fully returned, but there are still those moments when I'll be talking to someone about a past event and there will be a hole or crack that needs to get filled in.
Two months ago.
Remember when you were five and we bought you this cow costume for Halloween?
Honestly, I thought we'd never get you out of that thing. You wore it straight through to new year's.
HAPPY NEW

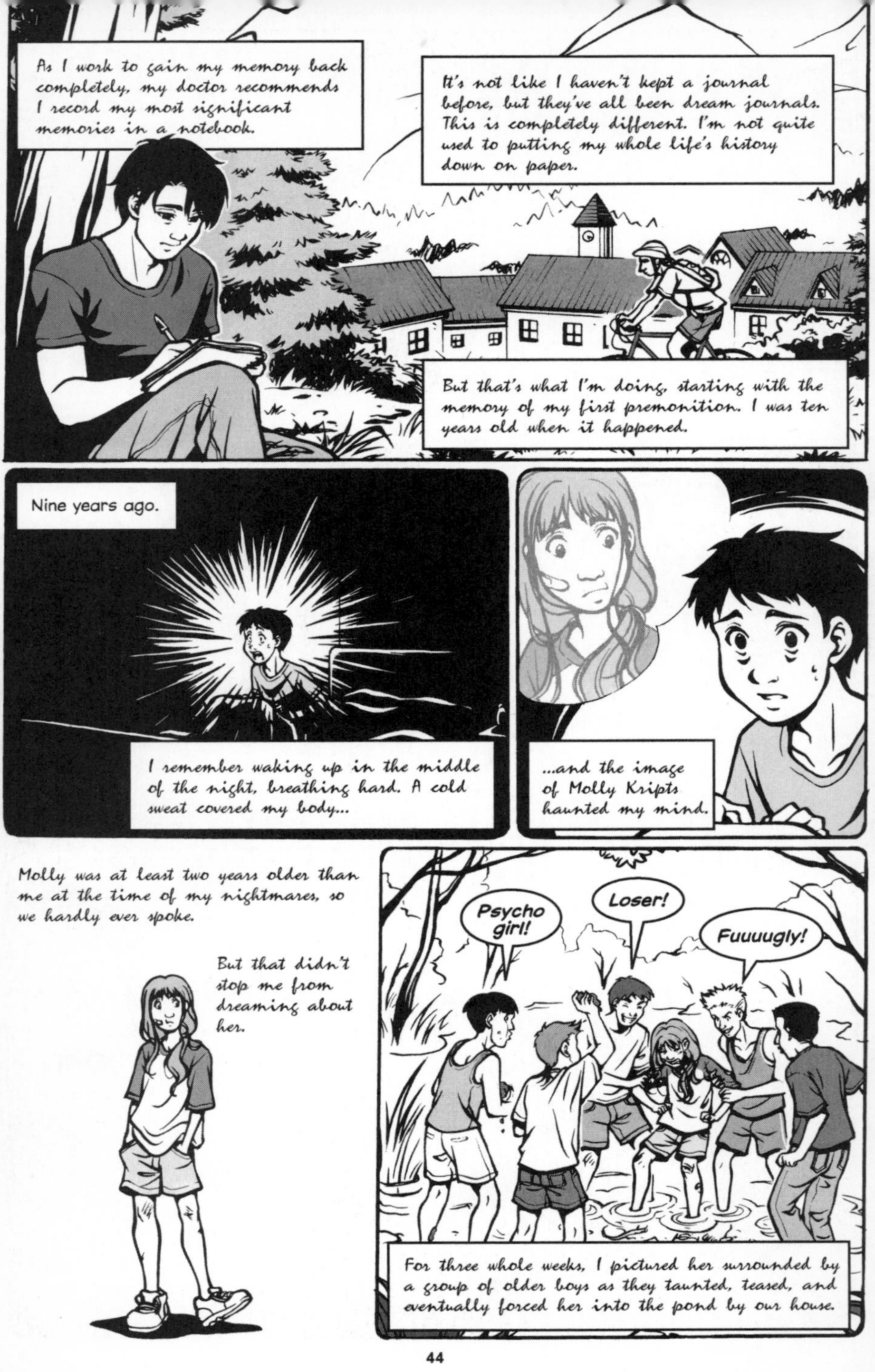
As I work to gain my memory back completely, my doctor recommends I record my most significant memories in a notebook.
It's not like I haven't kept a journal before, but they've all been dream journals. This is completely different. I'm not quite used to putting my whole life's history down on paper.
But that's what I'm doing, starting with the memory of my first premonition. I was ten years old when it happened.
Nine years ago.
I remember waking up in the middle of the night, breathing hard. A cold sweat covered my body...
...and the image of Molly Kripts haunted my mind.
Molly was at least two years older than me at the time of my nightmares, so we hardly ever spoke.
But that didn't stop me from dreaming about her.
Psycho girl!
Loser!
Fuuuugly!
For three whole weeks, I pictured her surrounded by a group of older boys as they taunted, teased, and eventually forced her into the pond by our house.

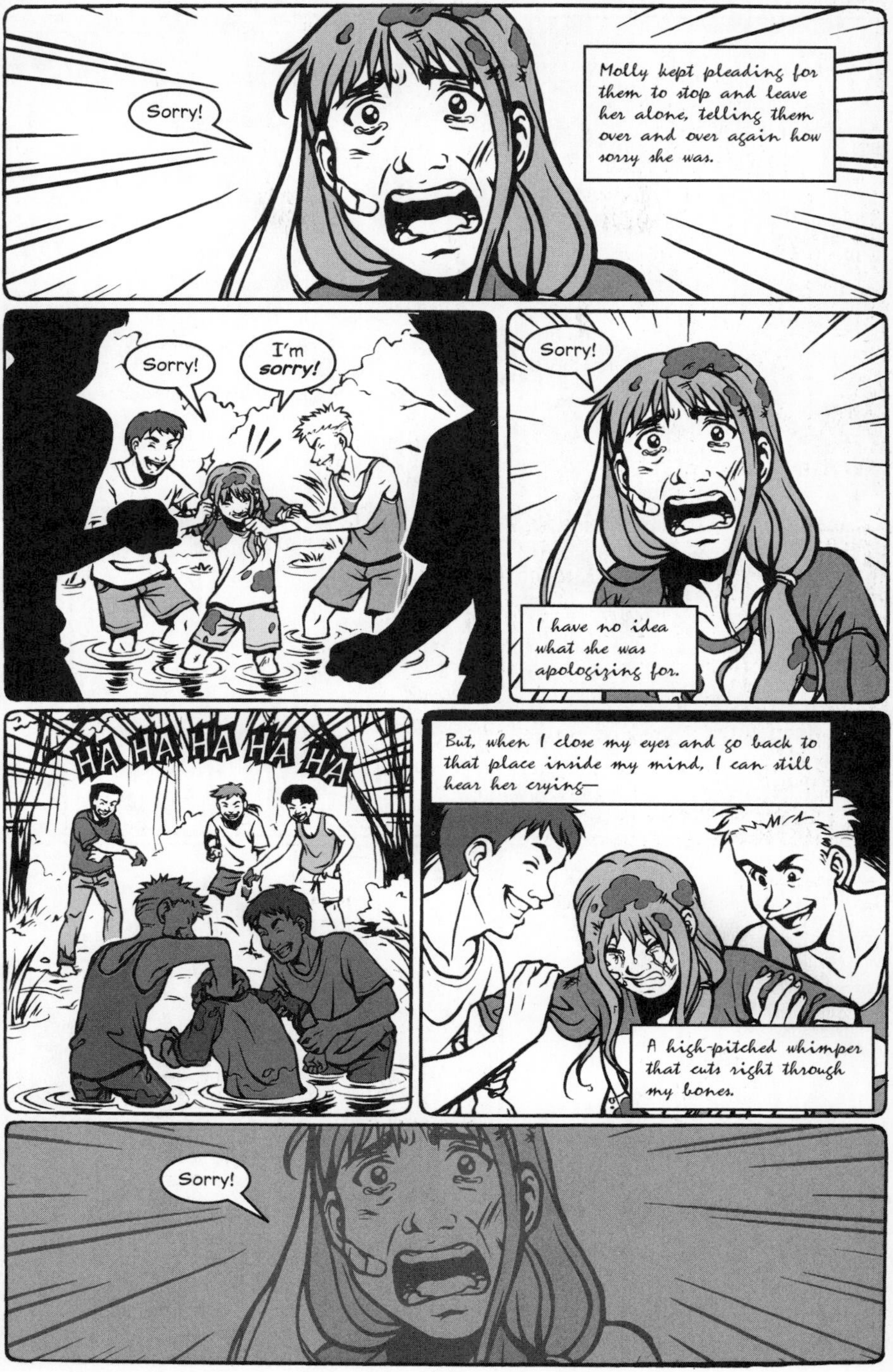
Sorry!
Molly kept pleading for them to stop and leave her alone, telling them over and over again how sorry she was.
Sorry!
I'm sorry!
Sorry!
I have no idea what she was apologizing for.
HA HA HA HA HA
But, when I close my eyes and go back to that place inside my mind, I can still hear her crying—
A high-pitched whimper that cuts right through my bones.
Sorry!

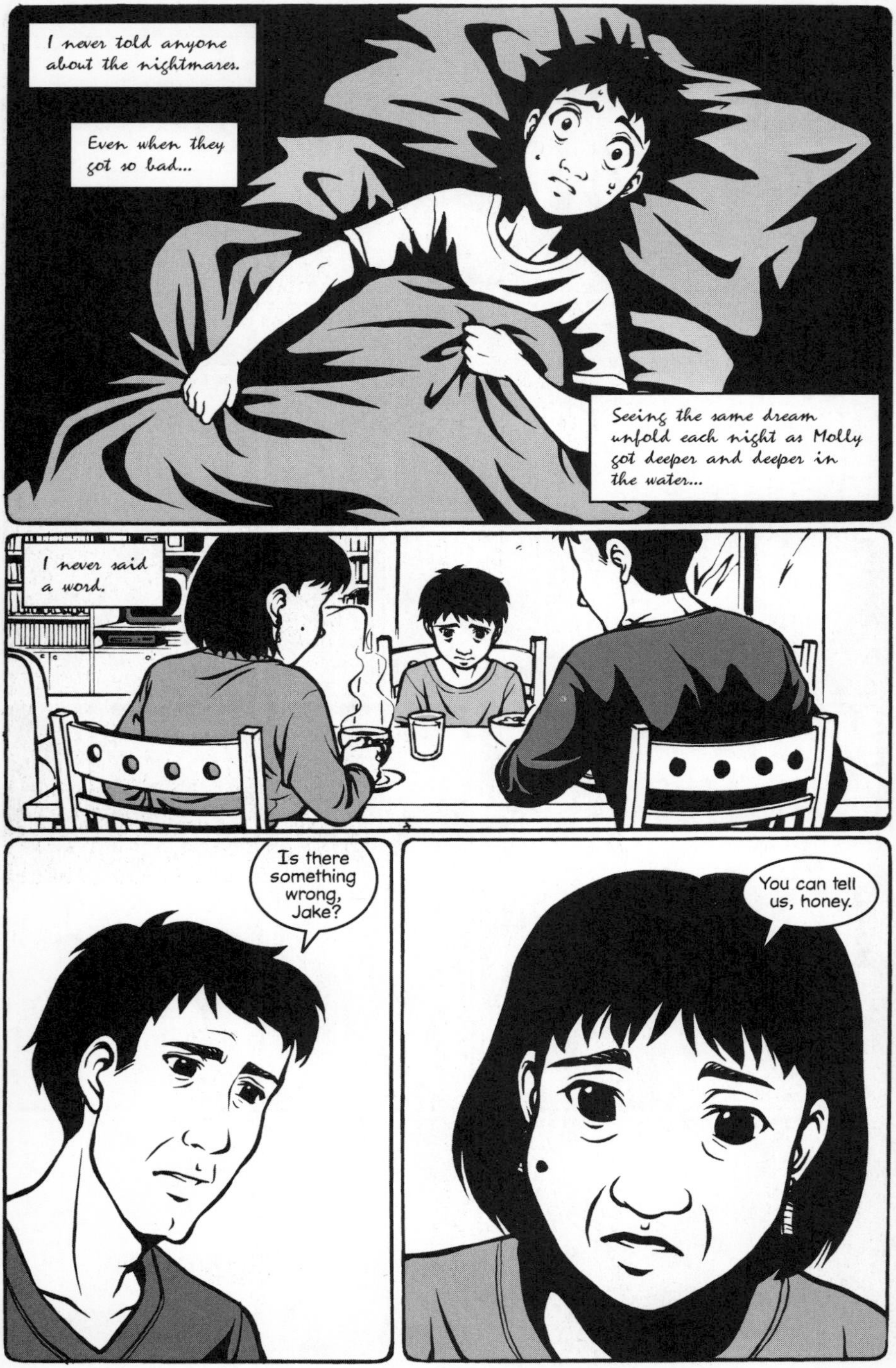
I never told anyone about the nightmares.
Even when they got so bad...
Seeing the same dream unfold each night as Molly got deeper and deeper in the water...
I never said a word.
Is there something wrong, Jake?
You can tell us, honey.

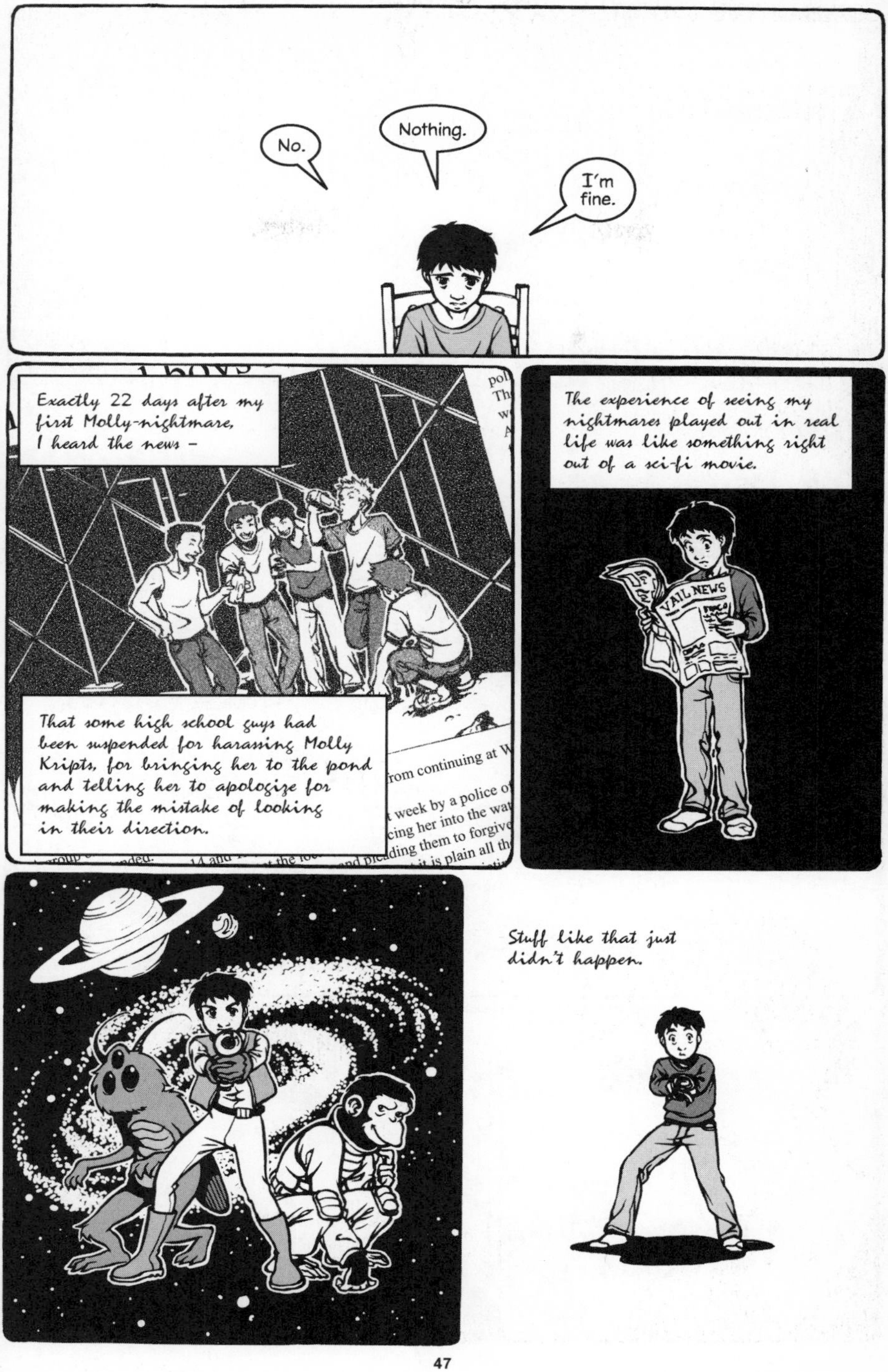
No.
Nothing.
I'm fine.
Exactly 22 days after my first Molly-nightmare, I heard the news –
That some high school guys had been suspended for harassing Molly Kripts, for bringing her to the pond and telling her to apologize for making the mistake of looking in their direction.
The experience of seeing my nightmares played out in real life was like something right out of a sci-fi movie.
VAIL NEWS
Stuff like that just didn't happen.

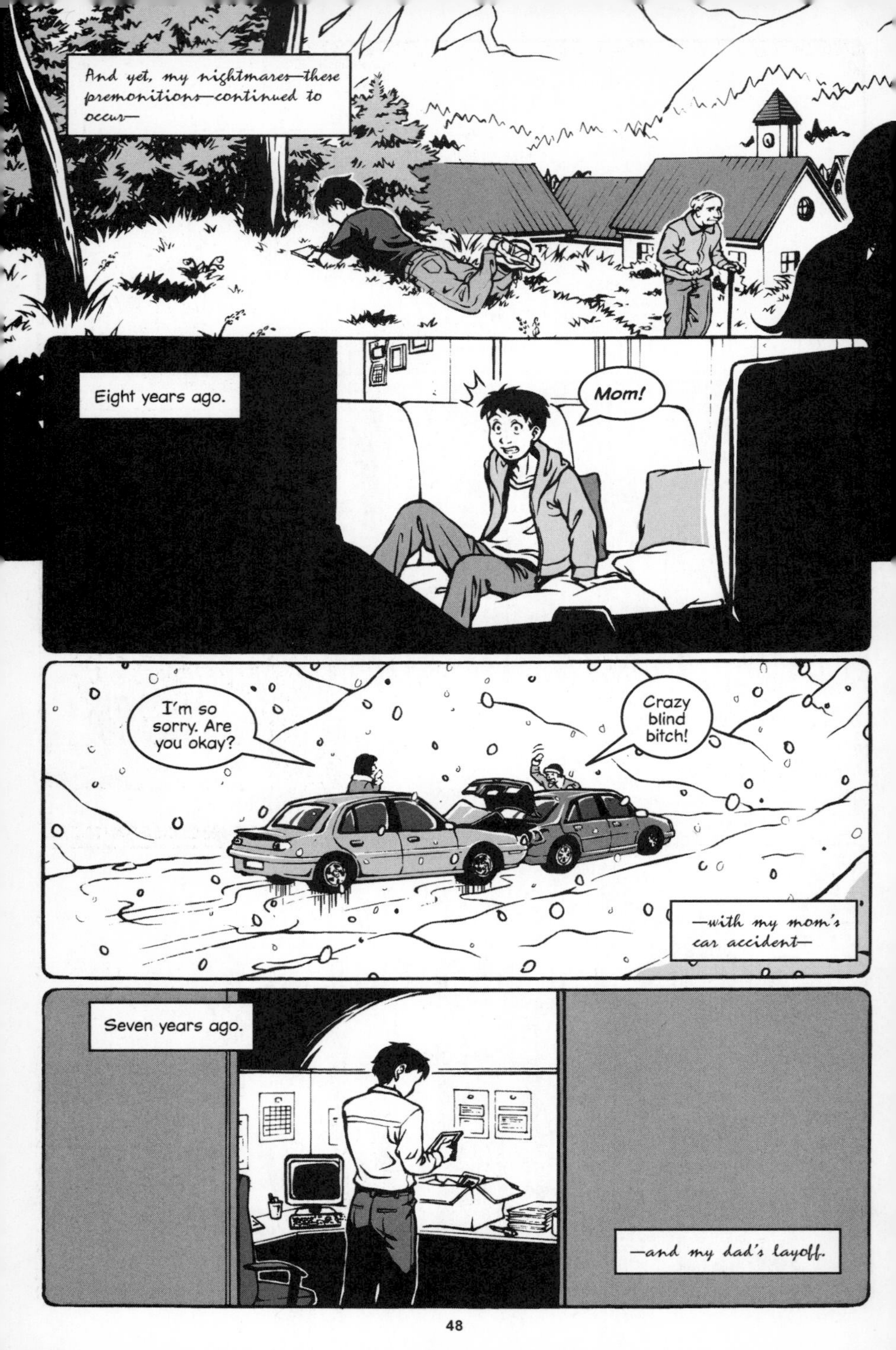
And yet, my nightmares—these premonitions—continued to occur—
Eight years ago.
Mom!
I'm so sorry. Are you okay?
Crazy blind bitch!
—with my mom's car accident—
Seven years ago.
—and my dad's layoff.

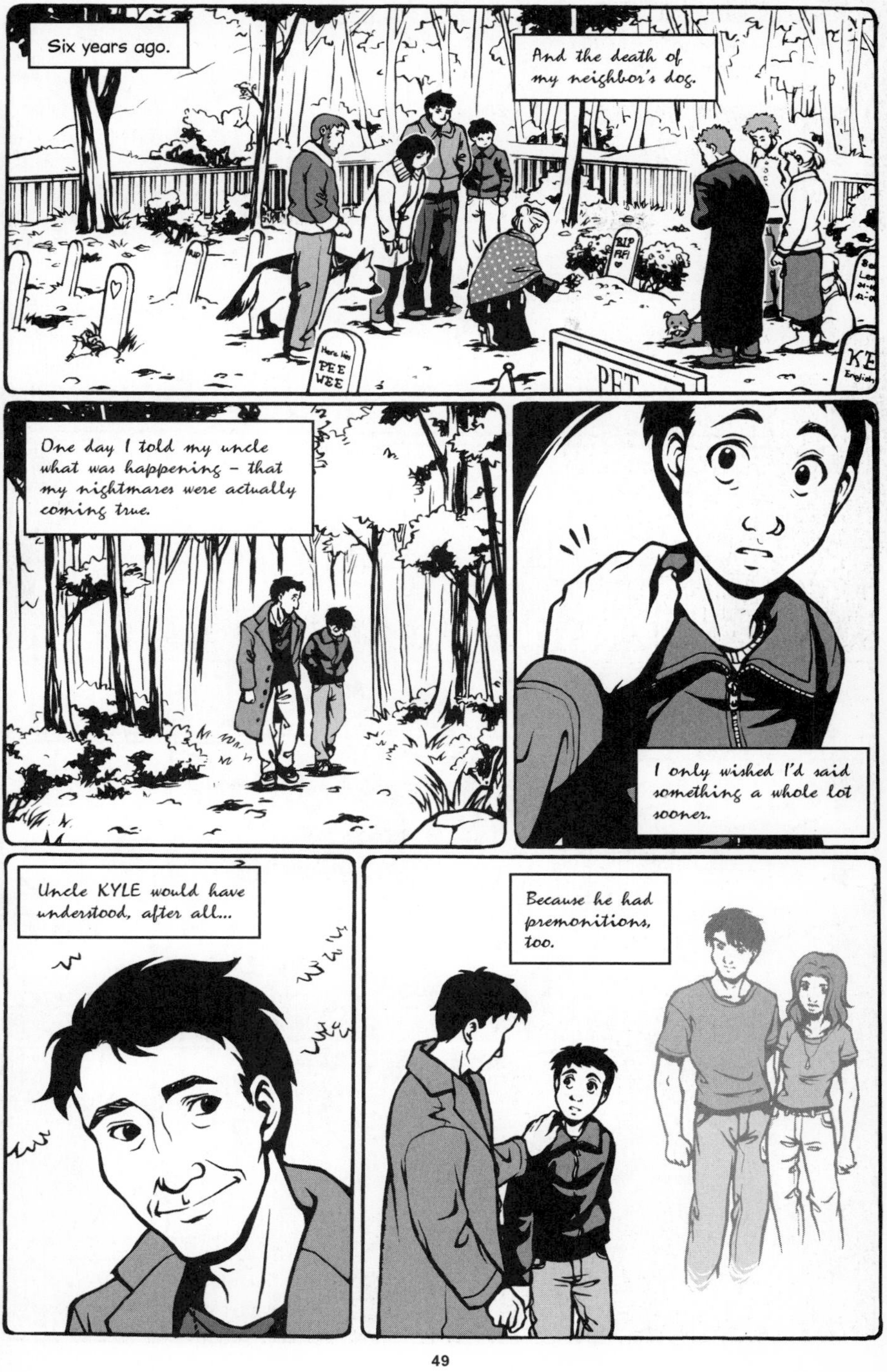
Six years ago.
And the death of my neighbor's dog.
RIP FIFI
PEE WEE
PET
One day I told my uncle what was happening – that my nightmares were actually coming true.
I only wished I'd said something a whole lot sooner.
Uncle KYLE would have understood, after all...
Because he had premonitions, too.

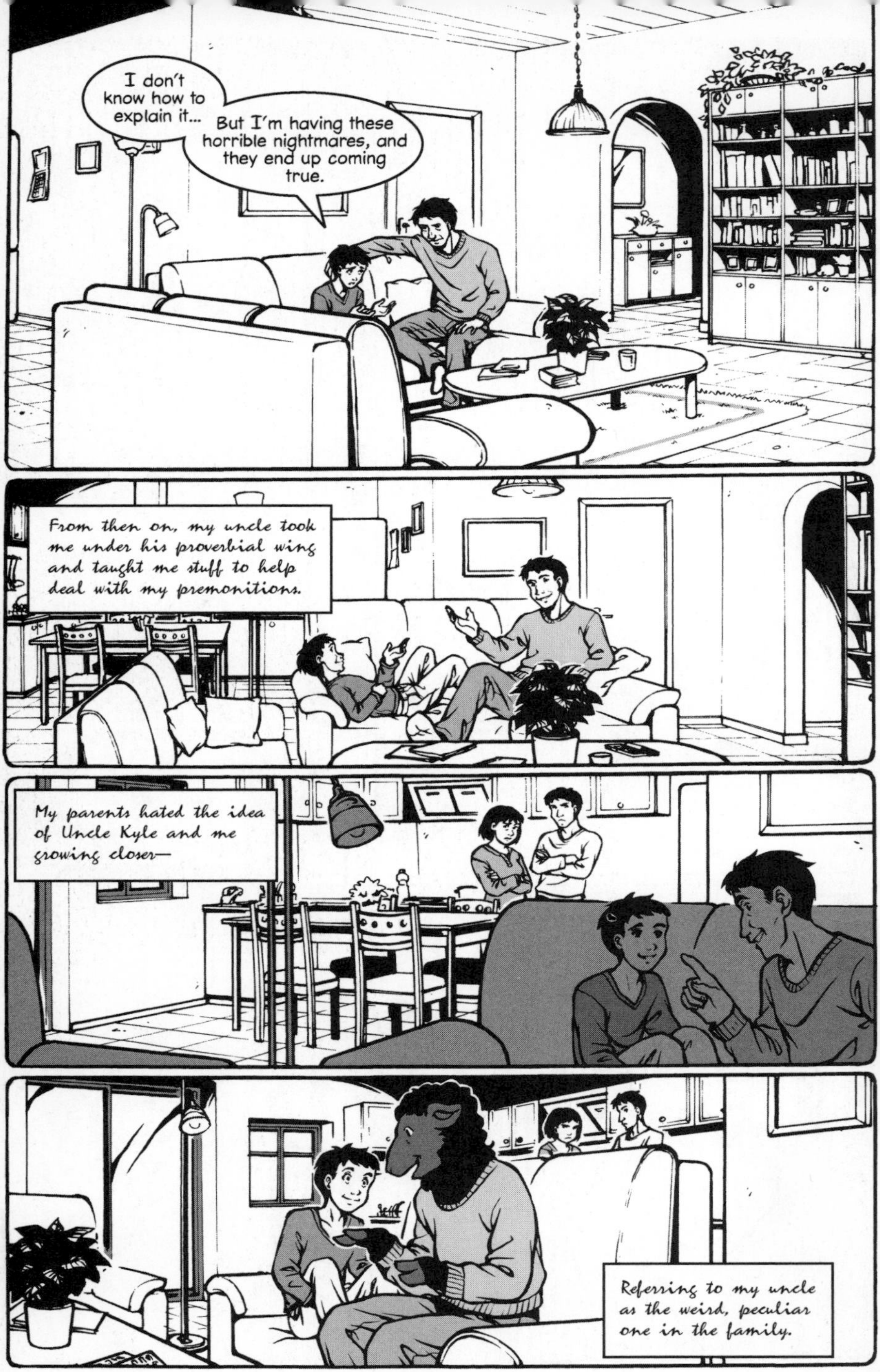
I don't know how to explain it...
But I'm having these horrible nightmares, and they end up coming true.
From then on, my uncle took me under his proverbial wing and taught me stuff to help deal with my premonitions.
My parents hated the idea of Uncle Kyle and me growing closer—
Referring to my uncle as the weird, peculiar one in the family.

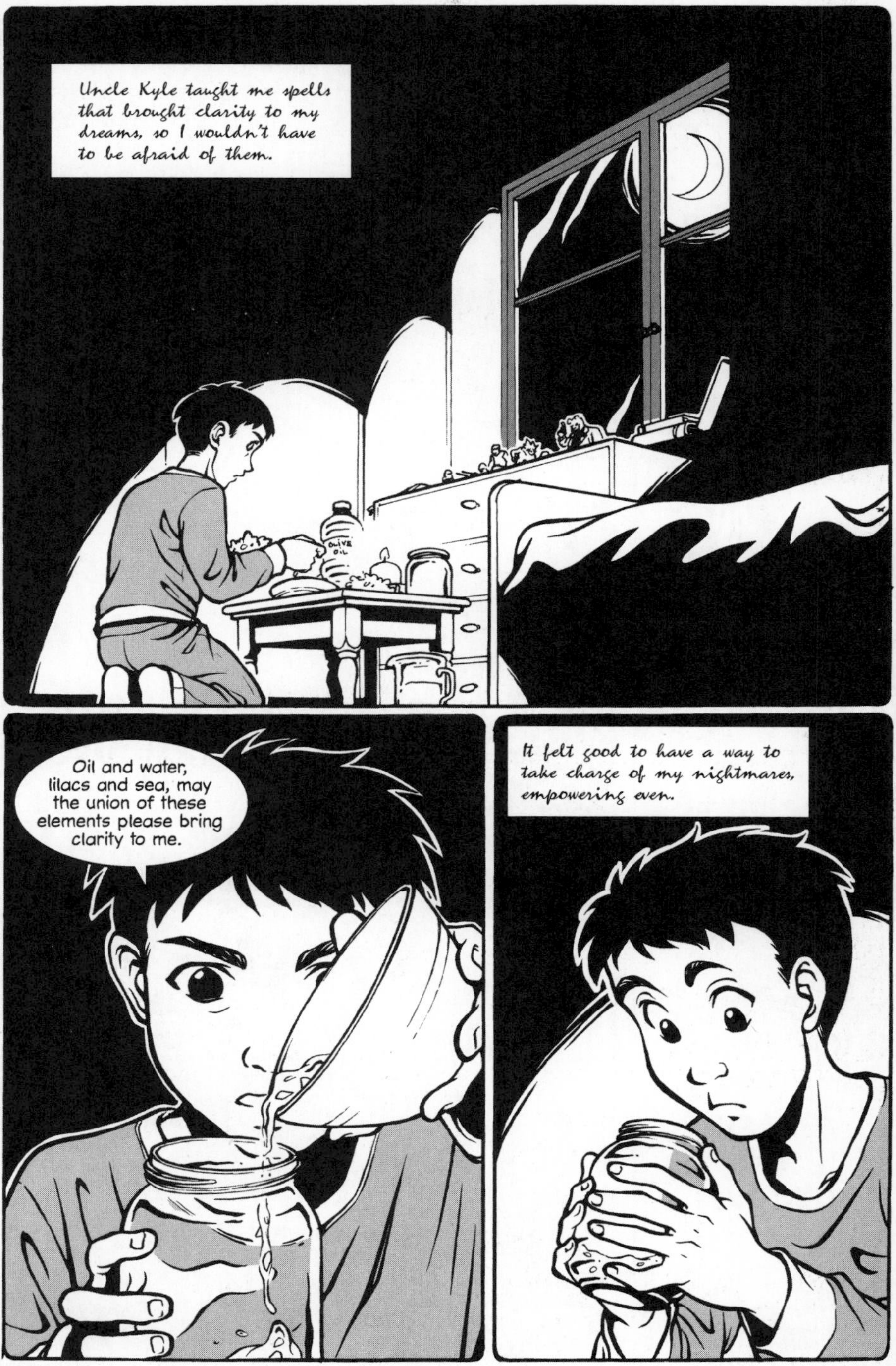
Uncle Kyle taught me spells that brought clarity to my dreams, so I wouldn't have to be afraid of them.
OLIVE OIL
Oil and water, lilacs and sea, may the union of these elements please bring clarity to me.
It felt good to have a way to take charge of my nightmares, empowering even.

UNCLE KYLE'S SCHOOL OF MAGIC

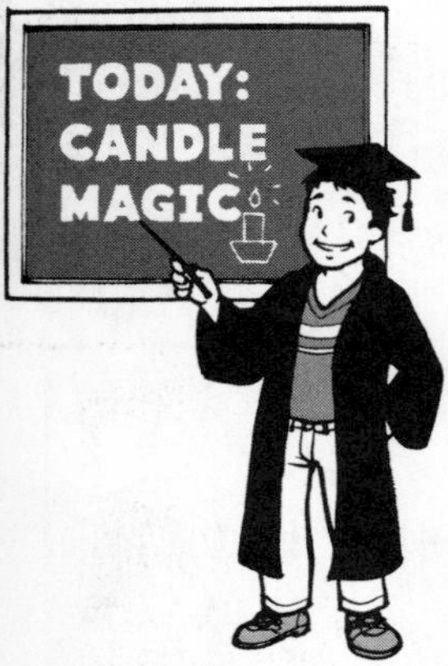
TODAY: CANDLE MAGIC

WHITE = MAGIC, PURITY, LOVE

SILVER = BANISHING SECRETS

GREEN = MONEY, GROWTH

GOLD = POSITIVE ENERGY

BLACK = CHANGES, BEGINNINGS

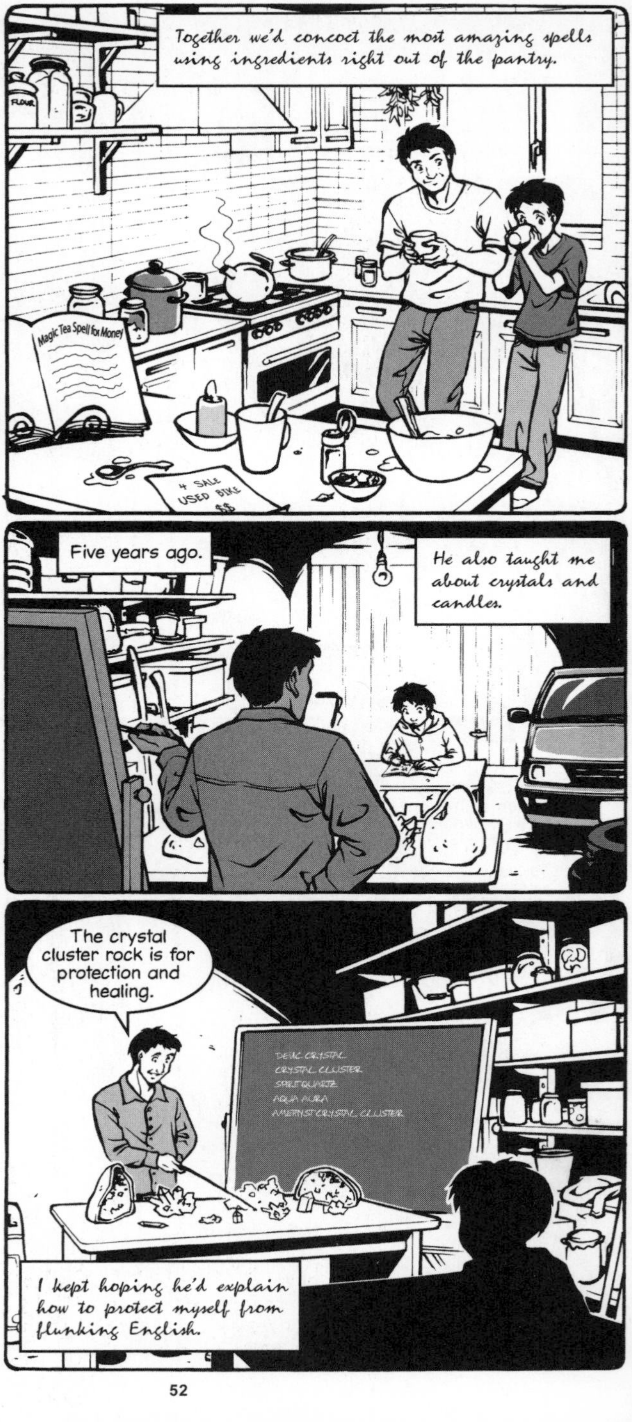
Together we'd concoct the most amazing spells using ingredients right out of the pantry.
Magic Tea Spell for Money
FLOUR
4 SALE USED BIKE $$
Five years ago.
He also taught me about crystals and candles.
The crystal cluster rock is for protection and healing.
DEVIC CRYSTAL
CRYSTAL CLUSTER
SPIRIT QUARTZ
AQUA AURA
AMETHYST CRYSTAL CLUSTER
I kept hoping he'd explain how to protect myself from flunking English.

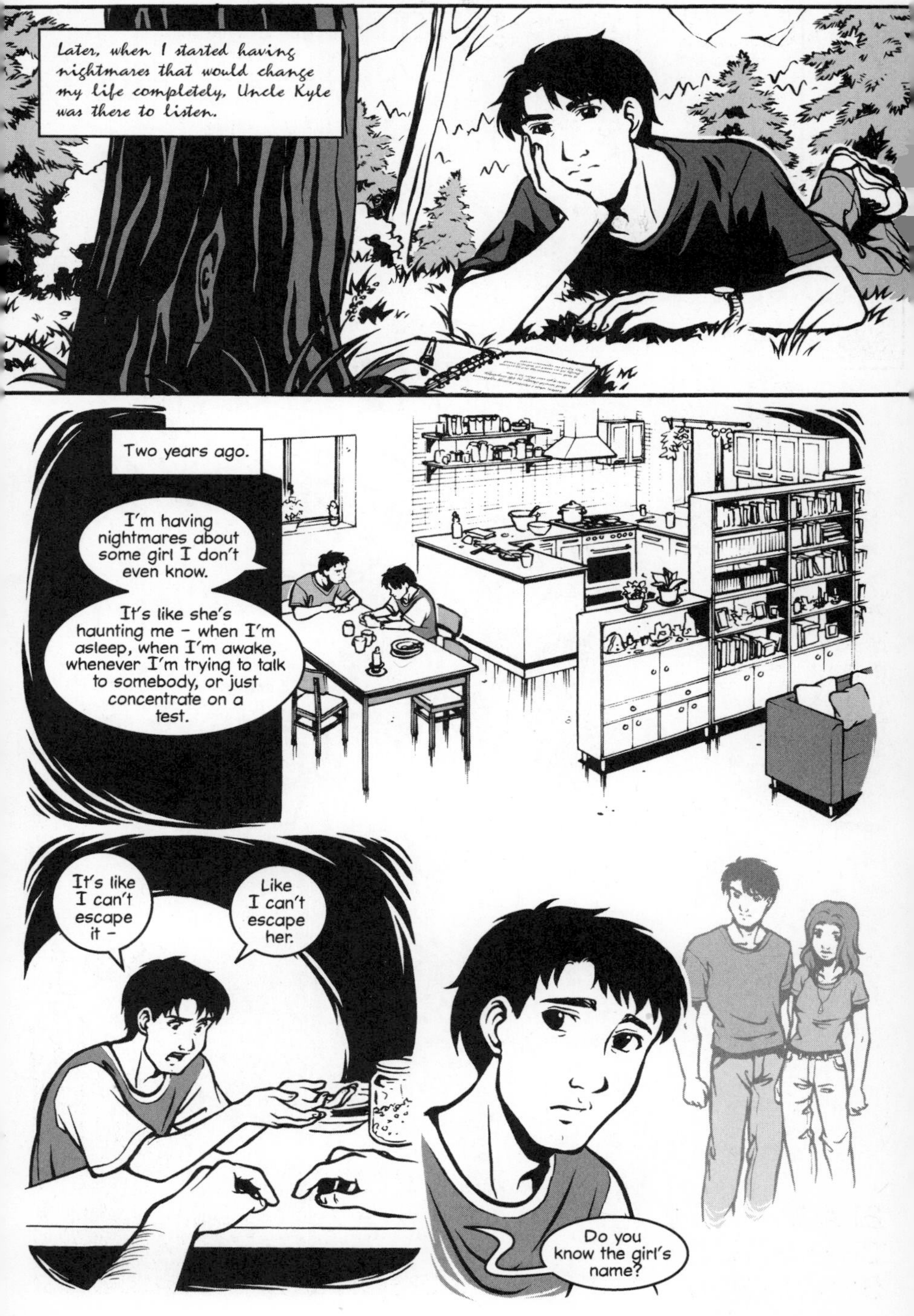
Later, when I started having nightmares that would change my life completely, Uncle Kyle was there to listen.
Two years ago.
I'm having nightmares about some girl I don't even know.
It's like she's haunting me – when I'm asleep, when I'm awake, whenever I'm trying to talk to somebody, or just concentrate on a test.
It's like I can't escape it –
Like I can't escape her.
Do you know the girl's name?

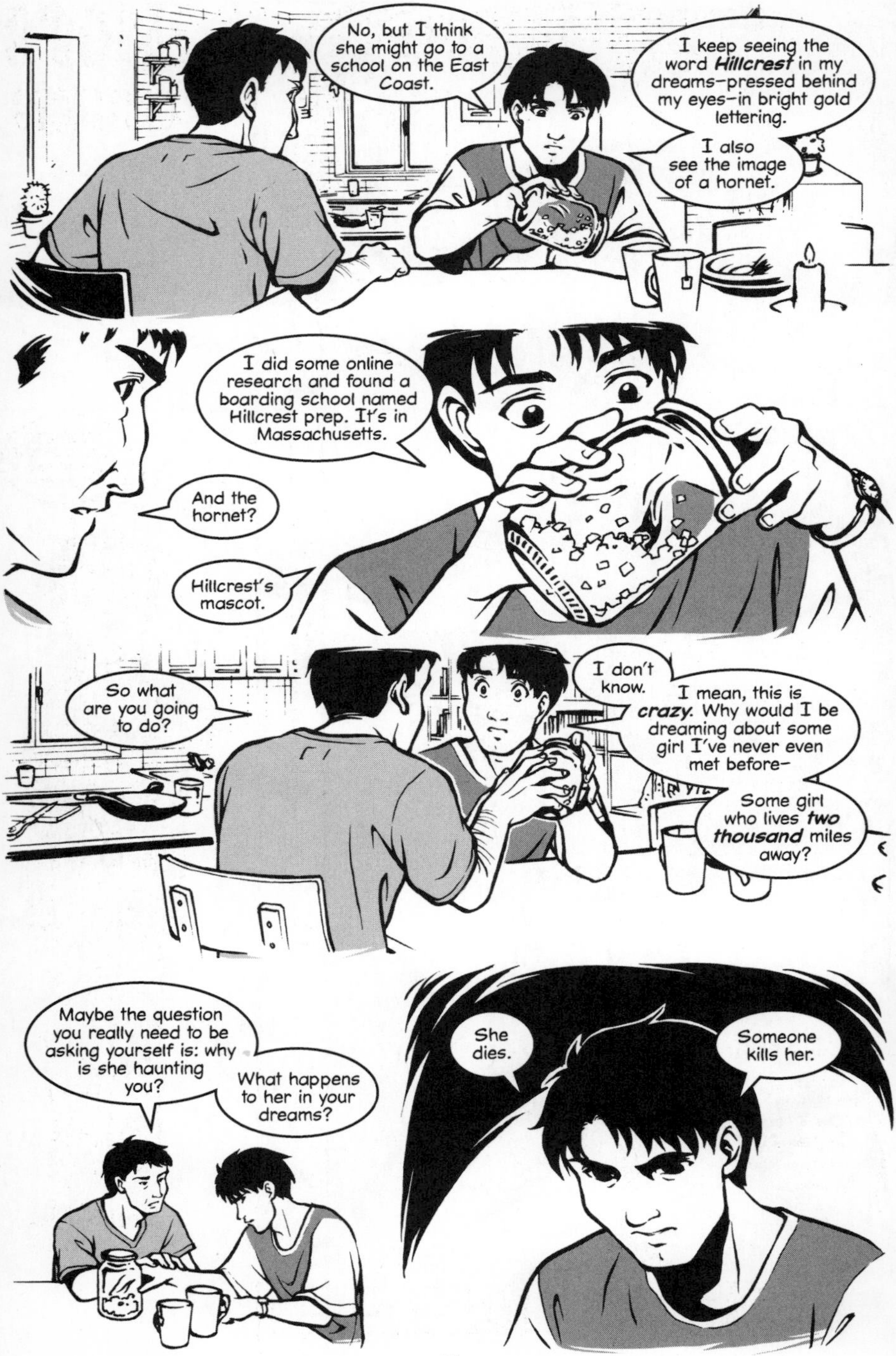
No, but I think she might go to a school on the East Coast.
I keep seeing the word Hillcrest in my dreams—pressed behind my eyes—in bright gold lettering.
I also see the image of a hornet.
I did some online research and found a boarding school named Hillcrest prep. It's in Massachusetts.
And the hornet?
Hillcrest's mascot.
So what are you going to do?
I don't know.
I mean, this is crazy. Why would I be dreaming about some girl I've never even met before—
Some girl who lives two thousand miles away?
Maybe the question you really need to be asking yourself is: why is she haunting you?
What happens to her in your dreams?
She dies.
Someone kills her.

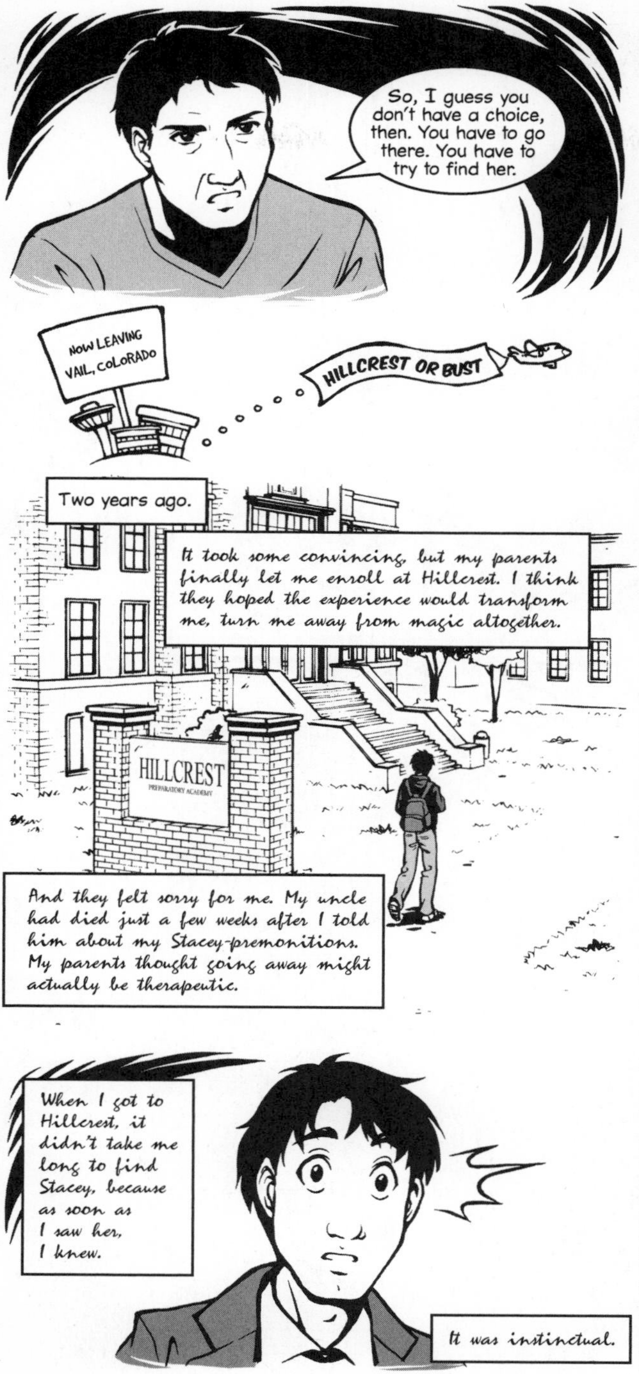
So, I guess you don't have a choice, then. You have to go there. You have to try to find her.
NOW LEAVING VAIL, COLORADO
HILLCREST OR BUST
Two years ago.
It took some convincing, but my parents finally let me enroll at Hillcrest. I think they hoped the experience would transform me, turn me away from magic altogether.
HILLCREST
PREPARATORY ACADEMY
And they felt sorry for me. My uncle had died just a few weeks after I told him about my Stacey-premonitions. My parents thought going away might actually be therapeutic.
When I got to Hillcrest, it didn't take me long to find Stacey, because as soon as I saw her, I knew.
It was instinctual.

JACOB'S INSTINCTS

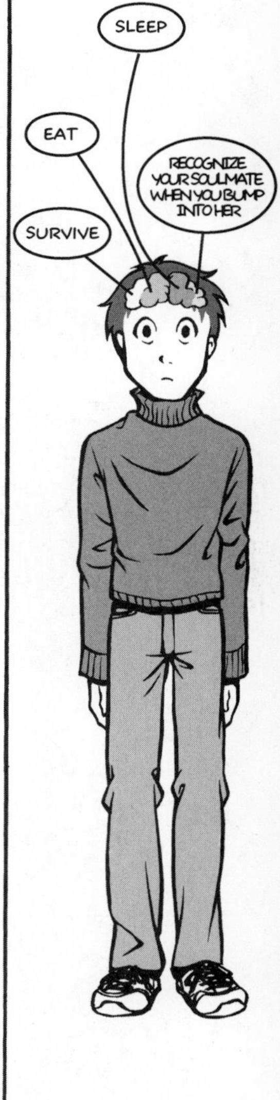
SLEEP
EAT
RECOGNIZE YOUR SOULMATE WHEN YOU BUMP INTO HER
SURVIVE

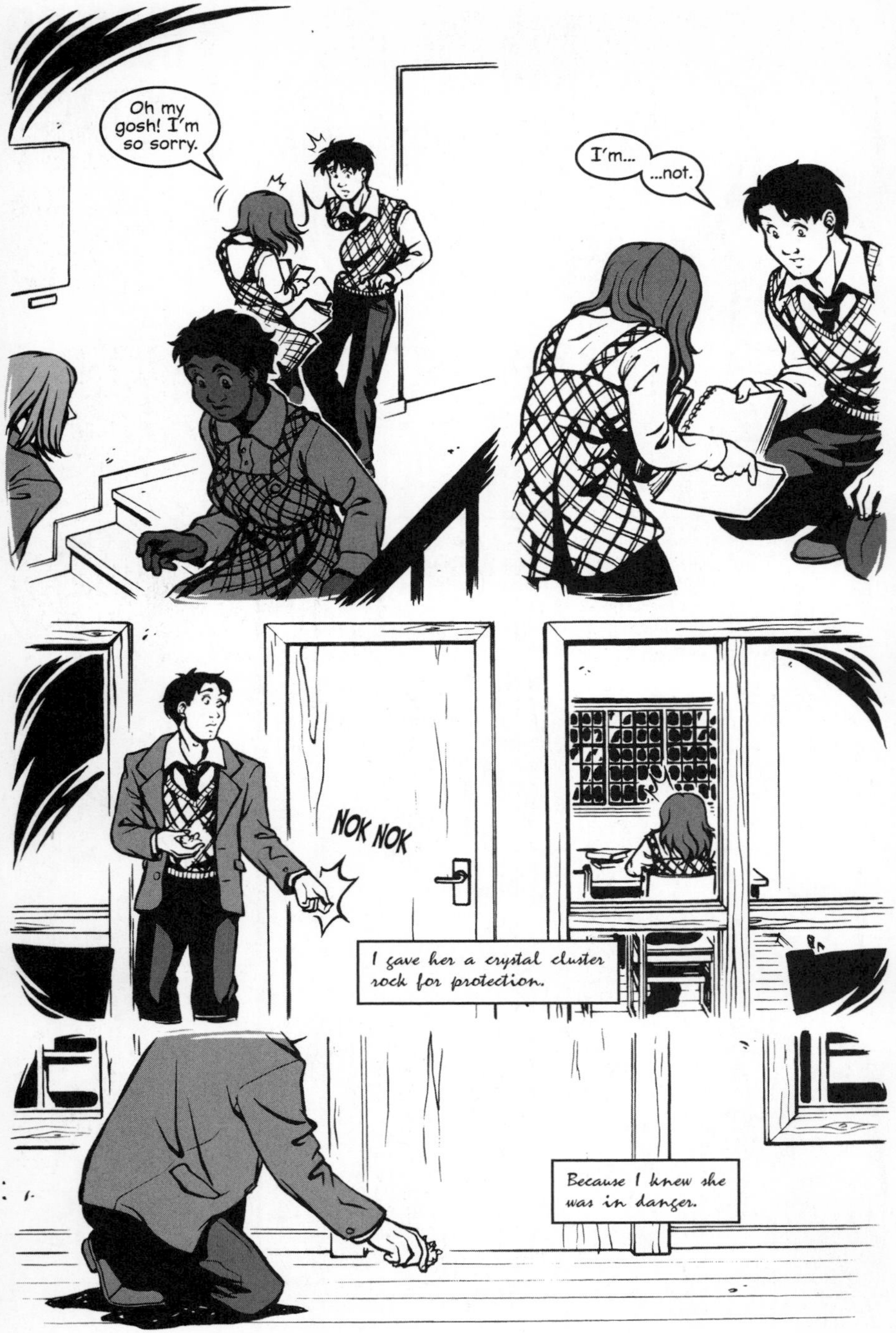
Oh my gosh! I'm so sorry.
I'm...
...not.
NOK NOK
I gave her a crystal cluster rock for protection.
Because I knew she was in danger.

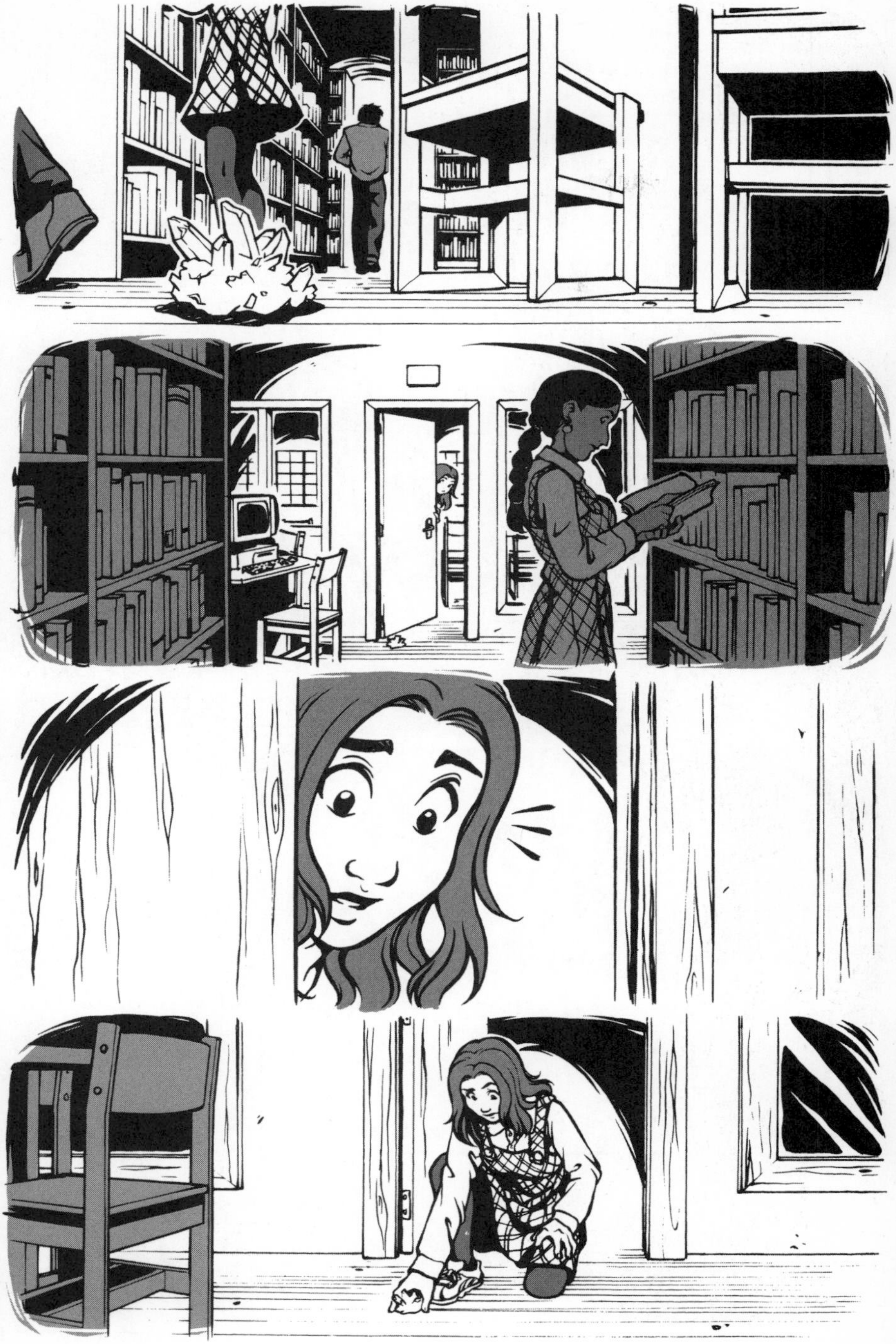

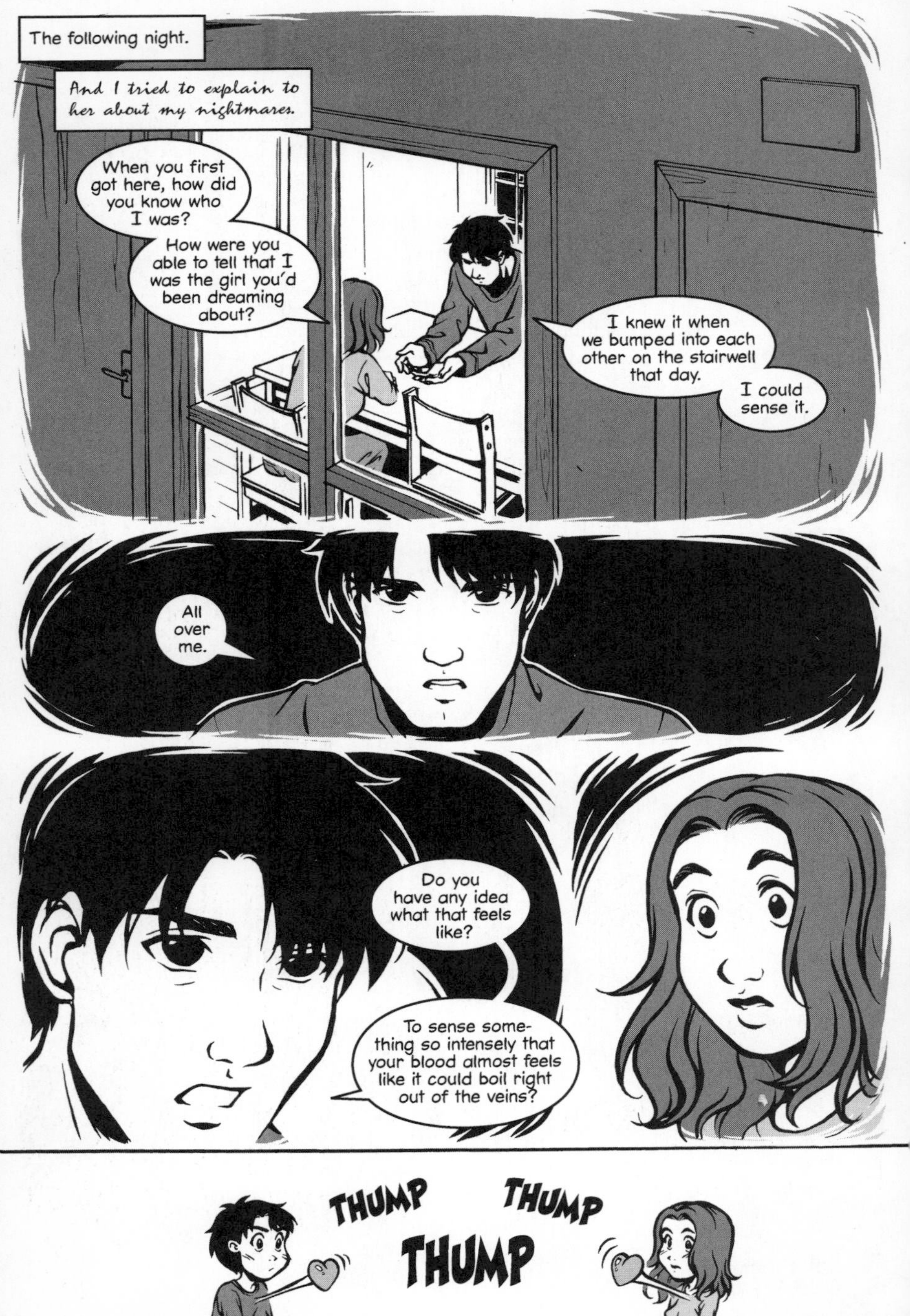
The following night.
And I tried to explain to her about my nightmares.
When you first got here, how did you know who I was?
How were you able to tell that I was the girl you'd been dreaming about?
I knew it when we bumped into each other on the stairwell that day.
I could sense it.
All over me.
Do you have any idea what that feels like?
To sense something so intensely that your blood almost feels like it could boil right out of the veins?
THUMP
THUMP
THUMP

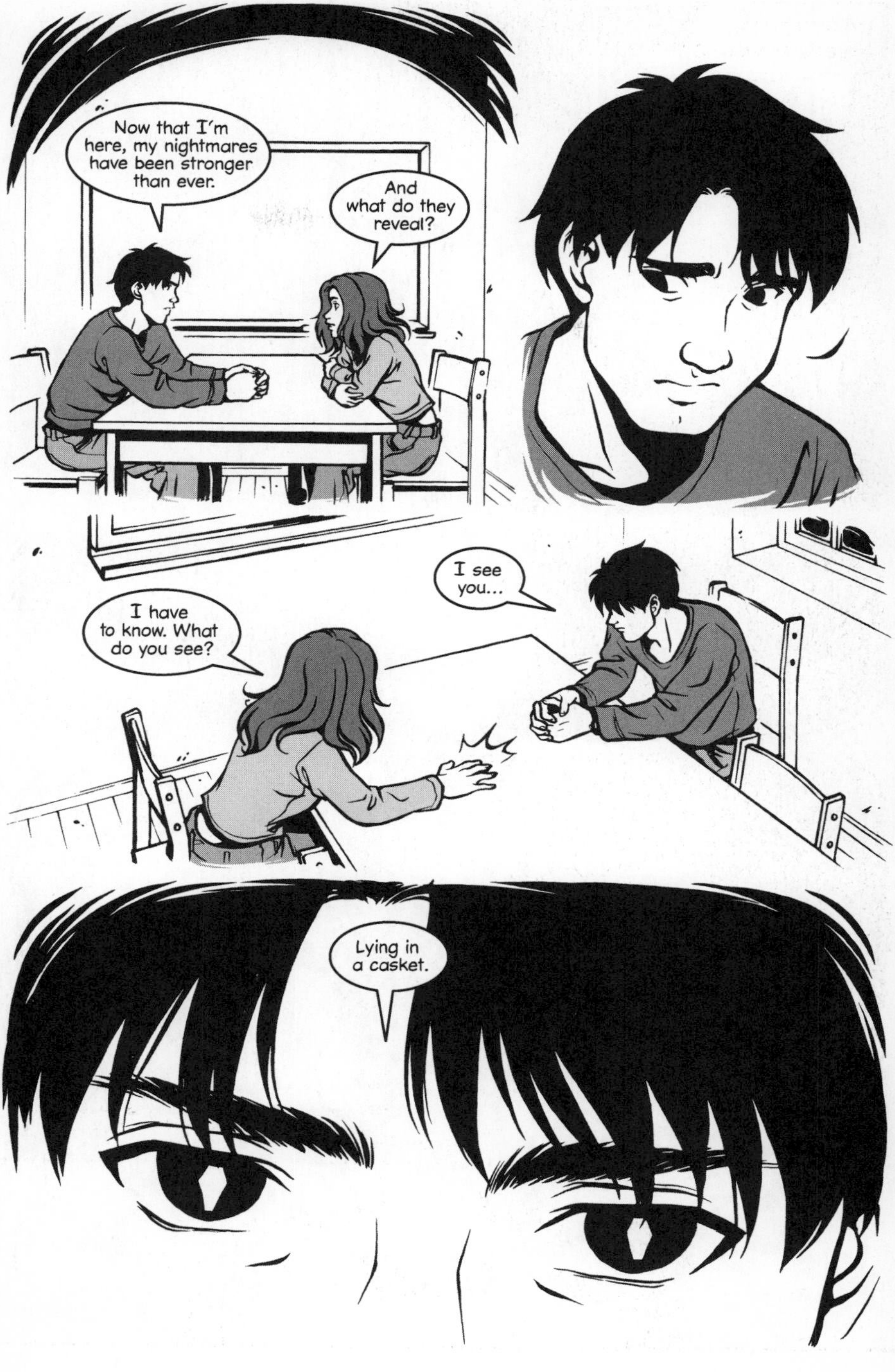
Now that I'm here, my nightmares have been stronger than ever.
And what do they reveal?
I have to know. What do you see?
I see you...
Lying in a casket.

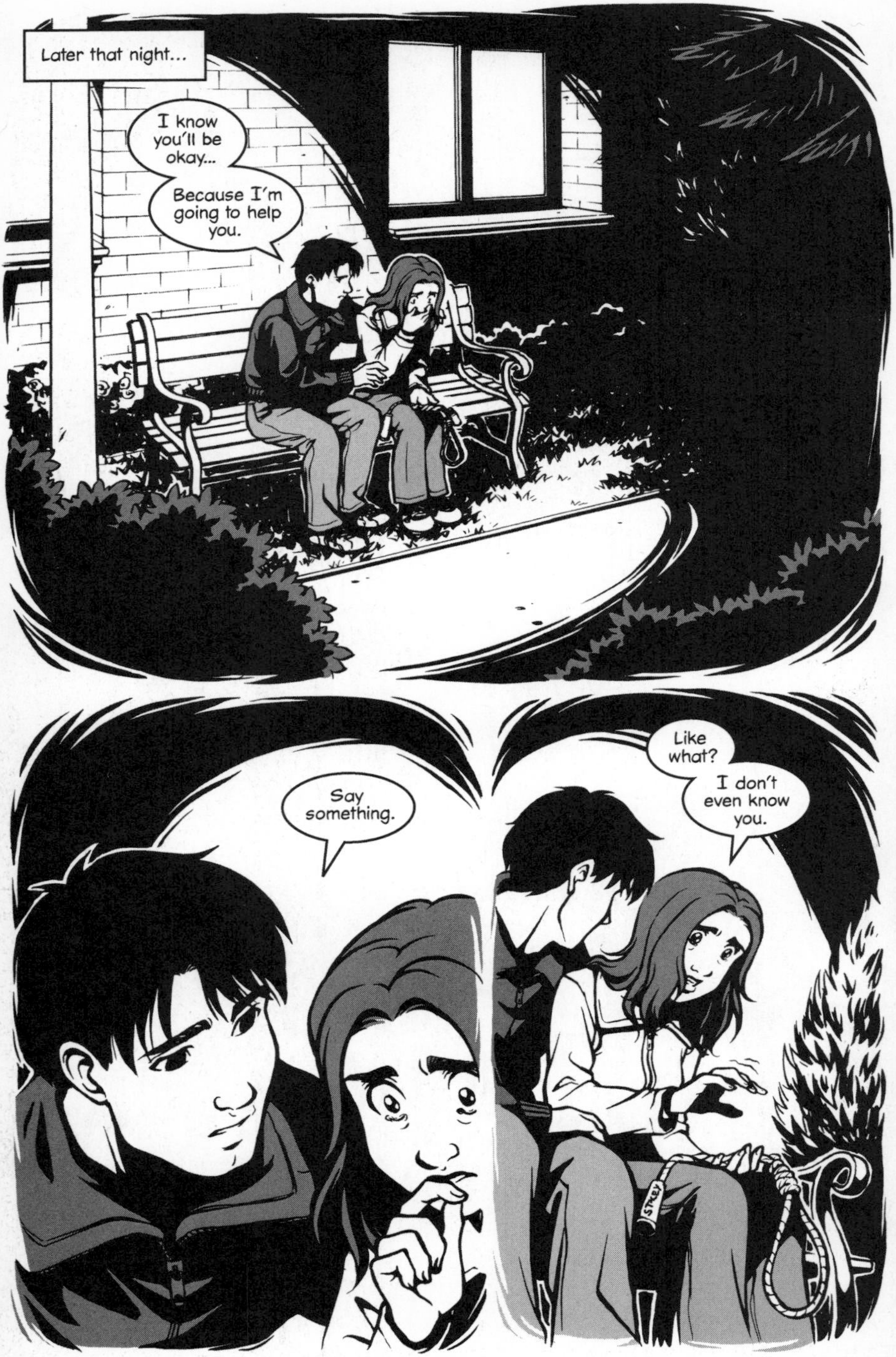
Later that night...
I know you'll be okay...
Because I'm going to help you.
Say something.
Like what?
I don't even know you.
STACEY

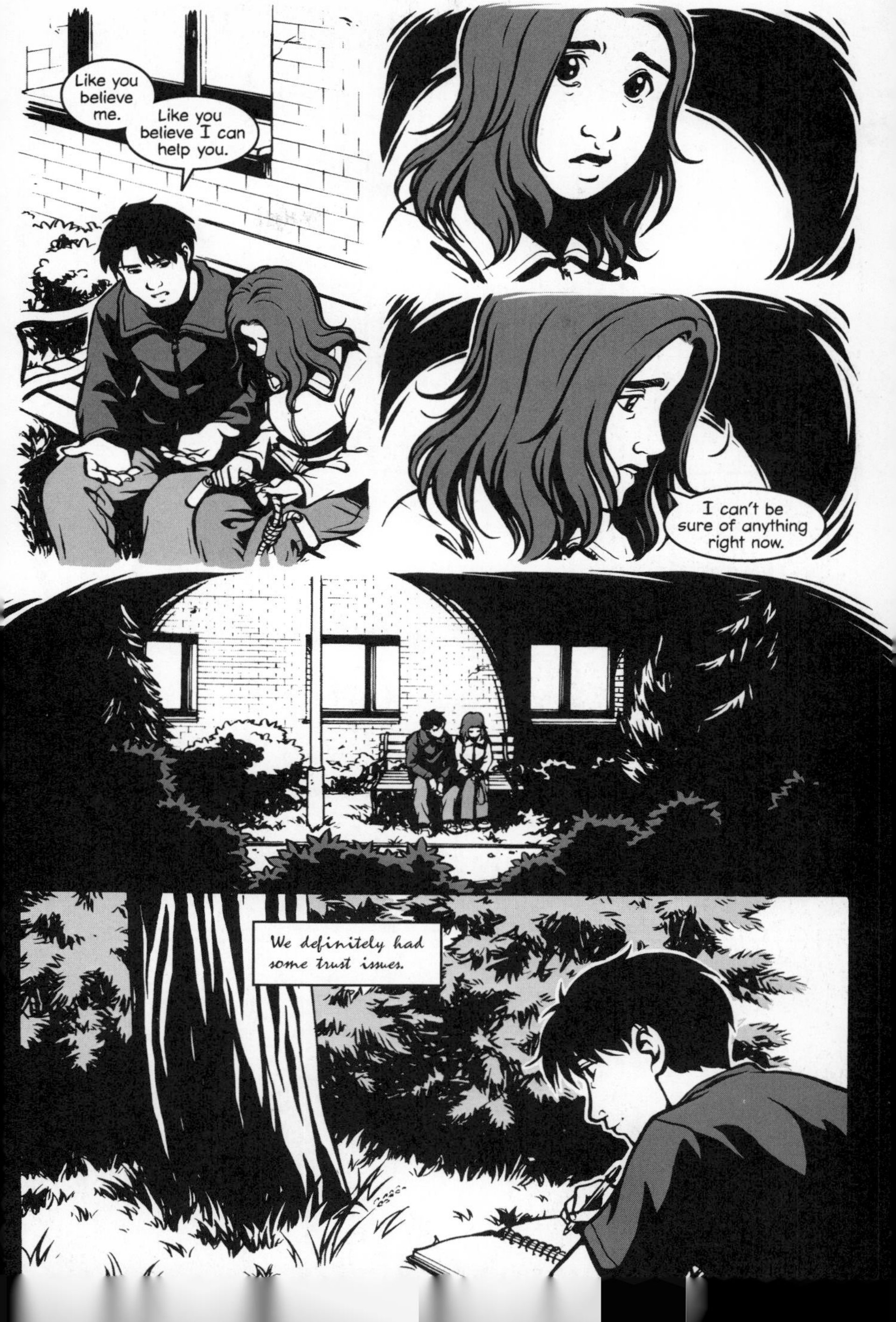
Like you believe me.
Like you believe I can help you.
I can't be sure of anything right now.
We definitely had some trust issues.

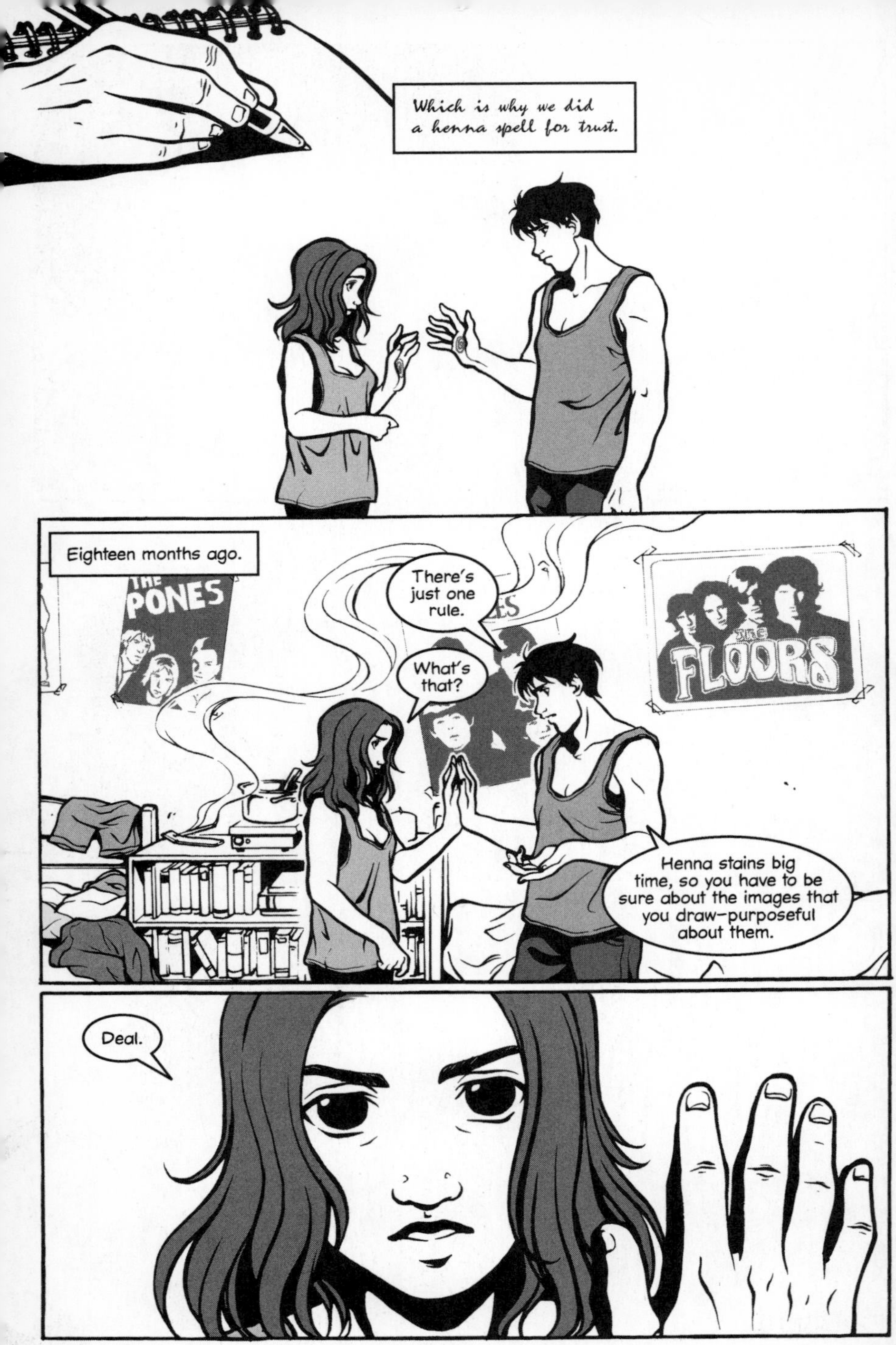
Which is why we did
a henna spell for trust.
Eighteen months ago.
THE PONES
There's just one rule.
What's that?
FLOORS
Henna stains big time, so you have to be sure about the images that you draw–purposeful about them.
Deal.

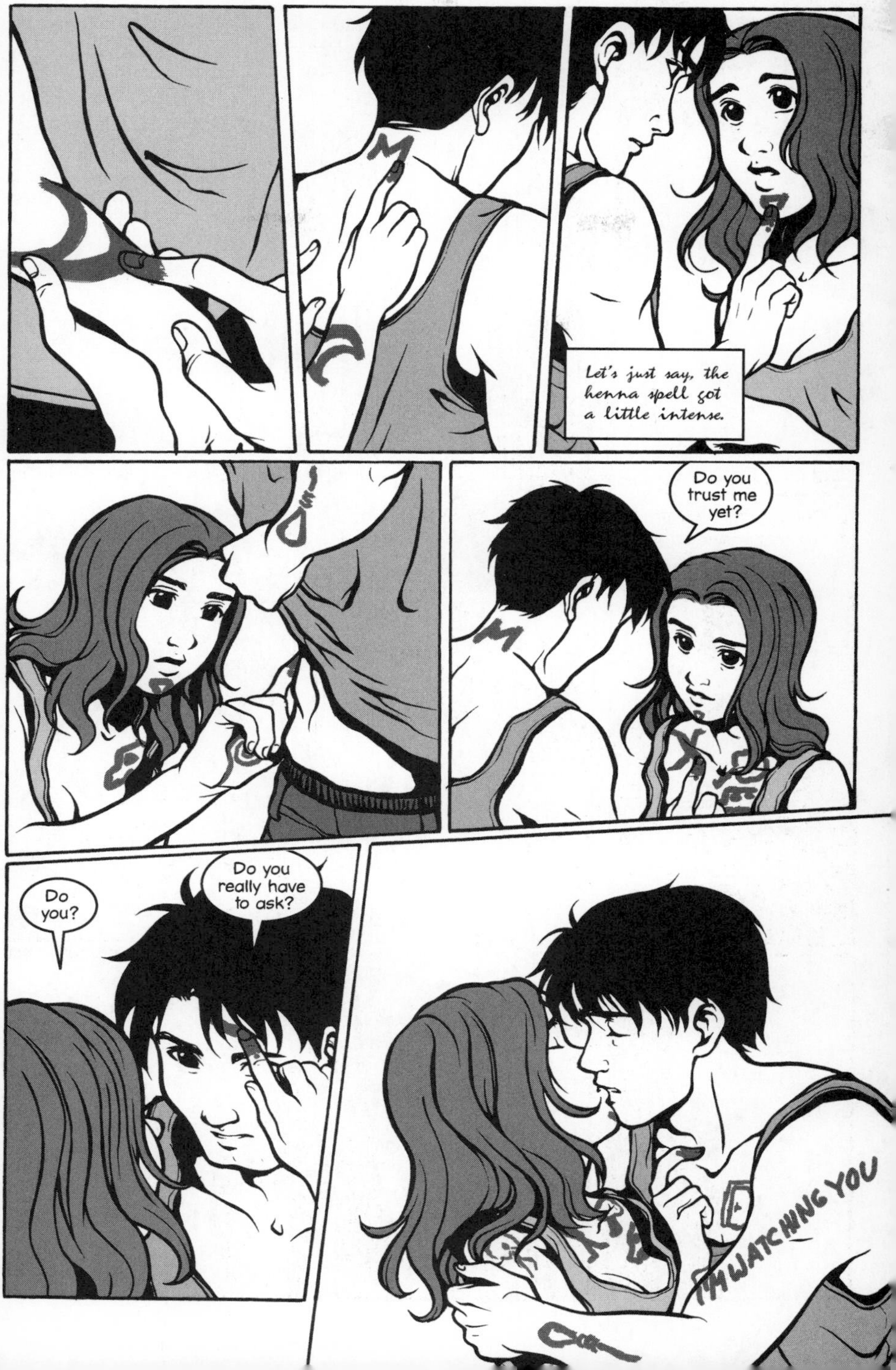
Let's just say, the henna spell got a little intense.
Do you trust me yet?
Do you?
Do you really have to ask?
I'M WATCHING YOU

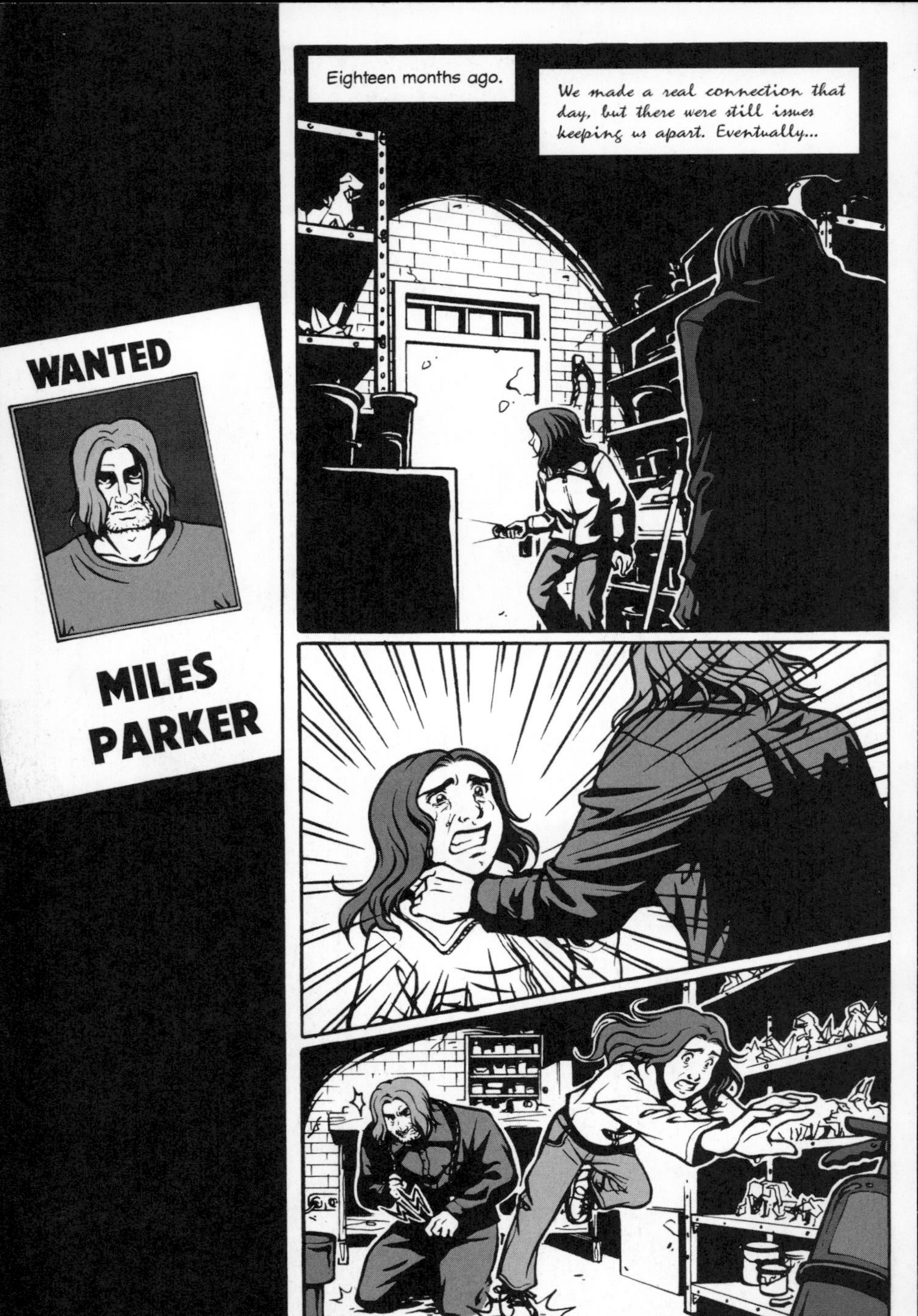
WANTED
MILES PARKER
Eighteen months ago.
We made a real connection that day, but there were still issues keeping us apart. Eventually...

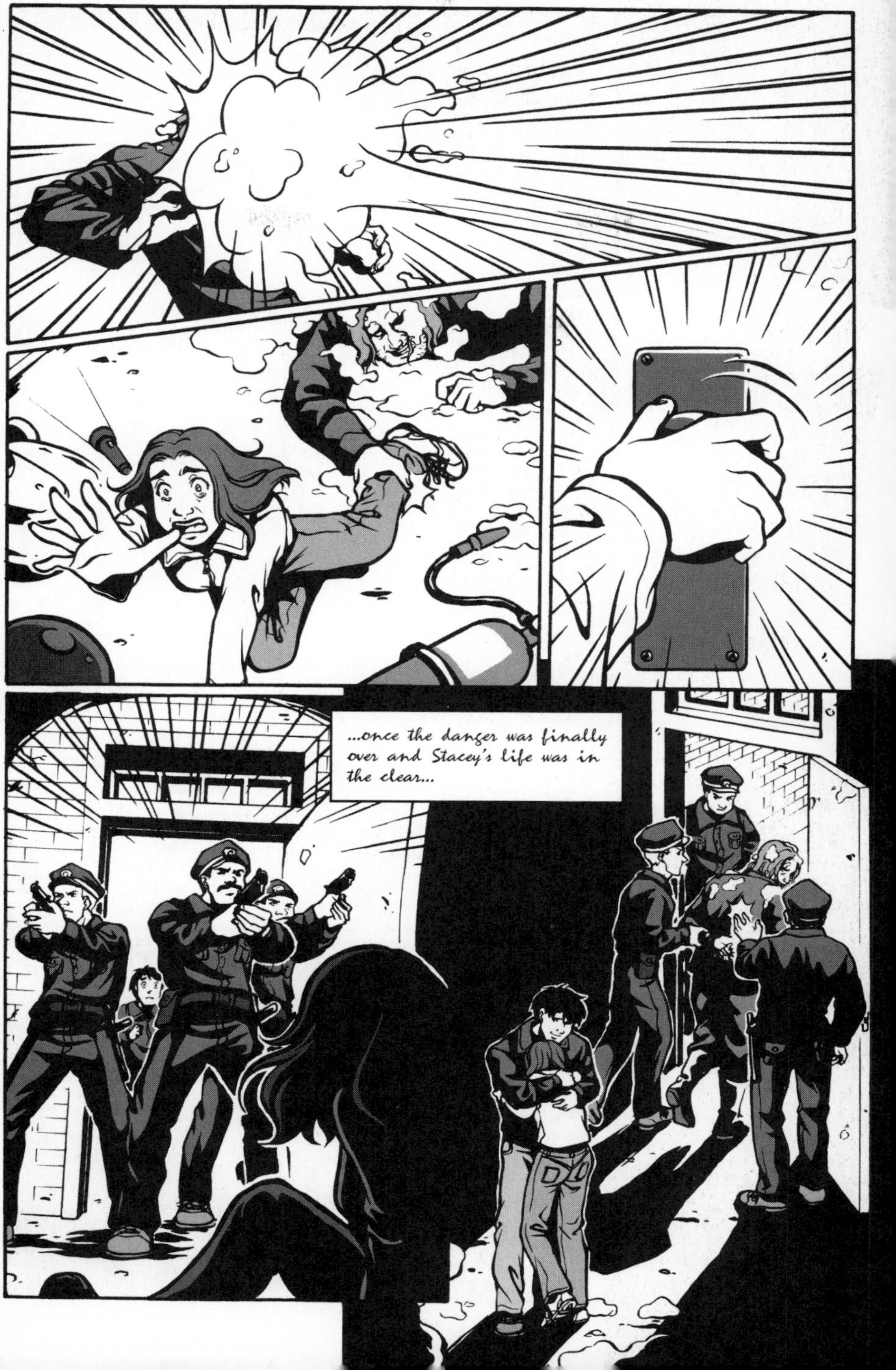
...once the danger was finally over and Stacey's life was in the clear...

...Stacey and I were able to embark upon more pleasurable pursuits.

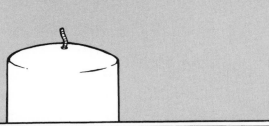

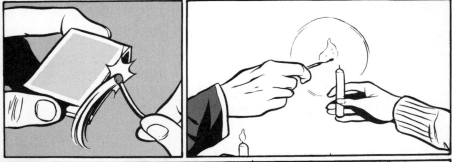

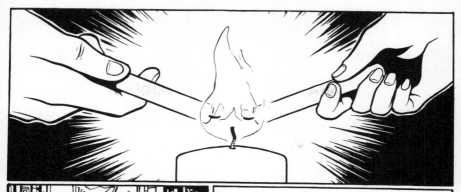

Blessed be.

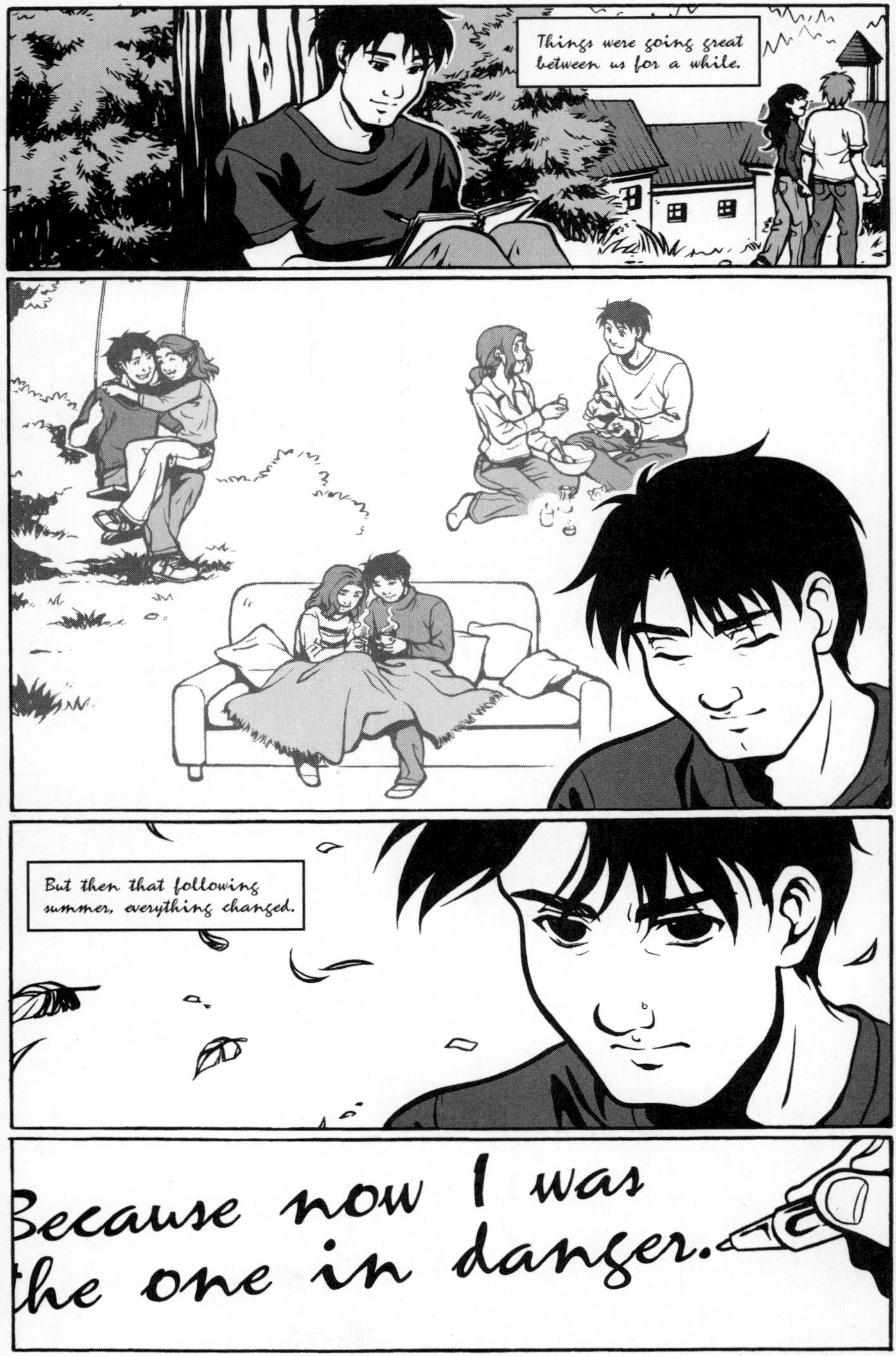
Things were going great between us for a while.
But then that following summer, everything changed.
Because now I was the one in danger...

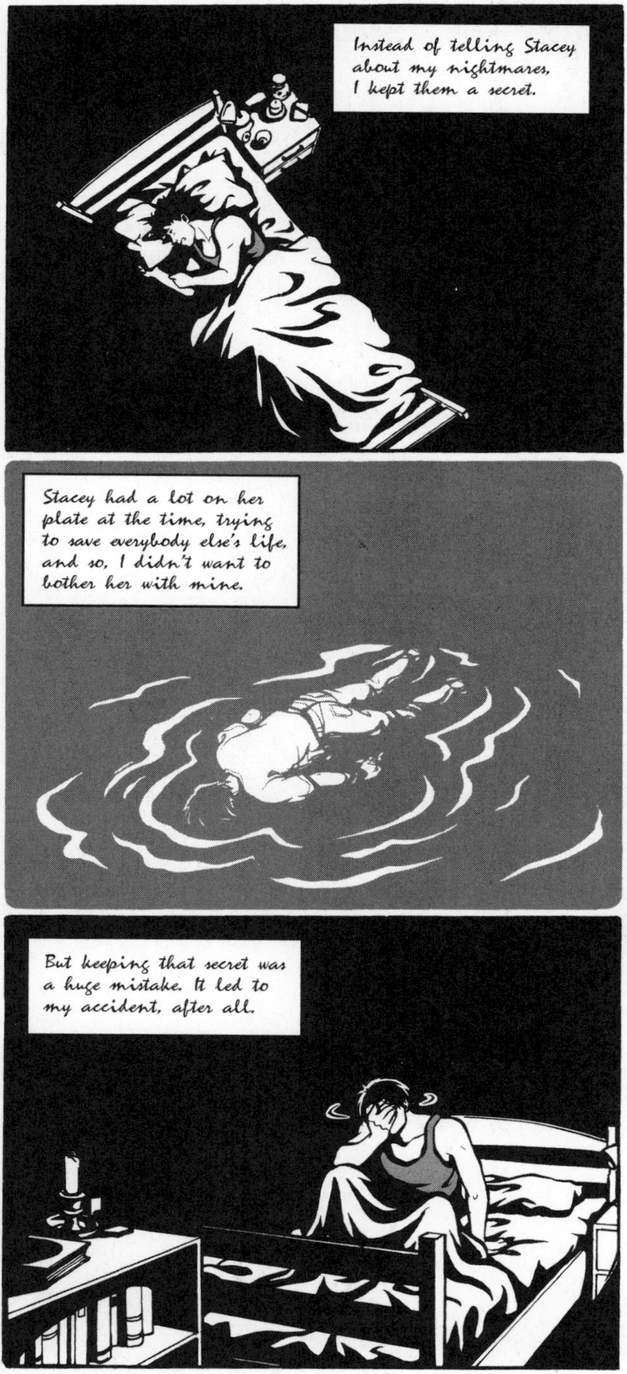
Instead of telling Stacey about my nightmares, I kept them a secret.
Stacey had a lot on her plate at the time, trying to save everybody else's life, and so, I didn't want to bother her with mine.
But keeping that secret was a huge mistake. It led to my accident, after all.

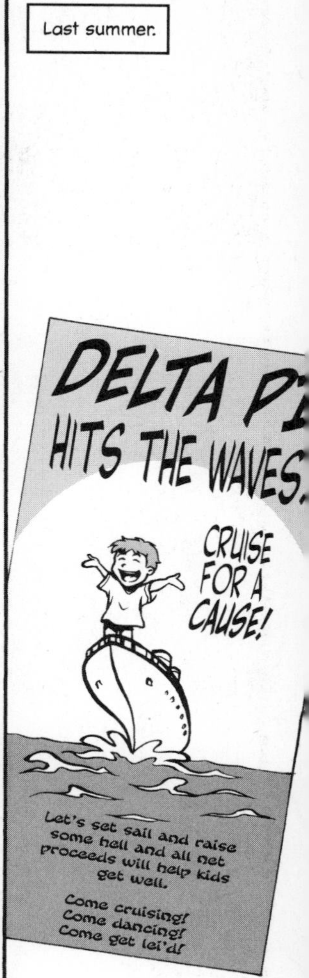
Last summer.
DELTA P
HITS THE WAVES.
CRUISE FOR A CAUSE!
Let's set sail and raise some hell and all net proceeds will help kids get well.
Come cruising!
Come dancing!
Come get lei'd!

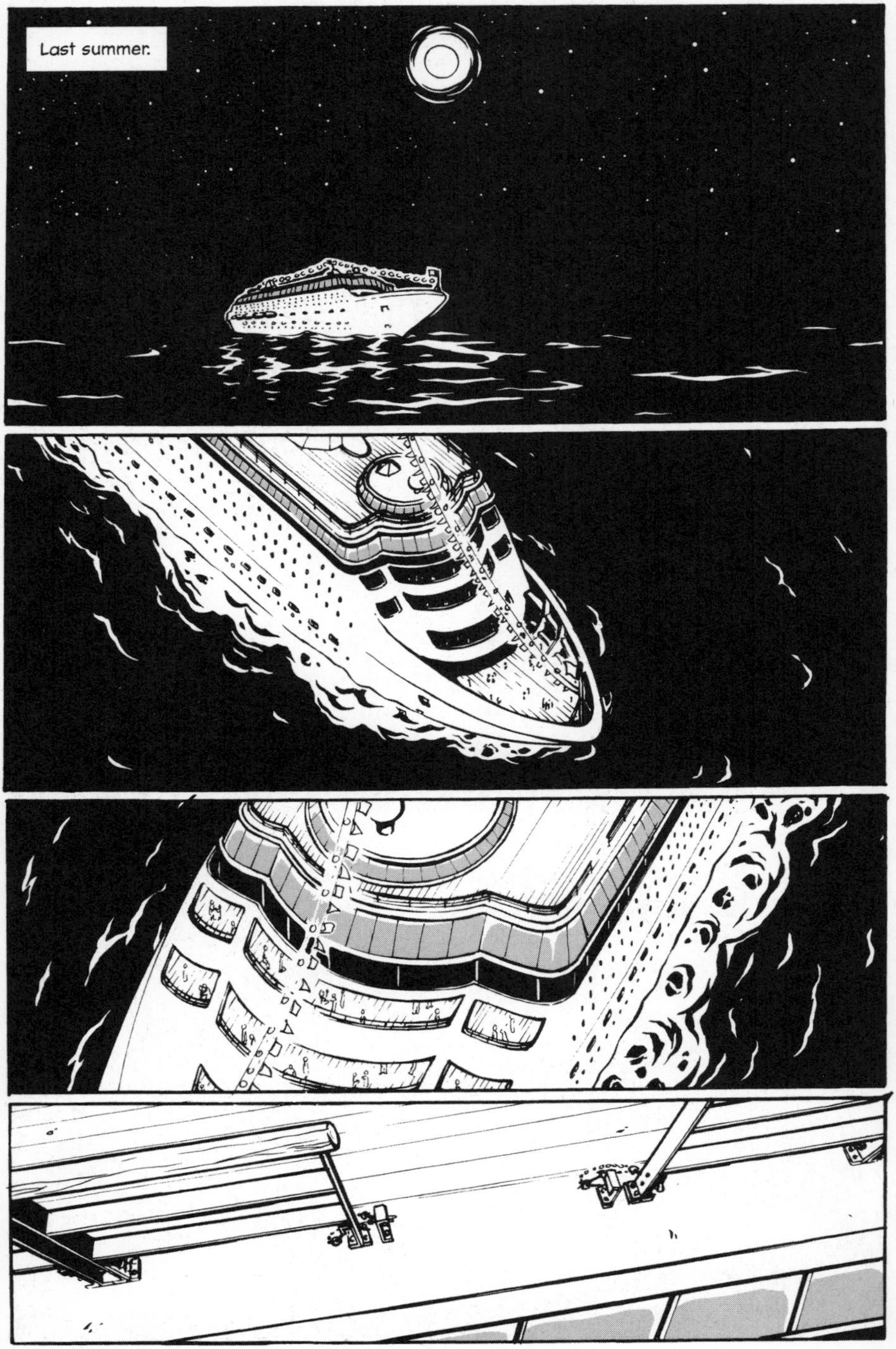
Last summer.

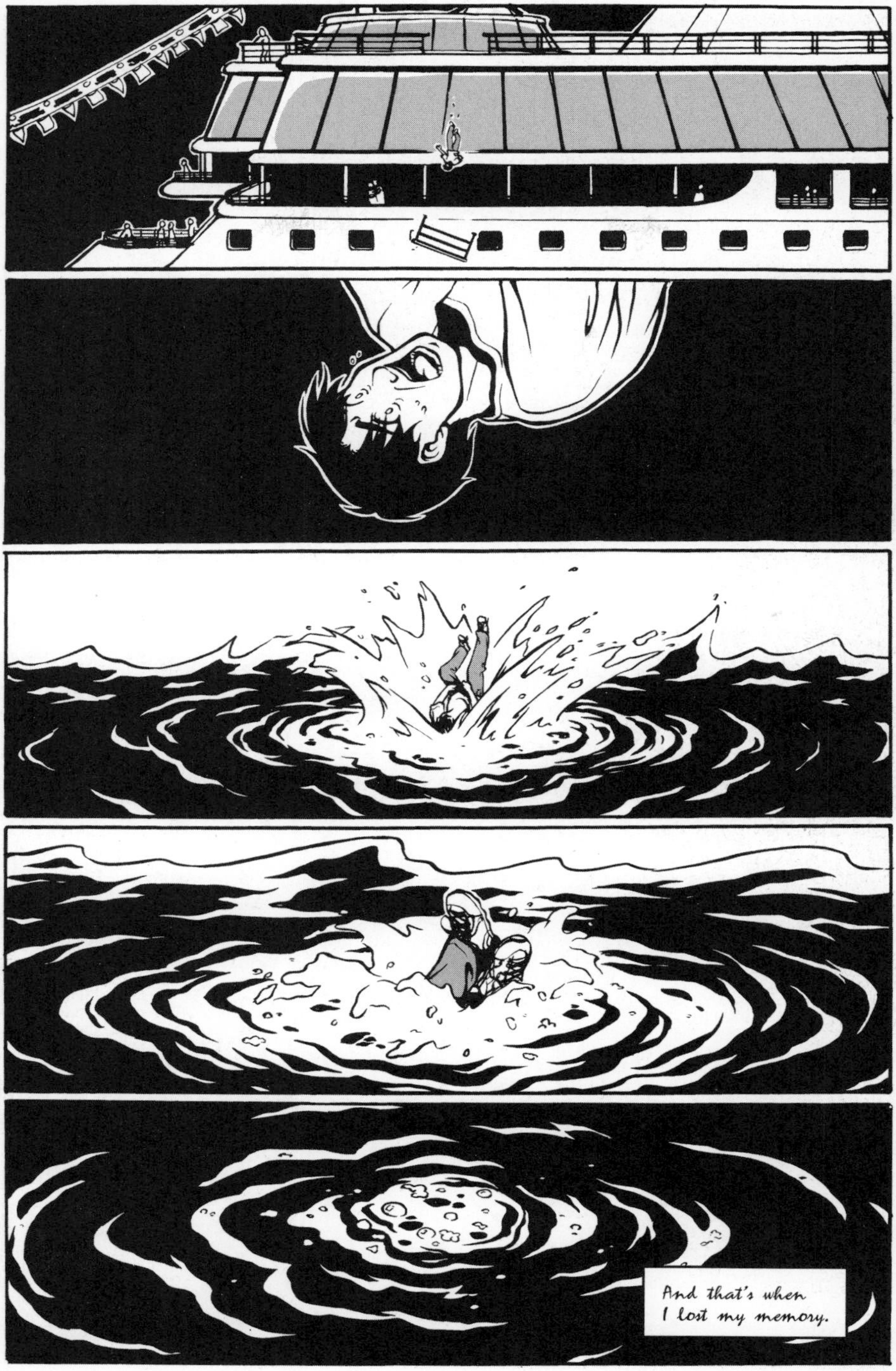
And that's when
I lost my memory.

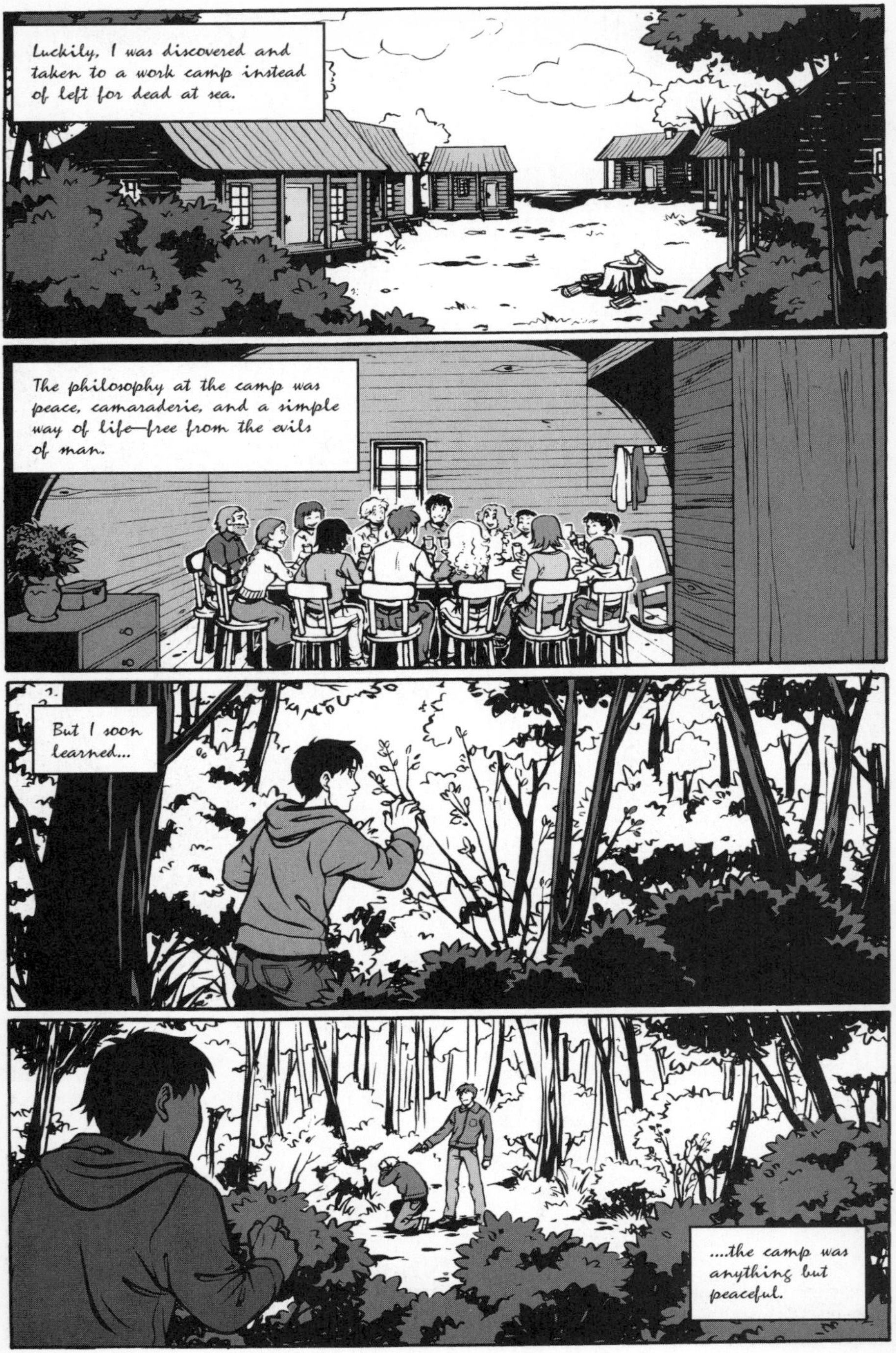
Luckily, I was discovered and taken to a work camp instead of left for dead at sea.
The philosophy at the camp was peace, camaraderie, and a simple way of life—free from the evils of man.
But I soon learned...
...the camp was anything but peaceful.

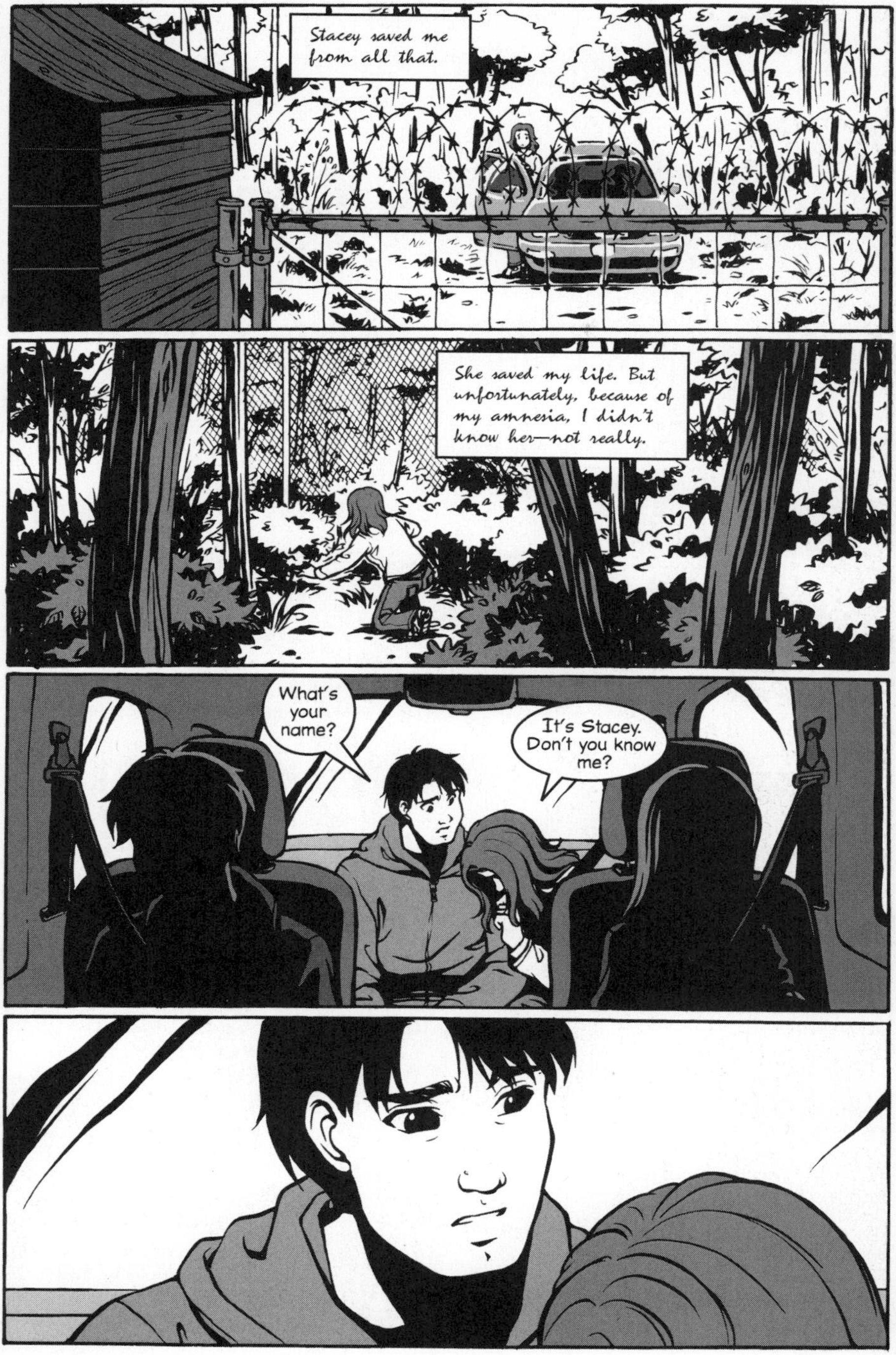

Stacey saved me from all that.
She saved my life. But unfortunately, because of my amnesia, I didn't know her—not really.
What's your name?
It's Stacey. Don't you know me?

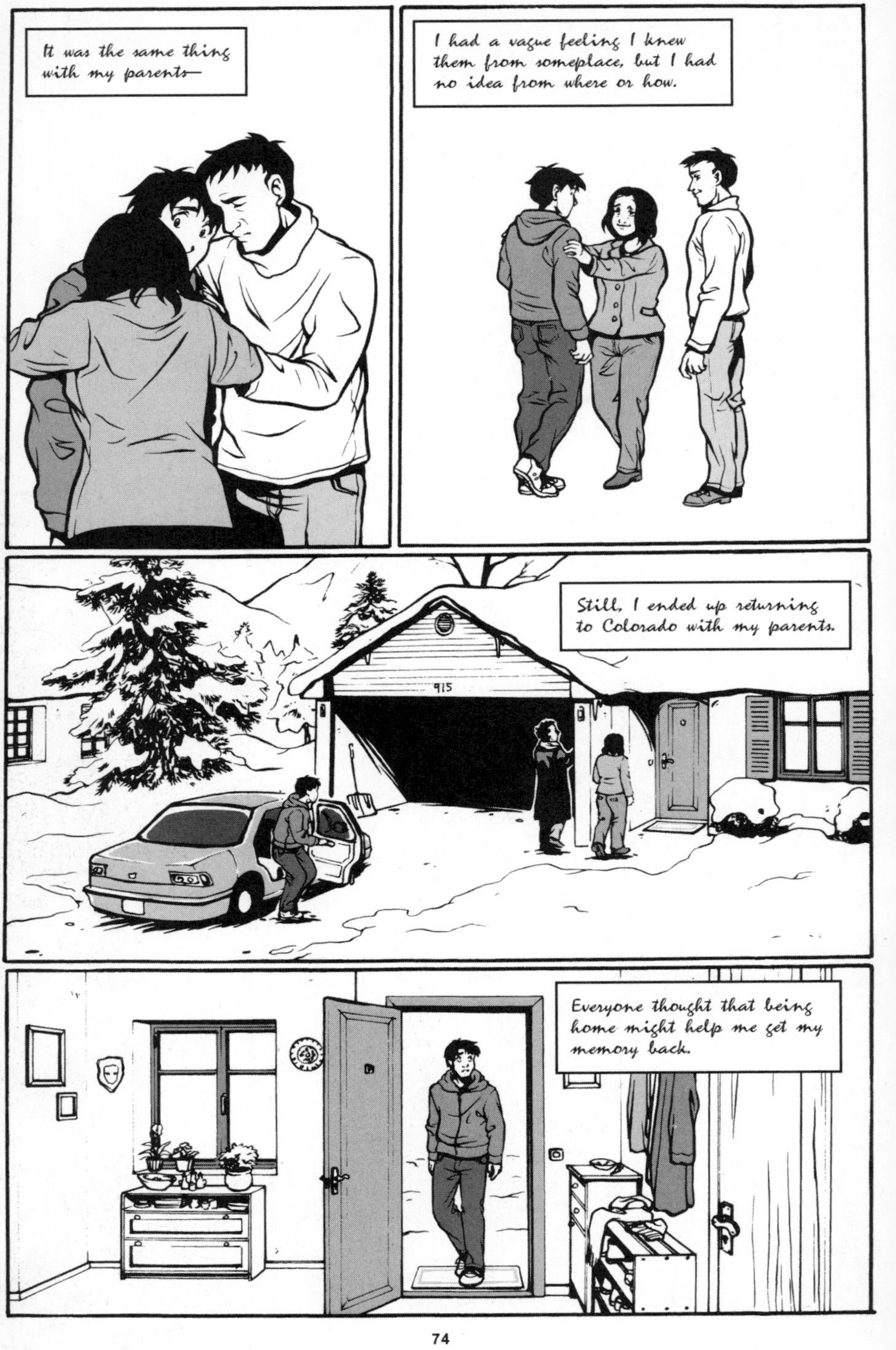
It was the same thing with my parents—
I had a vague feeling I knew them from someplace, but I had no idea from where or how.
Still, I ended up returning to Colorado with my parents.
Everyone thought that being home might help me get my memory back.

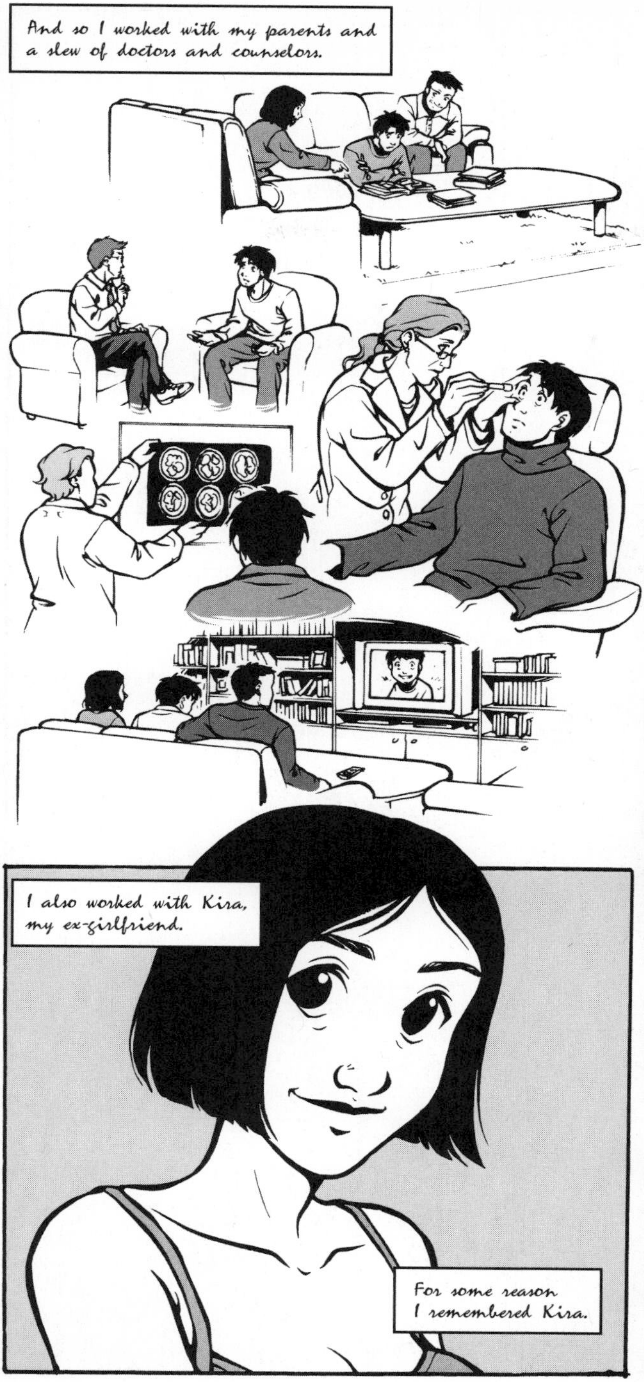
And so I worked with my parents and a slew of doctors and counselors.
I also worked with Kira, my ex-girlfriend.
For some reason I remembered Kira.

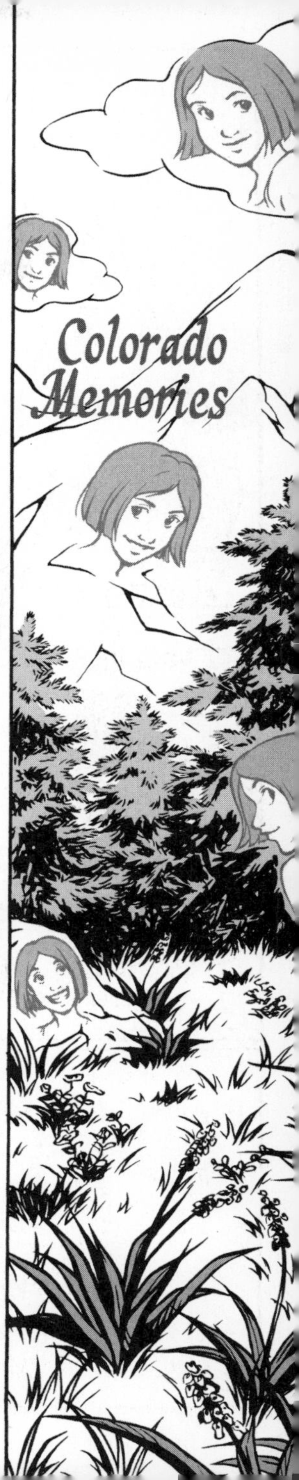
Colorado Memories

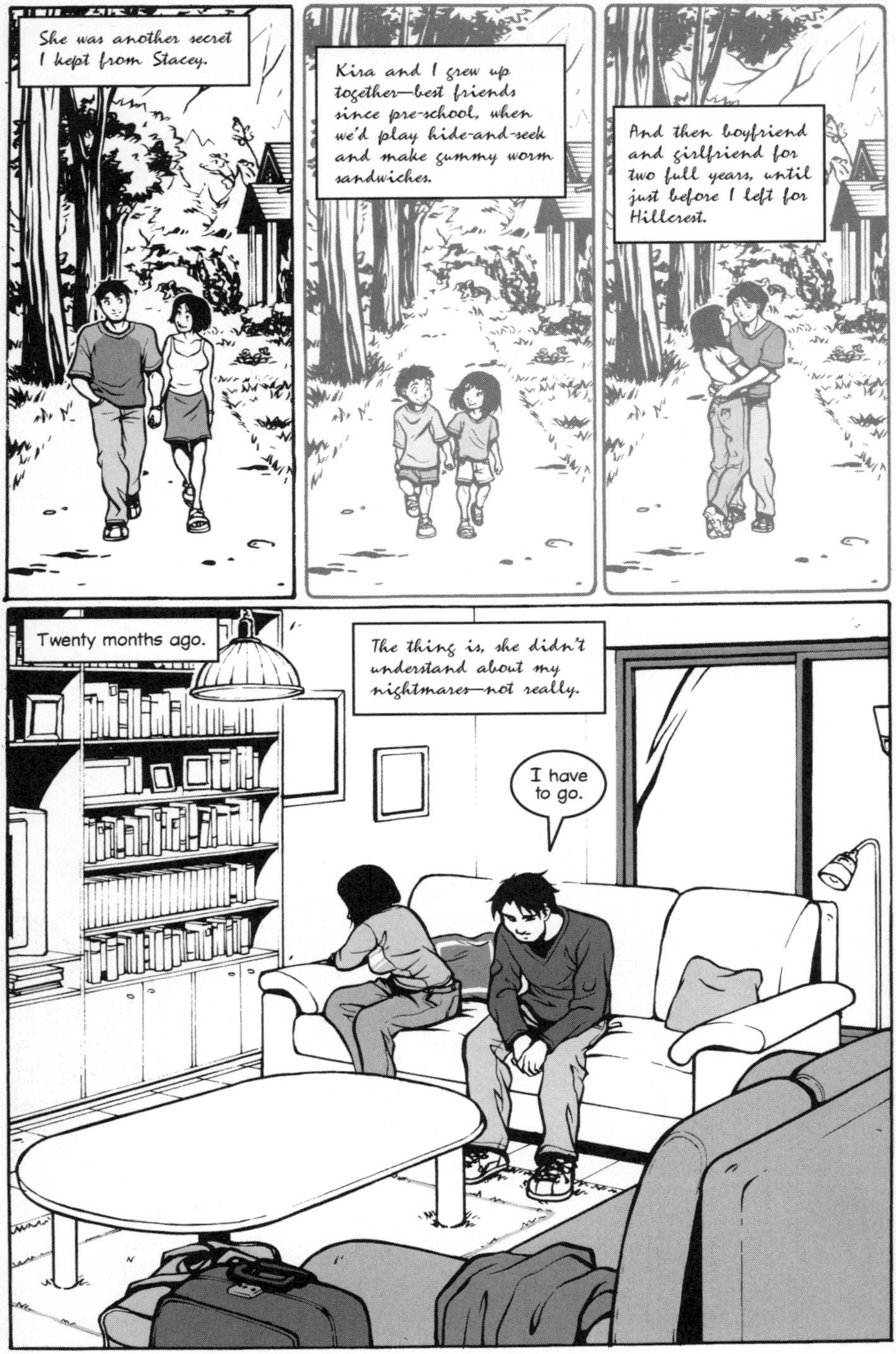
She was another secret I kept from Stacey.
Kira and I grew up together—best friends since pre-school, when we'd play hide-and-seek and make gummy worm sandwiches.
And then boyfriend and girlfriend for two full years, until just before I left for Hillcrest.
Twenty months ago.
The thing is, she didn't understand about my nightmares—not really.
I have to go.

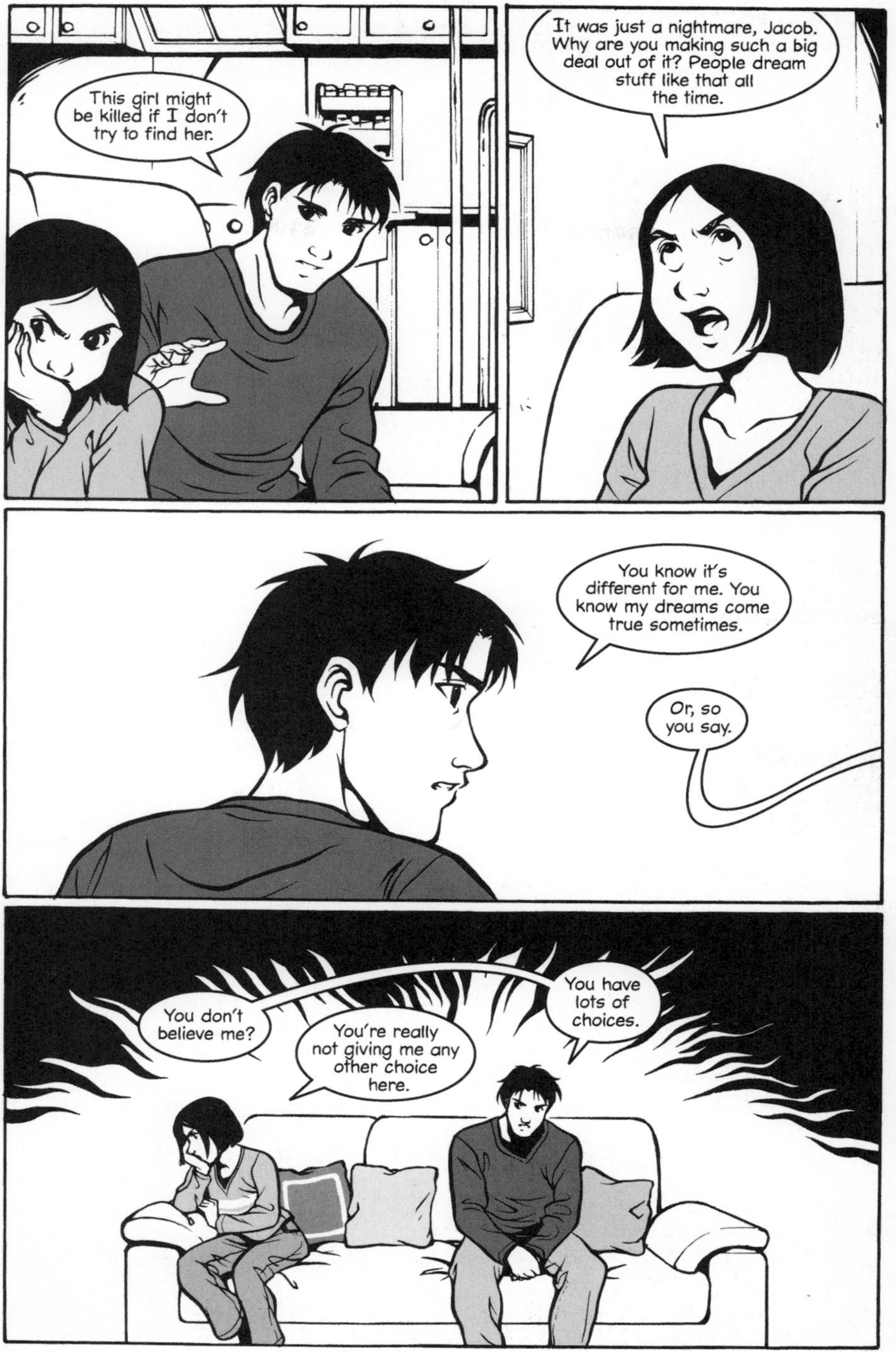
This girl might be killed if I don't try to find her.
It was just a nightmare, Jacob. Why are you making such a big deal out of it? People dream stuff like that all the time.
You know it's different for me. You know my dreams come true sometimes.
Or, so you say.
You don't believe me?
You have lots of choices.
You're really not giving me any other choice here.

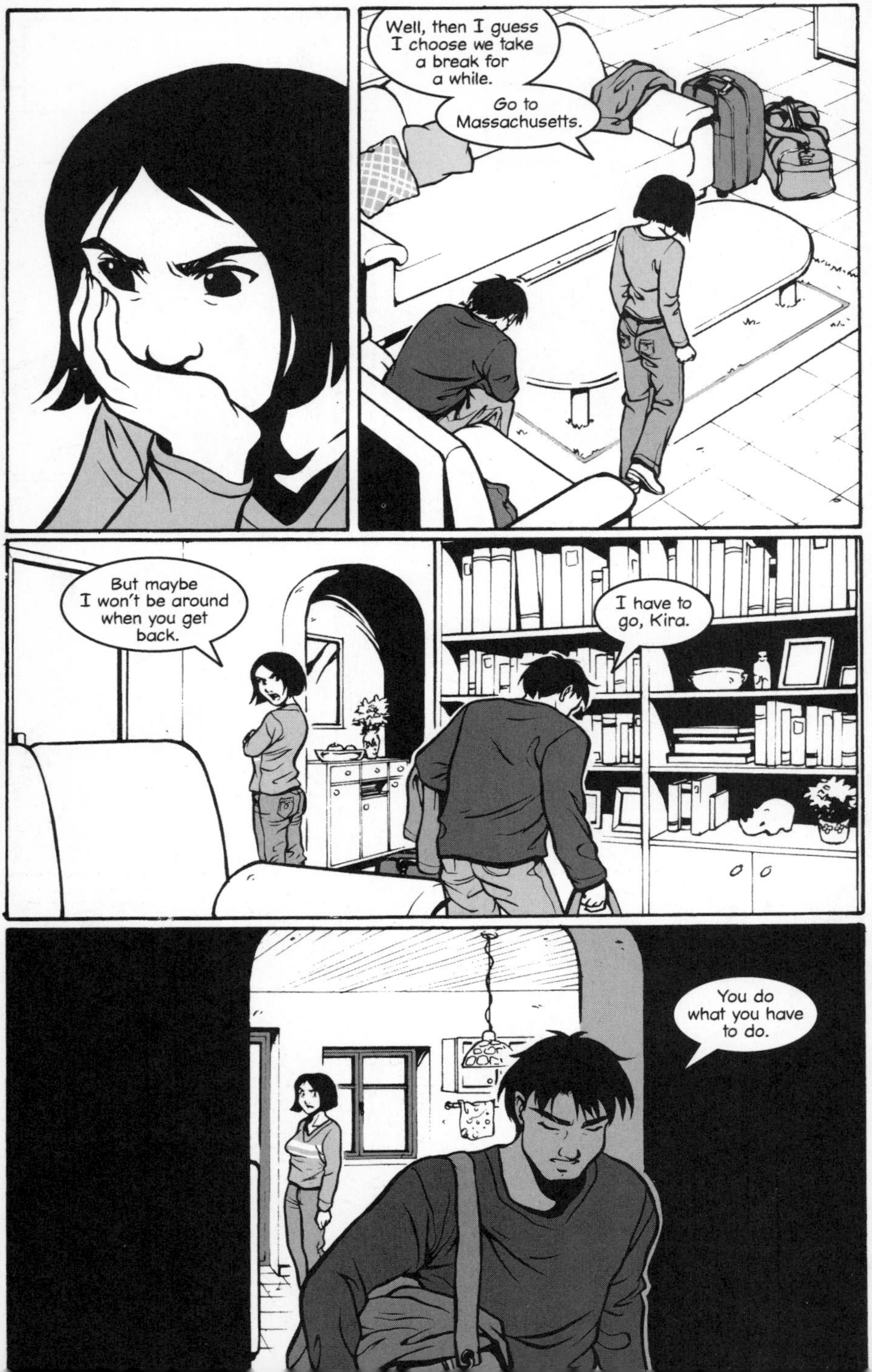
Well, then I guess I choose we take a break for a while.
Go to Massachusetts.
But maybe I won't be around when you get back.
I have to go, Kira.
You do what you have to do.

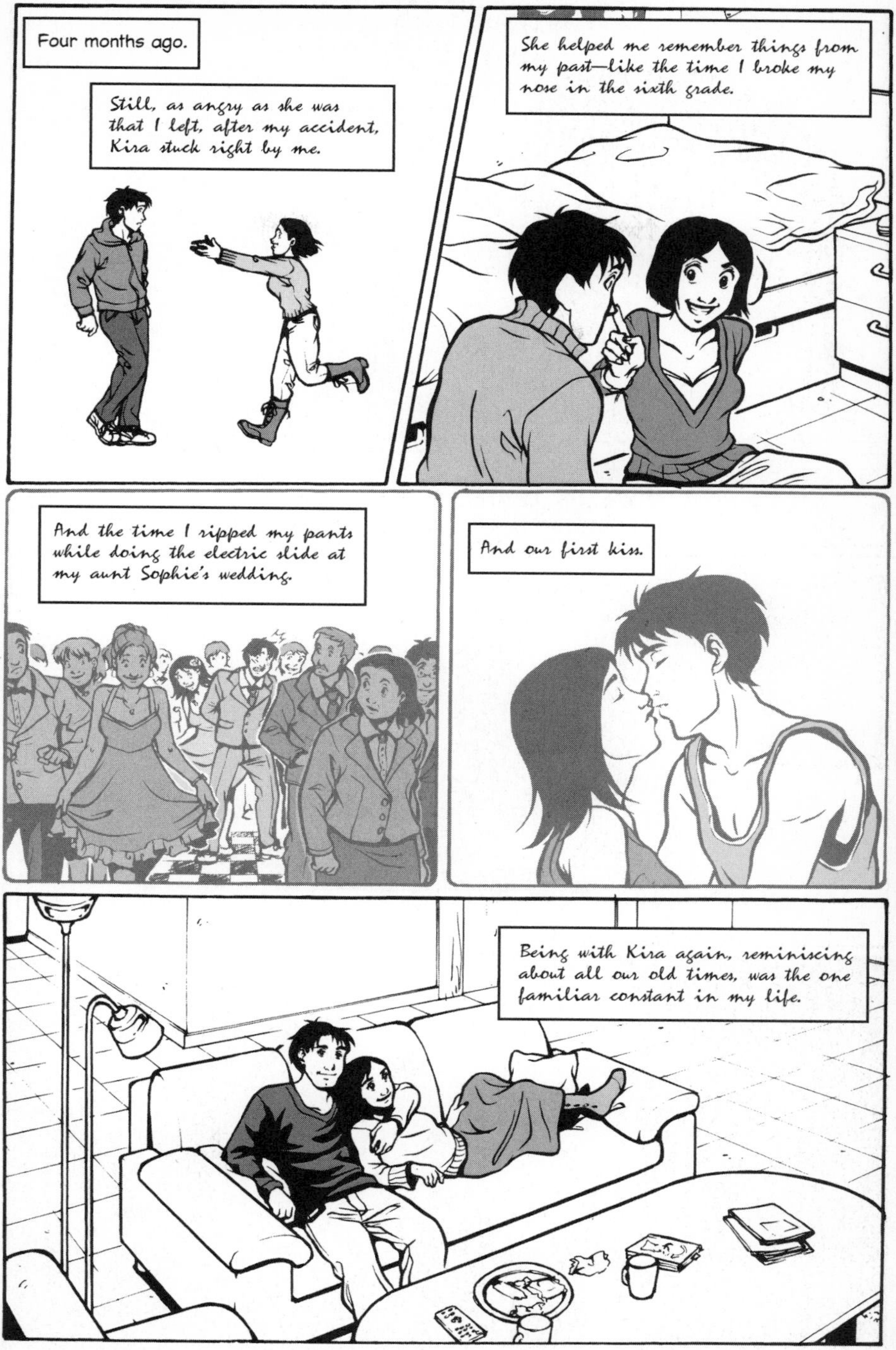
Four months ago.
Still, as angry as she was that I left, after my accident, Kira stuck right by me.
She helped me remember things from my past—like the time I broke my nose in the sixth grade.
And the time I ripped my pants while doing the electric slide at my aunt Sophie's wedding.
And our first kiss.
Being with Kira again, reminiscing about all our old times, was the one familiar constant in my life.

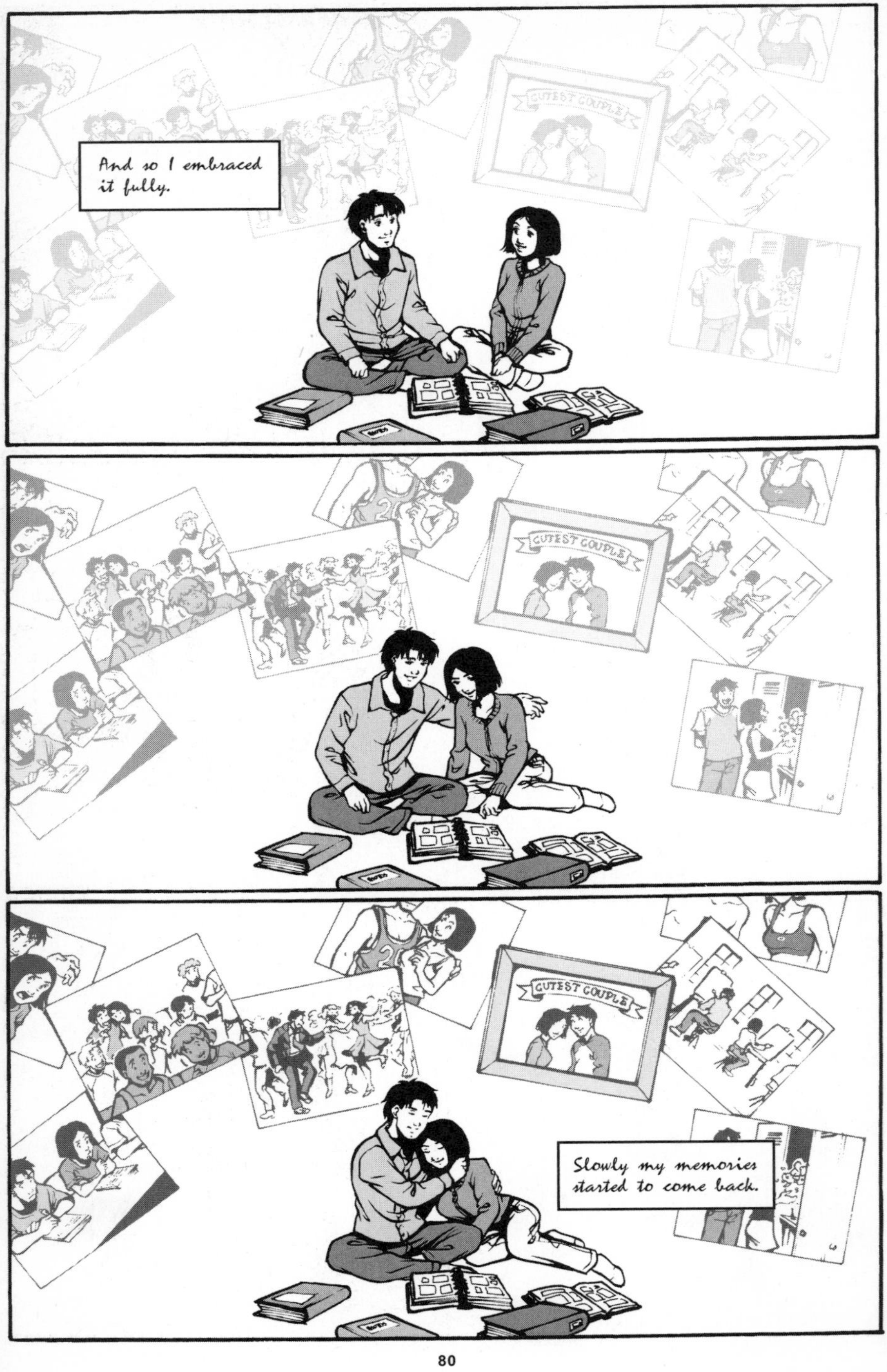
CUTEST COUPLE
And so I embraced it fully.
CUTEST COUPLE
CUTEST COUPLE
Slowly my memories started to come back.

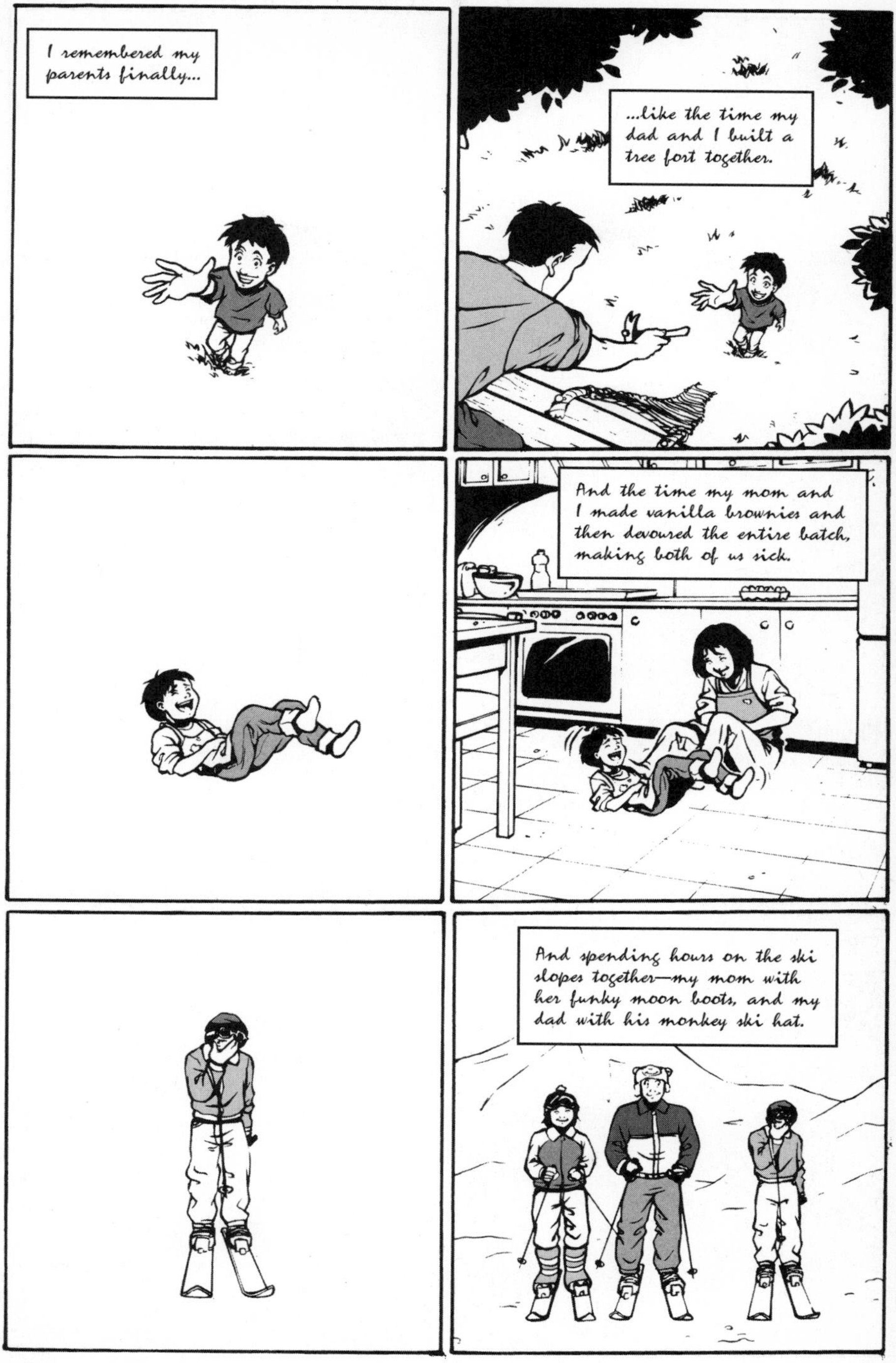
I remembered my parents finally...
...like the time my dad and I built a tree fort together.
And the time my mom and I made vanilla brownies and then devoured the entire batch, making both of us sick.
And spending hours on the ski slopes together—my mom with her funky moon boots, and my dad with his monkey ski hat.

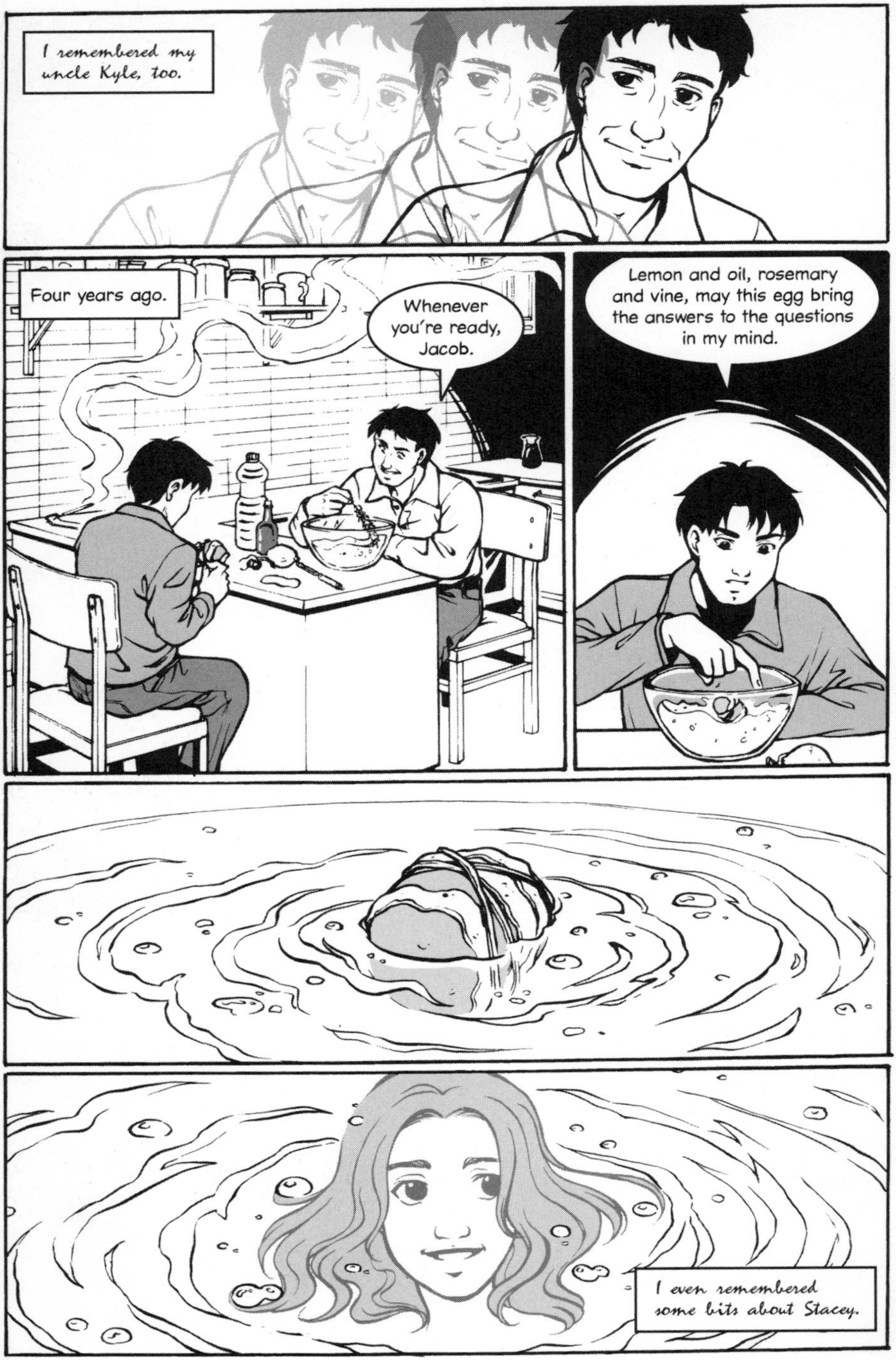
I remembered my uncle Kyle, too.
Four years ago.
Whenever you're ready, Jacob.
Lemon and oil, rosemary and vine, may this egg bring the answers to the questions in my mind.
I even remembered some bits about Stacey.

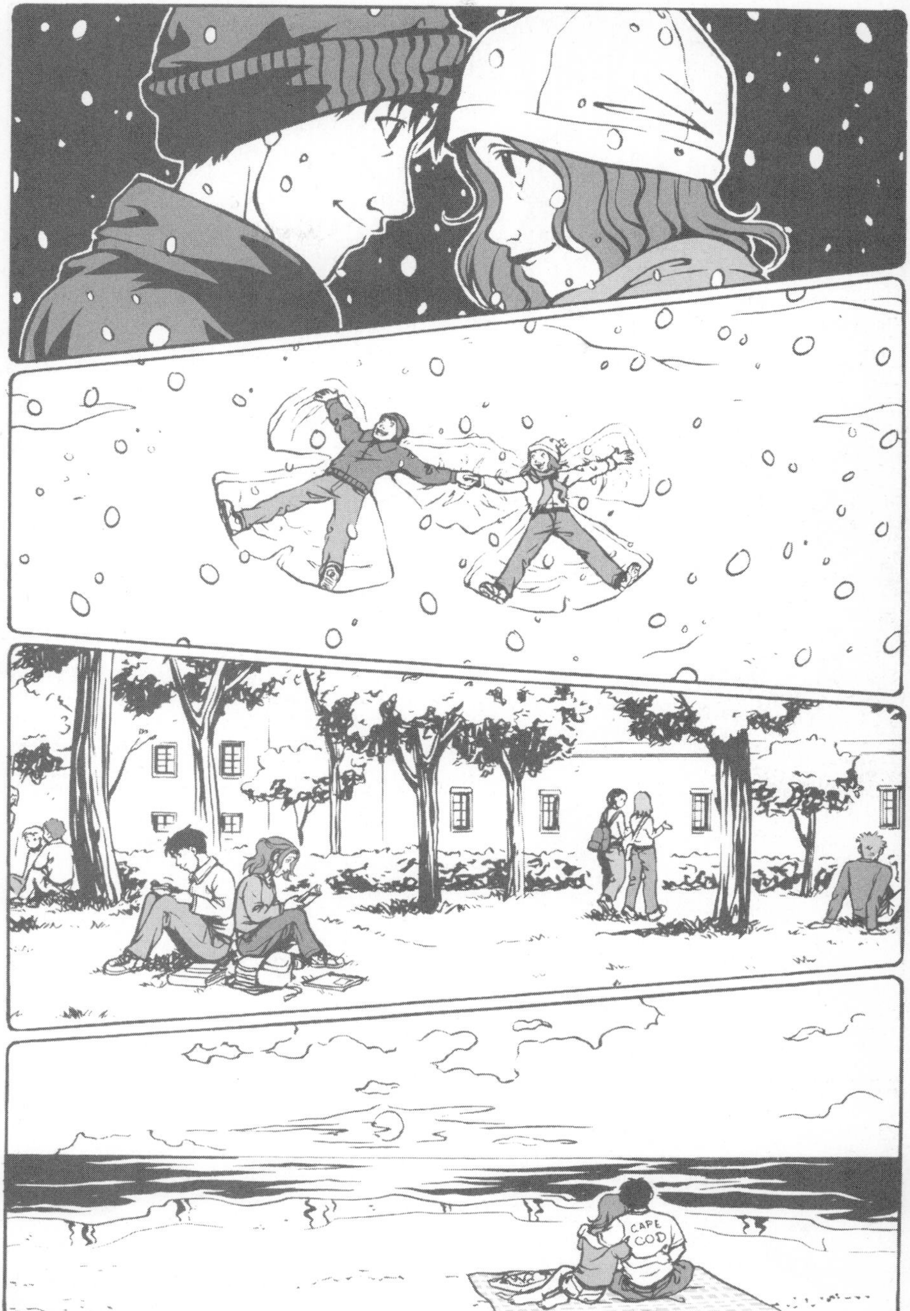
CAPE
COD

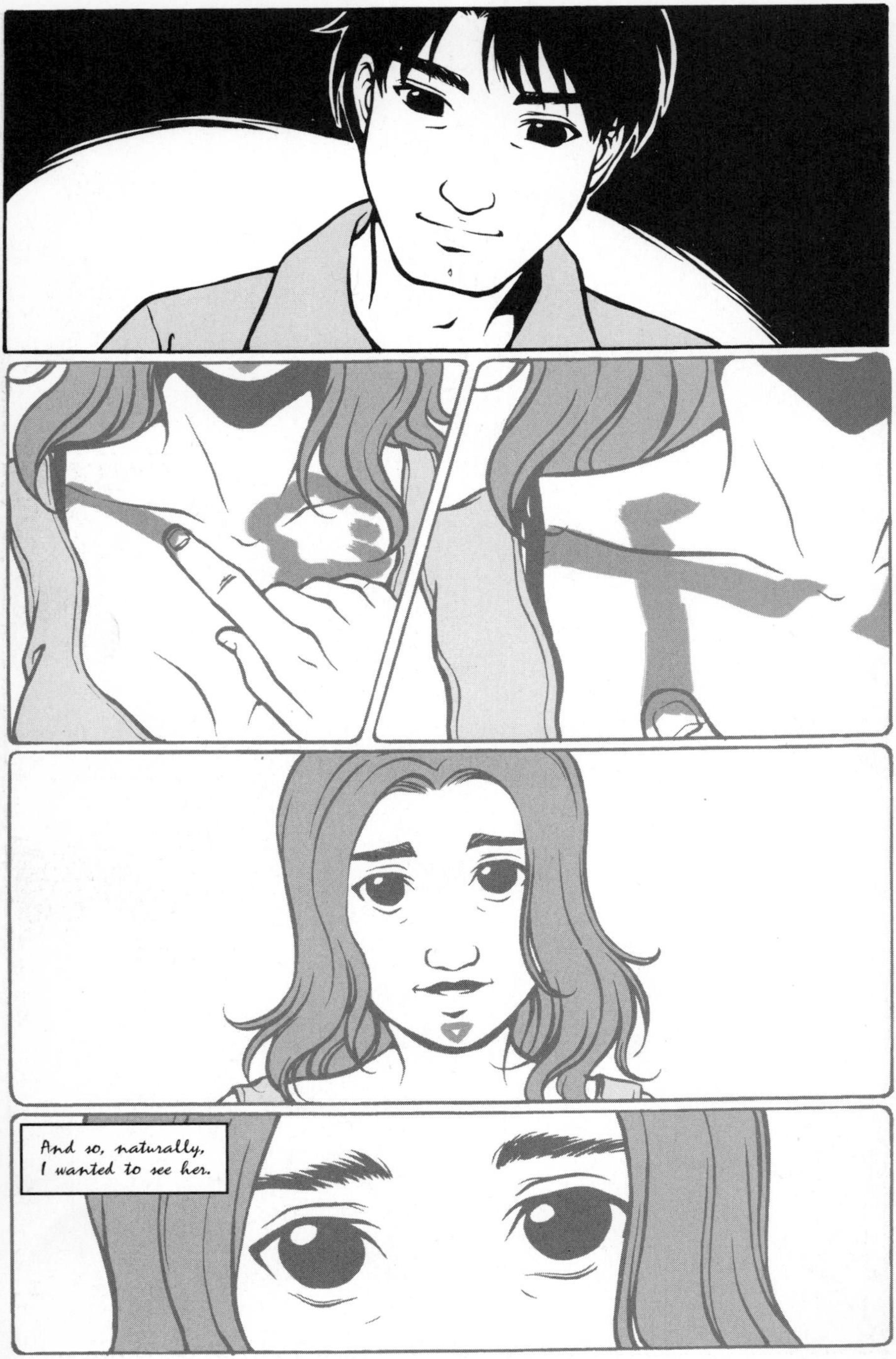
And so, naturally,
I wanted to see her.

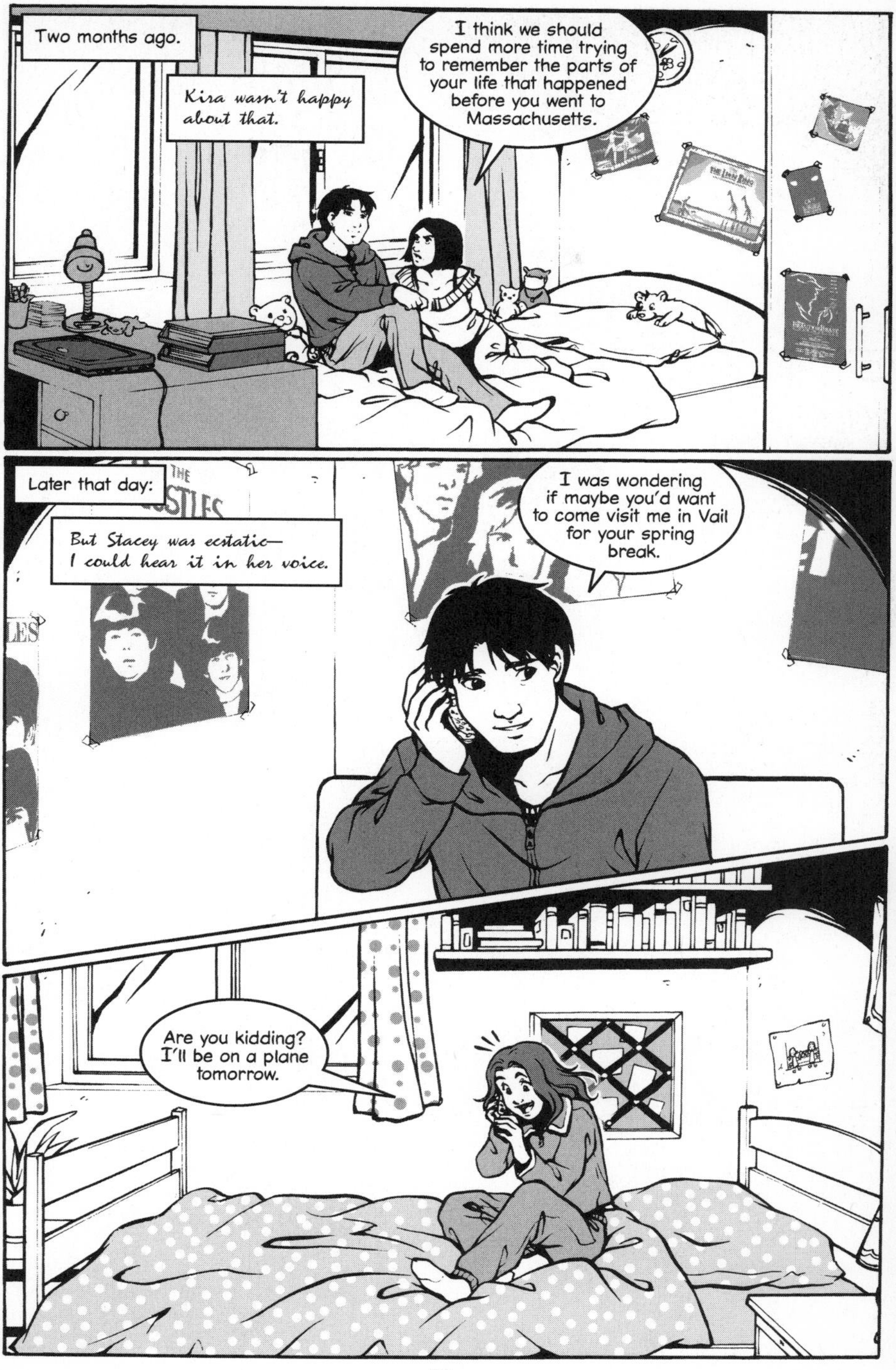
Two months ago.
Kira wasn't happy about that.
I think we should spend more time trying to remember the parts of your life that happened before you went to Massachusetts.
Later that day:
But Stacey was ecstatic—I could hear it in her voice.
I was wondering if maybe you'd want to come visit me in Vail for your spring break.
Are you kidding? I'll be on a plane tomorrow.

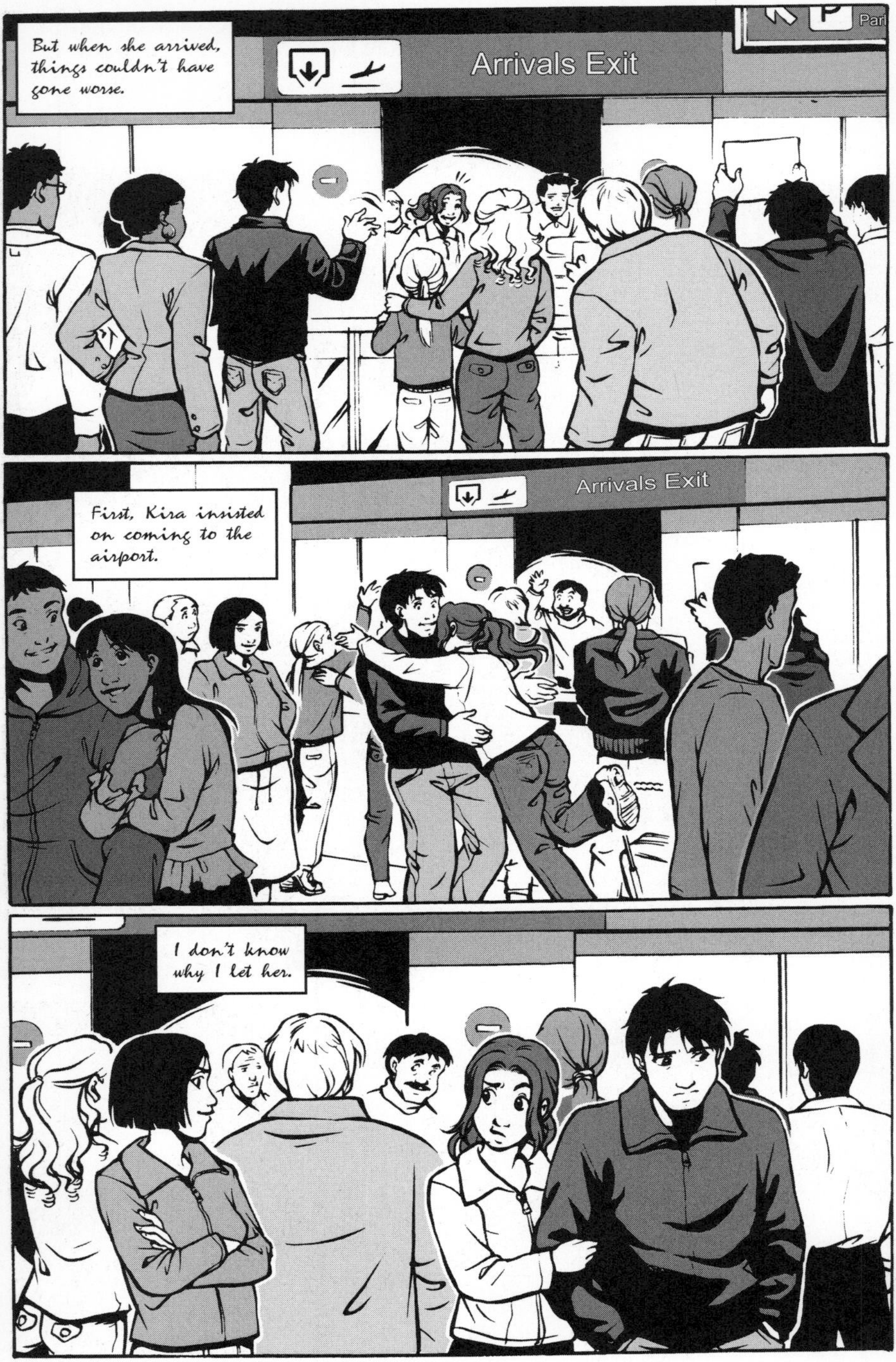
But when she arrived, things couldn't have gone worse.
Arrivals Exit
First, Kira insisted on coming to the airport.
Arrivals Exit
I don't know why I let her.

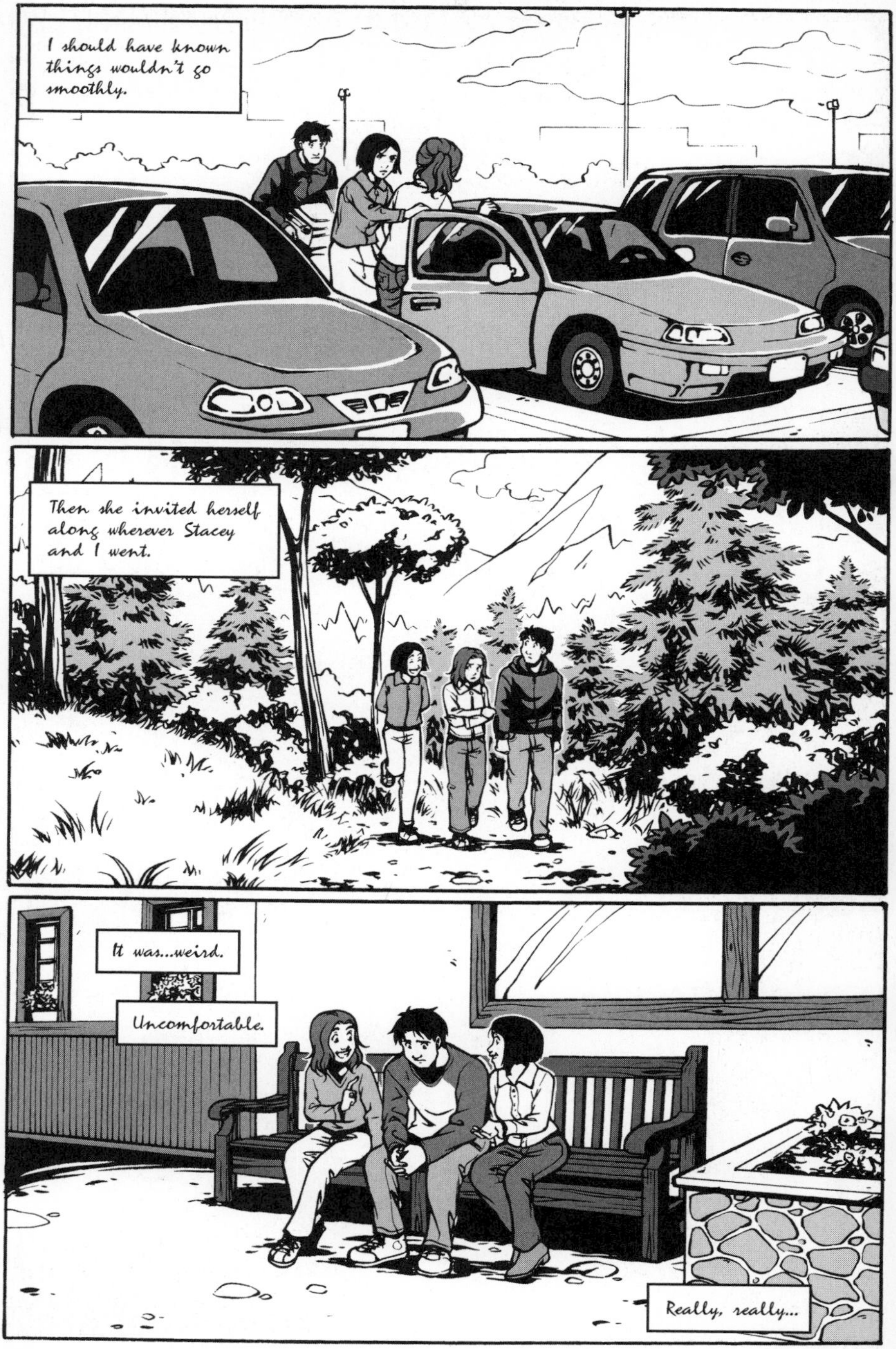
I should have known things wouldn't go smoothly.
Then she invited herself along wherever Stacey and I went.
It was...weird.
Uncomfortable.
Really, really...

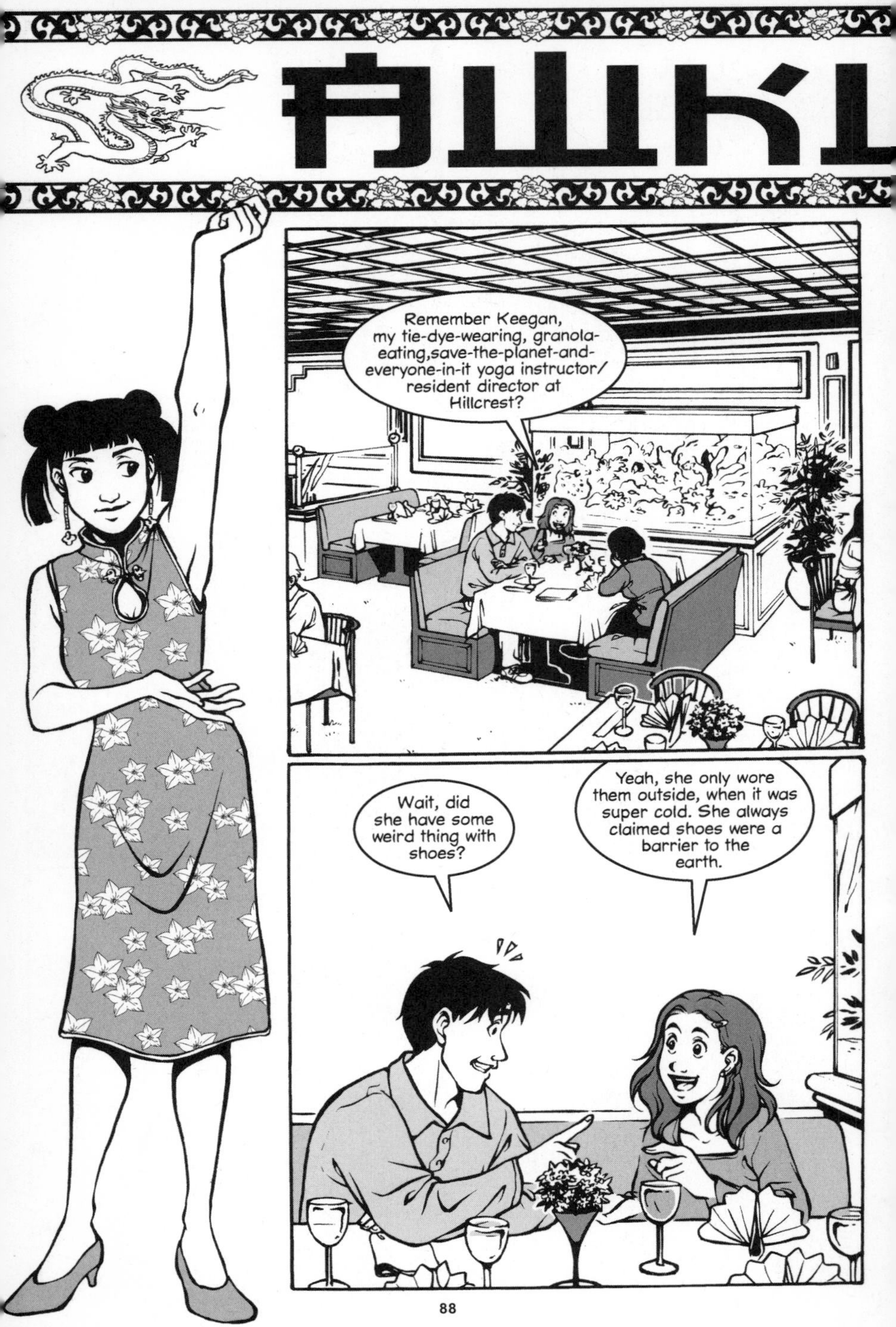
Remember Keegan, my tie-dye-wearing, granola-eating,save-the-planet-and-everyone-in-it yoga instructor/ resident director at Hillcrest?
Wait, did she have some weird thing with shoes?
Yeah, she only wore them outside, when it was super cold. She always claimed shoes were a barrier to the earth.

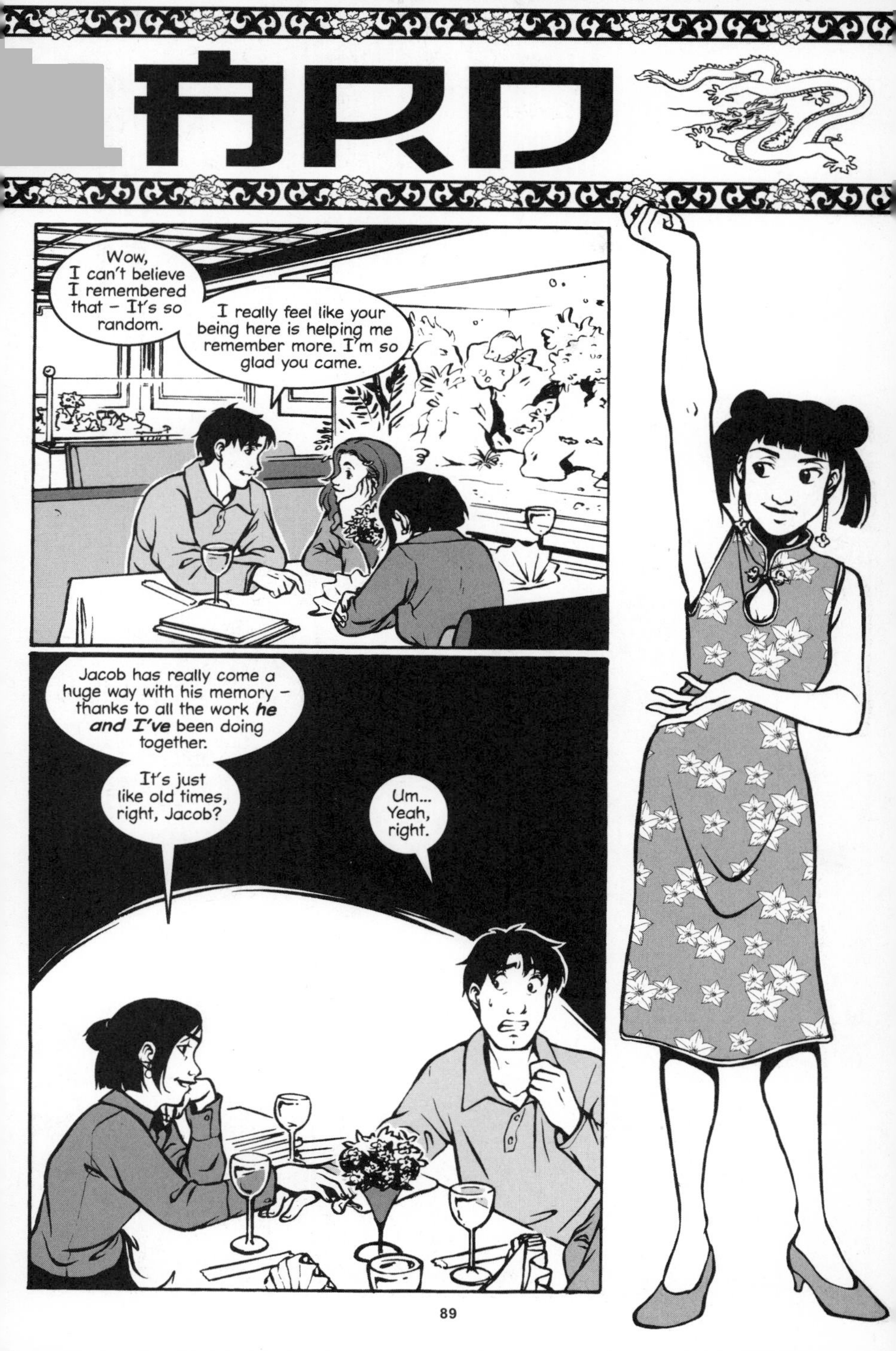

3RD
Wow, I can't believe I remembered that – It's so random.
I really feel like your being here is helping me remember more. I'm so glad you came.
Jacob has really come a huge way with his memory – thanks to all the work ***he and I've*** been doing together.
It's just like old times, right, Jacob?
Um... Yeah, right.

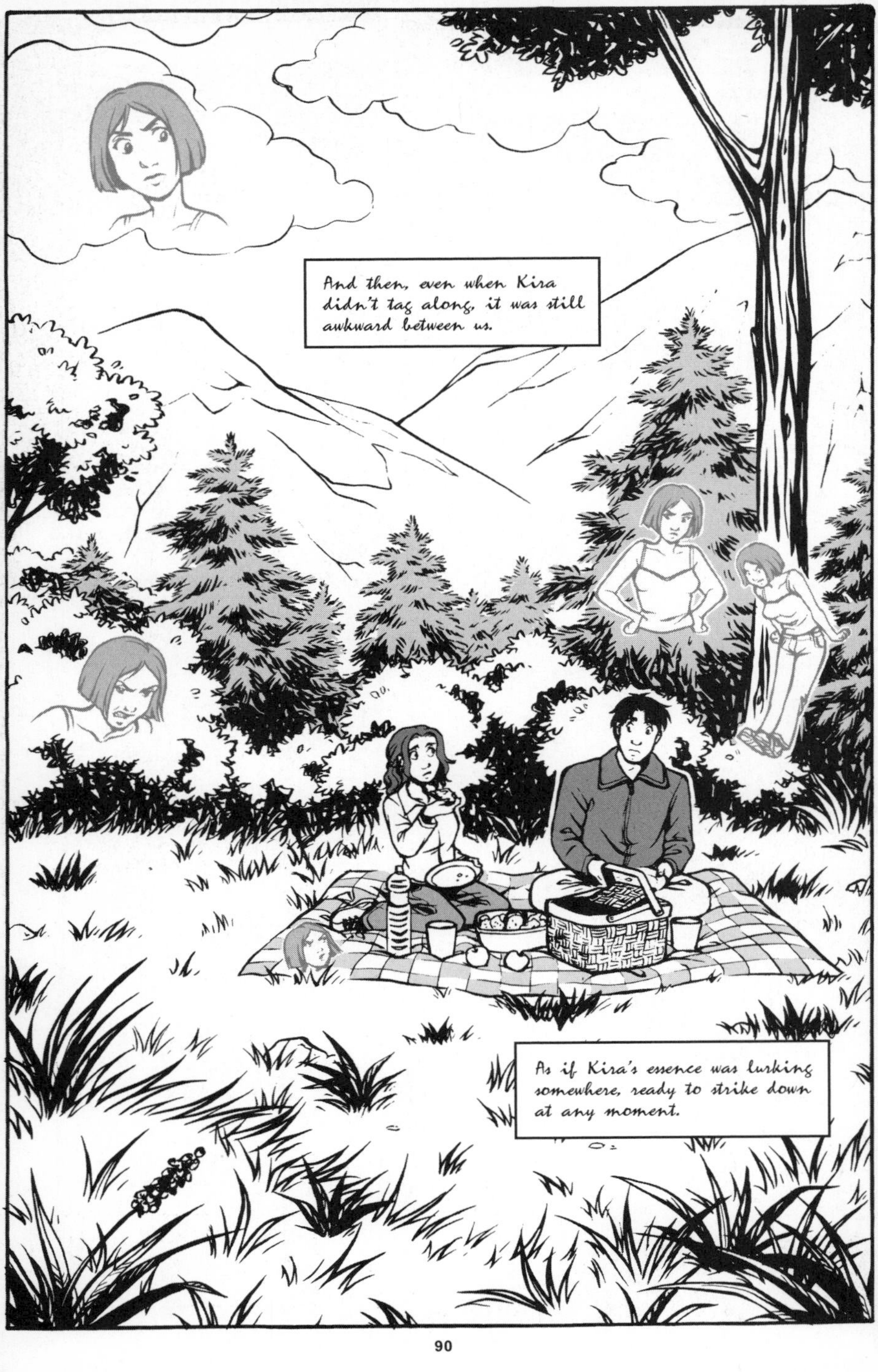
And then, even when Kira didn't tag along, it was still awkward between us.
As if Kira's essence was lurking somewhere, ready to strike down at any moment.

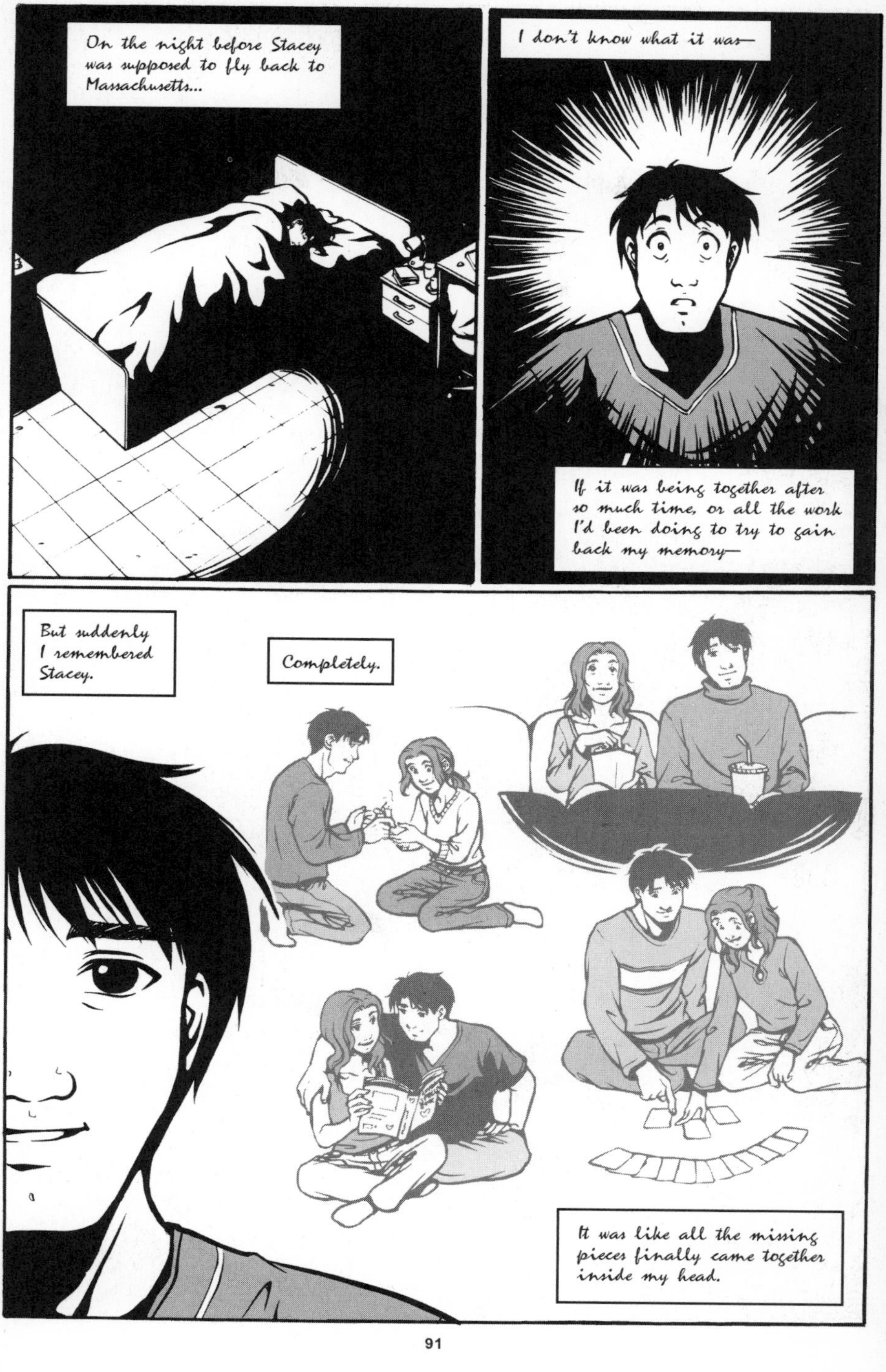
On the night before Stacey was supposed to fly back to Massachusetts...
I don't know what it was—
If it was being together after so much time, or all the work I'd been doing to try to gain back my memory—
But suddenly I remembered Stacey.
Completely.
It was like all the missing pieces finally came together inside my head.

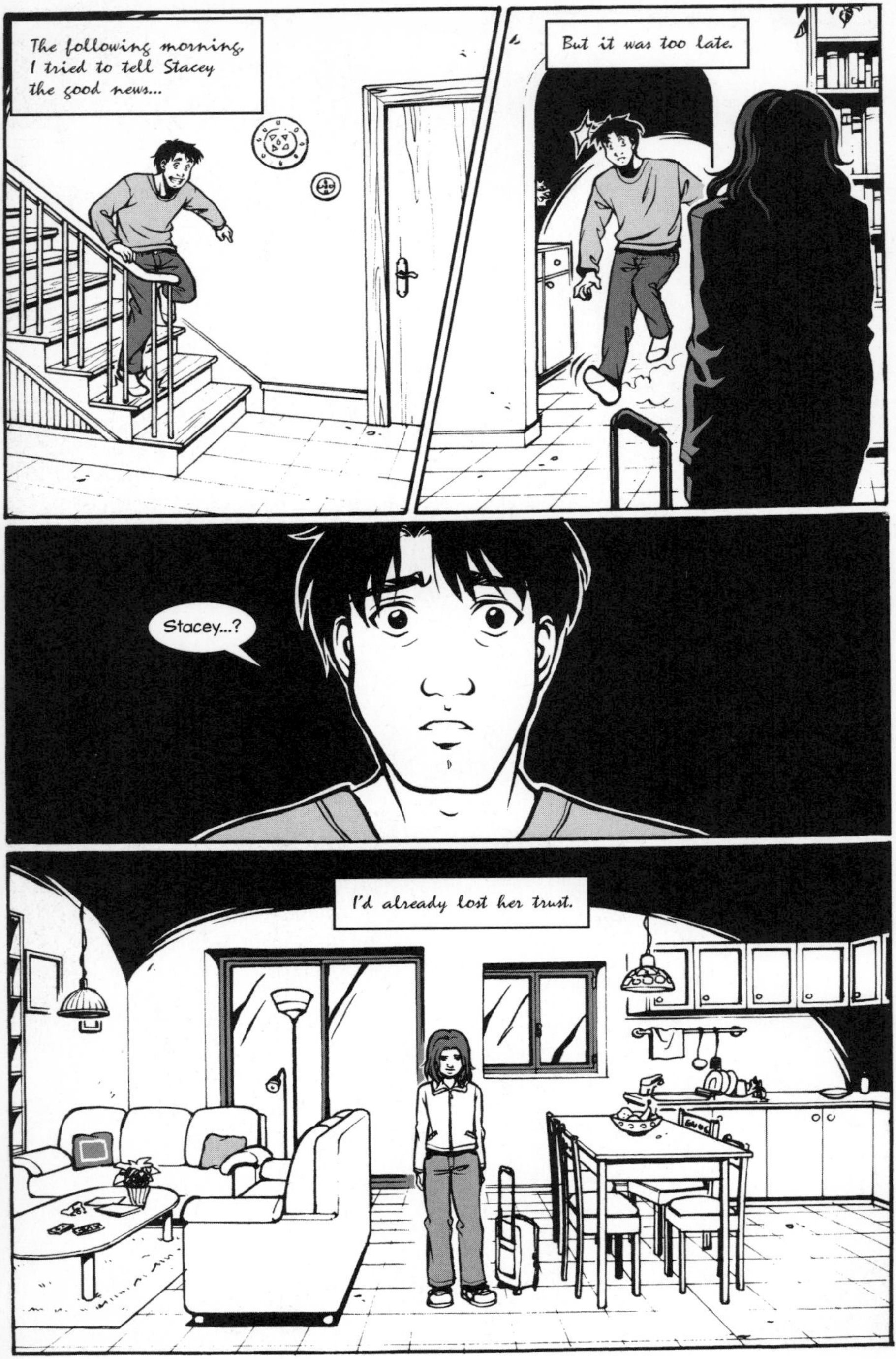

The following morning, I tried to tell Stacey the good news...
But it was too late.
Stacey...?
I'd already lost her trust.

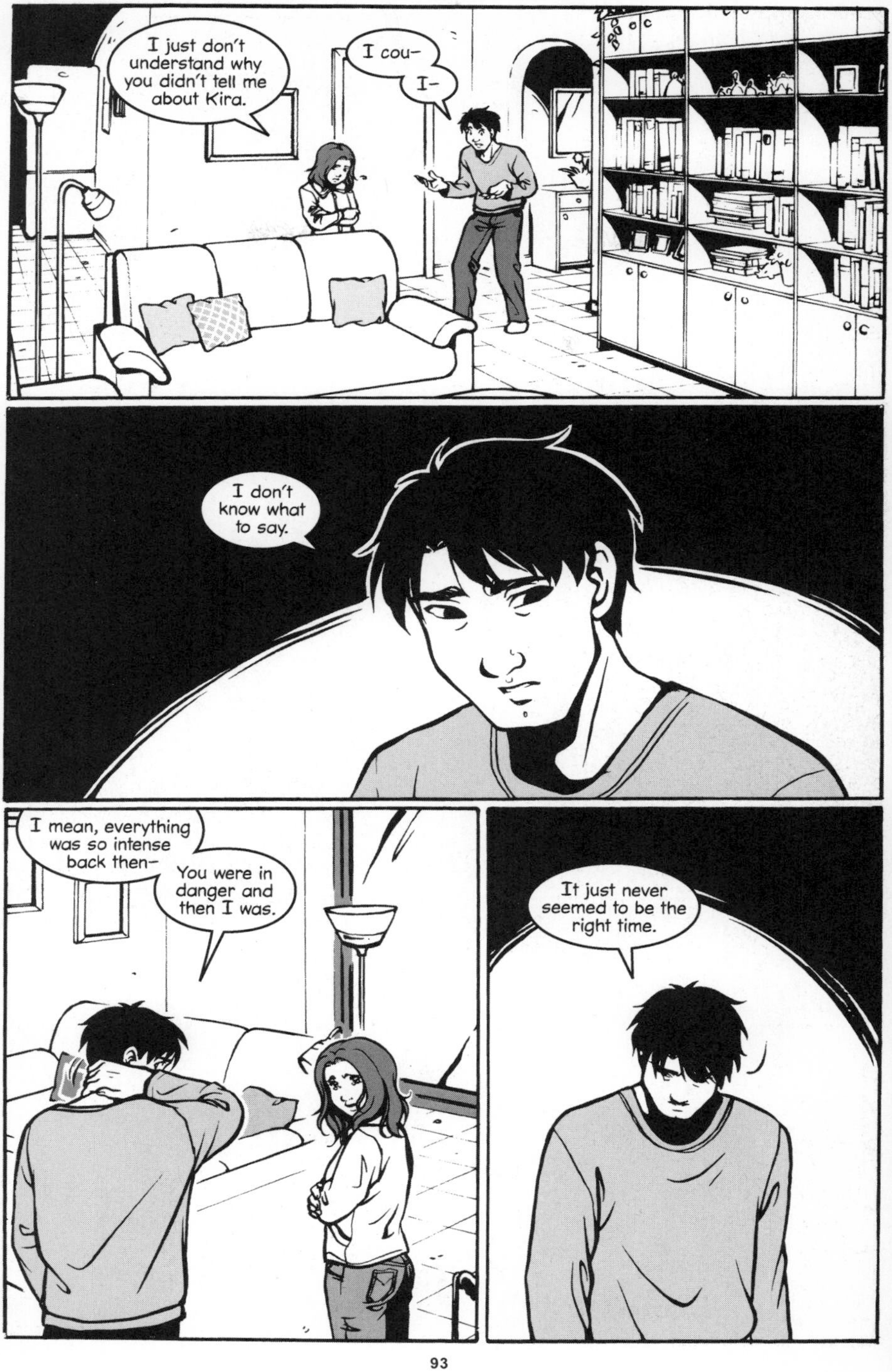
I just don't understand why you didn't tell me about Kira.
I cou-
I-
I don't know what to say.
I mean, everything was so intense back then-
You were in danger and then I was.
It just never seemed to be the right time.

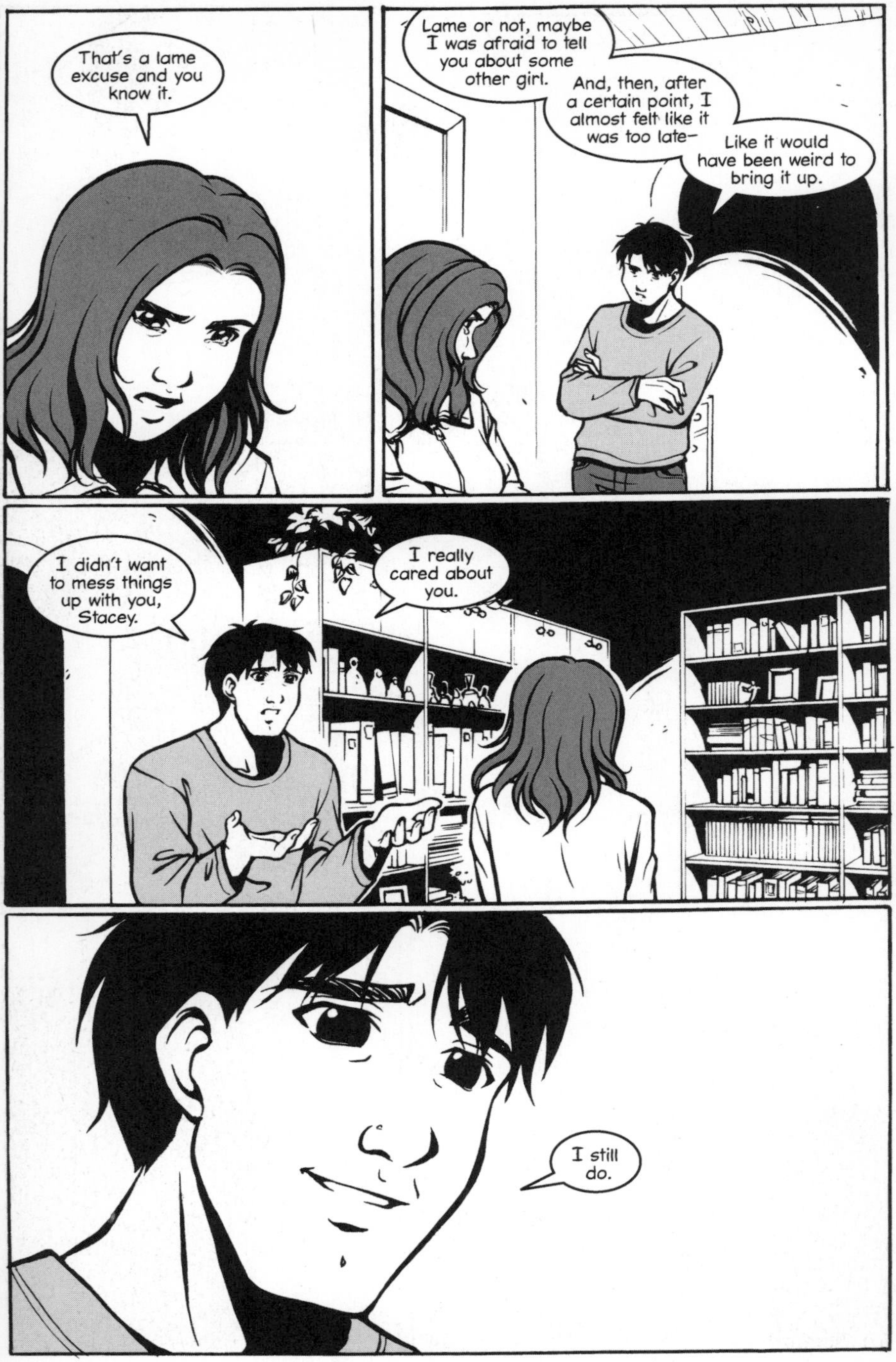
That's a lame excuse and you know it.
Lame or not, maybe I was afraid to tell you about some other girl.
And, then, after a certain point, I almost felt like it was too late–
Like it would have been weird to bring it up.
I didn't want to mess things up with you, Stacey.
I really cared about you.
I still do.

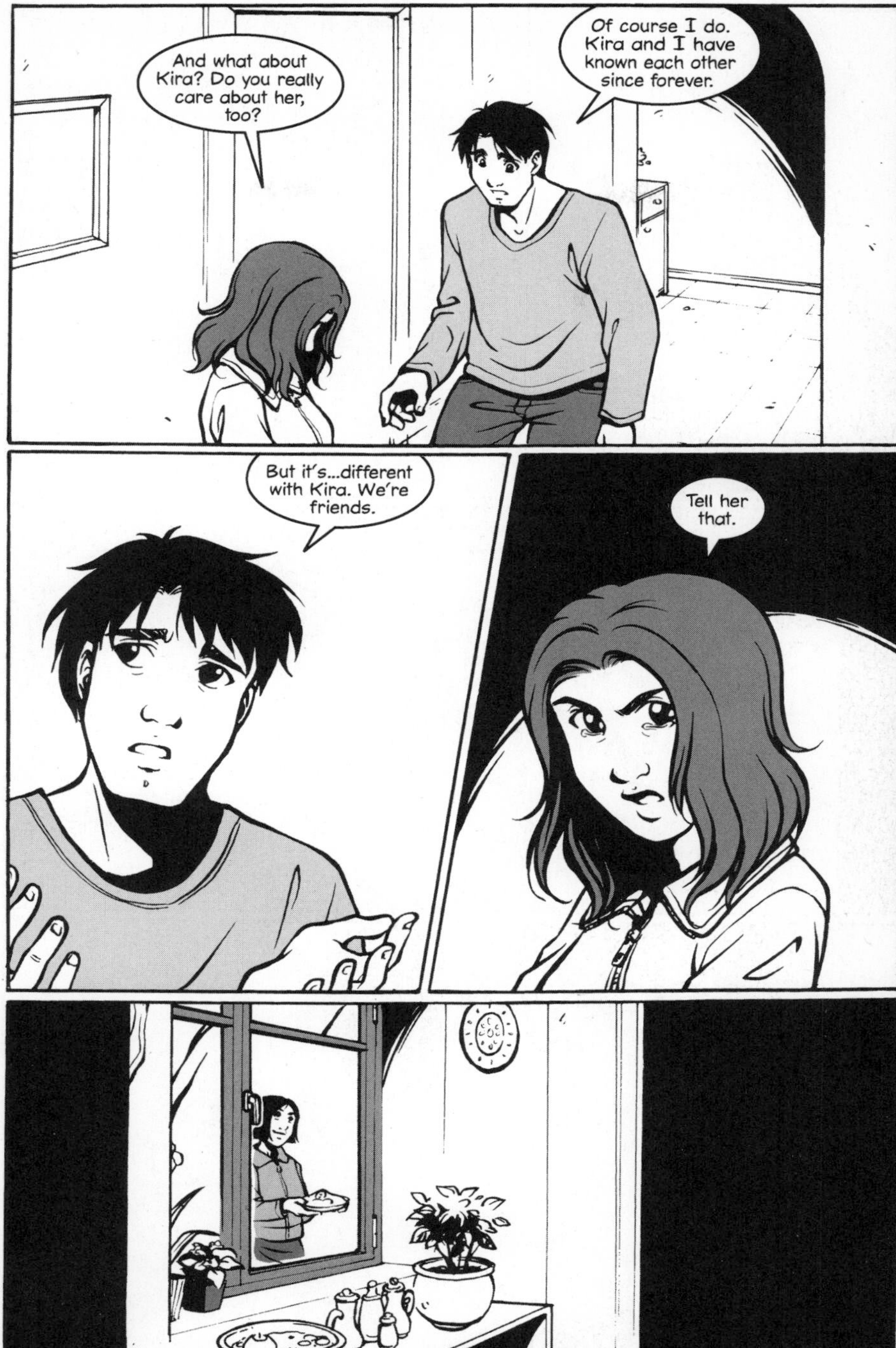
And what about Kira? Do you really care about her, too?
Of course I do. Kira and I have known each other since forever.
But it's...different with Kira. We're friends.
Tell her that.

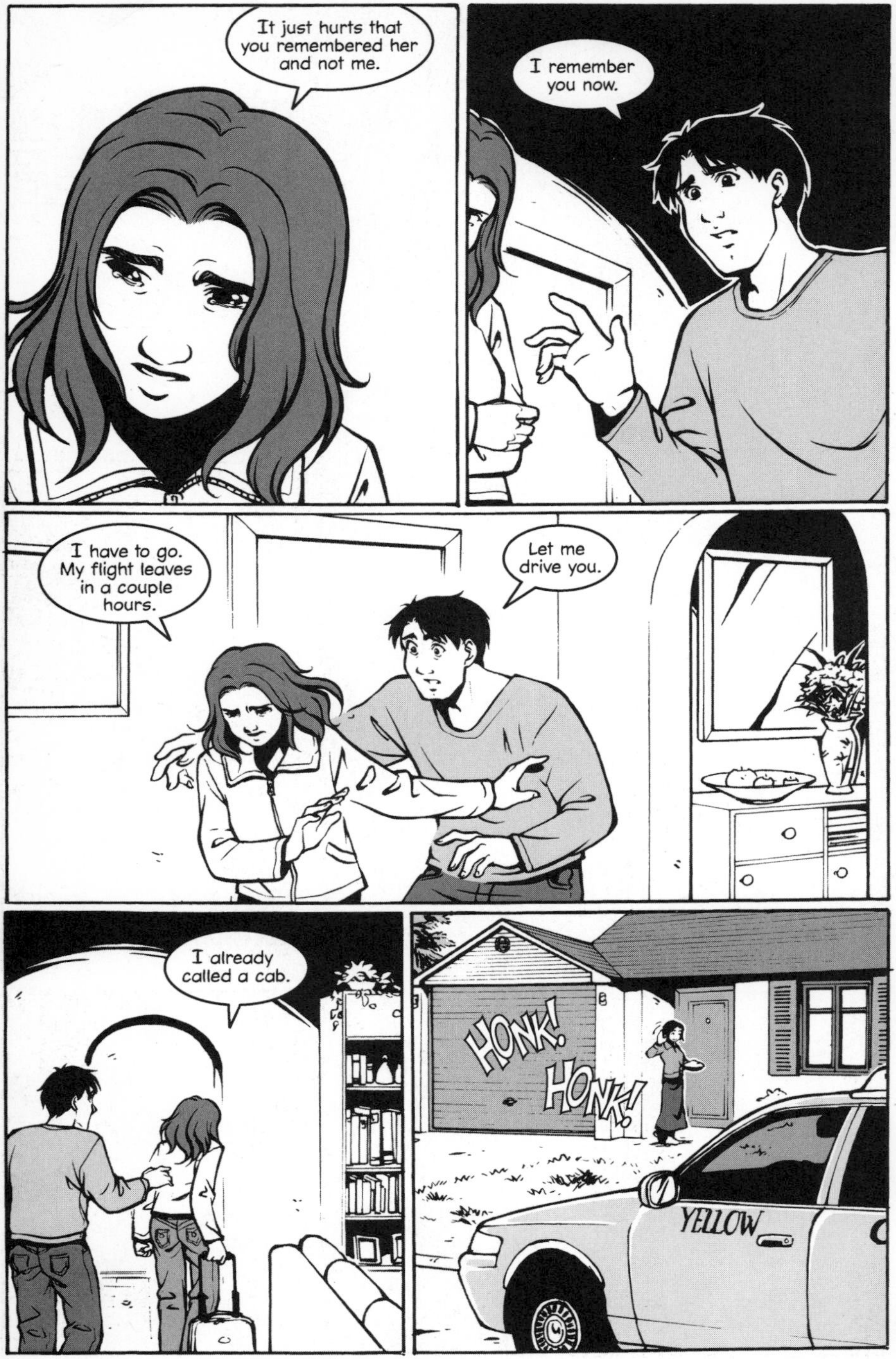
It just hurts that you remembered her and not me.
I remember you now.
I have to go. My flight leaves in a couple hours.
Let me drive you.
I already called a cab.
HONK!
HONK!
YELLOW

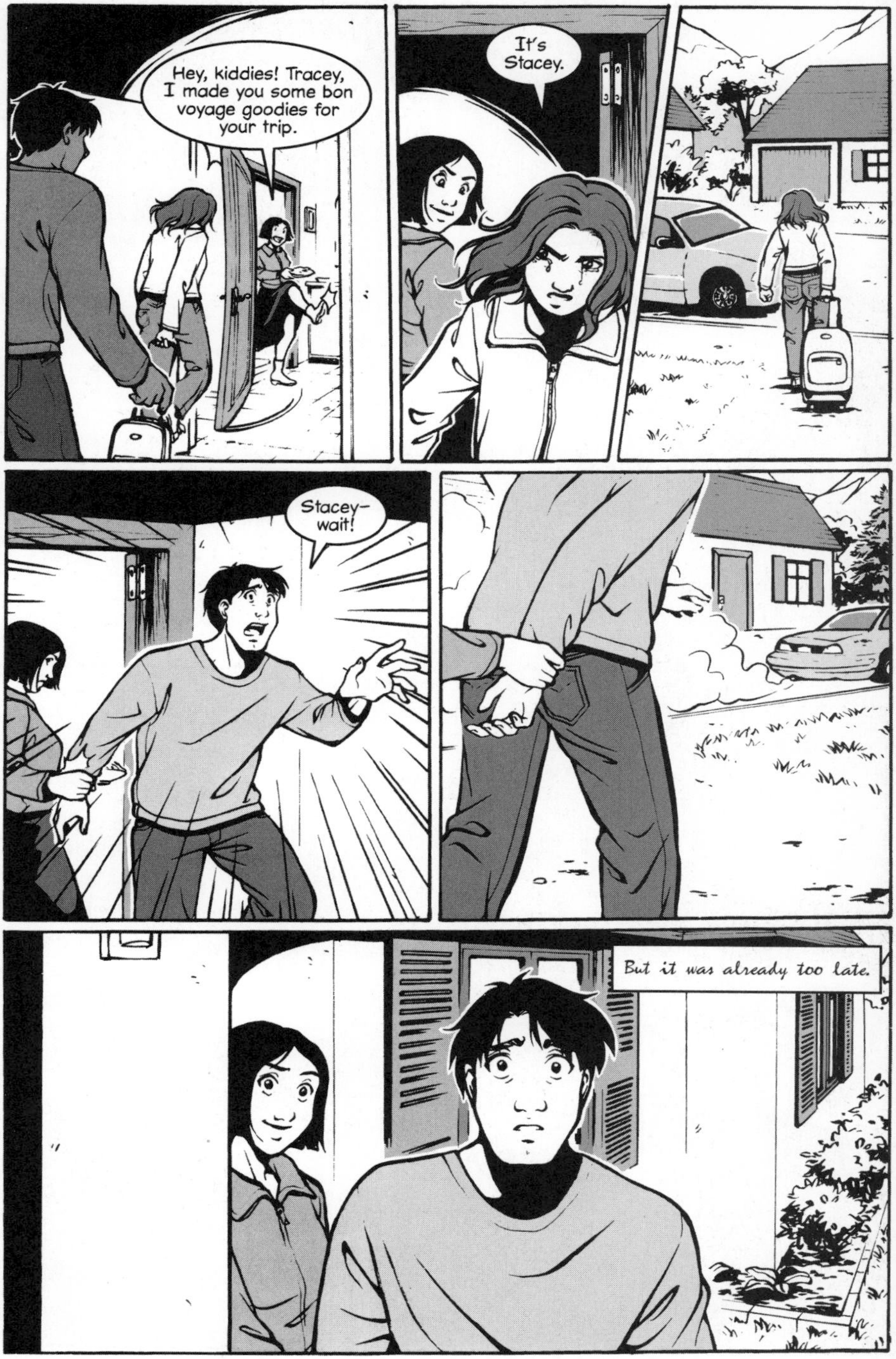
Hey, kiddies! Tracey, I made you some bon voyage goodies for your trip.
It's Stacey.
Stacey-wait!
But it was already too late.

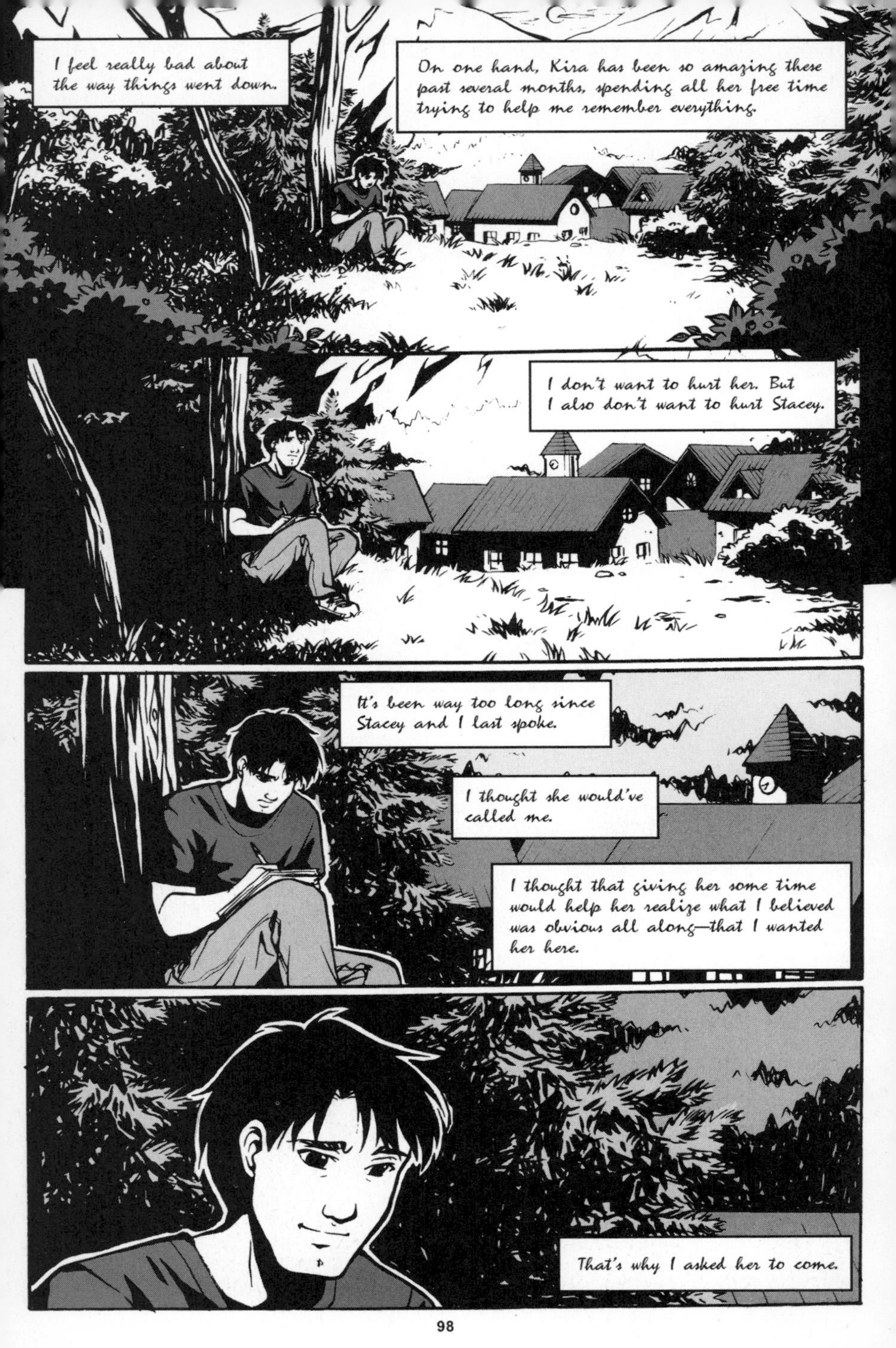
I feel really bad about the way things went down.
On one hand, Kira has been so amazing these past several months, spending all her free time trying to help me remember everything.
I don't want to hurt her. But I also don't want to hurt Stacey.
It's been way too long since Stacey and I last spoke.
I thought she would've called me.
I thought that giving her some time would help her realize what I believed was obvious all along—that I wanted her here.
That's why I asked her to come.

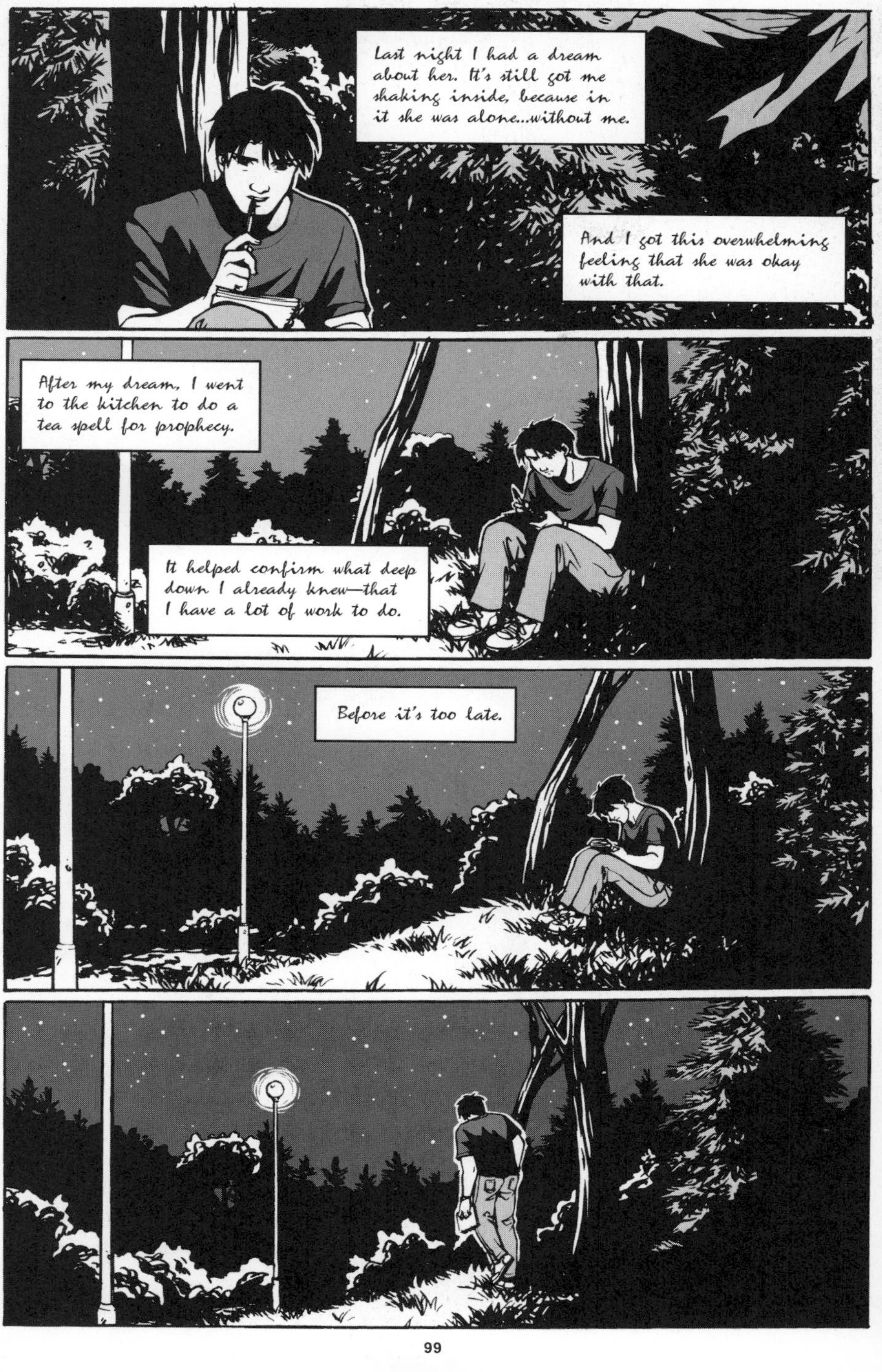
Last night I had a dream about her. It's still got me shaking inside, because in it she was alone...without me.
And I got this overwhelming feeling that she was okay with that.
After my dream, I went to the kitchen to do a tea spell for prophecy.
It helped confirm what deep down I already knew—that I have a lot of work to do.
Before it's too late.

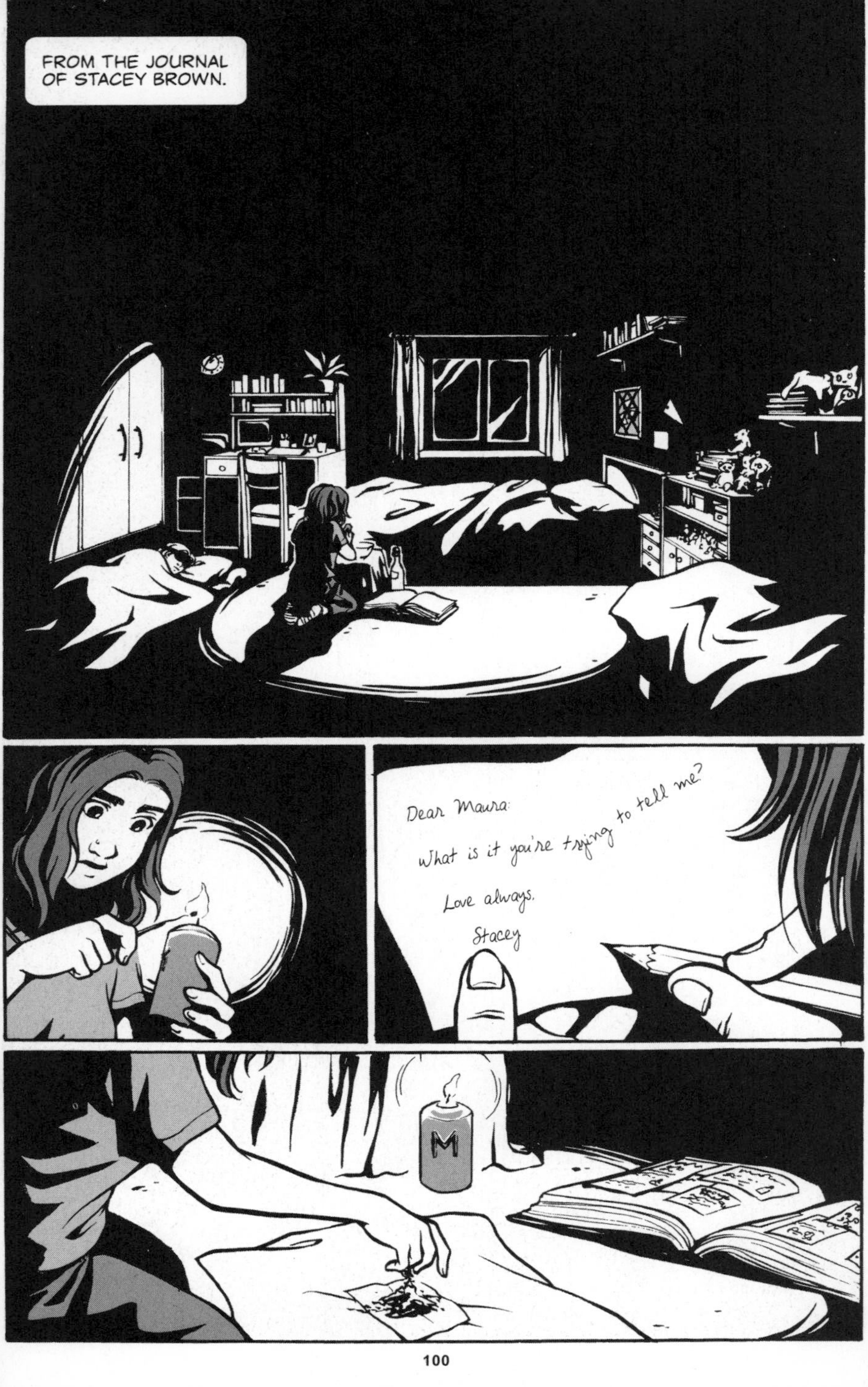
FROM THE JOURNAL OF STACEY BROWN.
Dear Maura:
What is it you're trying to tell me?
Love always,
Stacey

As grounded as the earth and as unruly as the sea, may the blending of both bring me clarity times three.

Blessed be the way.

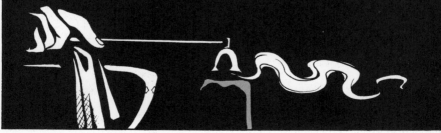

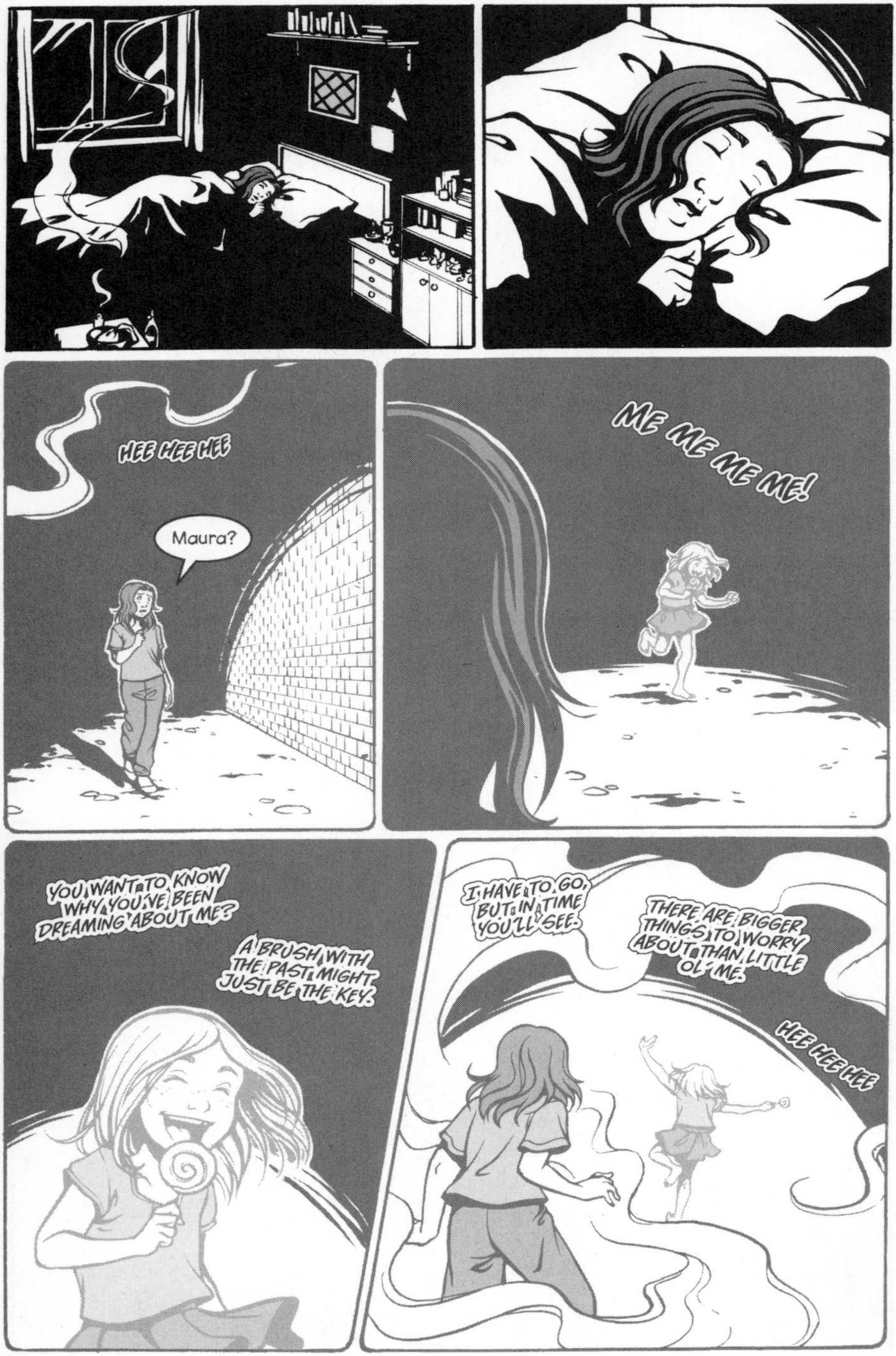
HEE HEE HEE
Maura?
ME ME ME ME!
YOU WANT TO KNOW WHY YOU'VE BEEN DREAMING ABOUT ME?
A BRUSH WITH THE PAST MIGHT JUST BE THE KEY.
I HAVE TO GO, BUT IN TIME YOU'LL SEE.
THERE ARE BIGGER THINGS TO WORRY ABOUT THAN LITTLE OL' ME.
HEE HEE HEE

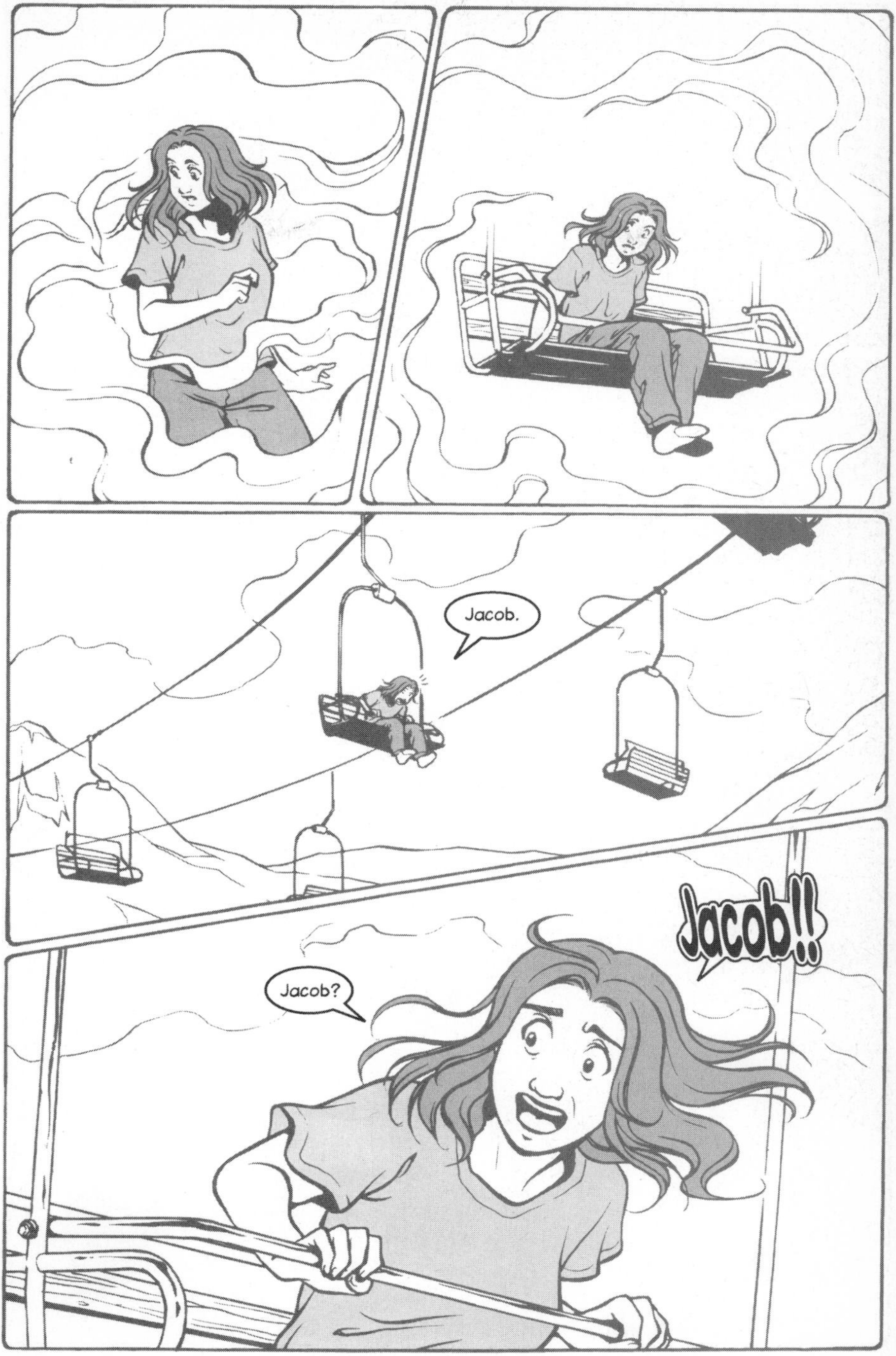
Jacob.
Jacob!!
Jacob?

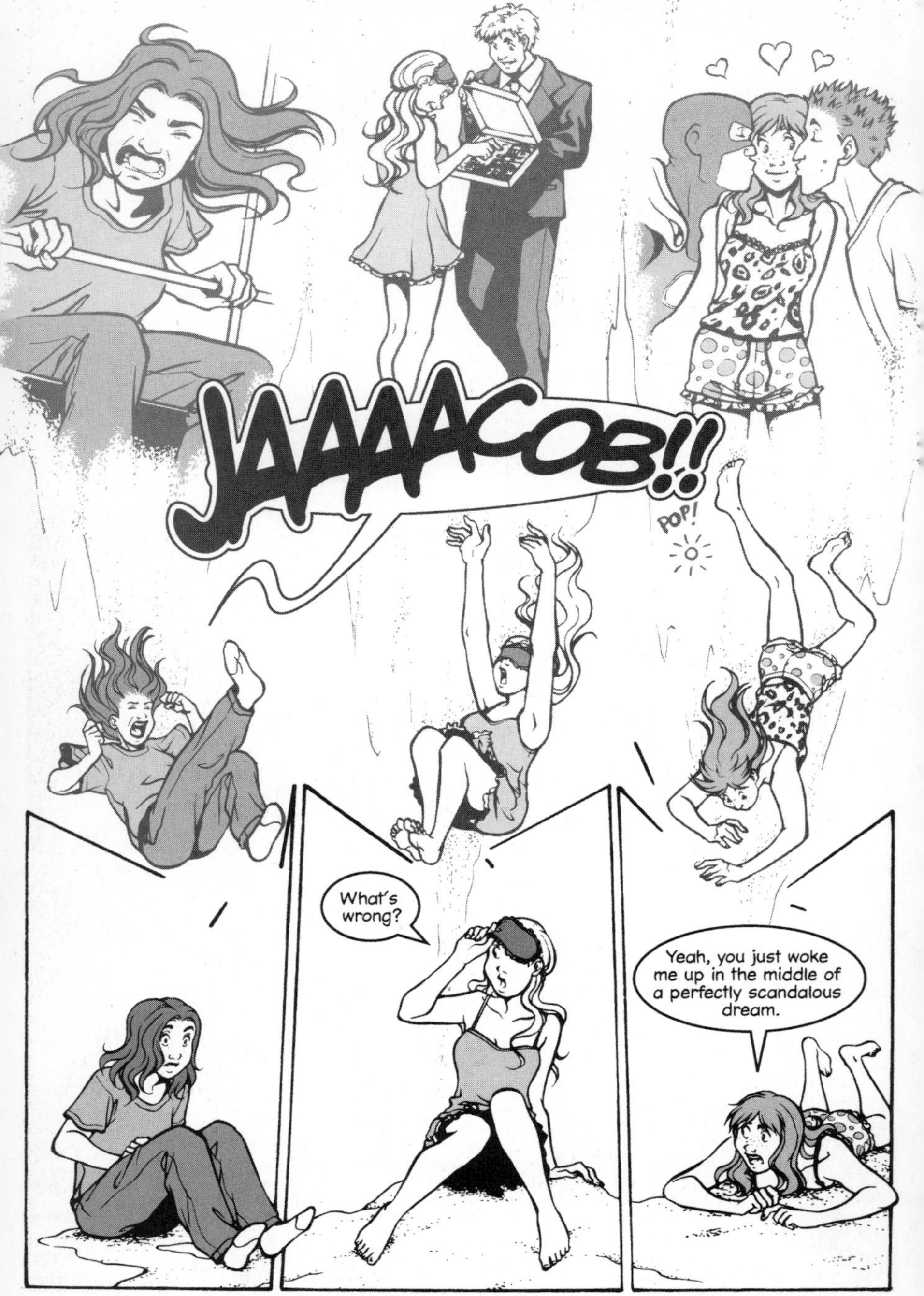
JAAAACOB!!
POP!
What's wrong?
Yeah, you just woke me up in the middle of a perfectly scandalous dream.

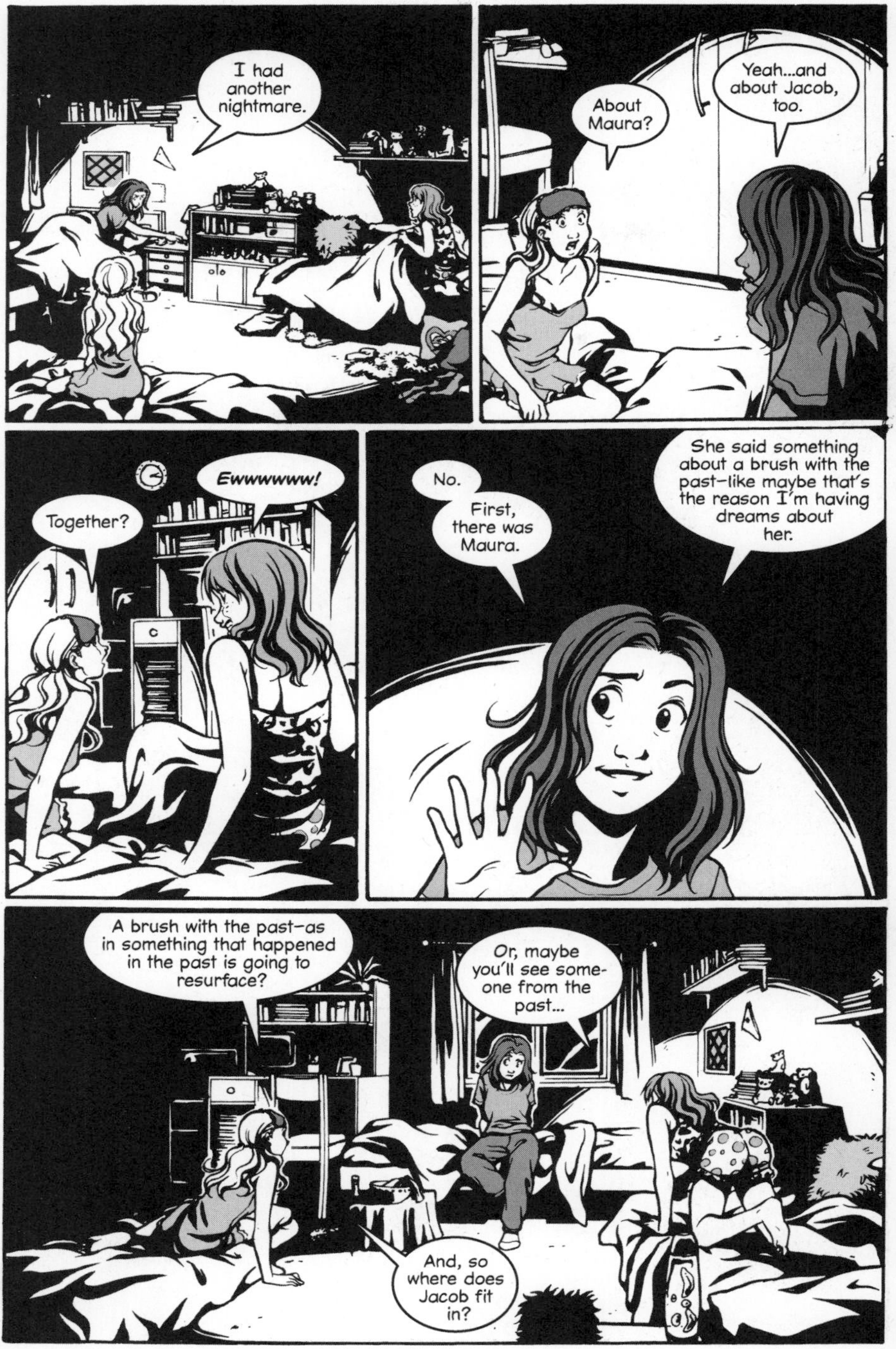
I had another nightmare.
About Maura?
Yeah...and about Jacob, too.
Together?
Ewwwwww!
No.
First, there was Maura.
She said something about a brush with the past–like maybe that's the reason I'm having dreams about her.
A brush with the past–as in something that happened in the past is going to resurface?
Or, maybe you'll see someone from the past...
And, so where does Jacob fit in?

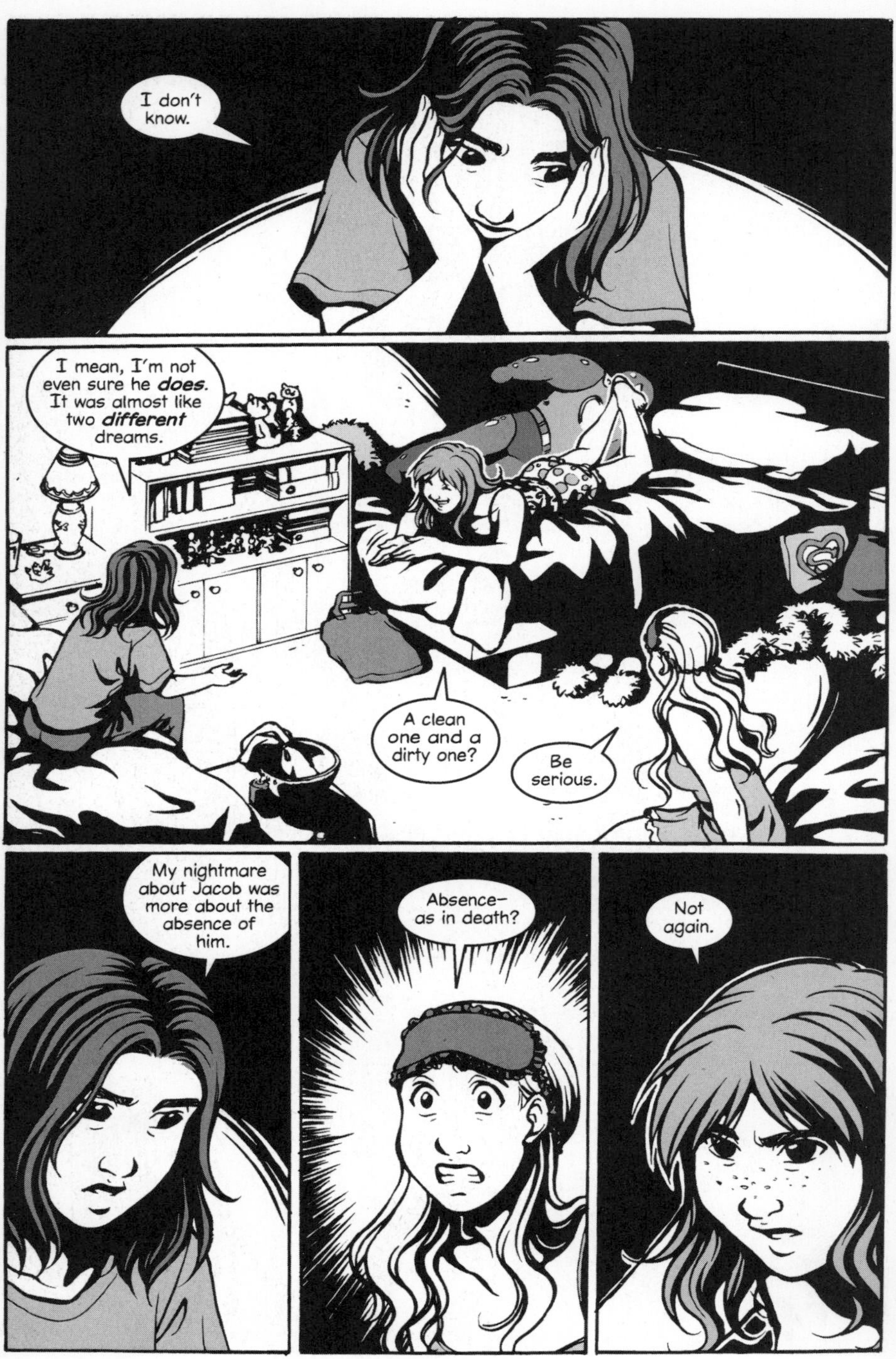
I don't know.
I mean, I'm not even sure he ***does***. It was almost like two ***different*** dreams.
A clean one and a dirty one?
Be serious.
My nightmare about Jacob was more about the absence of him.
Absence—as in death?
Not again.

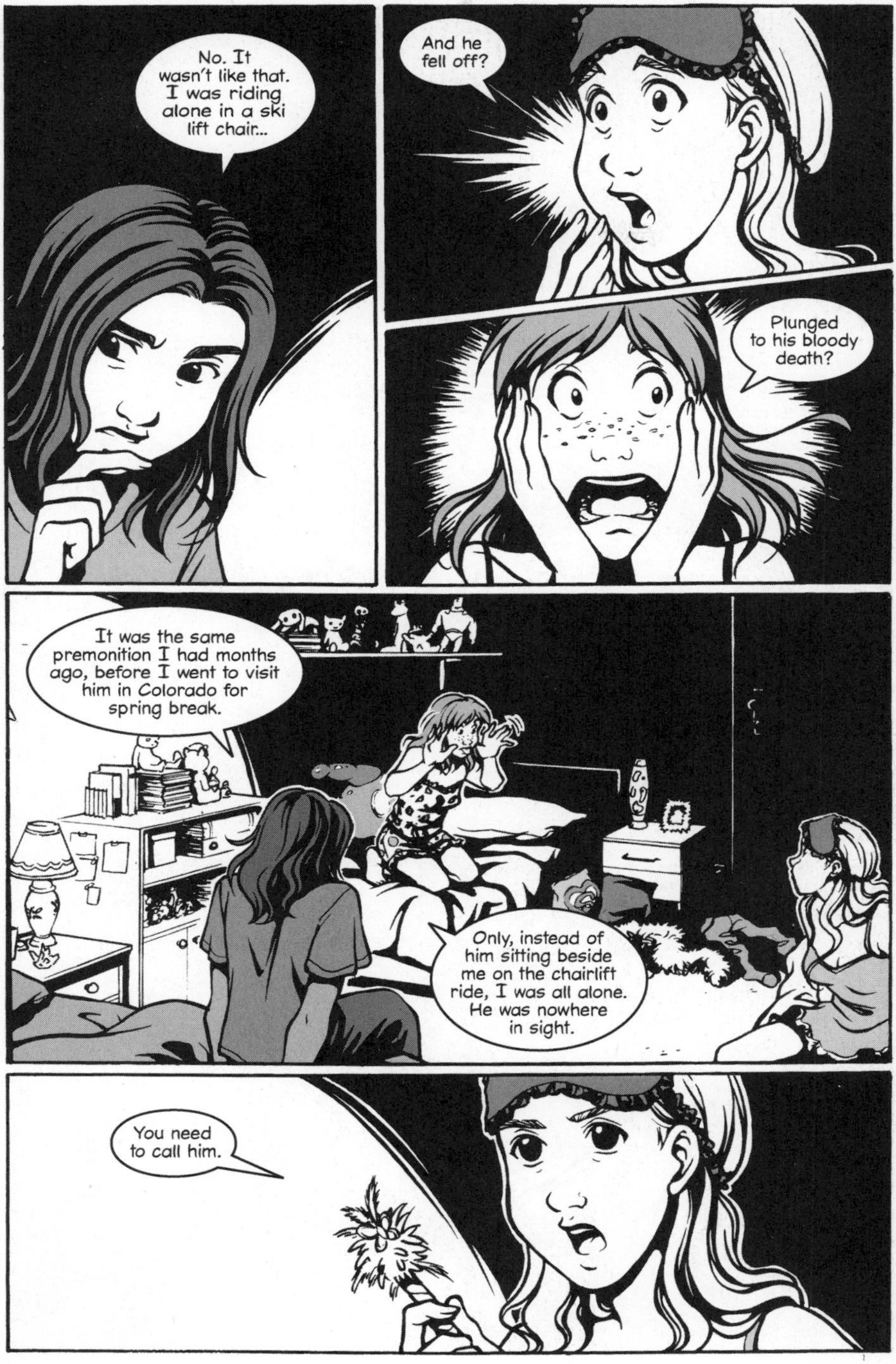
No. It wasn't like that. I was riding alone in a ski lift chair...
And he fell off?
Plunged to his bloody death?
It was the same premonition I had months ago, before I went to visit him in Colorado for spring break.
Only, instead of him sitting beside me on the chairlift ride, I was all alone. He was nowhere in sight.
You need to call him.

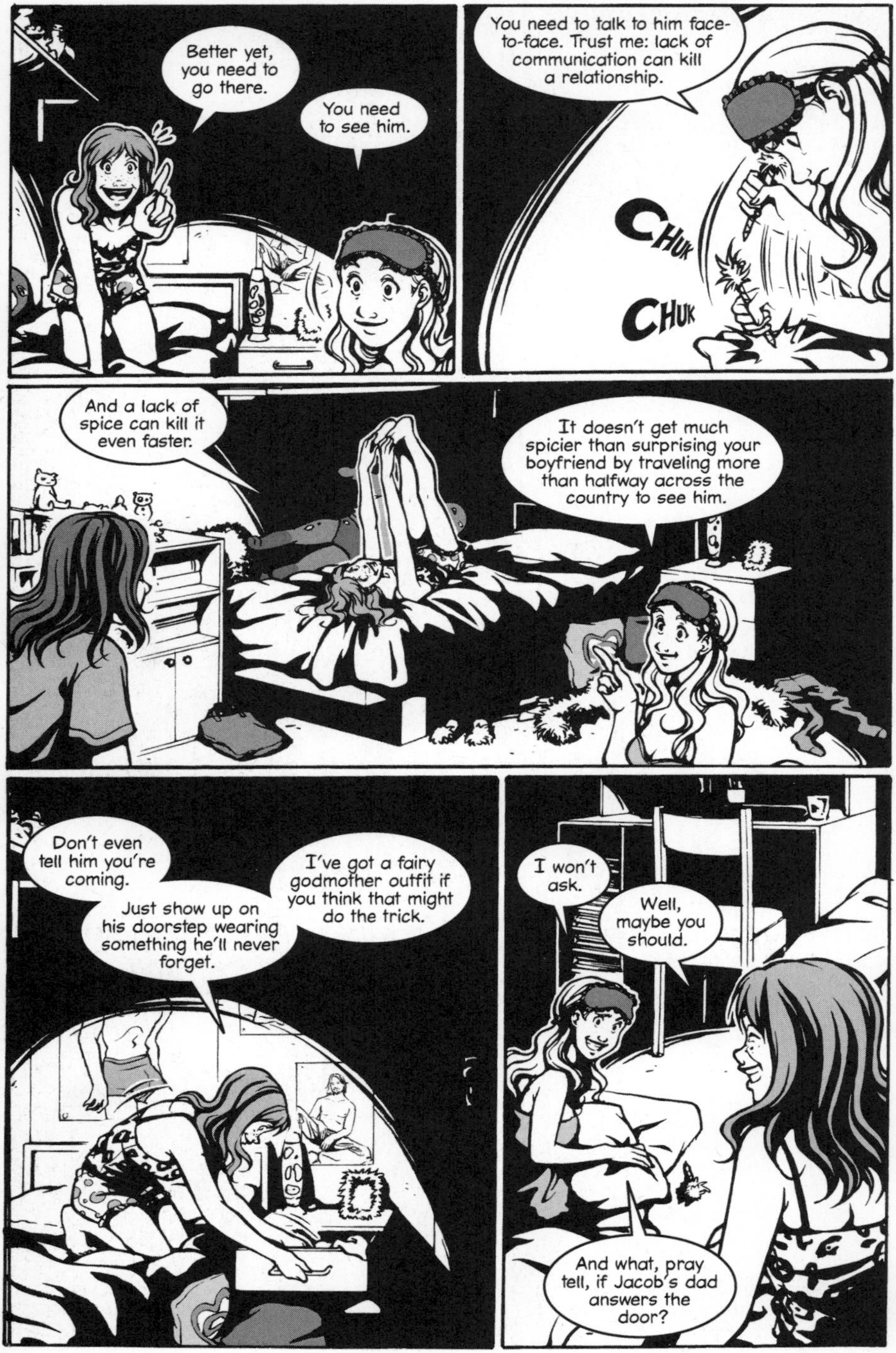

Better yet, you need to go there.
You need to see him.
You need to talk to him face-to-face. Trust me: lack of communication can kill a relationship.
CHUK
CHUK
And a lack of spice can kill it even faster.
It doesn't get much spicier than surprising your boyfriend by traveling more than halfway across the country to see him.
Don't even tell him you're coming.
Just show up on his doorstep wearing something he'll never forget.
I've got a fairy godmother outfit if you think that might do the trick.
I won't ask.
Well, maybe you should.
And what, pray tell, if Jacob's dad answers the door?

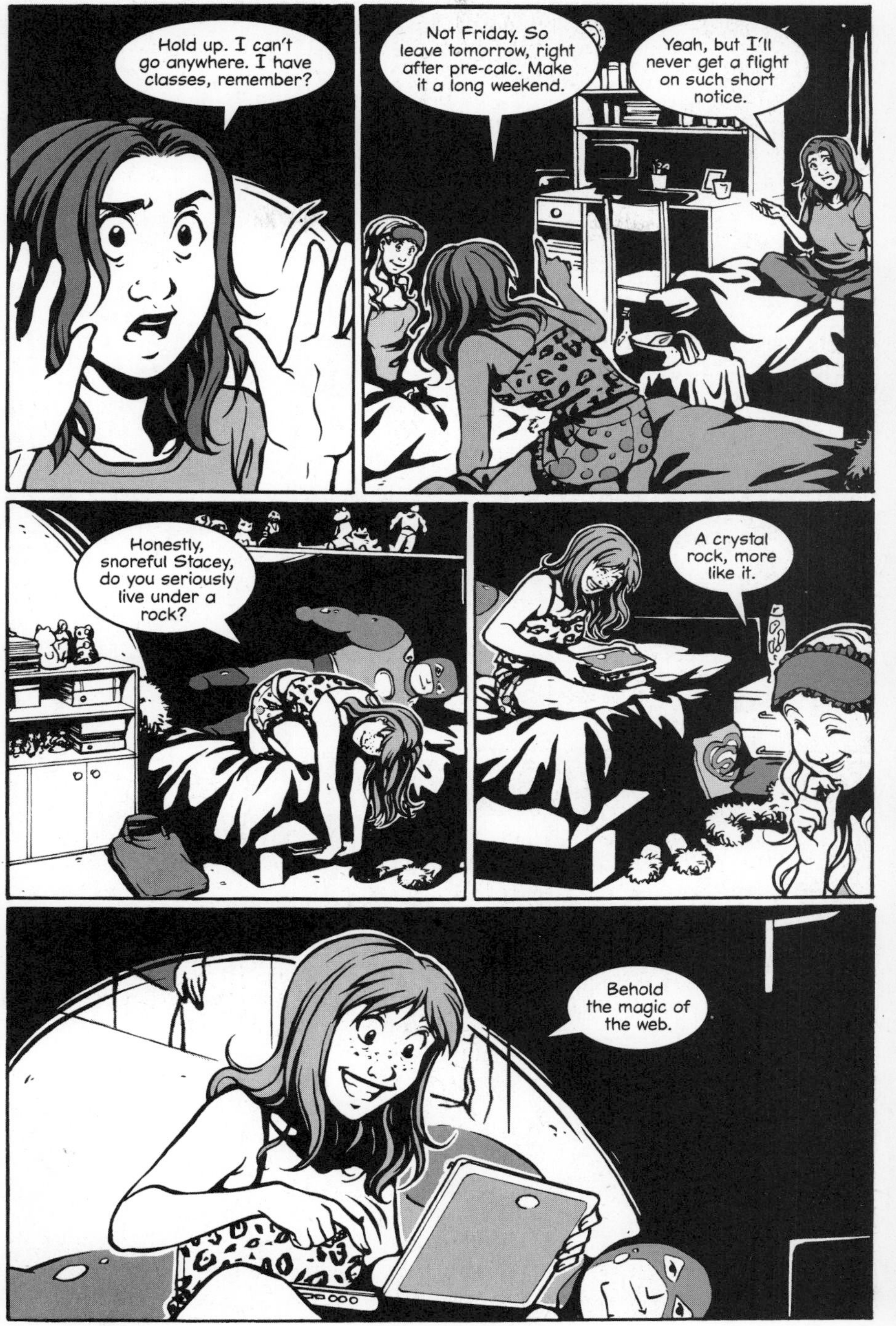

Hold up. I can't go anywhere. I have classes, remember?
Not Friday. So leave tomorrow, right after pre-calc. Make it a long weekend.
Yeah, but I'll never get a flight on such short notice.
Honestly, snoreful Stacey, do you seriously live under a rock?
A crystal rock, more like it.
Behold the magic of the web.

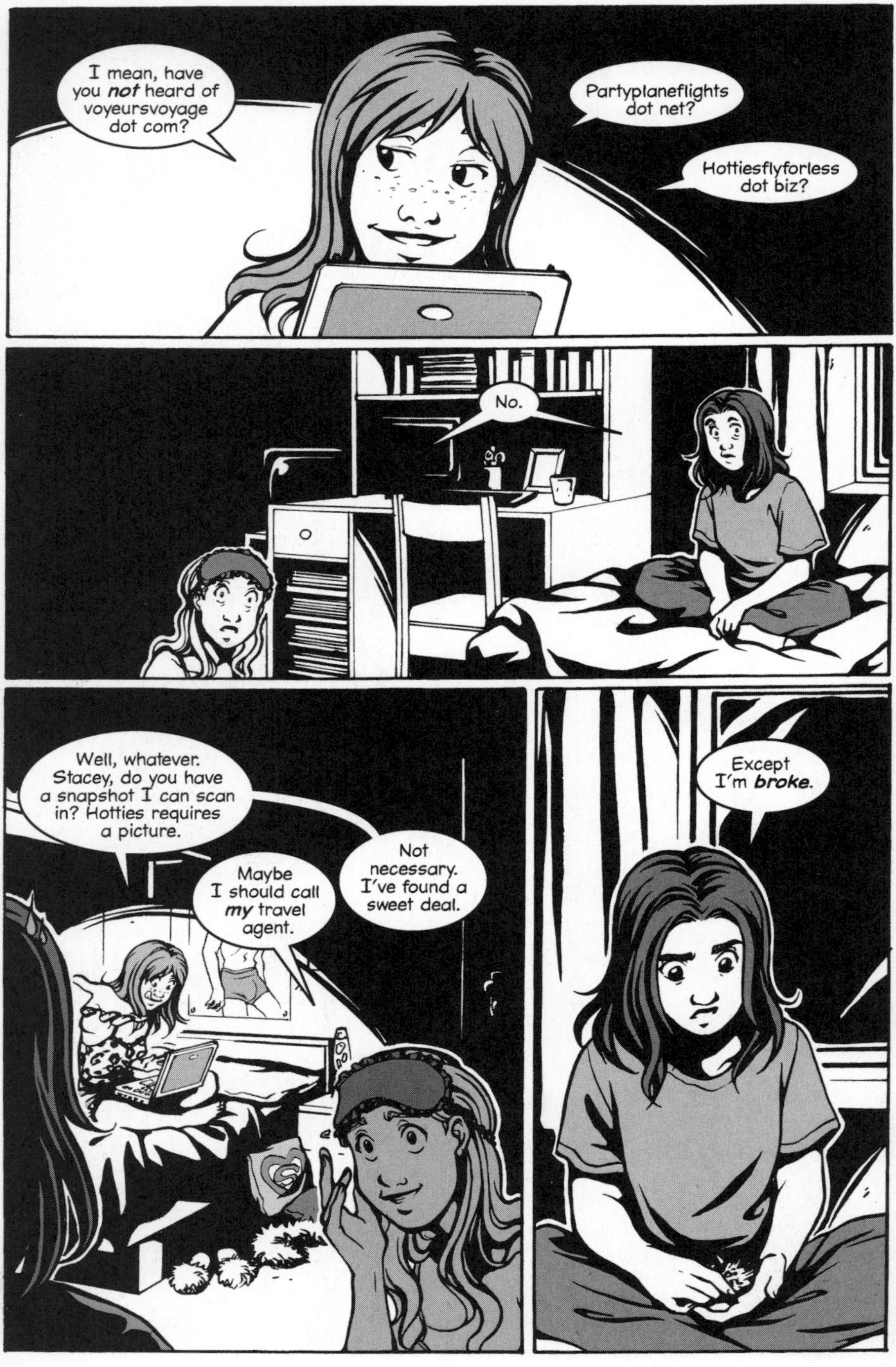

I mean, have you *not* heard of voyeursvoyage dot com?
Partyplaneflights dot net?
Hottiesflyforless dot biz?
No.
Well, whatever. Stacey, do you have a snapshot I can scan in? Hotties requires a picture.
Maybe I should call *my* travel agent.
Not necessary. I've found a sweet deal.
Except I'm ***broke.***

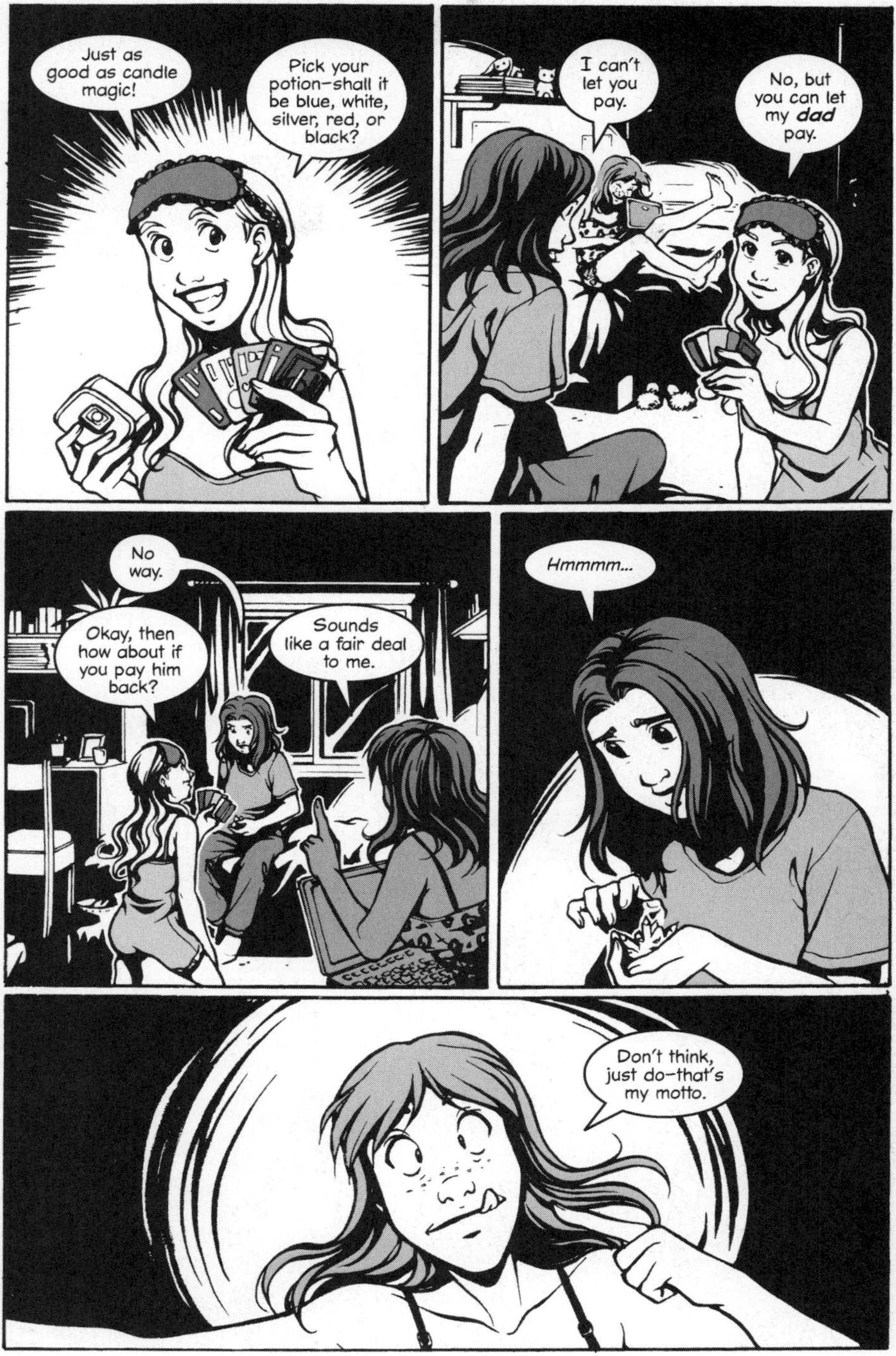
Just as good as candle magic!
Pick your potion—shall it be blue, white, silver, red, or black?
I can't let you pay.
No, but you can let my ***dad*** pay.
No way.
Okay, then how about if you pay him back?
Sounds like a fair deal to me.
Hmmmm...
Don't think, just do—that's my motto.

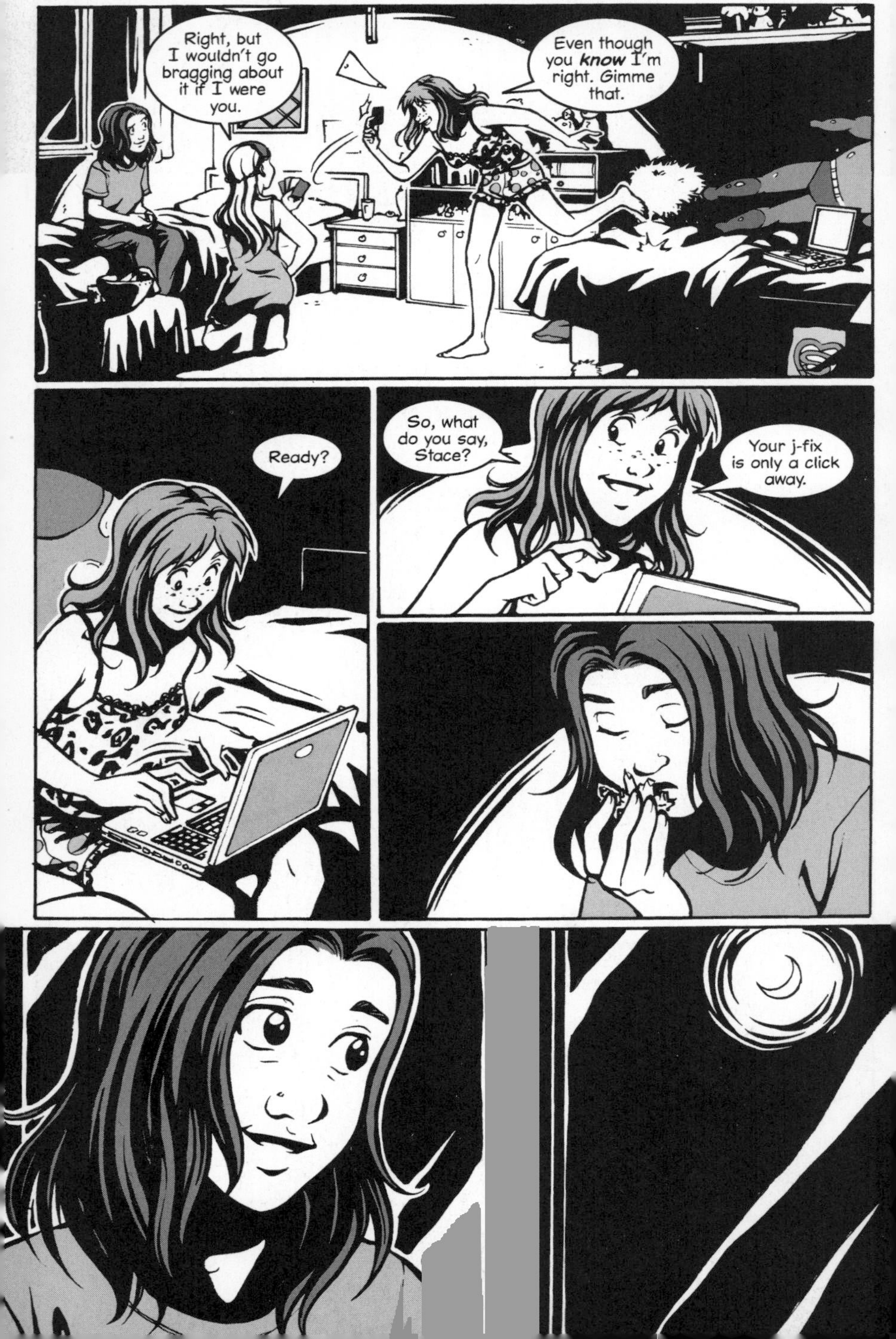
Right, but I wouldn't go bragging about it if I were you.
Even though you *know* I'm right. Gimme that.
Ready?
So, what do you say, Stace?
Your j-fix is only a click away.

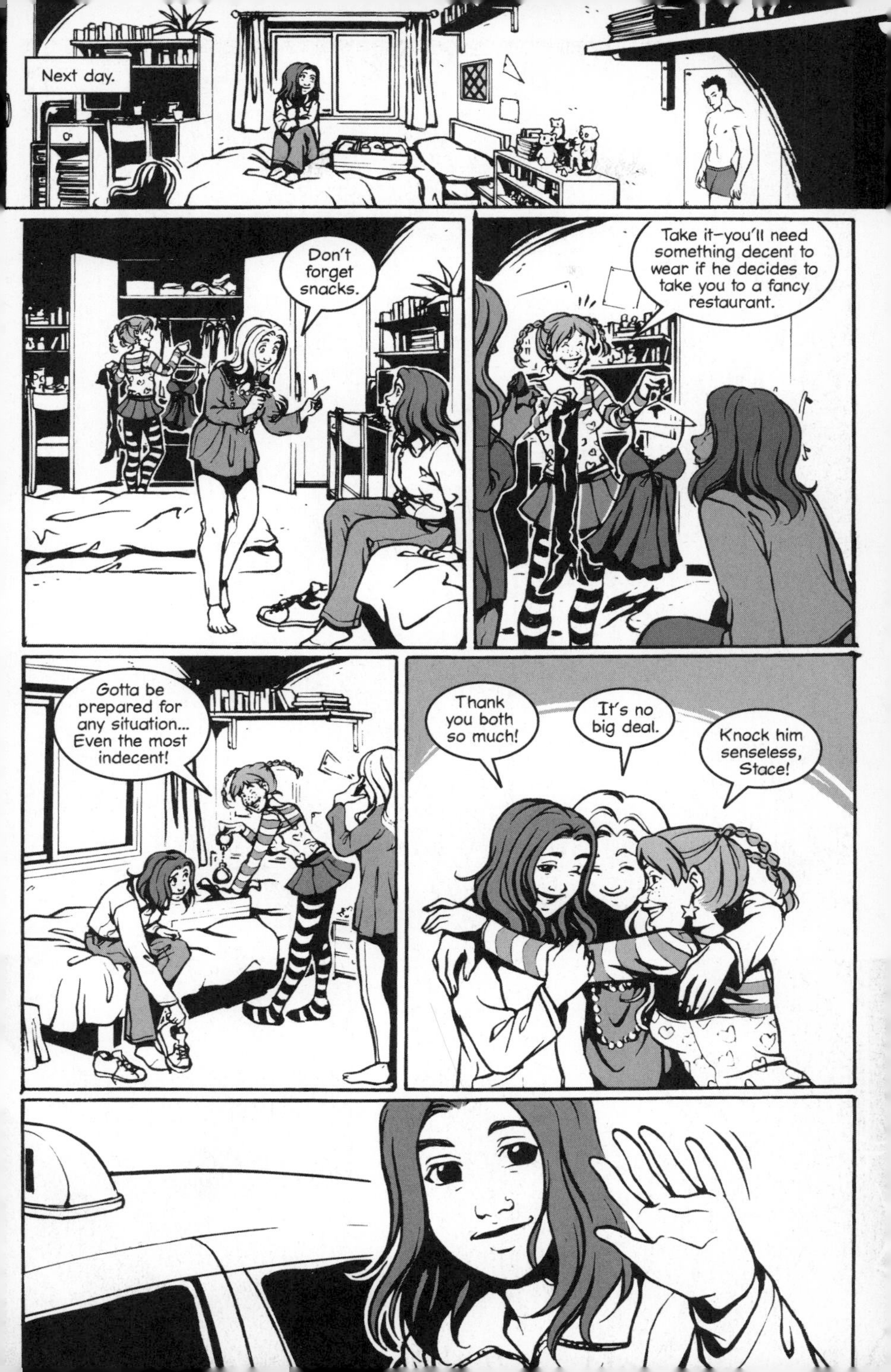
Next day.
Don't forget snacks.
Take it—you'll need something decent to wear if he decides to take you to a fancy restaurant.
Gotta be prepared for any situation... Even the most indecent!
Thank you both so much!
It's no big deal.
Knock him senseless, Stace!

STACEY'S TRAVEL SAFETY TIPS

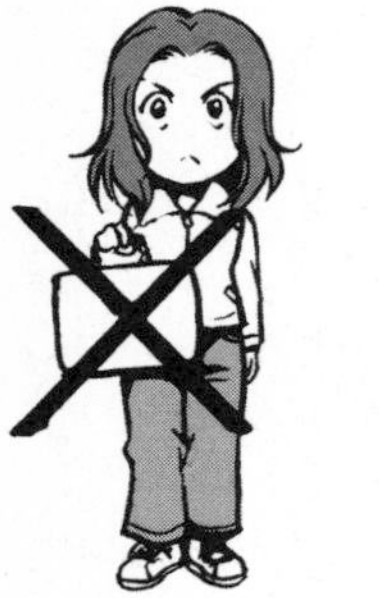

Don't let friends put the following items in your luggage:

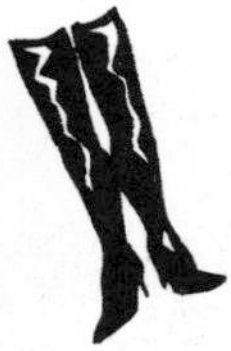

Unusual footwear.

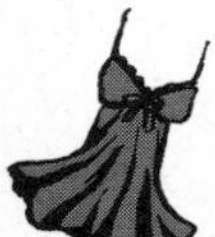

Exotic lingerie.

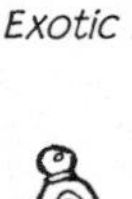

Questionable liquids.

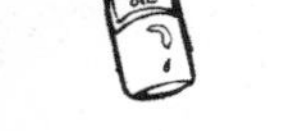

Handcuffs!

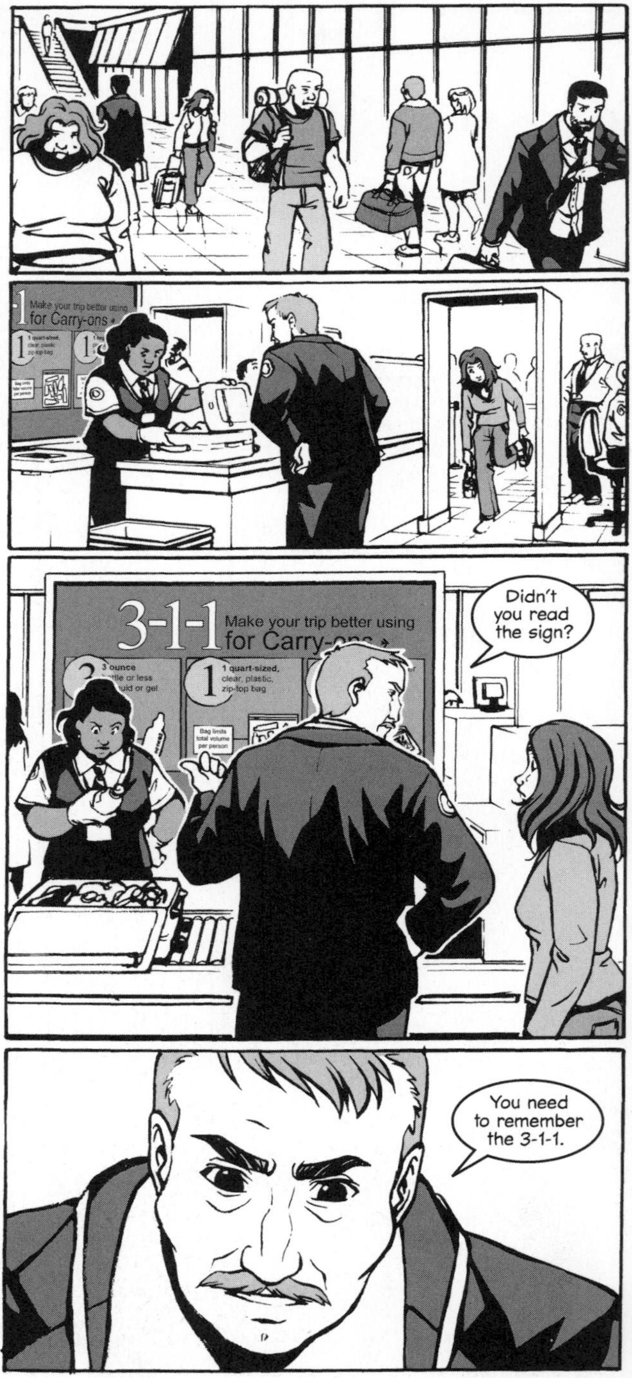
Make your trip better using
for Carry-ons
3-1-1
Make your trip better using
for Carry-ons
1 quart-sized,
clear, plastic,
zip-top bag
Bag limits
total volume
per person
Didn't you read the sign?
You need to remember the 3-1-1.

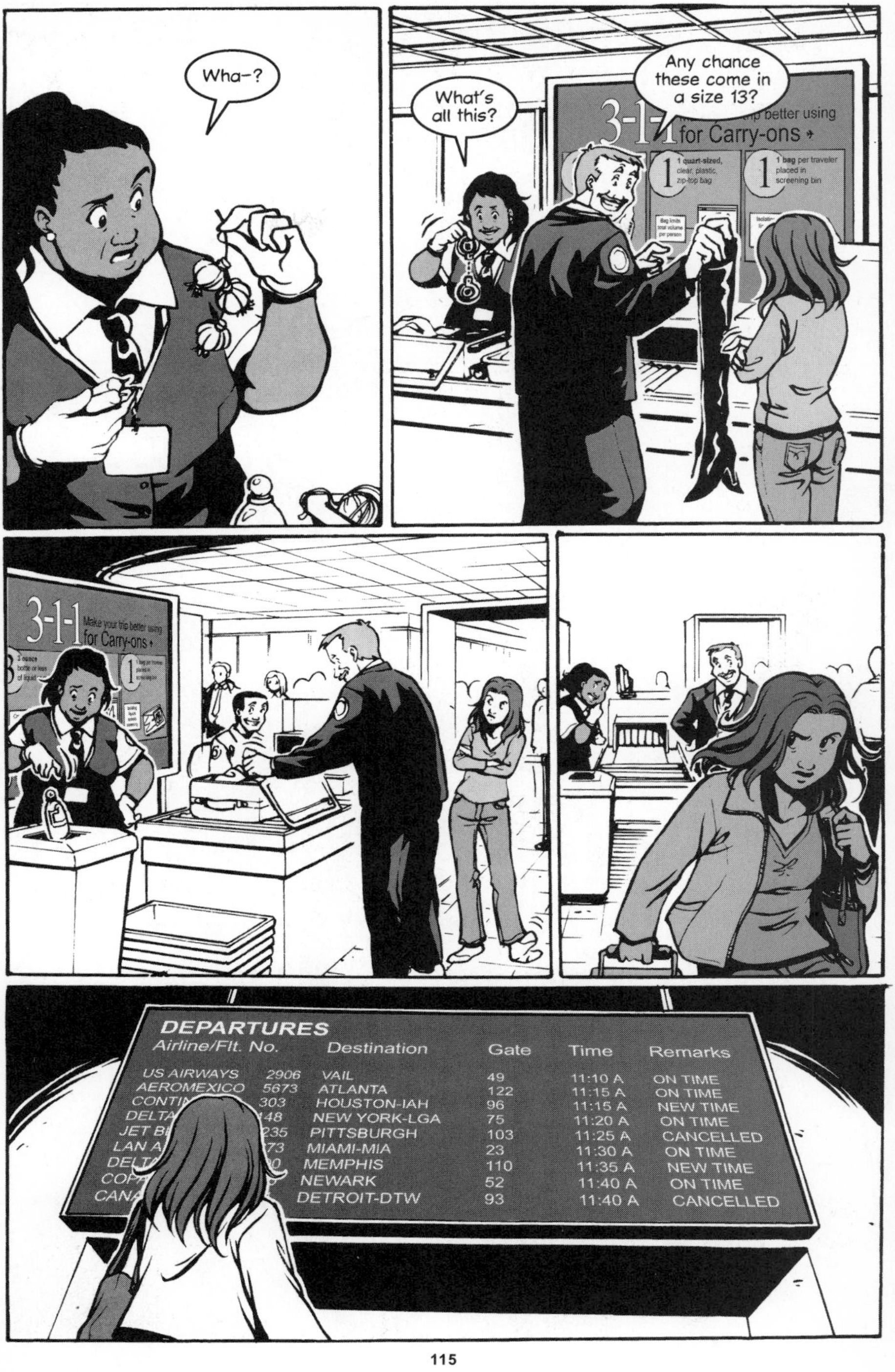
Wha-?
What's all this?
Any chance these come in a size 13?
3-1-1
for Carry-ons
1 quart-sized, clear, plastic, zip-top bag
1 bag per traveler placed in screening bin
3-1-1 Make your trip better using for Carry-ons
DEPARTURES
Airline/Flt. No. Destination Gate Time Remarks
US AIRWAYS 2906 VAIL 49 11:10 A ON TIME
AEROMEXICO 5673 ATLANTA 122 11:15 A ON TIME
HOUSTON-IAH 96 11:15 A NEW TIME
NEW YORK-LGA 75 11:20 A ON TIME
PITTSBURGH 103 11:25 A CANCELLED
MIAMI-MIA 23 11:30 A ON TIME
MEMPHIS 110 11:35 A NEW TIME
NEWARK 52 11:40 A ON TIME
DETROIT-DTW 93 11:40 A CANCELLED

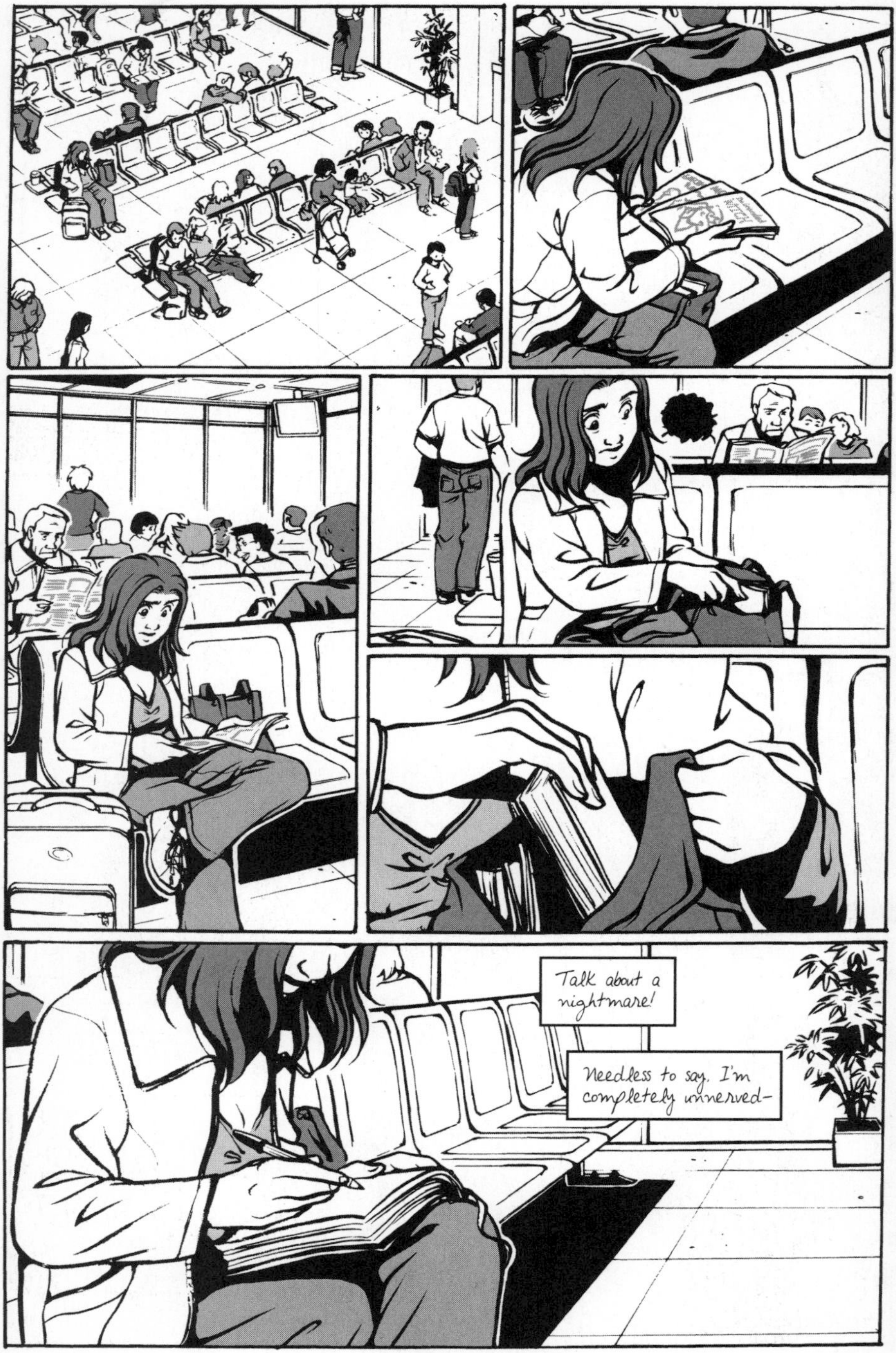

Talk about a nightmare!
Needless to say, I'm completely unnerved–

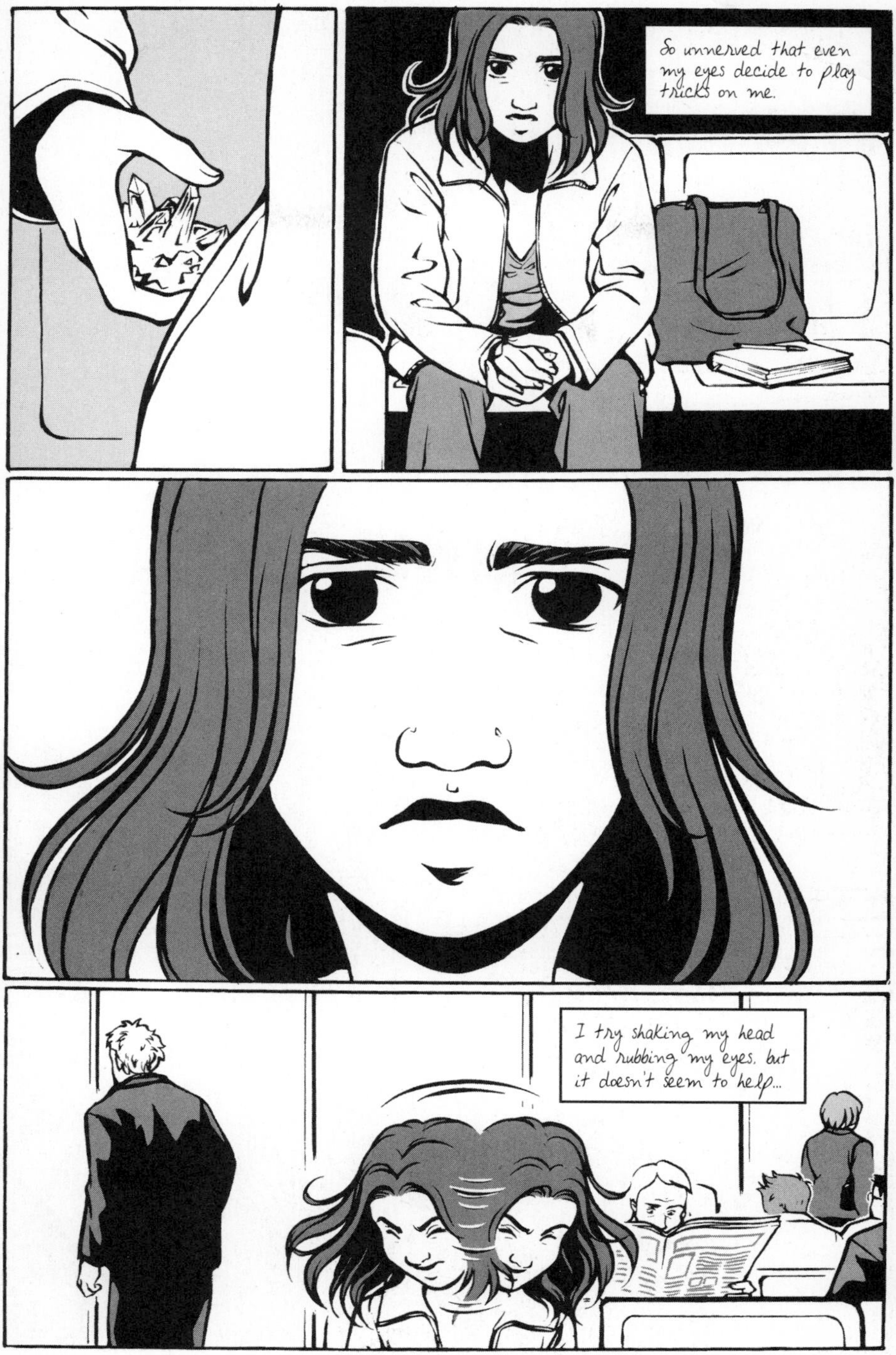
So unnerved that even my eyes decide to play tricks on me.
I try shaking my head and rubbing my eyes, but it doesn't seem to help...

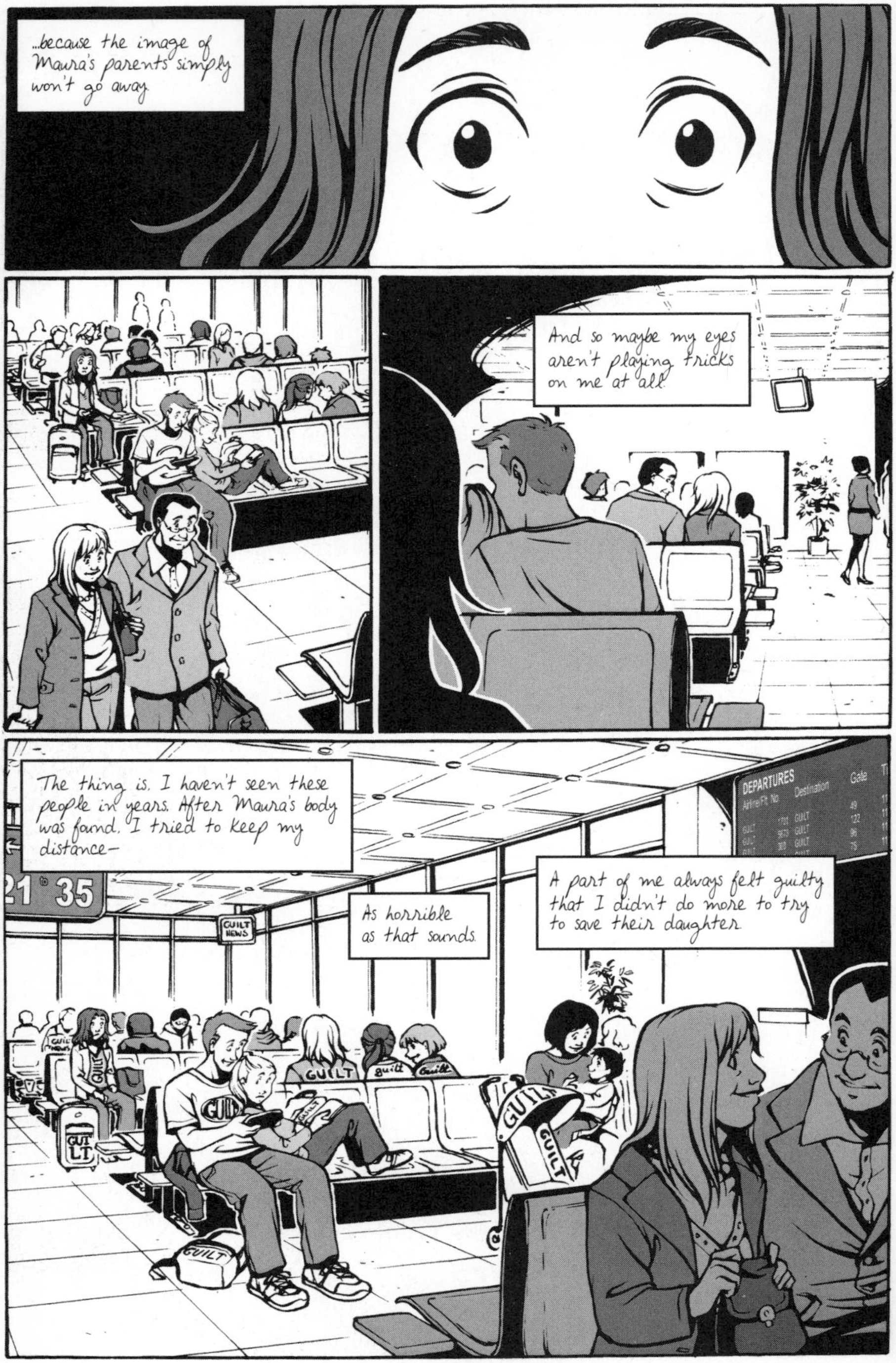
...because the image of Maura's parents simply won't go away.
And so maybe my eyes aren't playing tricks on me at all.
The thing is, I haven't seen these people in years. After Maura's body was found, I tried to keep my distance—
DEPARTURES
Destination
Gate
21 to 35
GUILT NEWS
As horrible as that sounds.
A part of me always felt guilty that I didn't do more to try to save their daughter.
GUILT
GUILT
GUILT
GUILT
GUILT

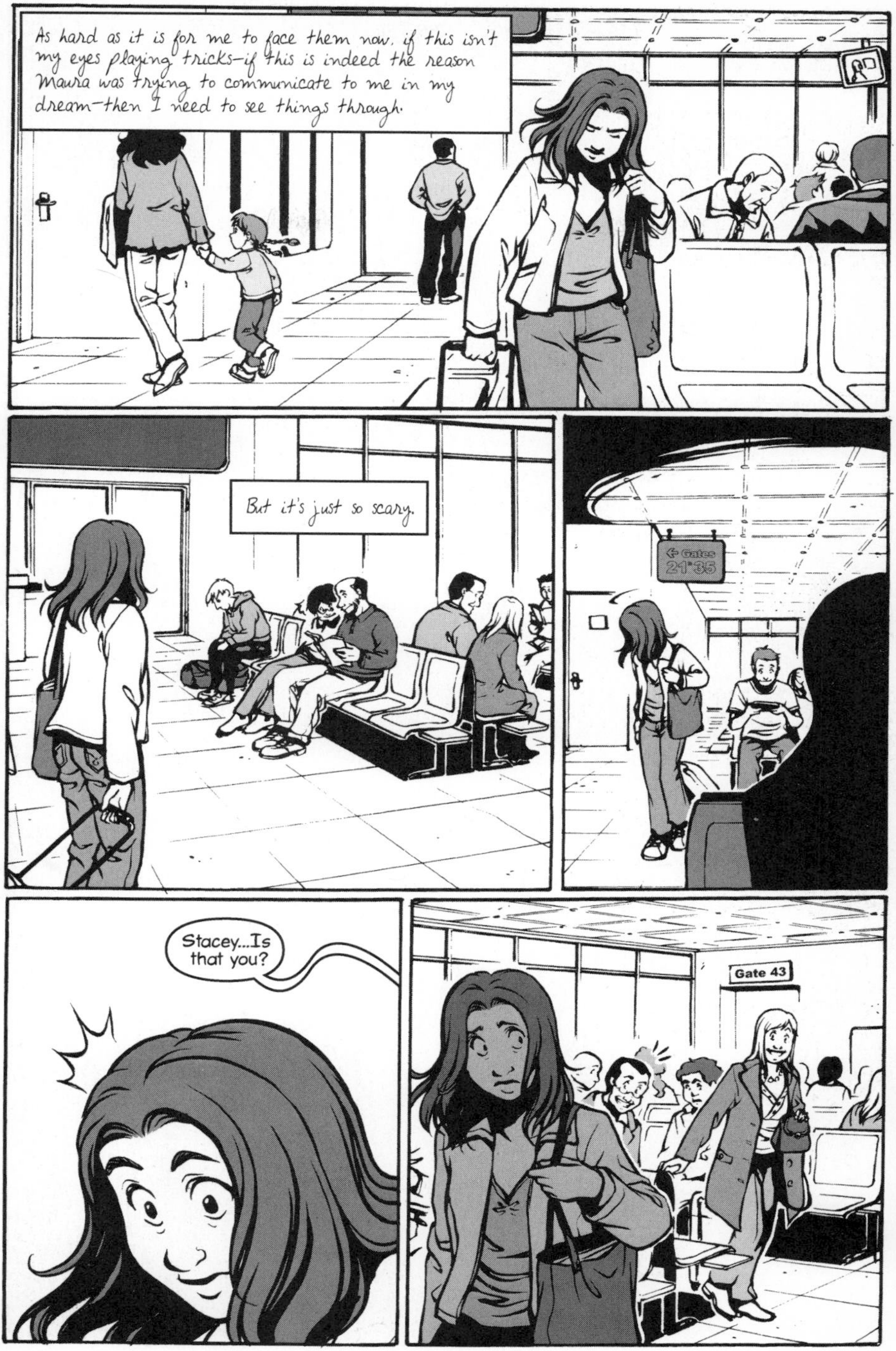

As hard as it is for me to face them now, if this isn't my eyes playing tricks—if this is indeed the reason Maura was trying to communicate to me in my dream—then I need to see things through.
But it's just so scary.
Gates 21-35
Stacey...Is that you?
Gate 43

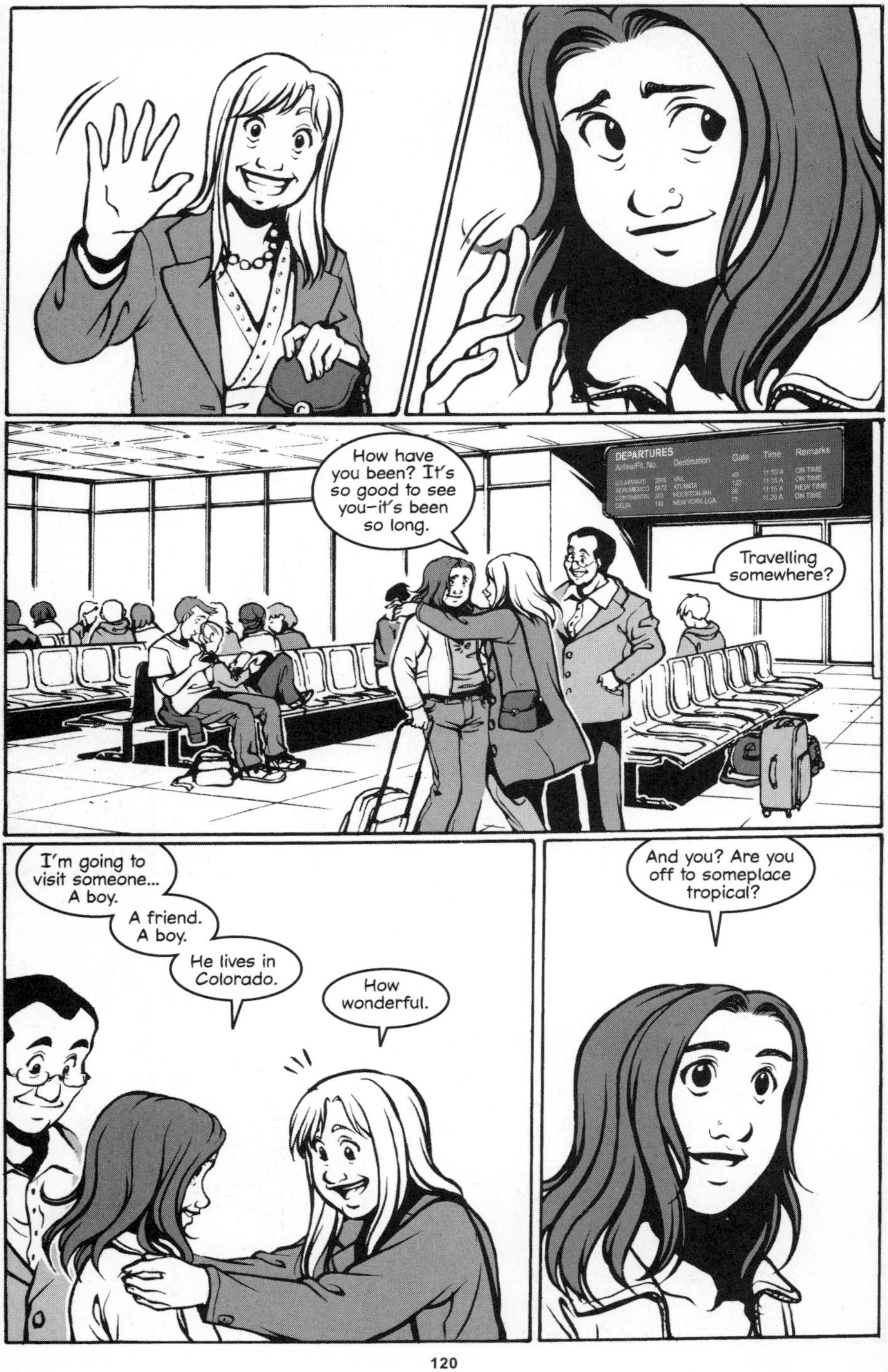
DEPARTURES
Airline/Flt. No. Destination Gate Time Remarks
How have you been? It's so good to see you–it's been so long.
Travelling somewhere?
I'm going to visit someone... A boy.
A friend. A boy.
He lives in Colorado.
How wonderful.
And you? Are you off to someplace tropical?

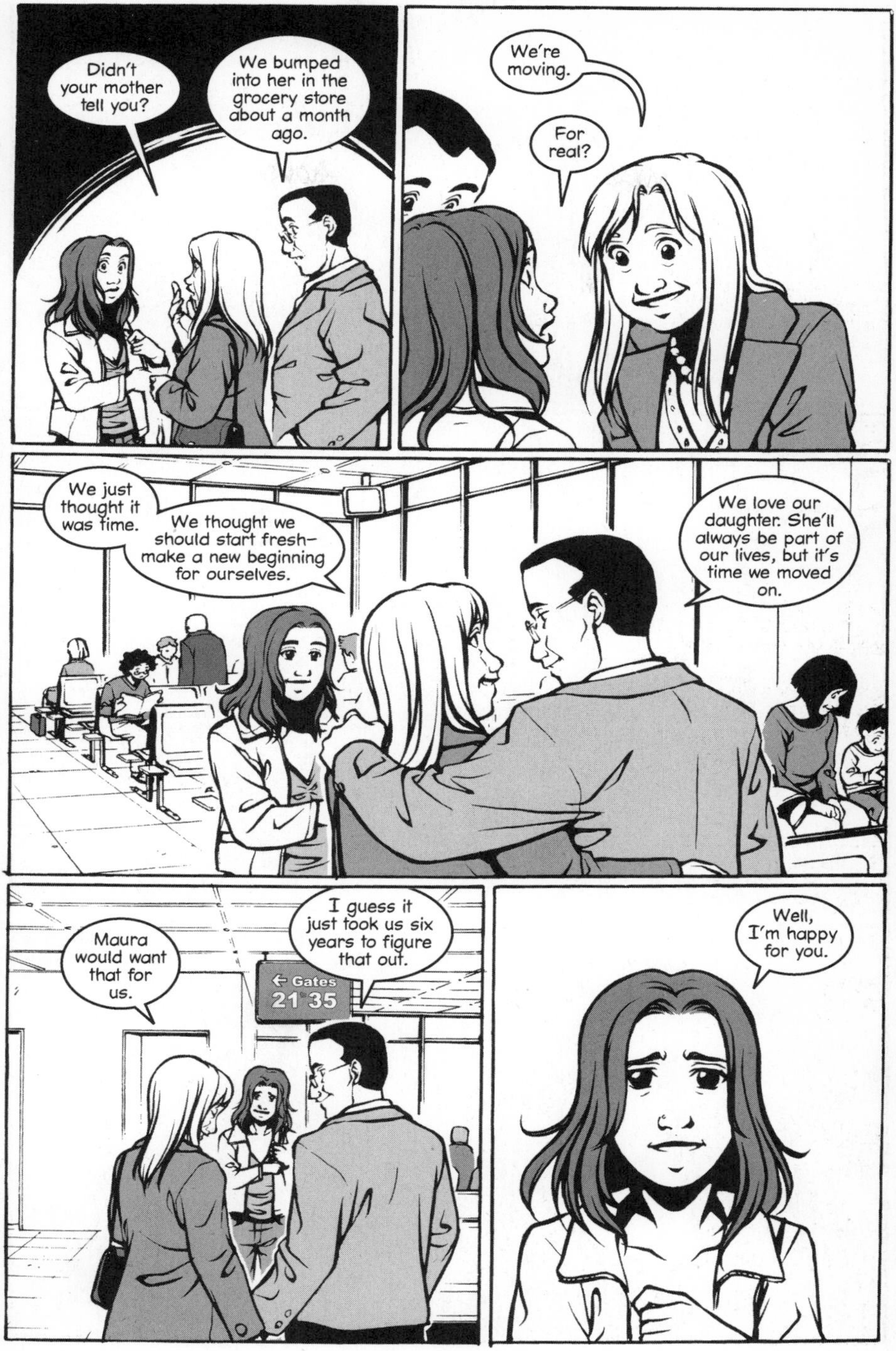
Didn't your mother tell you?
We bumped into her in the grocery store about a month ago.
We're moving.
For real?
We just thought it was time.
We thought we should start fresh- make a new beginning for ourselves.
We love our daughter. She'll always be part of our lives, but it's time we moved on.
Maura would want that for us.
← Gates 21-35
I guess it just took us six years to figure that out.
Well, I'm happy for you.

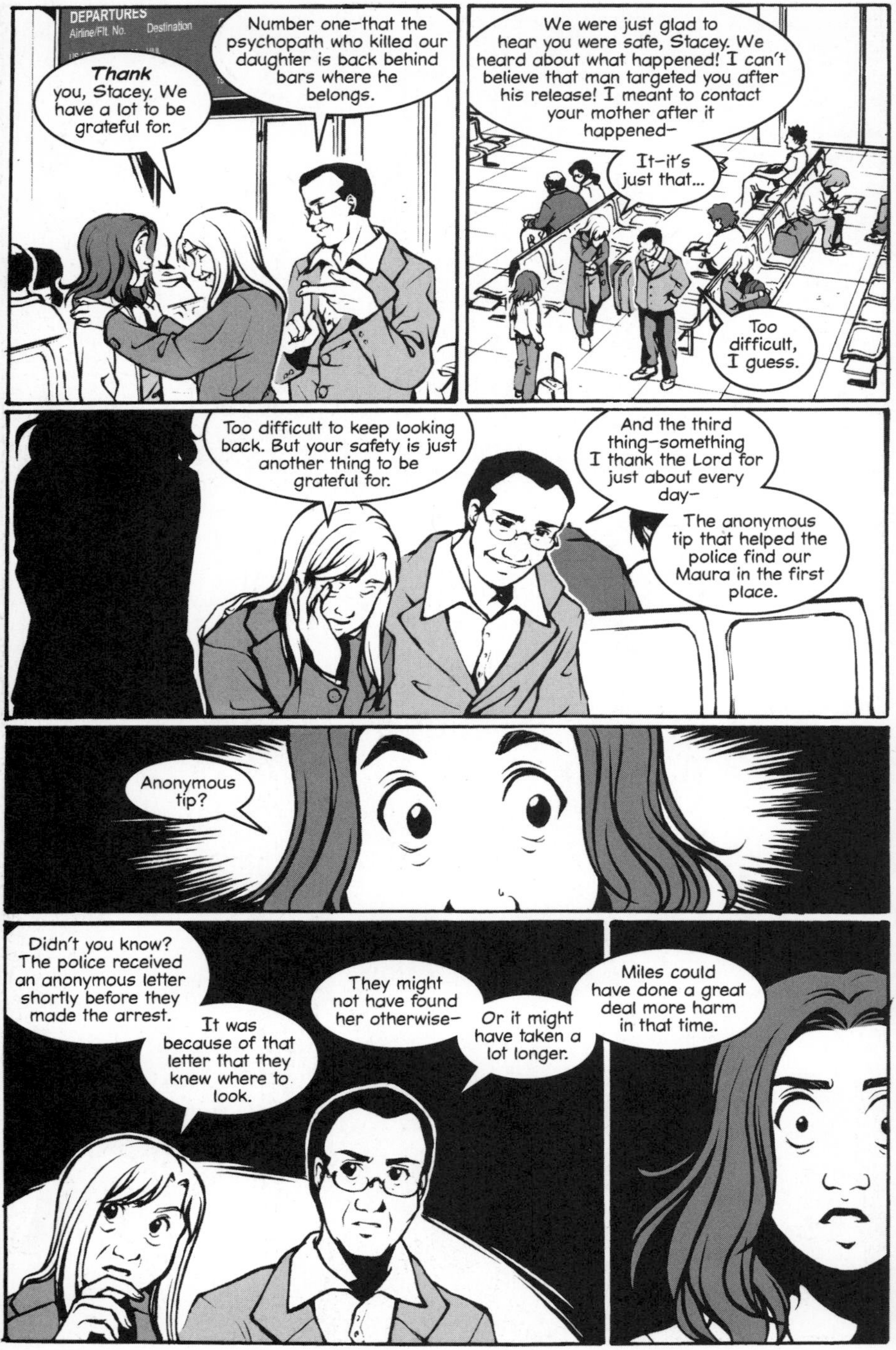
DEPARTURES
Airline/Flt. No. Destination
Thank you, Stacey. We have a lot to be grateful for.
Number one—that the psychopath who killed our daughter is back behind bars where he belongs.
We were just glad to hear you were safe, Stacey. We heard about what happened! I can't believe that man targeted you after his release! I meant to contact your mother after it happened—
It—it's just that...
Too difficult, I guess.
Too difficult to keep looking back. But your safety is just another thing to be grateful for.
And the third thing—something I thank the Lord for just about every day—
The anonymous tip that helped the police find our Maura in the first place.
Anonymous tip?
Didn't you know? The police received an anonymous letter shortly before they made the arrest.
It was because of that letter that they knew where to look.
They might not have found her otherwise—
Or it might have taken a lot longer.
Miles could have done a great deal more harm in that time.

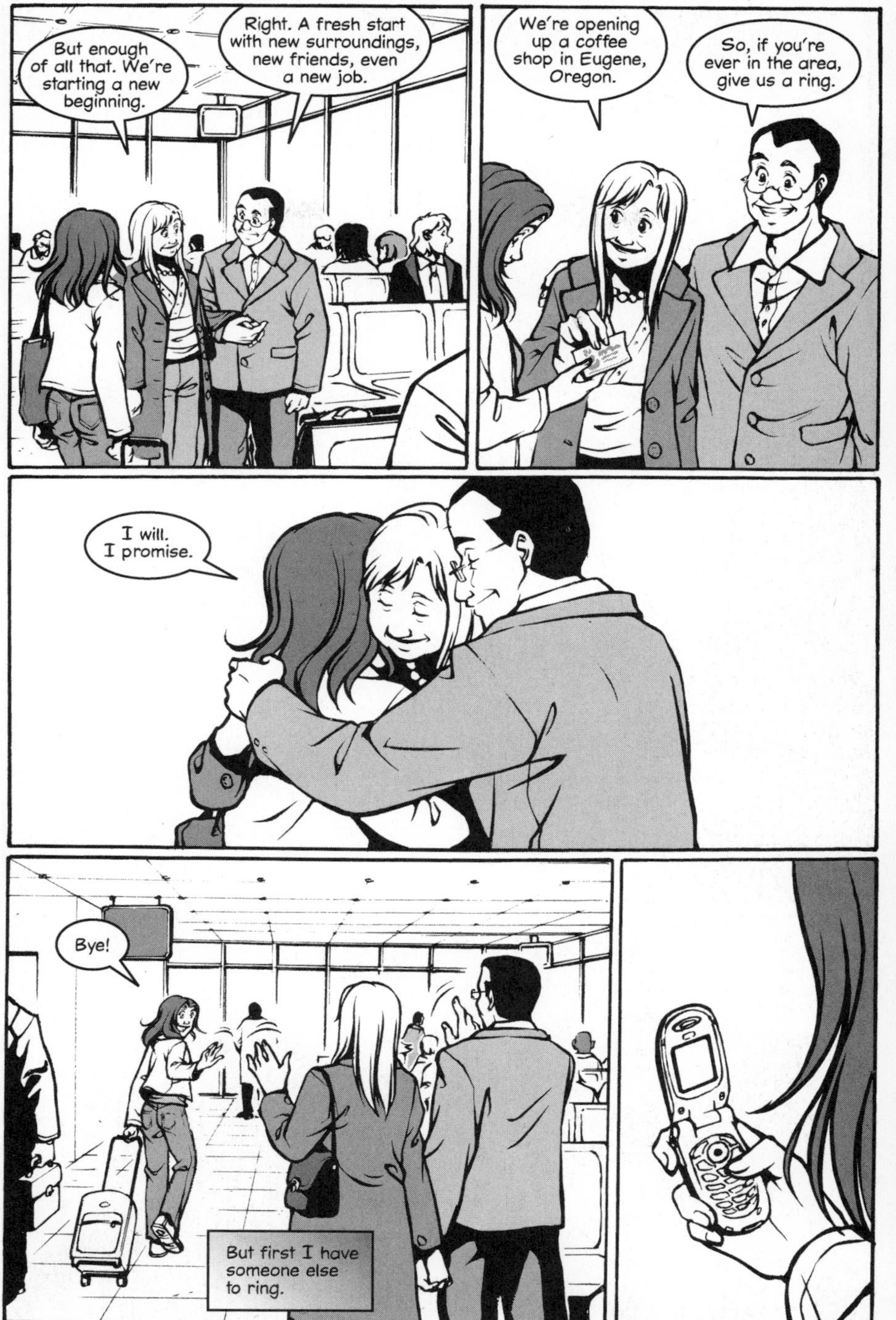

But enough of all that. We're starting a new beginning.
Right. A fresh start with new surroundings, new friends, even a new job.
We're opening up a coffee shop in Eugene, Oregon.
So, if you're ever in the area, give us a ring.
I will. I promise.
Bye!
But first I have someone else to ring.

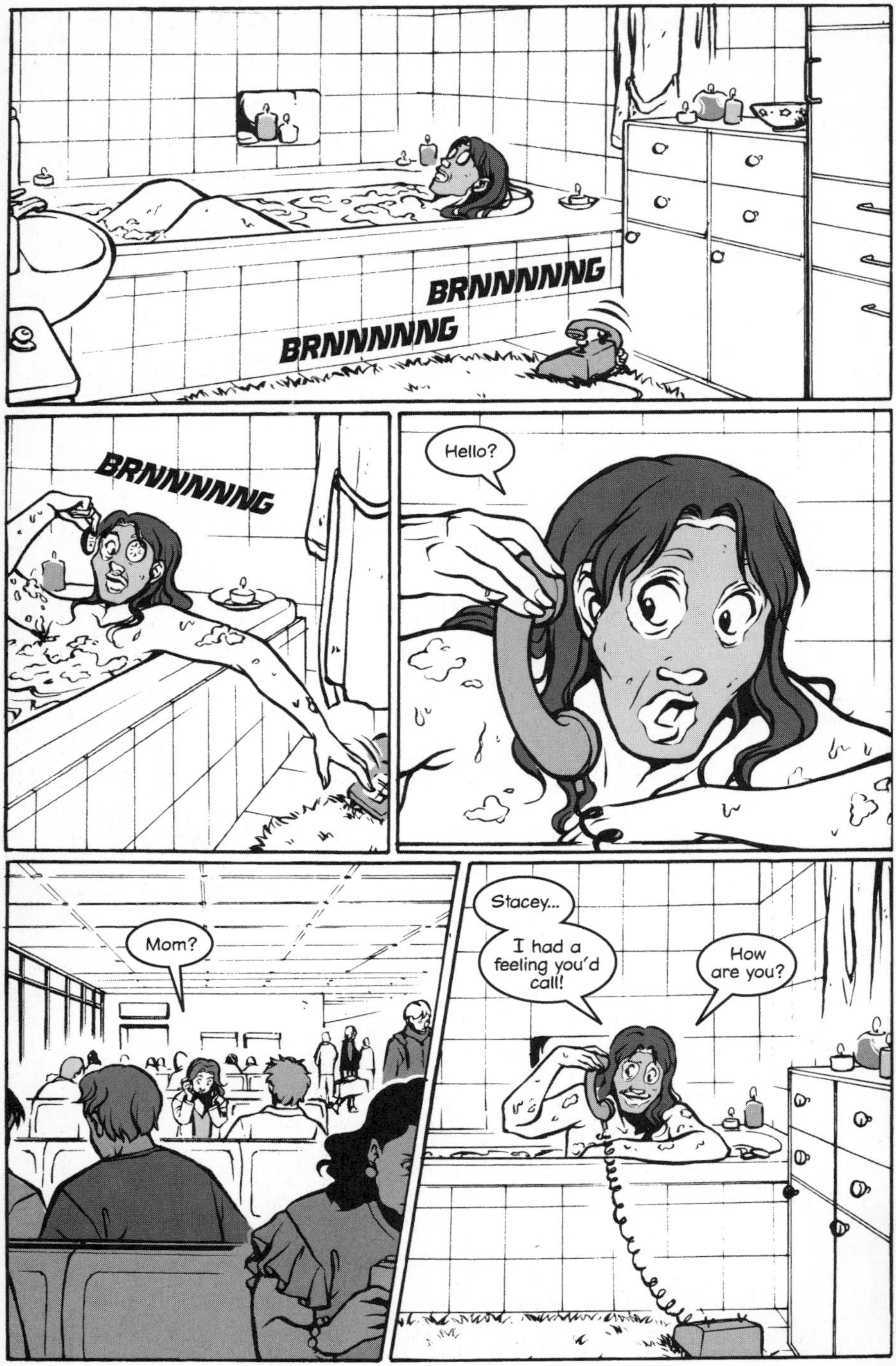
BRNNNNNG
BRNNNNNG
BRNNNNNNG
Hello?
Mom?
Stacey...
I had a feeling you'd call!
How are you?

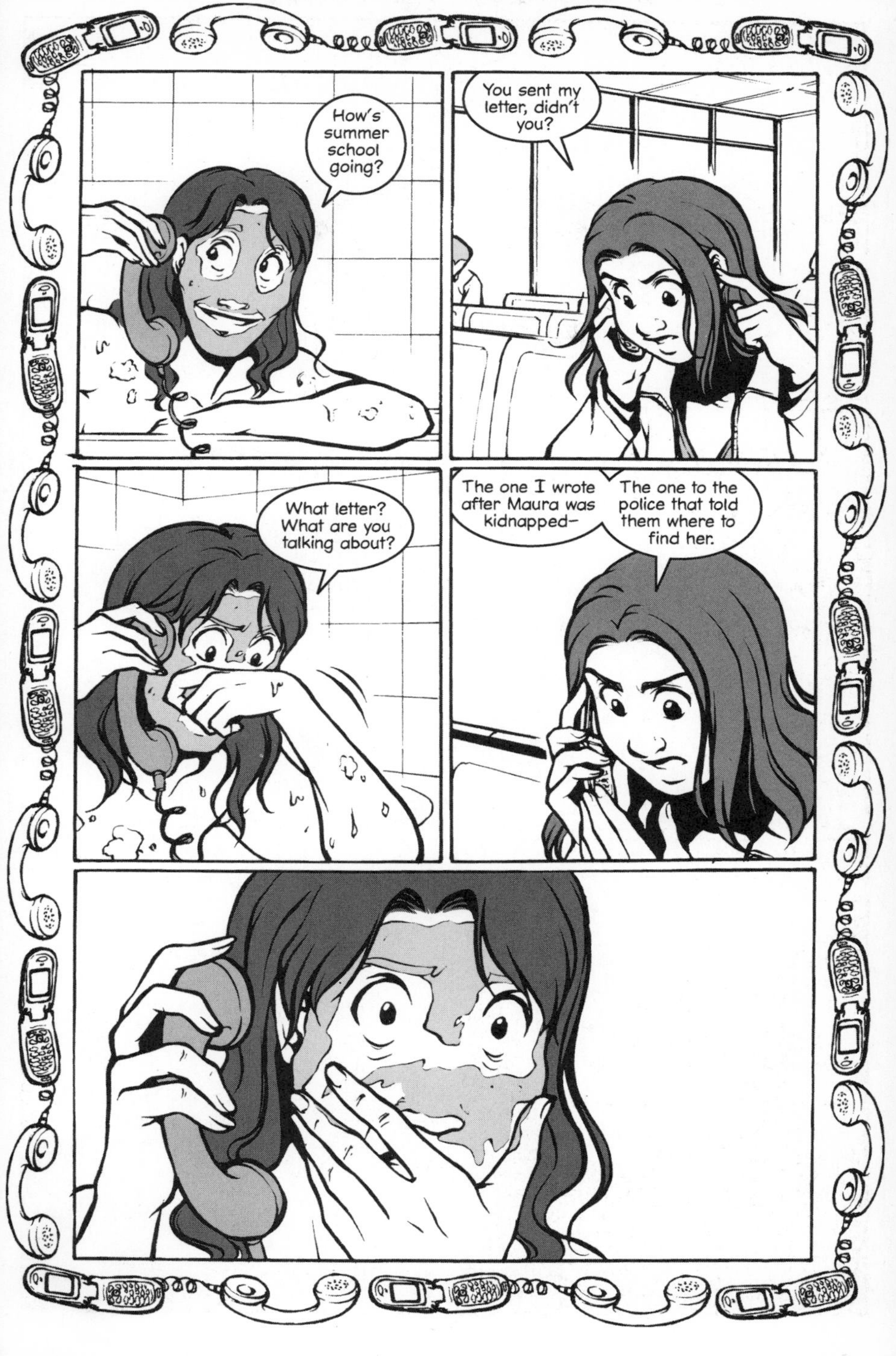
How's summer school going?
You sent my letter, didn't you?
What letter? What are you talking about?
The one I wrote after Maura was kidnapped–
The one to the police that told them where to find her.

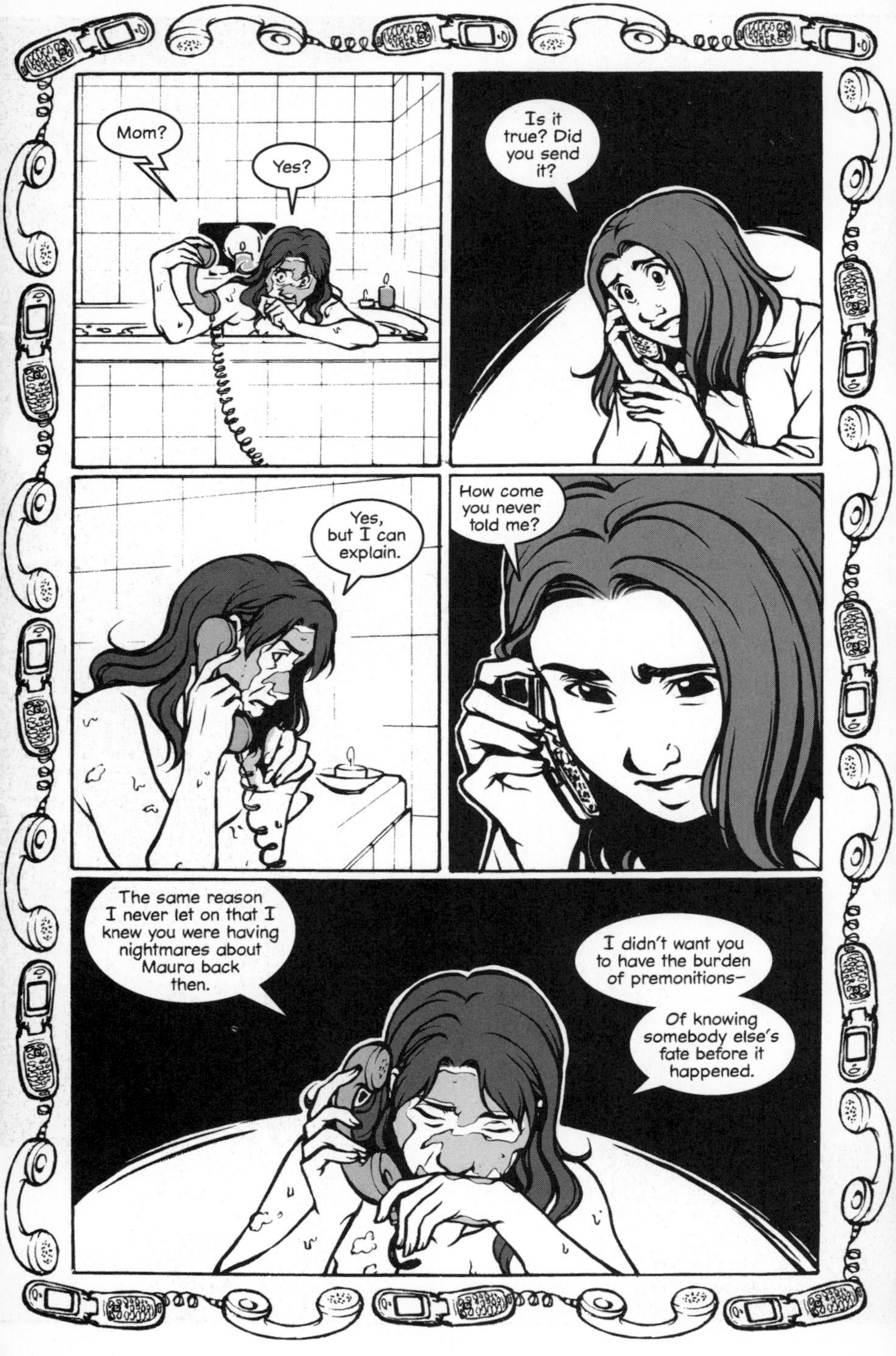
Mom?
Yes?
Is it true? Did you send it?
Yes, but I can explain.
How come you never told me?
The same reason I never let on that I knew you were having nightmares about Maura back then.
I didn't want you to have the burden of premonitions–
Of knowing somebody else's fate before it happened.

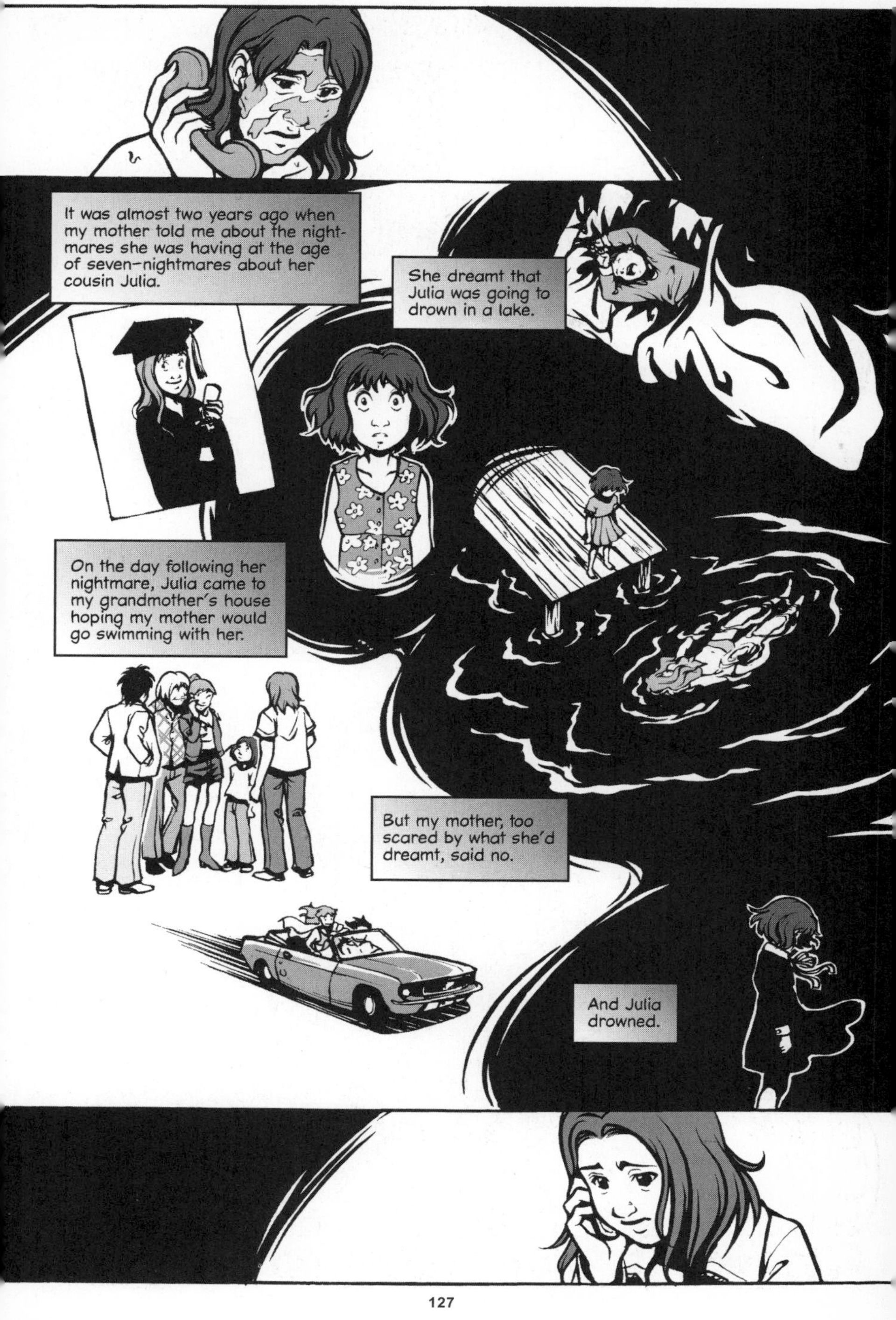
It was almost two years ago when my mother told me about the nightmares she was having at the age of seven—nightmares about her cousin Julia.
She dreamt that Julia was going to drown in a lake.
On the day following her nightmare, Julia came to my grandmother's house hoping my mother would go swimming with her.
But my mother, too scared by what she'd dreamt, said no.
And Julia drowned.

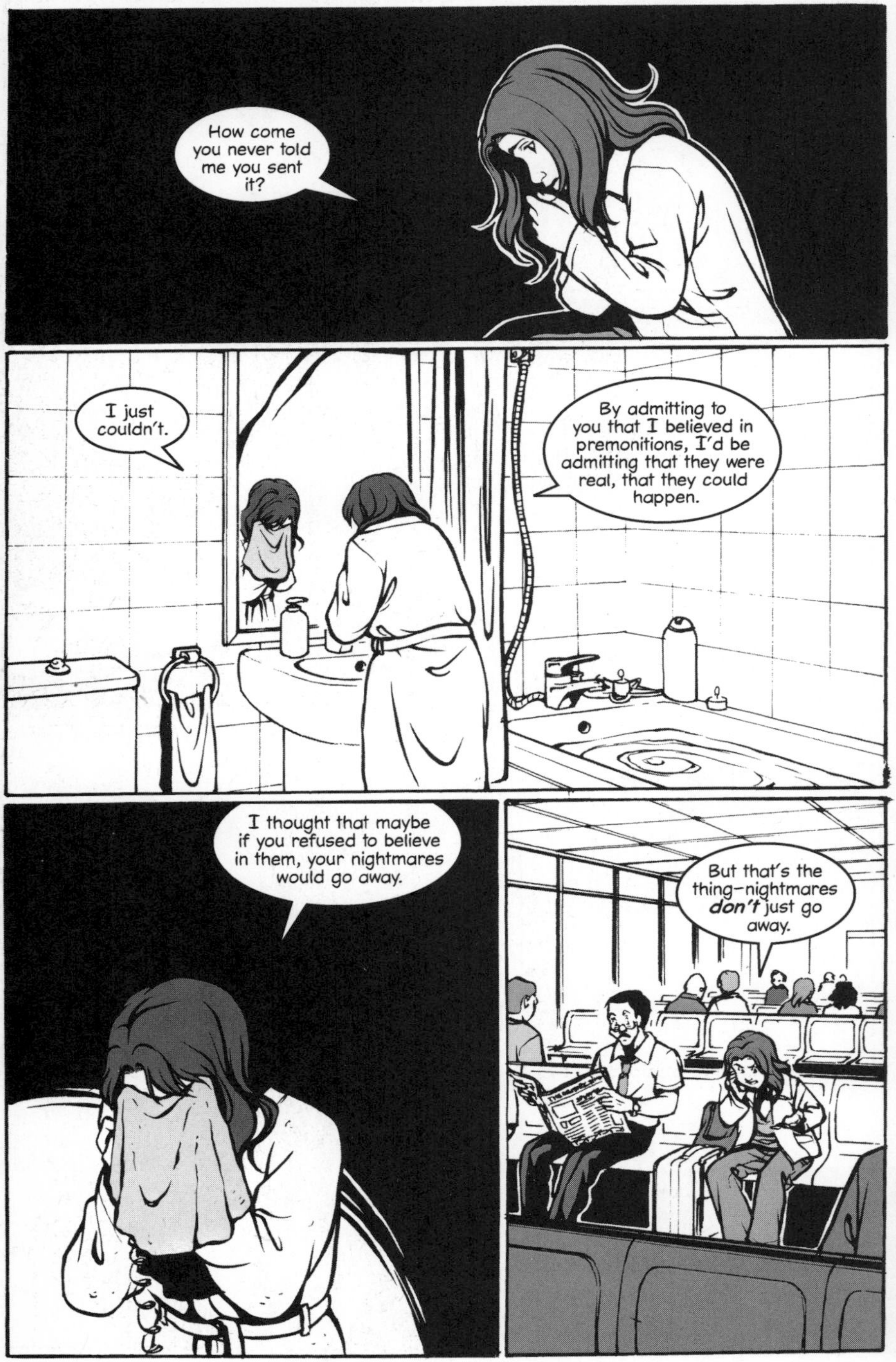
How come you never told me you sent it?
I just couldn't.
By admitting to you that I believed in premonitions, I'd be admitting that they were real, that they could happen.
I thought that maybe if you refused to believe in them, your nightmares would go away.
But that's the thing–nightmares ***don't*** just go away.

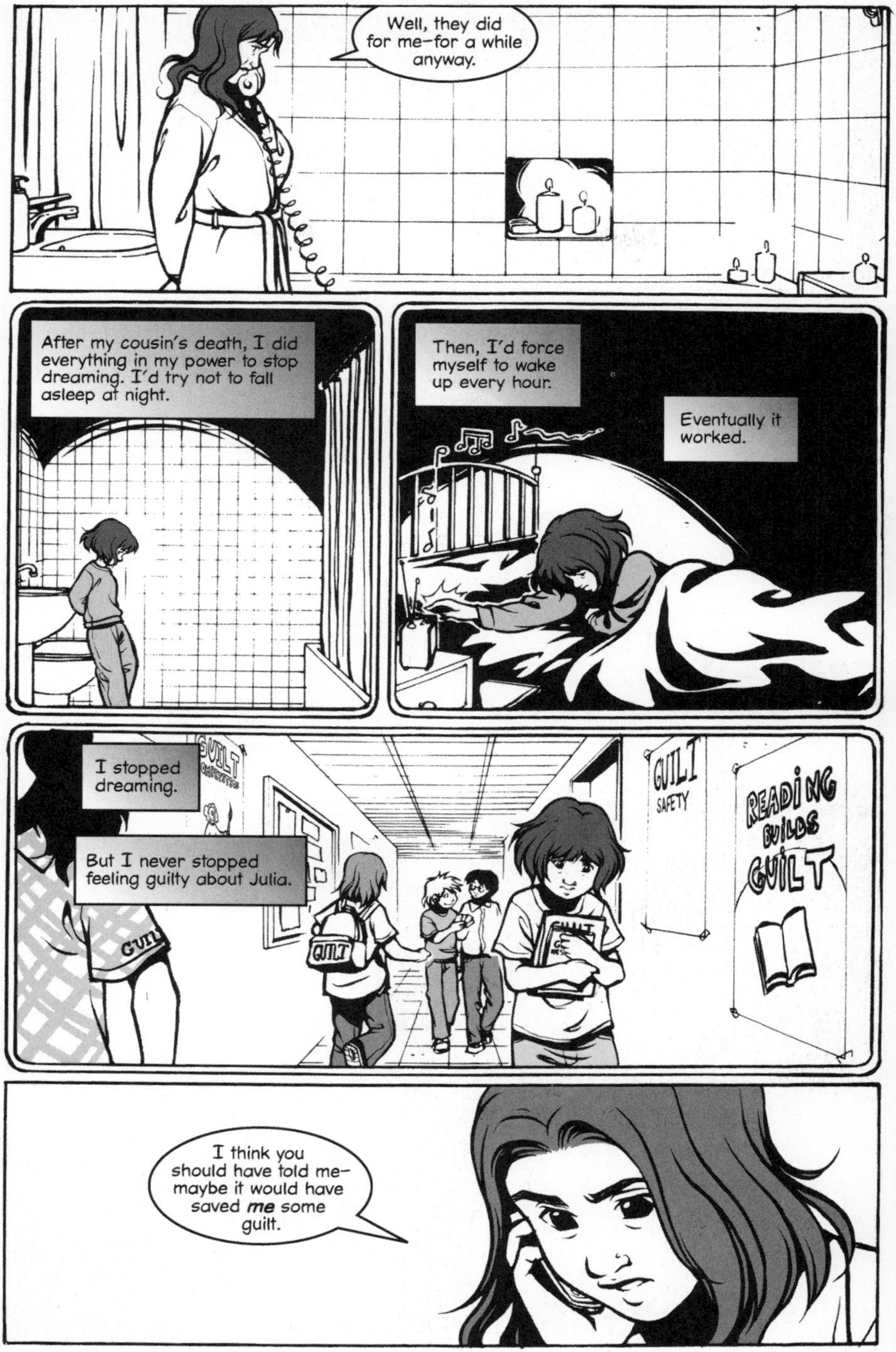
Well, they did for me—for a while anyway.
After my cousin's death, I did everything in my power to stop dreaming. I'd try not to fall asleep at night.
Then, I'd force myself to wake up every hour.
Eventually it worked.
I stopped dreaming.
But I never stopped feeling guilty about Julia.
GUILT
GUILT
SAFETY
READING BUILDS GUILT
GUILT
GUILT
I think you should have told me—maybe it would have saved *me* some guilt.

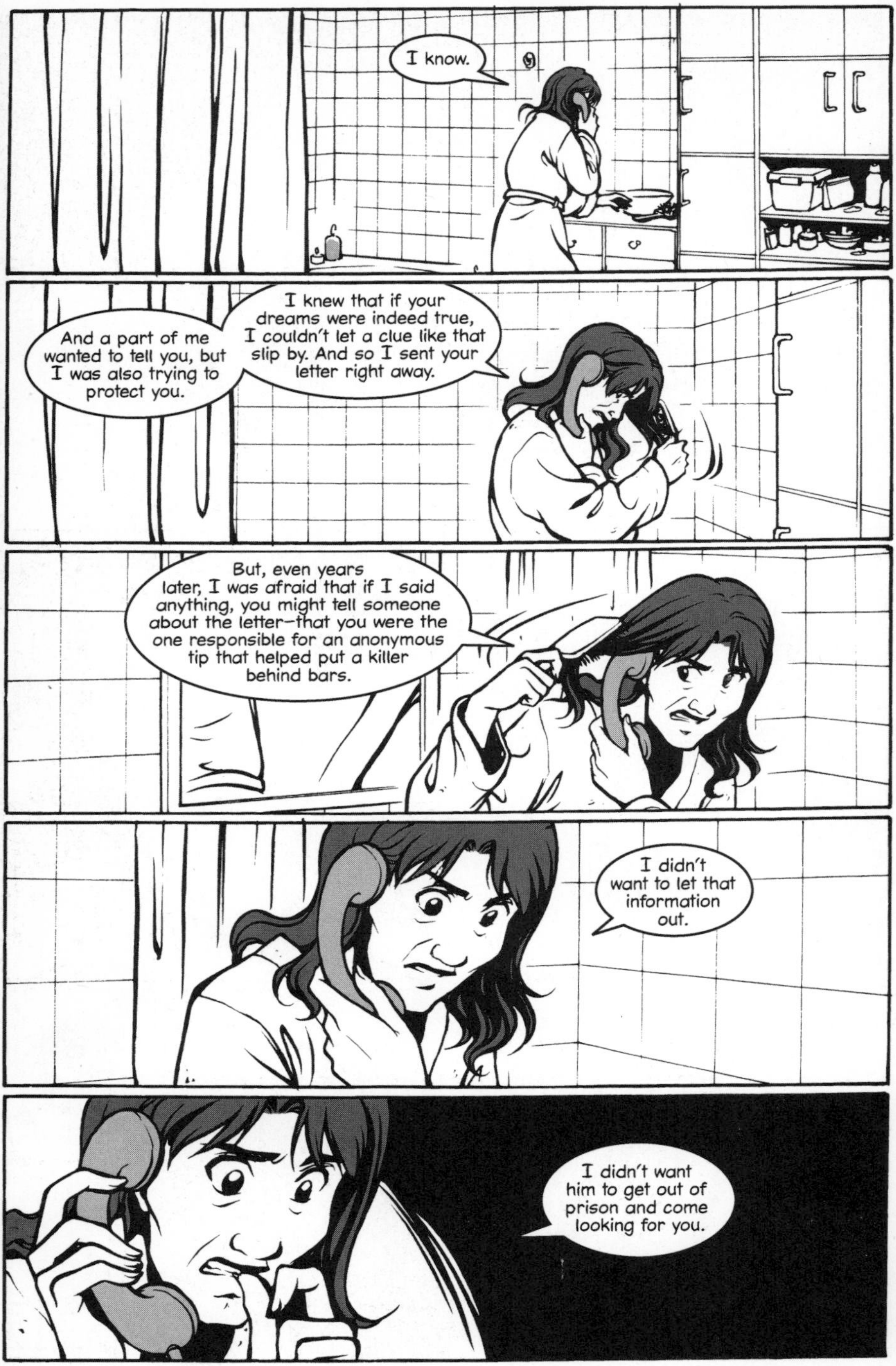
I know.
And a part of me wanted to tell you, but I was also trying to protect you.
I knew that if your dreams were indeed true, I couldn't let a clue like that slip by. And so I sent your letter right away.
But, even years later, I was afraid that if I said anything, you might tell someone about the letter—that you were the one responsible for an anonymous tip that helped put a killer behind bars.
I didn't want to let that information out.
I didn't want him to get out of prison and come looking for you.

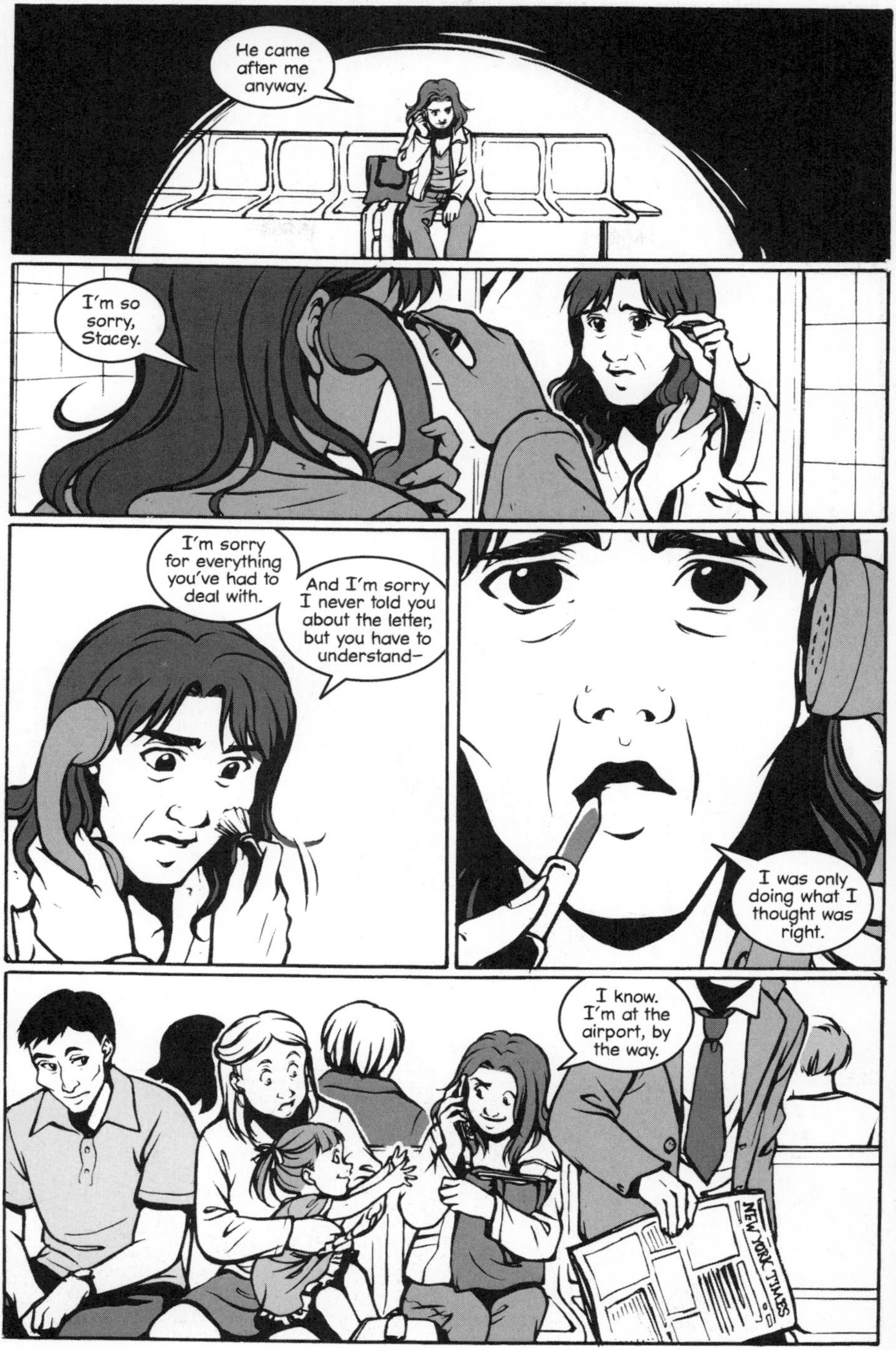
He came after me anyway.
I'm so sorry, Stacey.
I'm sorry for everything you've had to deal with.
And I'm sorry I never told you about the letter, but you have to understand–
I was only doing what I thought was right.
I know. I'm at the airport, by the way.
NEW YORK TIMES

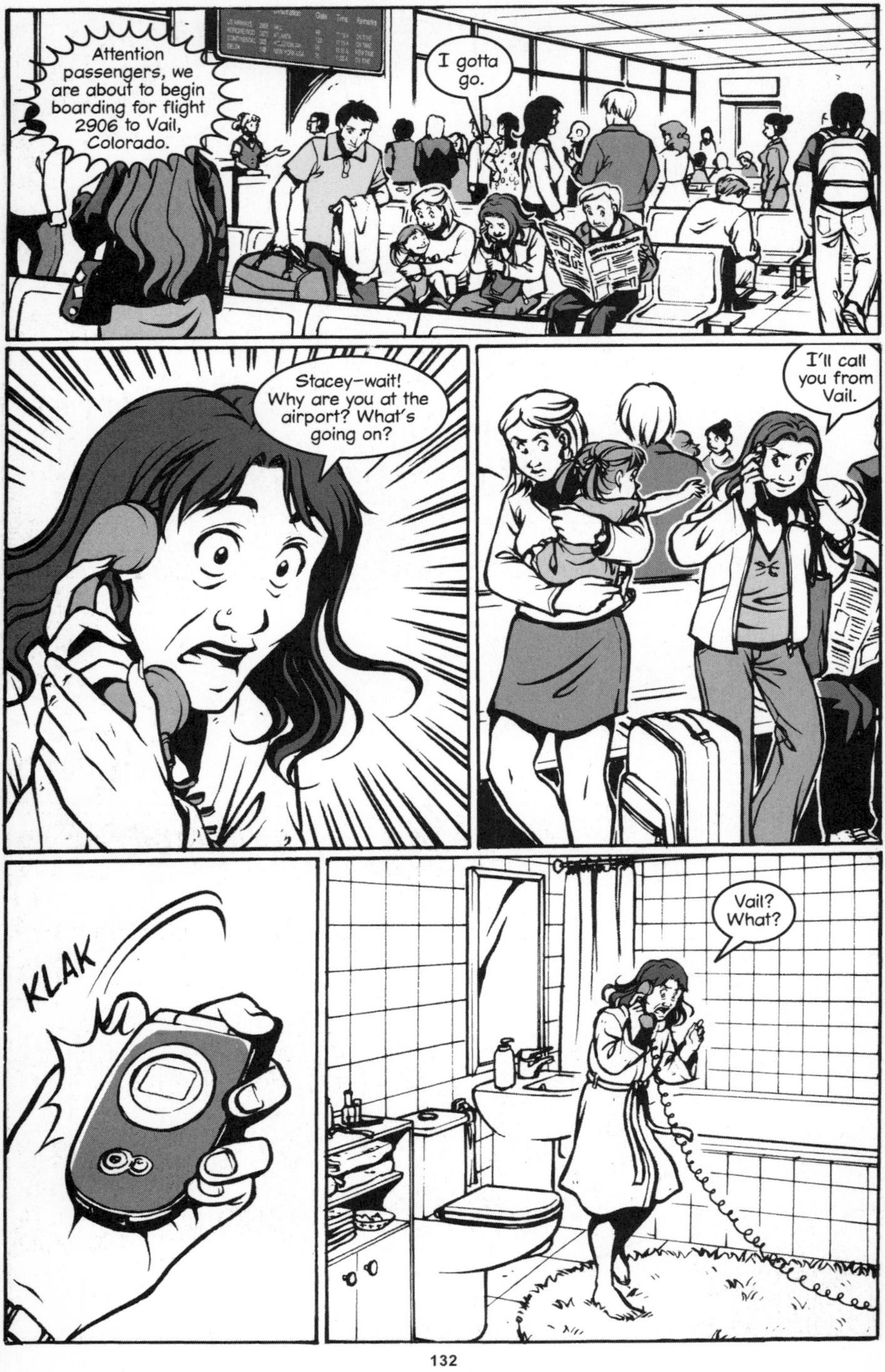
Attention passengers, we are about to begin boarding for flight 2906 to Vail, Colorado.
I gotta go.
Stacey—wait! Why are you at the airport? What's going on?
I'll call you from Vail.
KLAK
Vail? What?

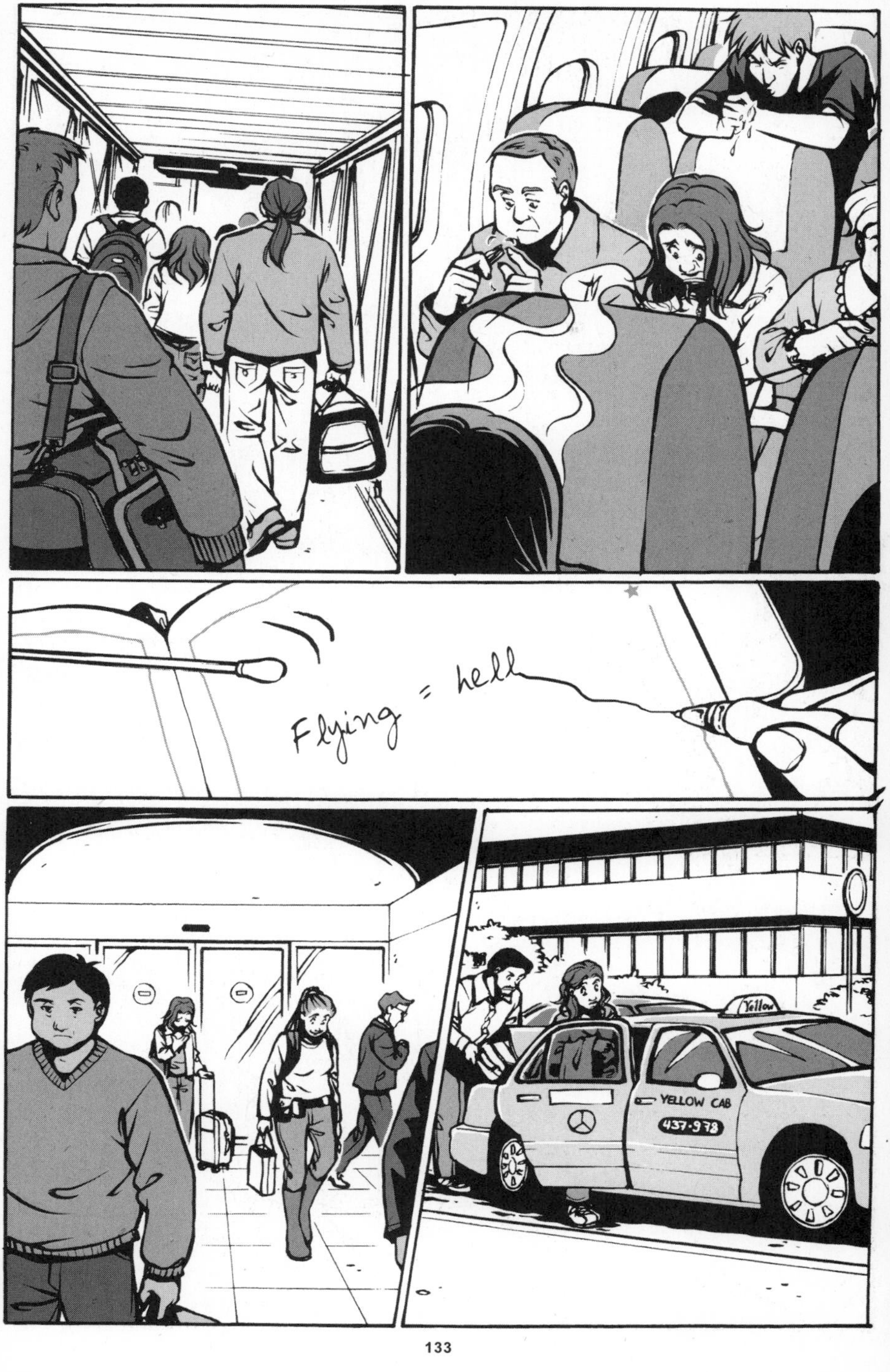

Flying = hell
Yellow
YELLOW CAB
437-978

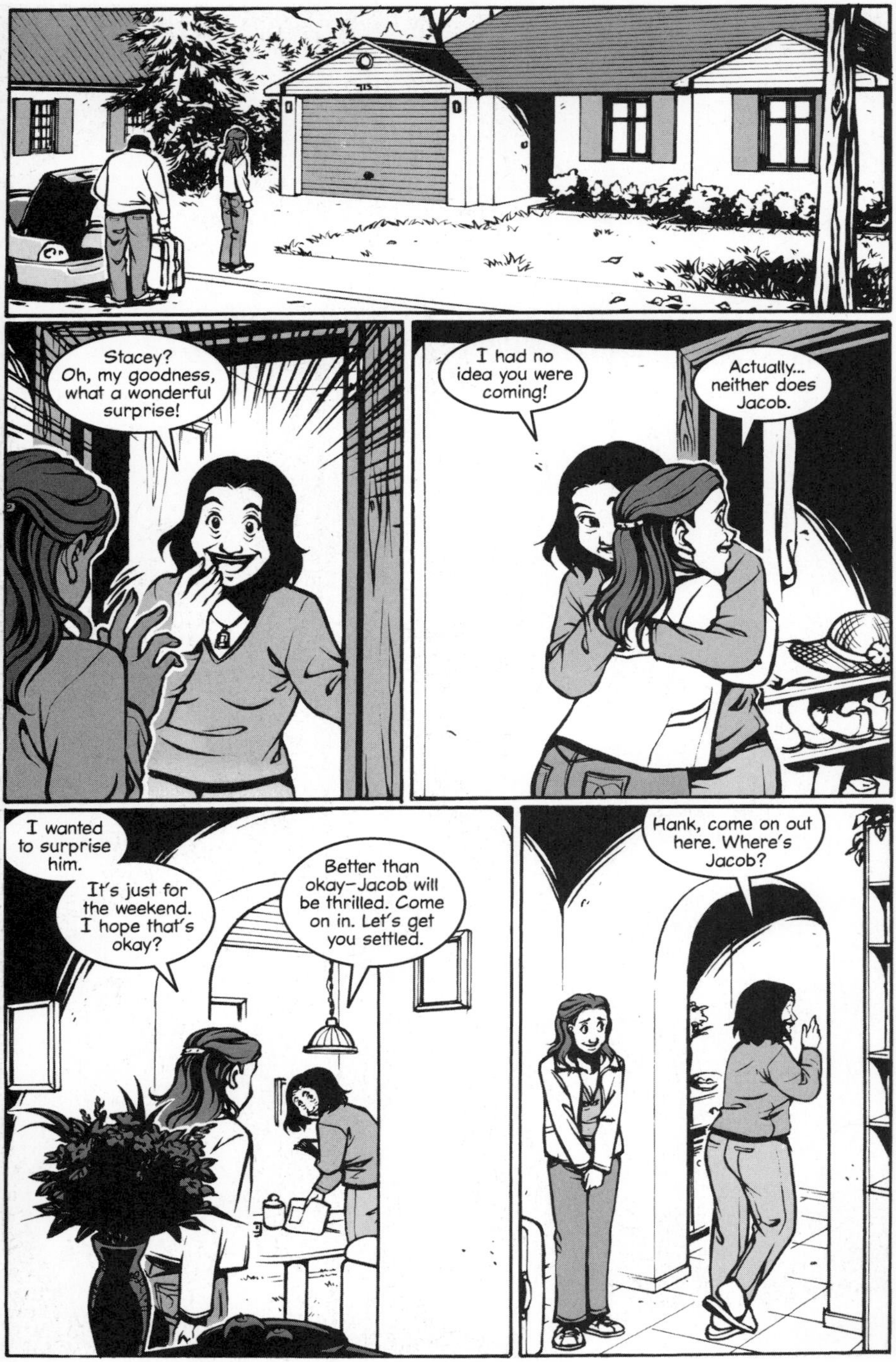
Stacey? Oh, my goodness, what a wonderful surprise!
I had no idea you were coming!
Actually... neither does Jacob.
I wanted to surprise him.
It's just for the weekend. I hope that's okay?
Better than okay–Jacob will be thrilled. Come on in. Let's get you settled.
Hank, come on out here. Where's Jacob?

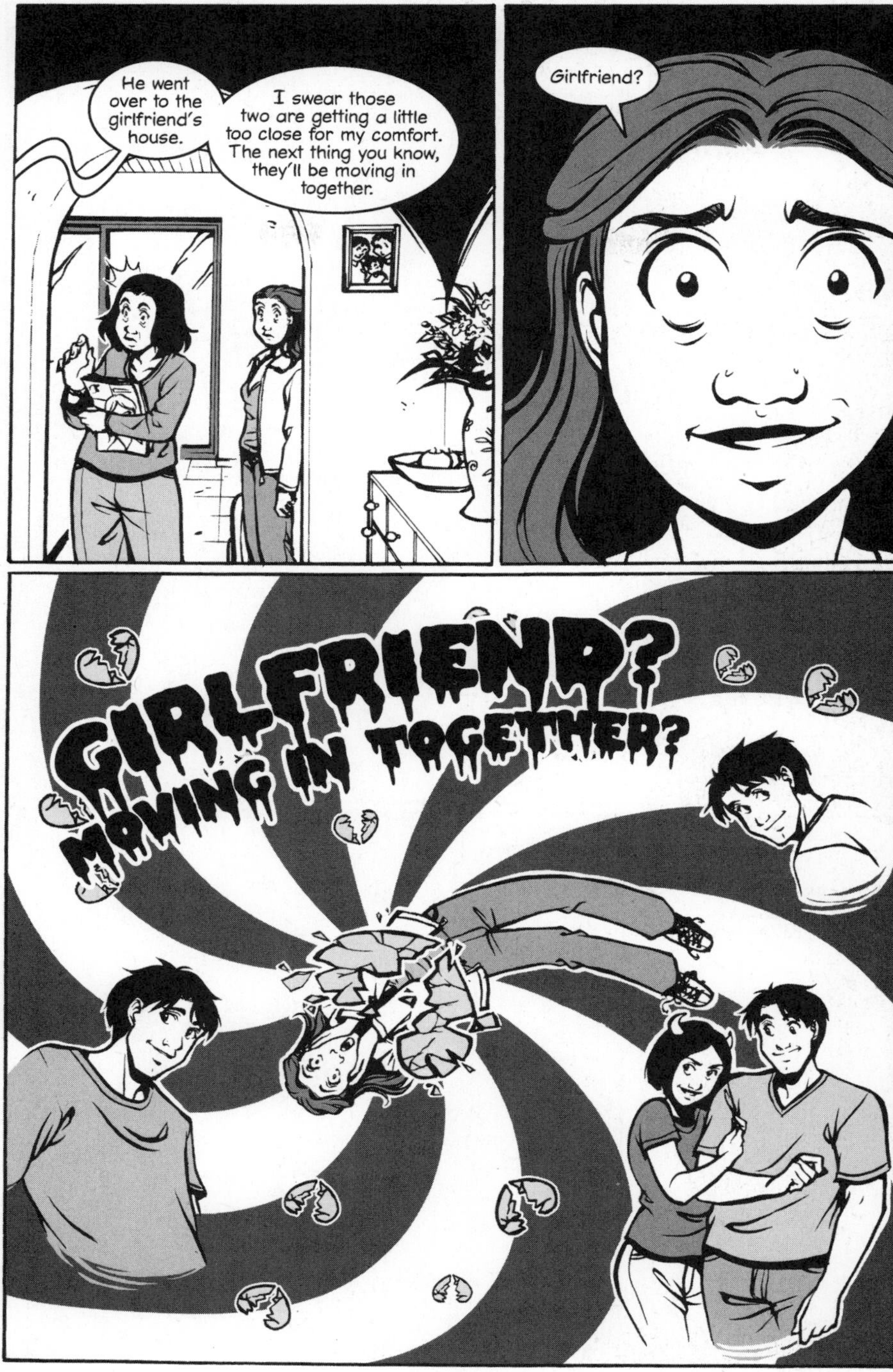
He went over to the girlfriend's house.
I swear those two are getting a little too close for my comfort. The next thing you know, they'll be moving in together.
Girlfriend?
GIRLFRIEND?
MOVING IN TOGETHER?

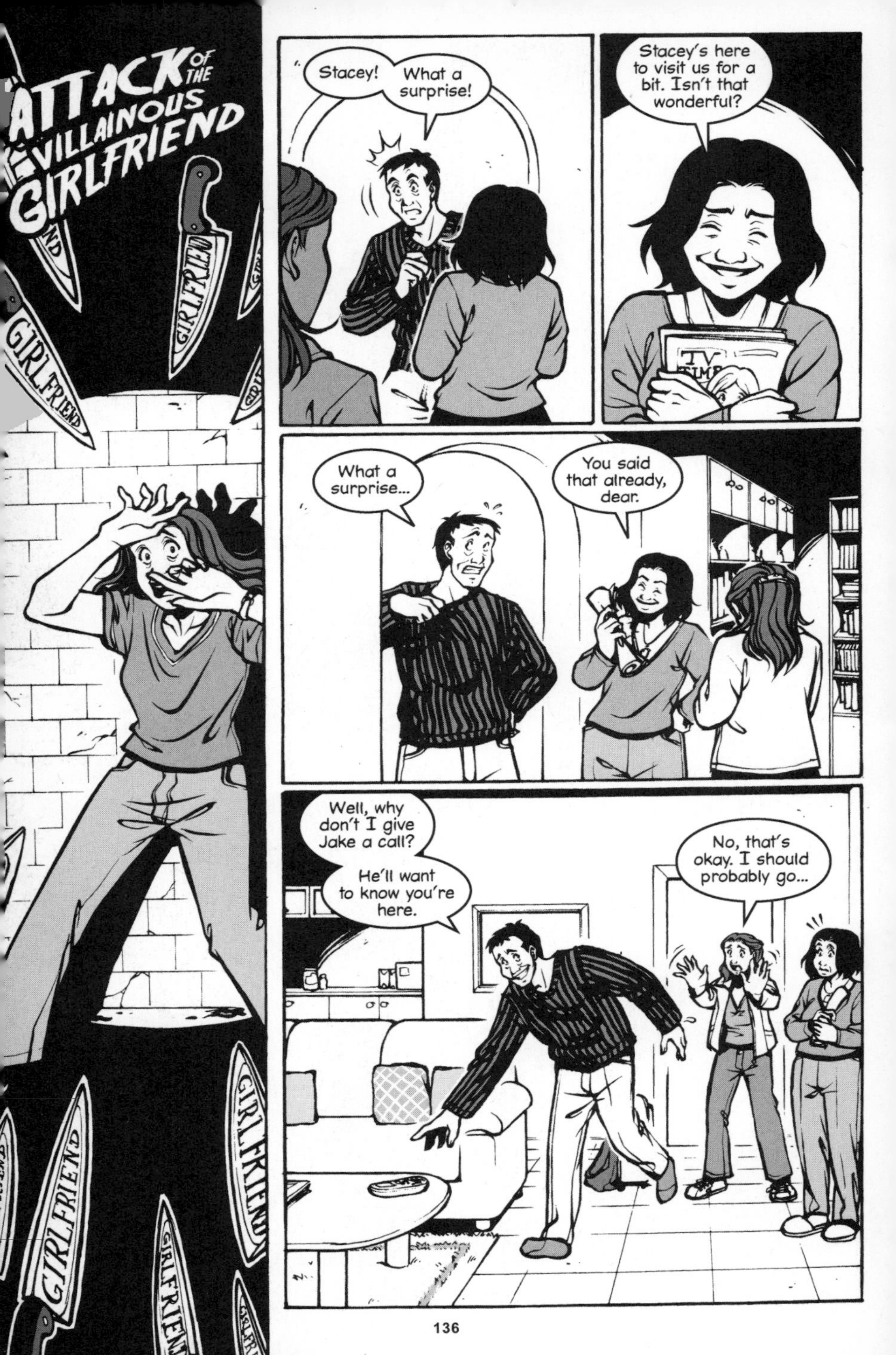
ATTACK OF THE VILLAINOUS GIRLFRIEND
Stacey!
What a surprise!
Stacey's here to visit us for a bit. Isn't that wonderful?
What a surprise...
You said that already, dear.
Well, why don't I give Jake a call?
He'll want to know you're here.
No, that's okay. I should probably go...

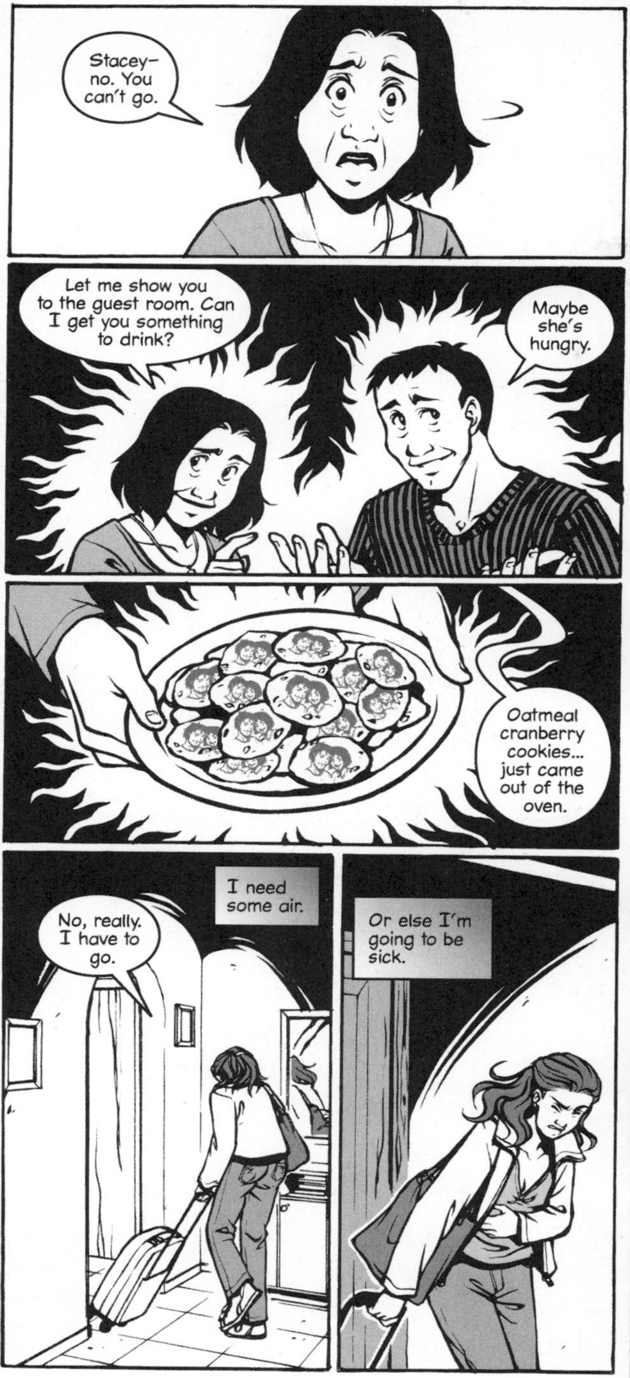
Stacey—no. You can't go.
Let me show you to the guest room. Can I get you something to drink?
Maybe she's hungry.
Oatmeal cranberry cookies... just came out of the oven.
No, really. I have to go.
I need some air.
Or else I'm going to be sick.

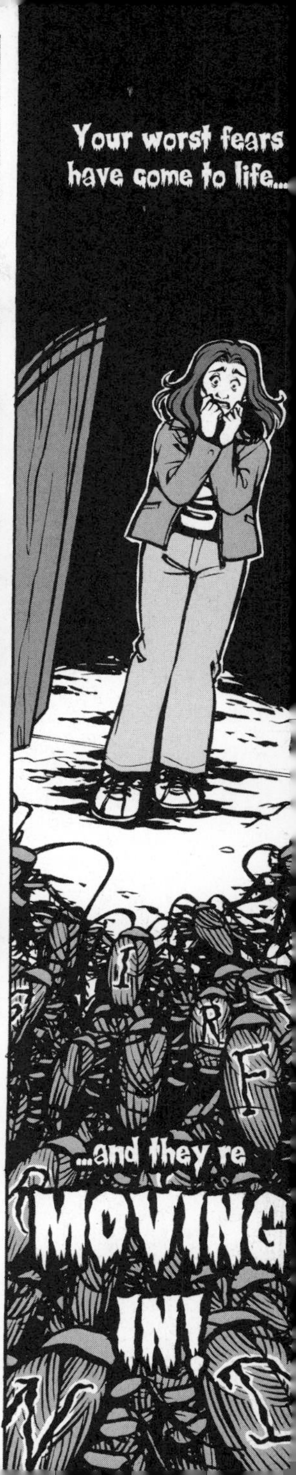
Your worst fears have come to life...
...and they're
MOVING IN!

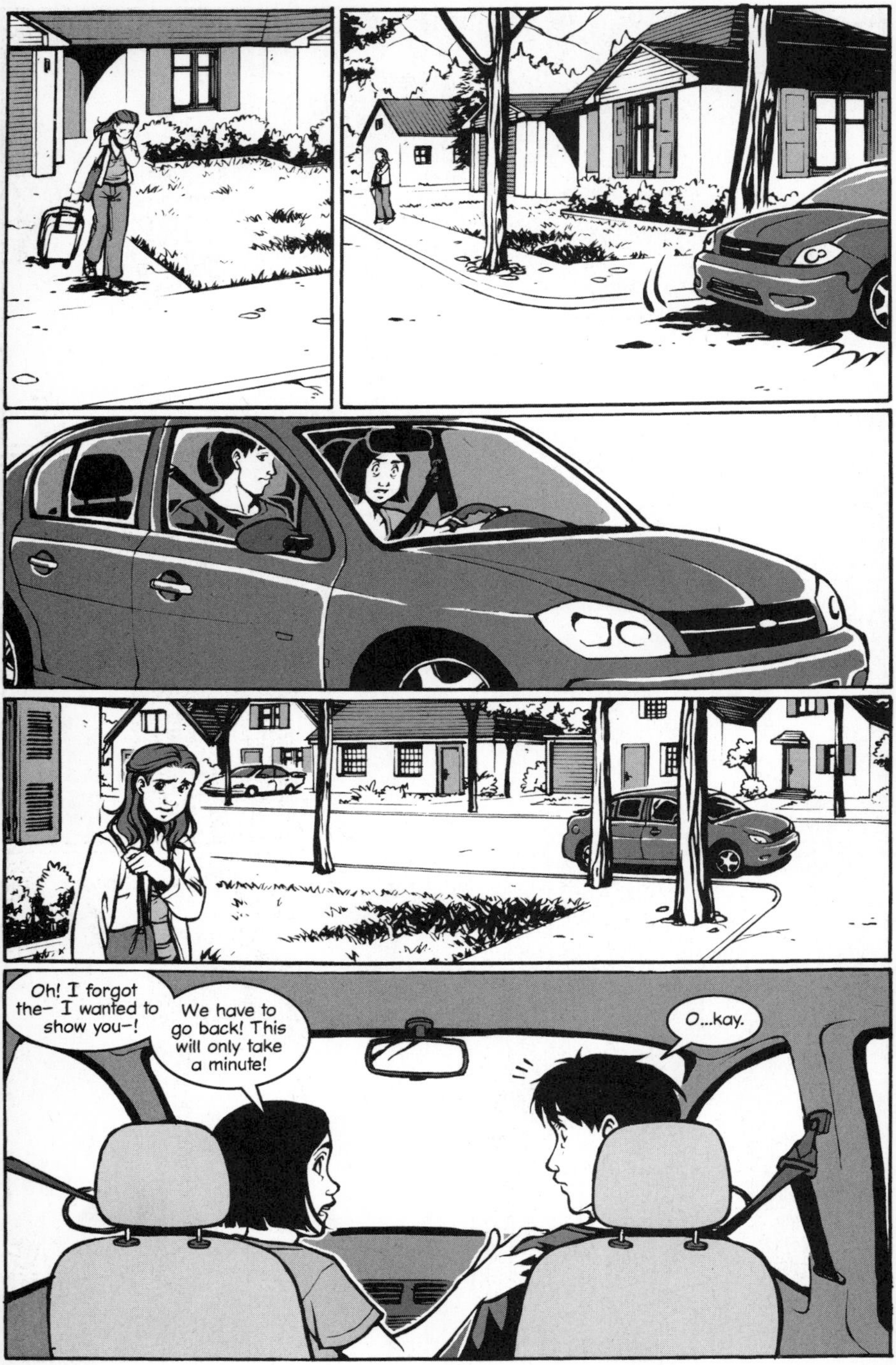
Oh! I forgot the– I wanted to show you–!
We have to go back! This will only take a minute!
O...kay.

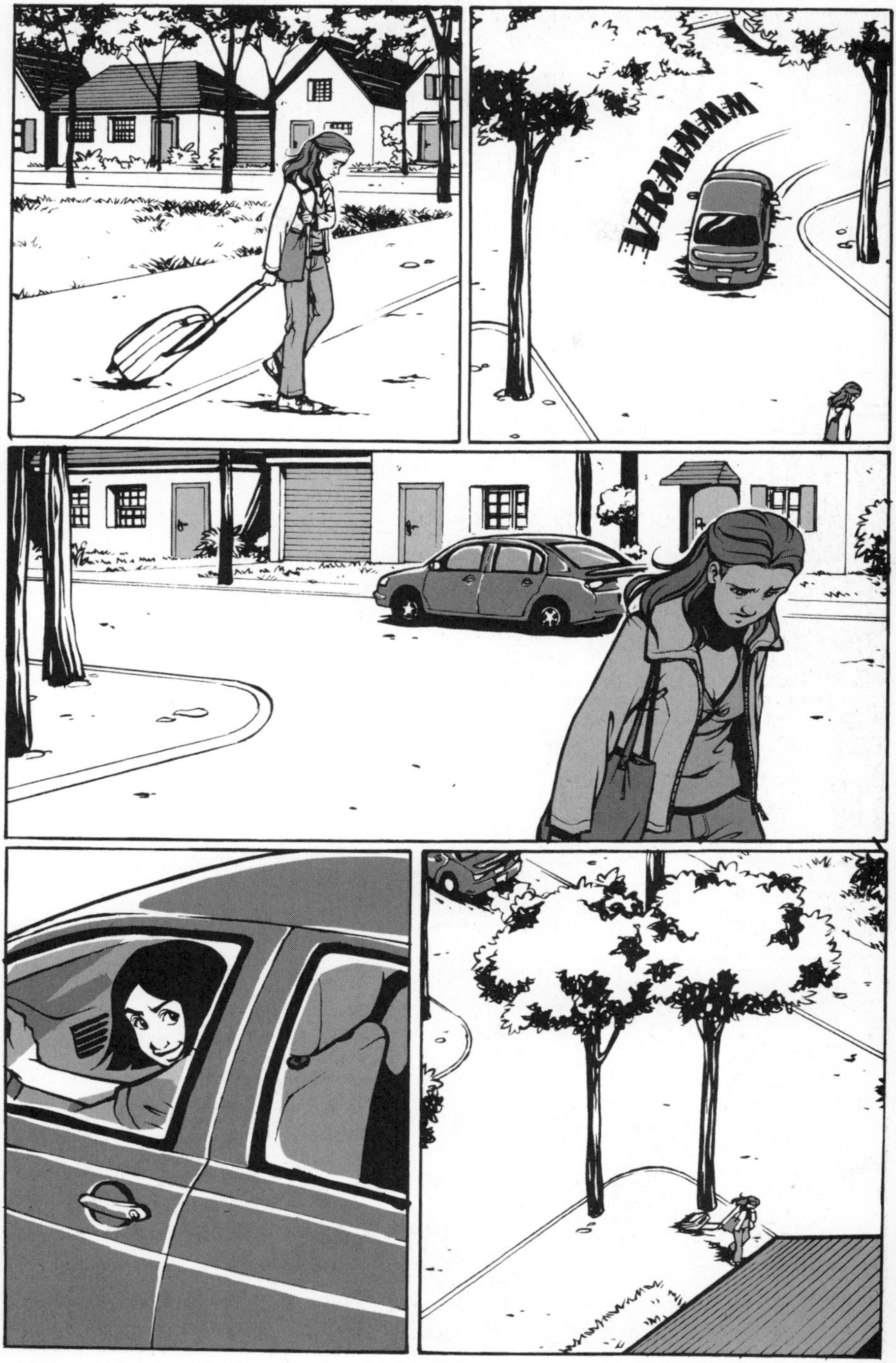
VRMMMMM

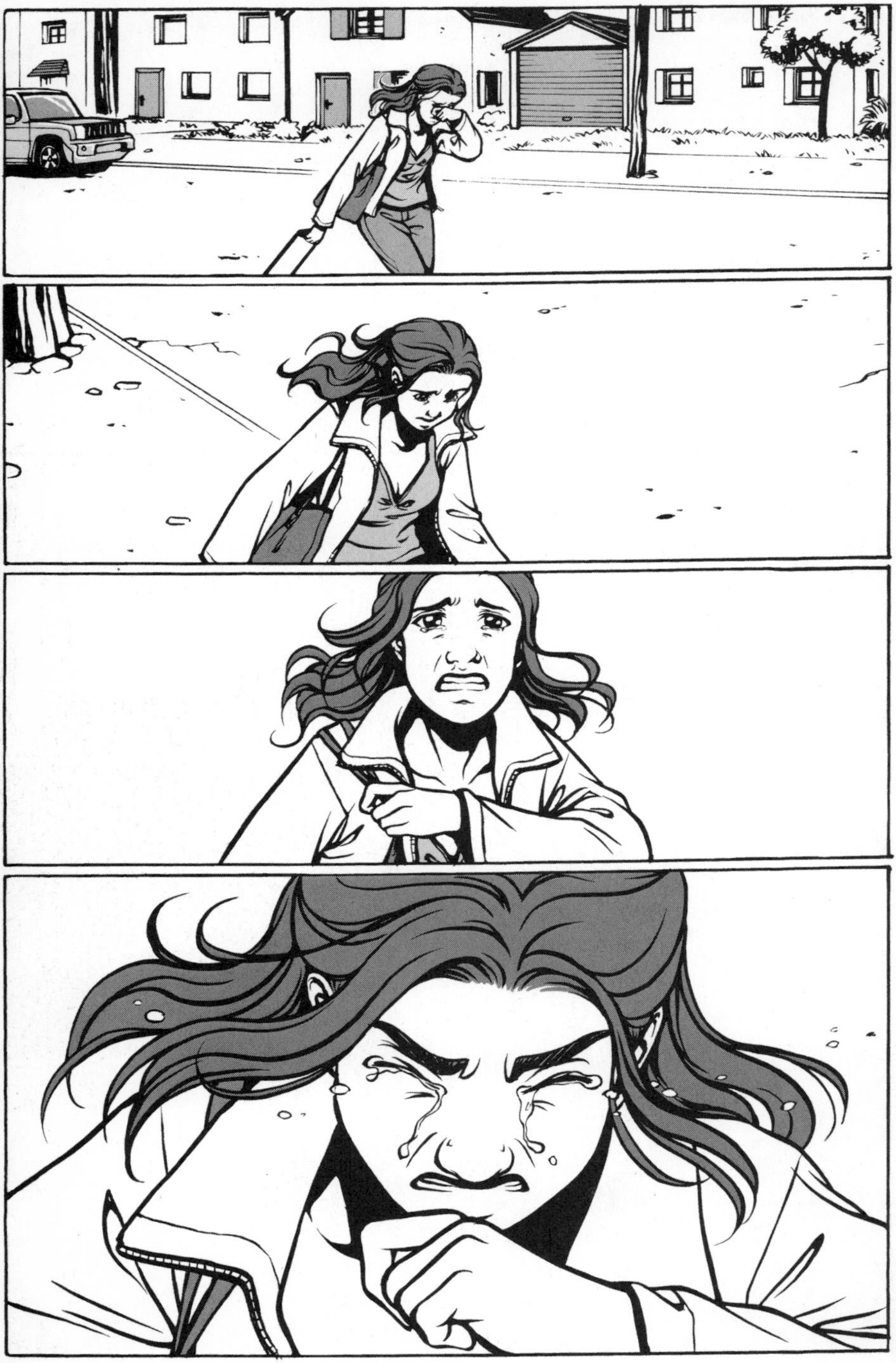

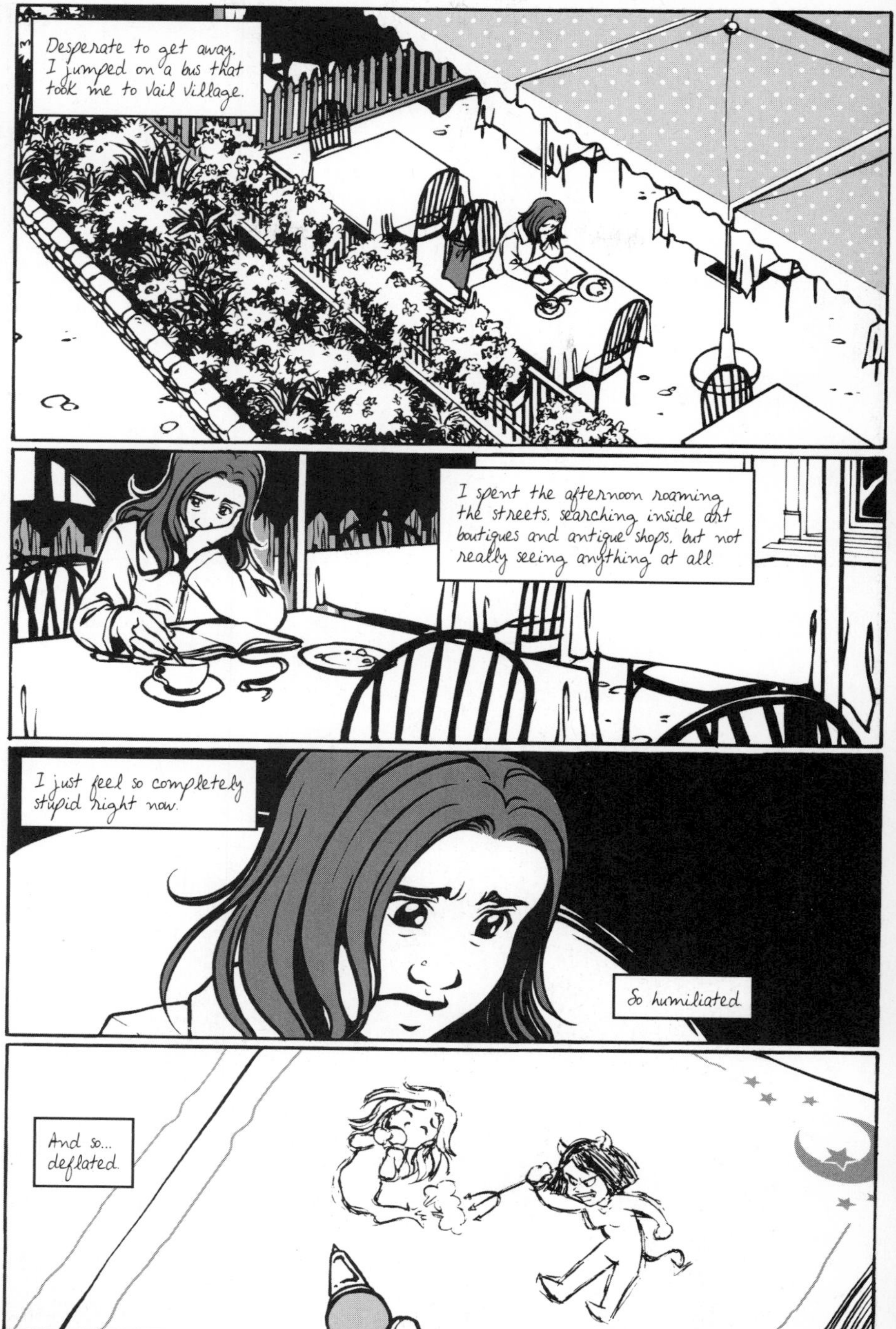
Desperate to get away, I jumped on a bus that took me to Vail Village.
I spent the afternoon roaming the streets, searching inside art boutiques and antique shops, but not really seeing anything at all.
I just feel so completely stupid right now.
So humiliated.
And so... deflated.

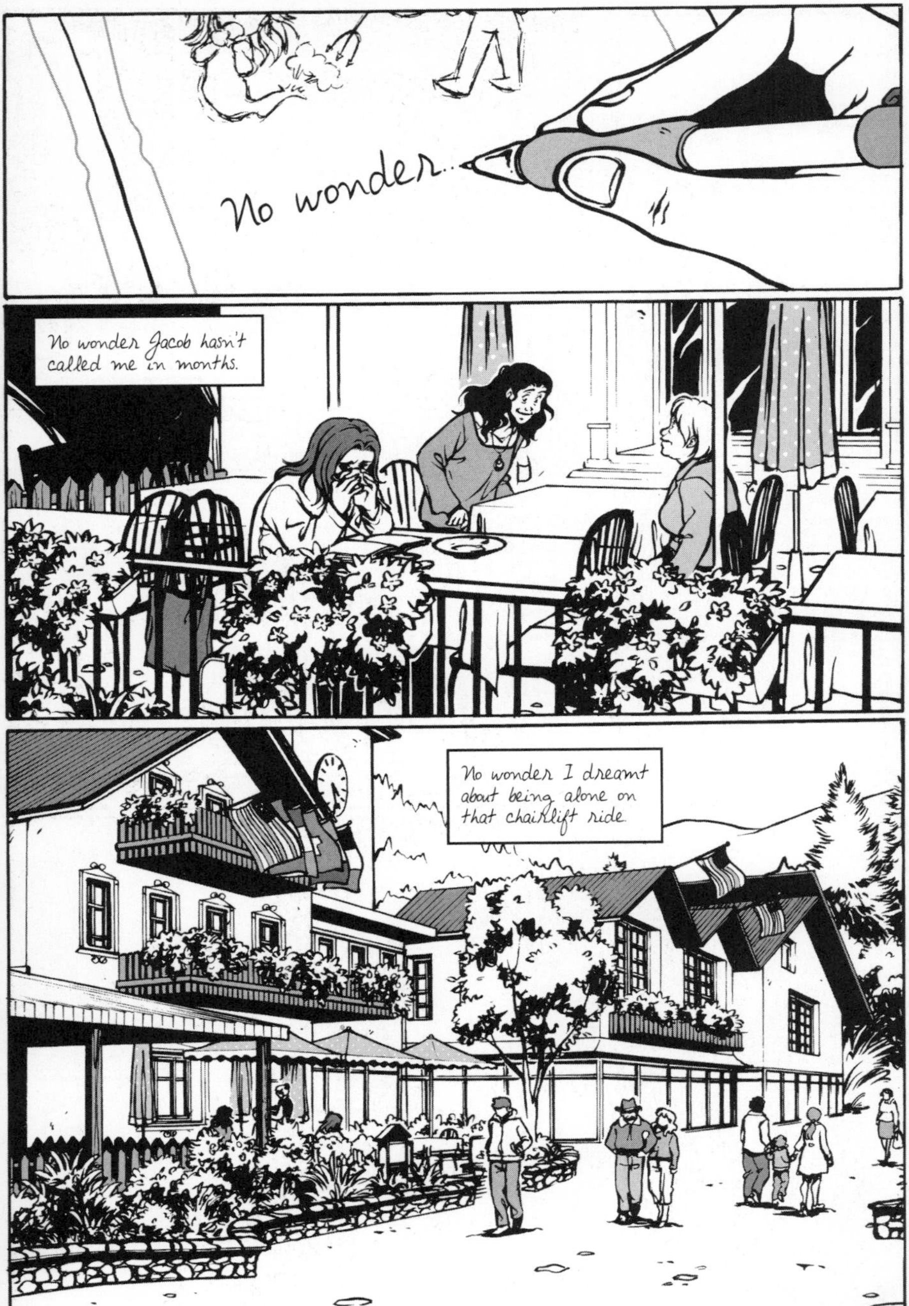
No wonder...
No wonder Jacob hasn't called me in months.
No wonder I dreamt about being alone on that chairlift ride.

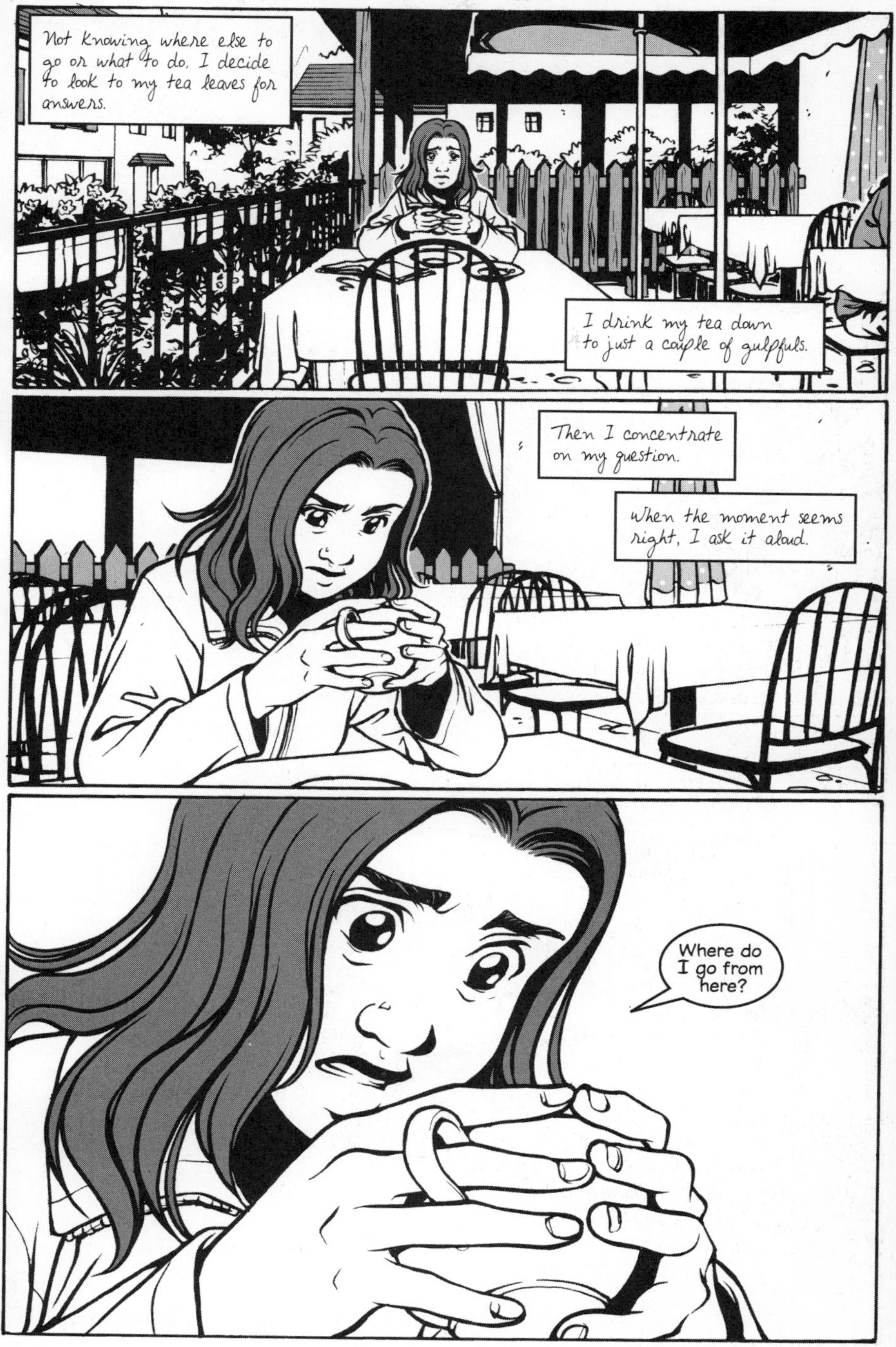
Not knowing where else to go or what to do, I decide to look to my tea leaves for answers.
I drink my tea down to just a couple of gulpfuls.
Then I concentrate on my question.
When the moment seems right, I ask it aloud.
Where do I go from here?

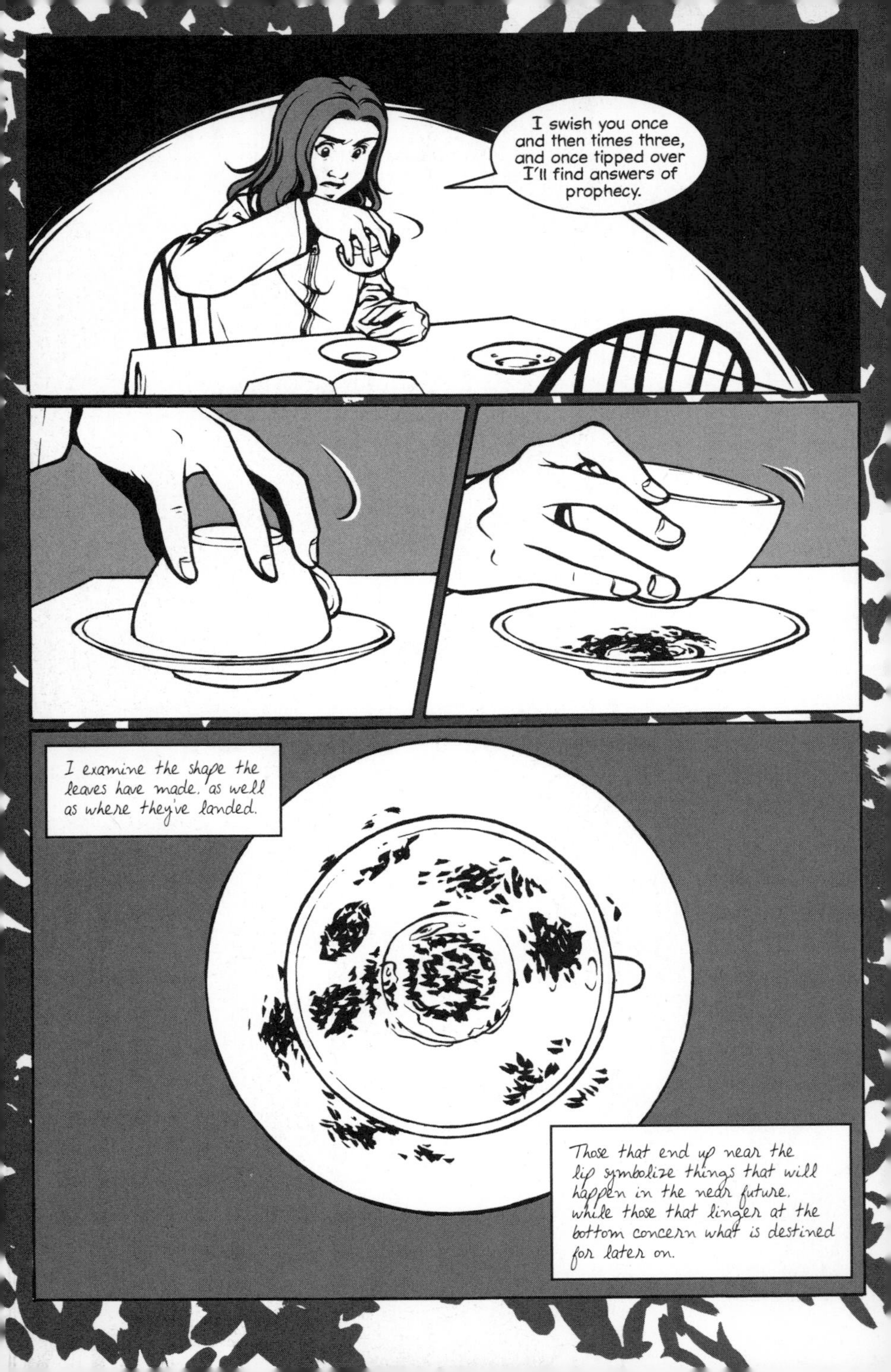
I swish you once and then times three, and once tipped over I'll find answers of prophecy.
I examine the shape the leaves have made, as well as where they've landed.
Those that end up near the lip symbolize things that will happen in the near future, while those that linger at the bottom concern what is destined for later on.

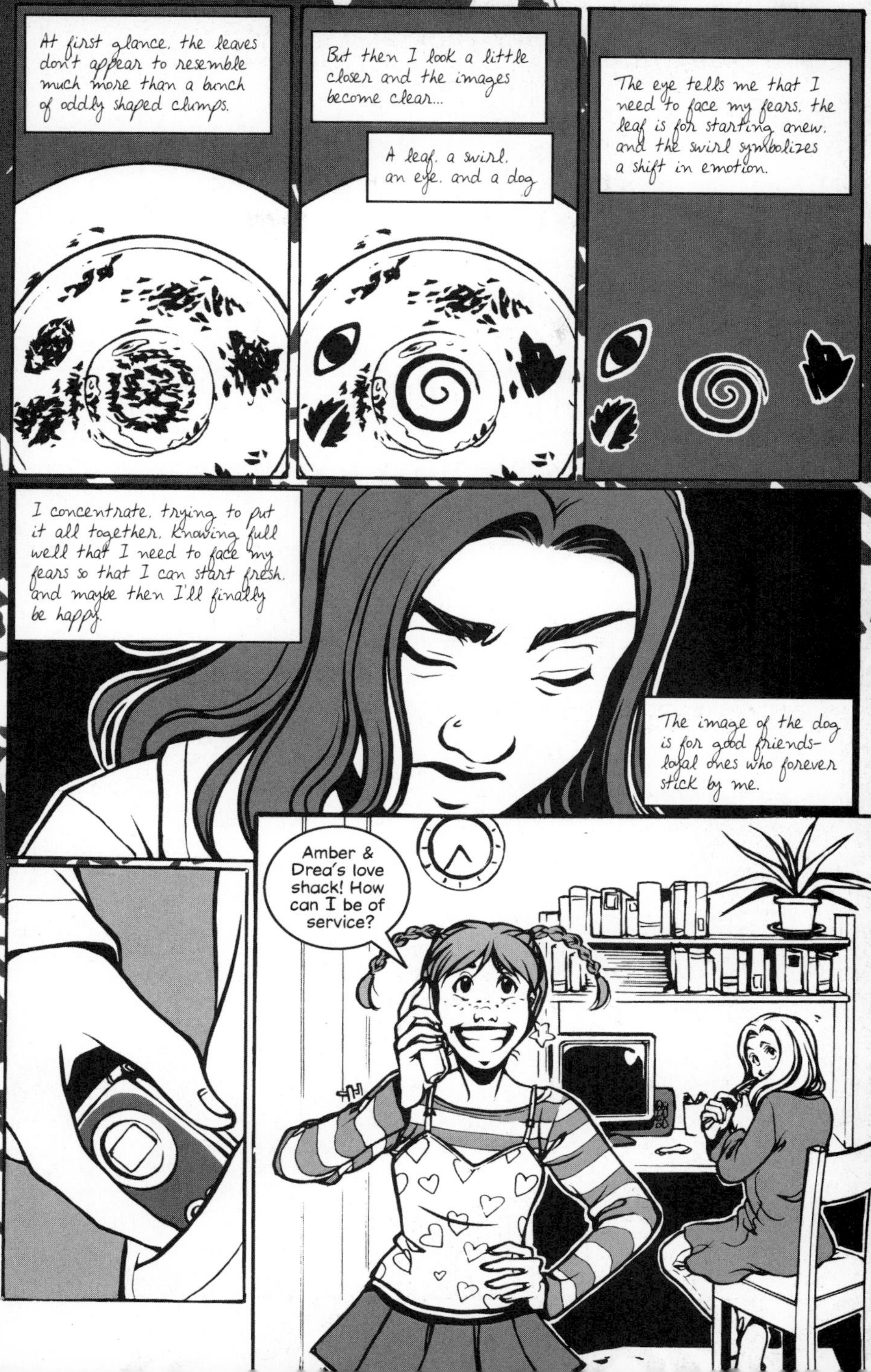
At first glance, the leaves don't appear to resemble much more than a bunch of oddly shaped clumps.
But then I look a little closer and the images become clear...
A leaf, a swirl, an eye, and a dog
The eye tells me that I need to face my fears, the leaf is for starting anew, and the swirl symbolizes a shift in emotion.
I concentrate, trying to put it all together. Knowing full well that I need to face my fears so that I can start fresh, and maybe then I'll finally be happy.
The image of the dog is for good friends- loyal ones who forever stick by me.
Amber & Drea's love shack! How can I be of service?

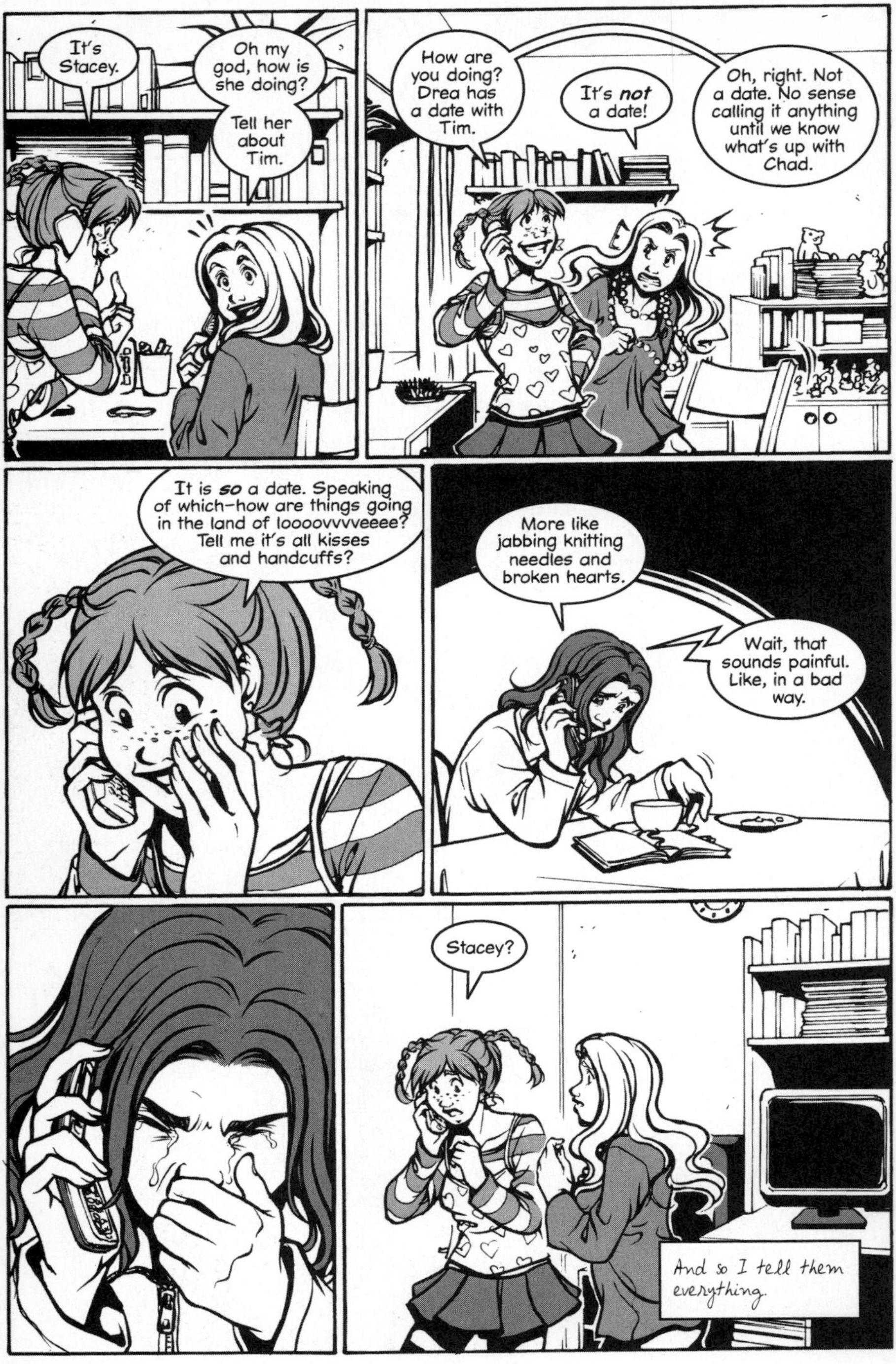
It's Stacey.
Oh my god, how is she doing?
Tell her about Tim.
How are you doing? Drea has a date with Tim.
It's **not** a date!
Oh, right. Not a date. No sense calling it anything until we know what's up with Chad.
It is **so** a date. Speaking of which–how are things going in the land of loooovvvveeee? Tell me it's all kisses and handcuffs?
More like jabbing knitting needles and broken hearts.
Wait, that sounds painful. Like, in a bad way.
Stacey?
And so I tell them everything.

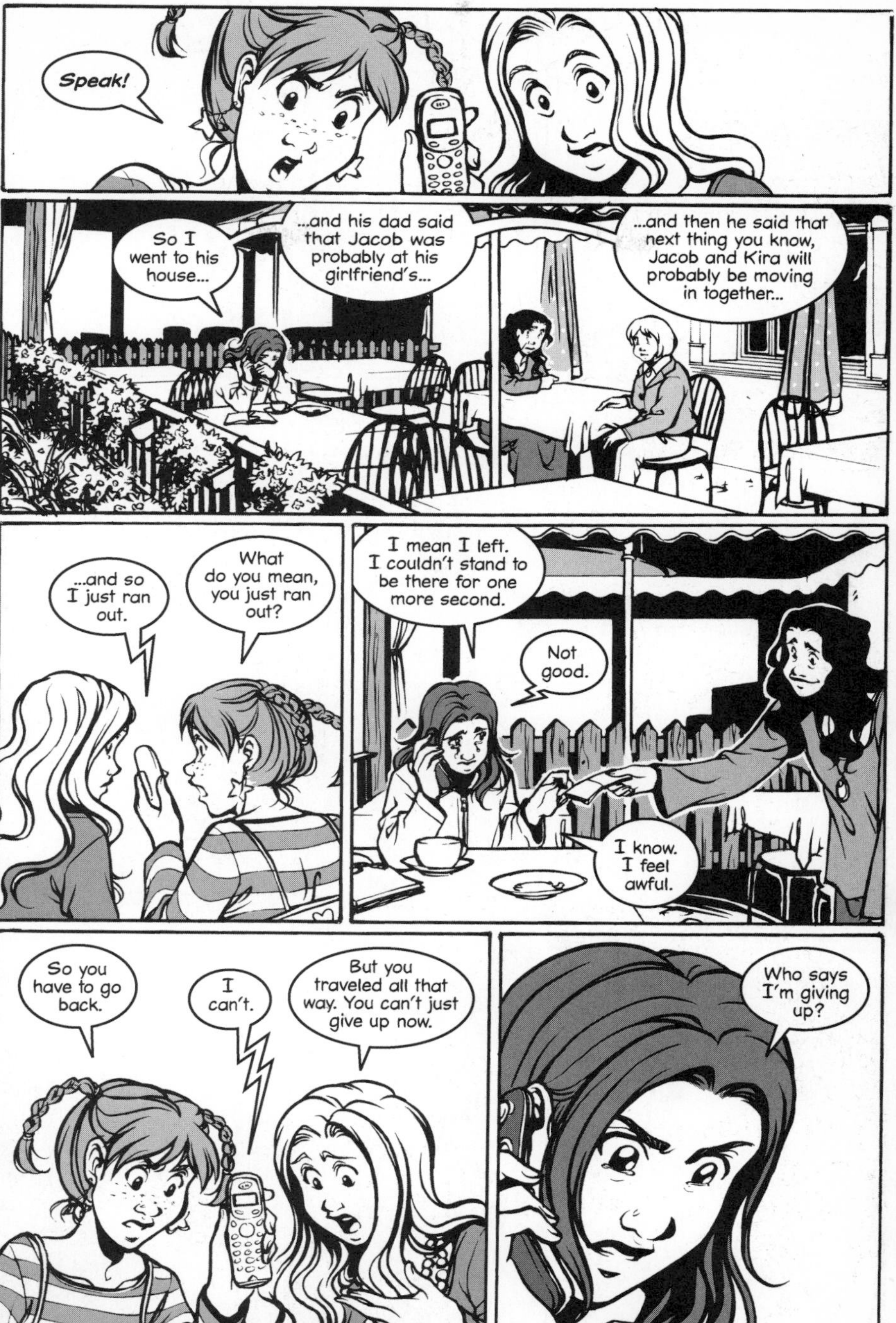
Speak!
So I went to his house...
...and his dad said that Jacob was probably at his girlfriend's...
...and then he said that next thing you know, Jacob and Kira will probably be moving in together...
...and so I just ran out.
What do you mean, you just ran out?
I mean I left. I couldn't stand to be there for one more second.
Not good.
I know. I feel awful.
So you have to go back.
I can't.
But you traveled all that way. You can't just give up now.
Who says I'm giving up?

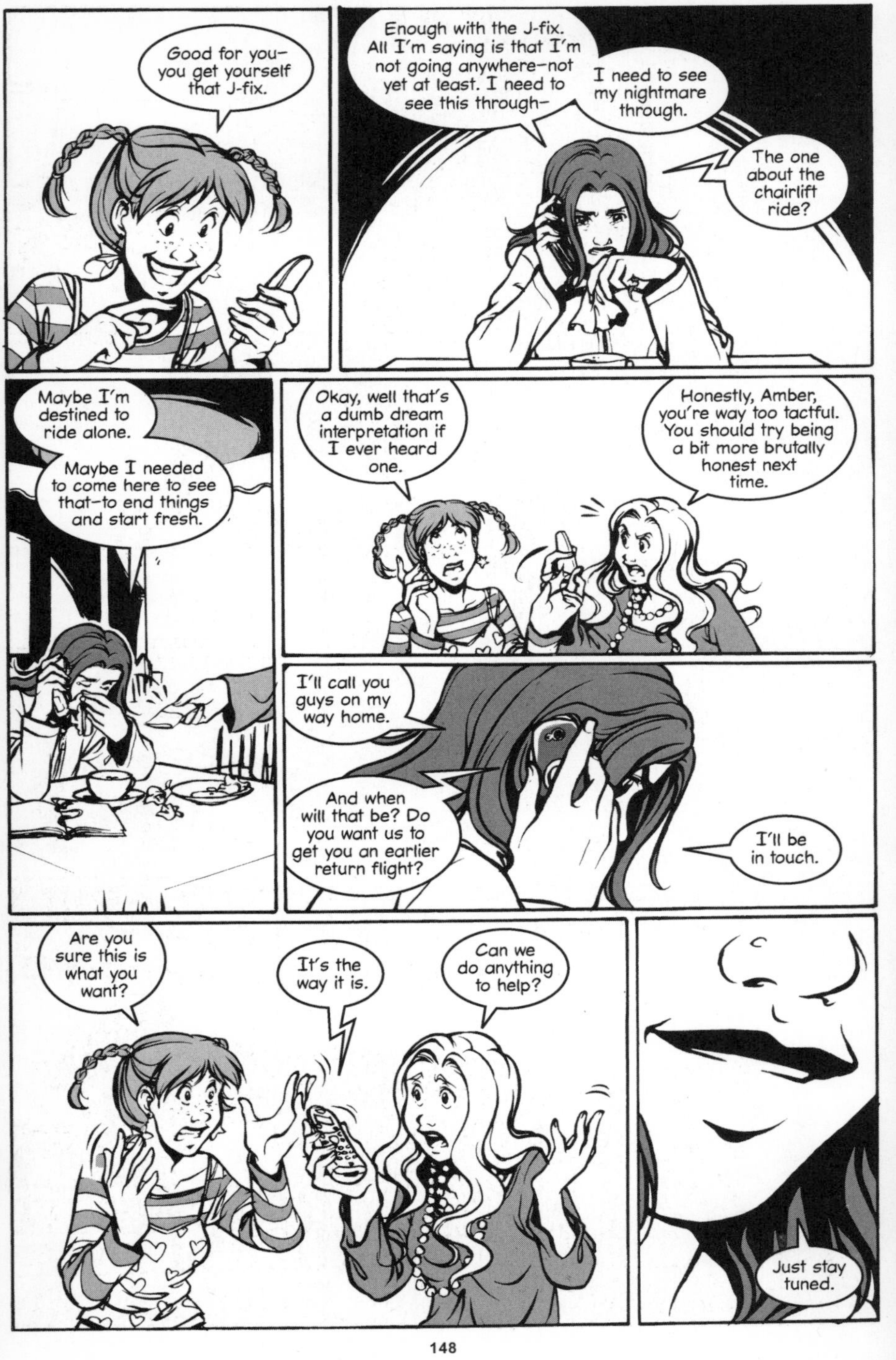
Good for you–you get yourself that J-fix.
Enough with the J-fix. All I'm saying is that I'm not going anywhere–not yet at least. I need to see this through–
I need to see my nightmare through.
The one about the chairlift ride?
Maybe I'm destined to ride alone.
Maybe I needed to come here to see that–to end things and start fresh.
Okay, well that's a dumb dream interpretation if I ever heard one.
Honestly, Amber, you're way too tactful. You should try being a bit more brutally honest next time.
I'll call you guys on my way home.
And when will that be? Do you want us to get you an earlier return flight?
I'll be in touch.
Are you sure this is what you want?
It's the way it is.
Can we do anything to help?
Just stay tuned.

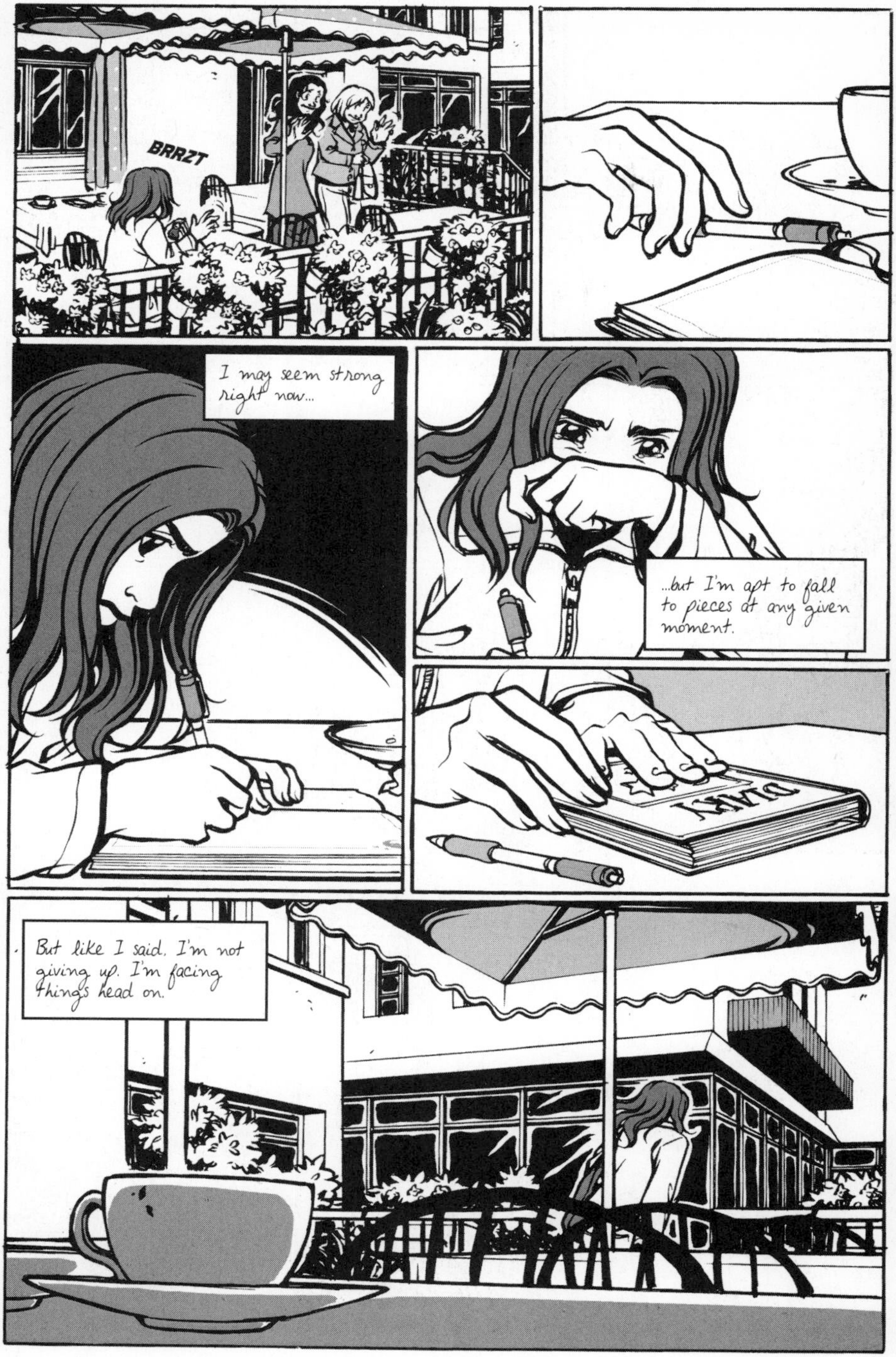
BRRZT
I may seem strong right now...
...but I'm apt to fall to pieces at any given moment.
DIARY
But like I said, I'm not giving up. I'm facing things head on.

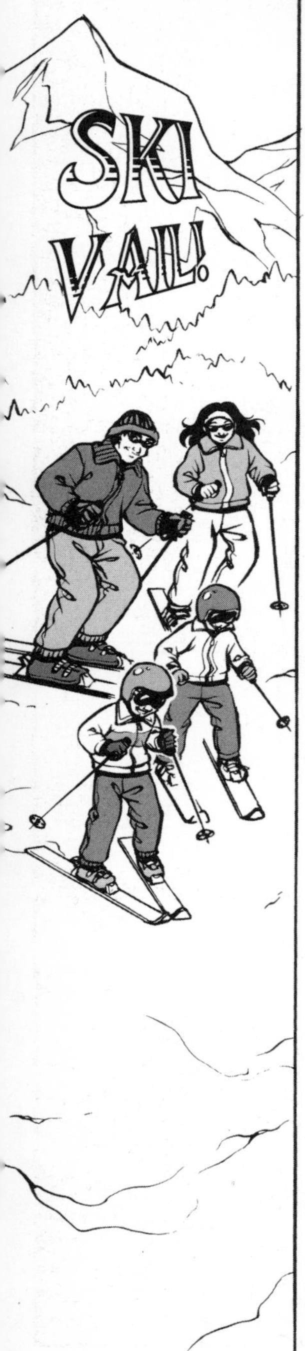
SKI VAIL!

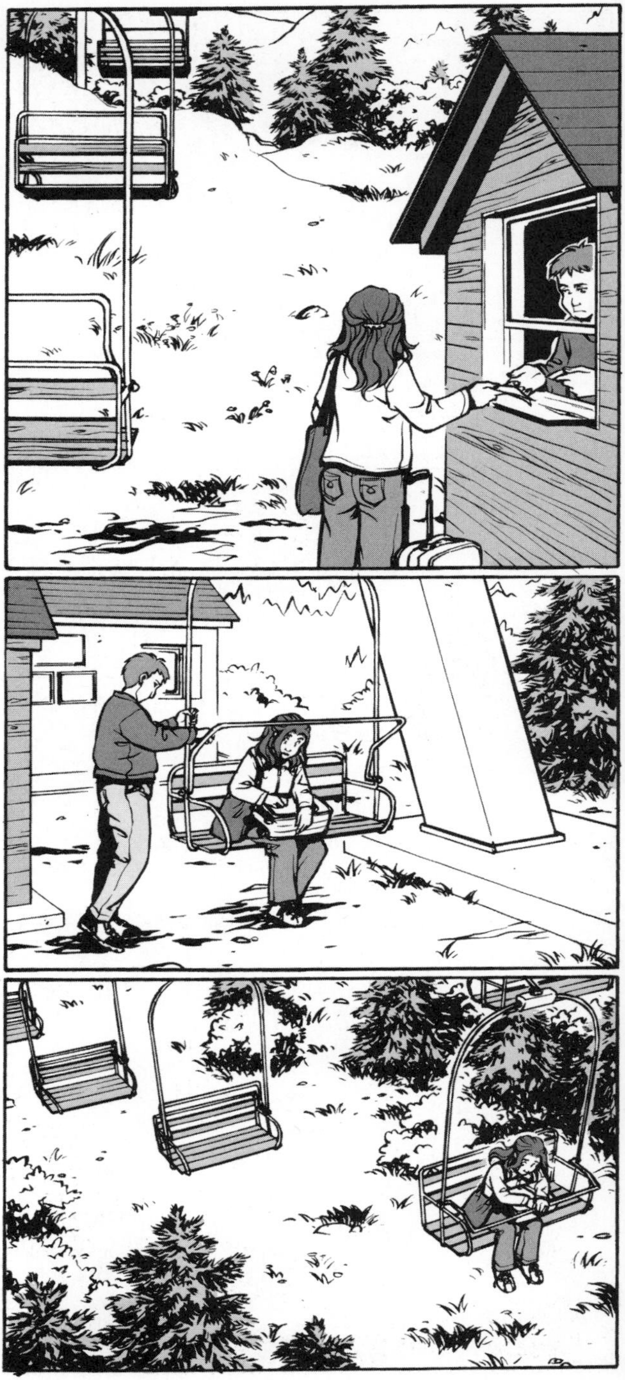

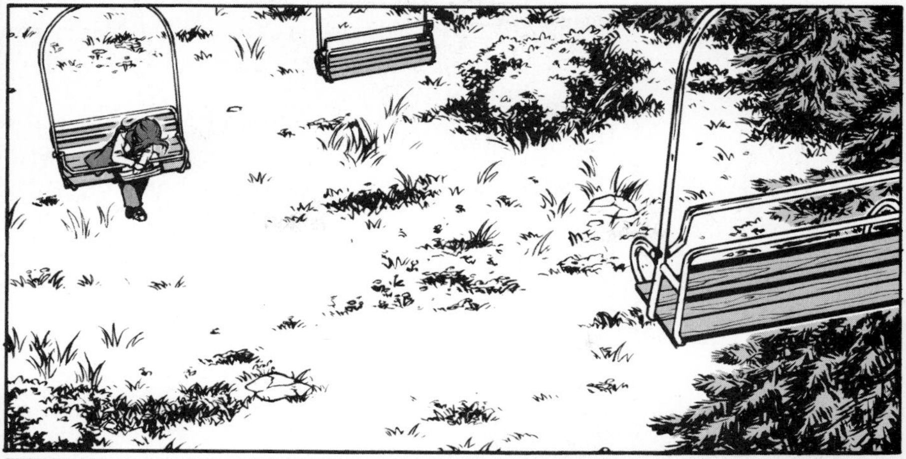

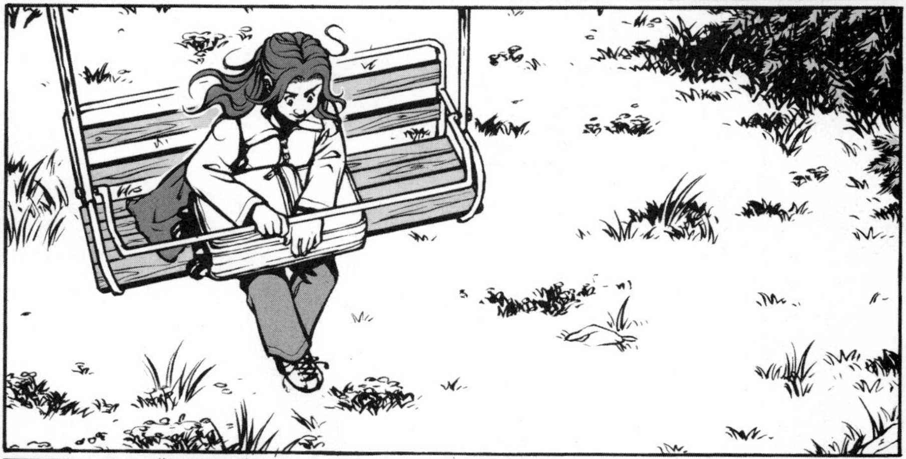

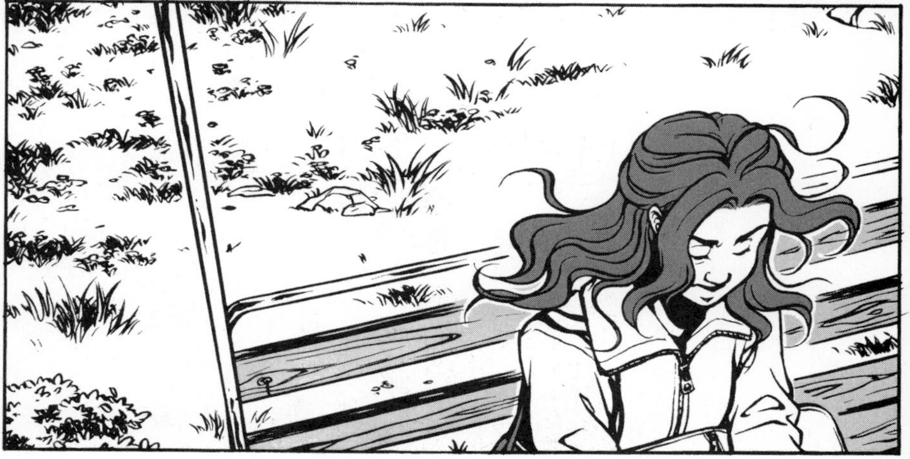

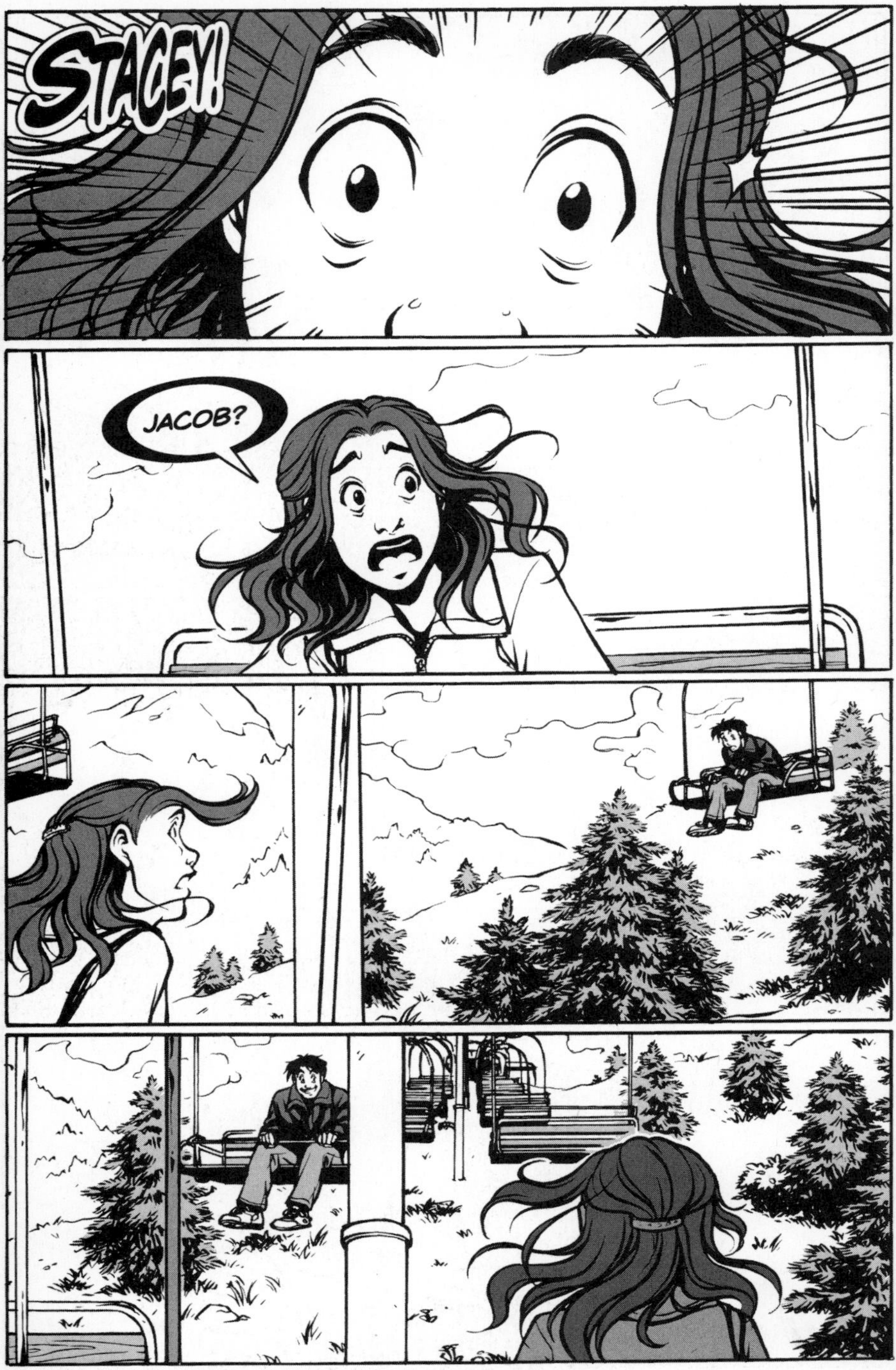
STACEY!
JACOB?

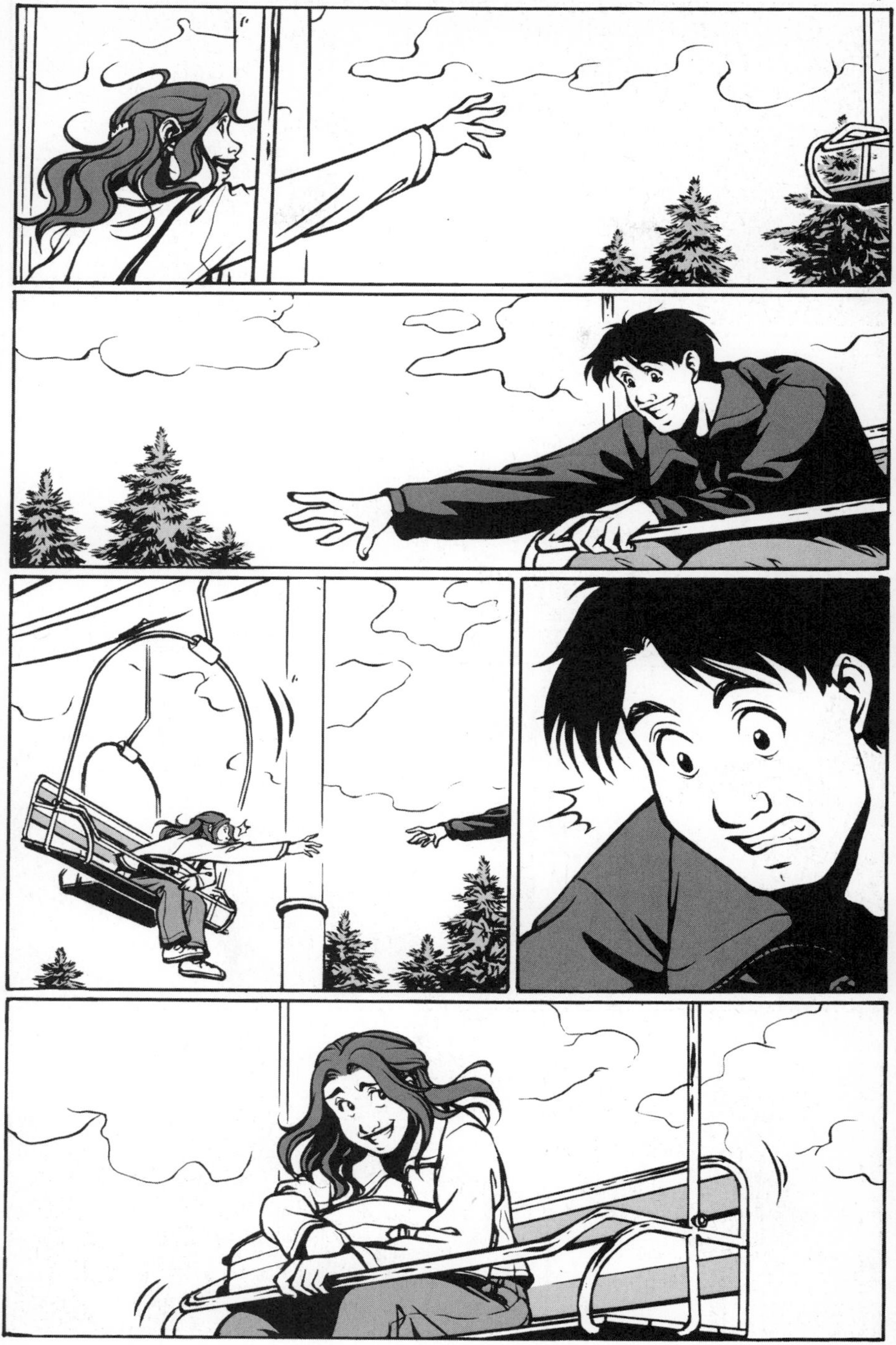

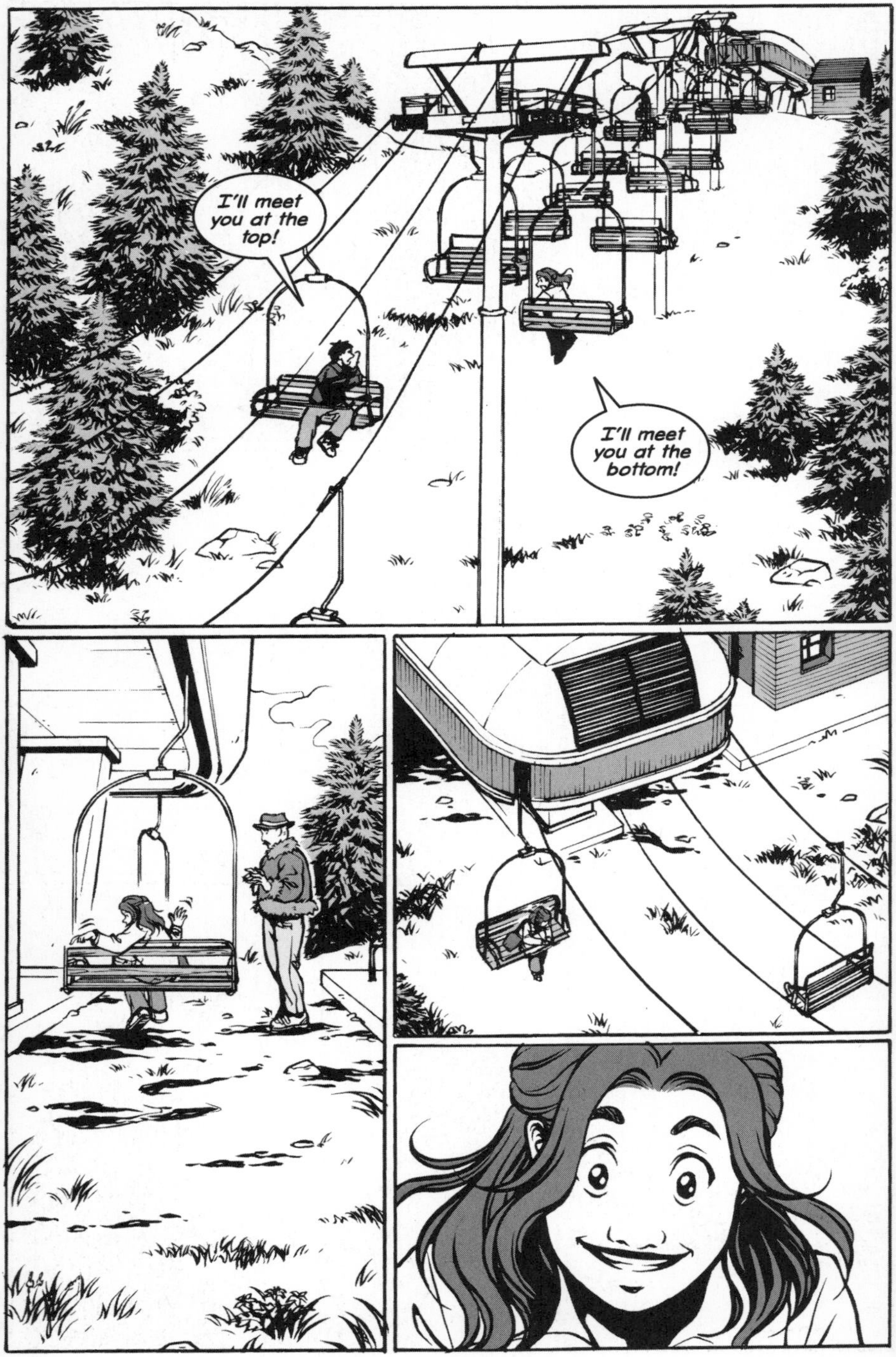
I'll meet you at the top!
I'll meet you at the bottom!

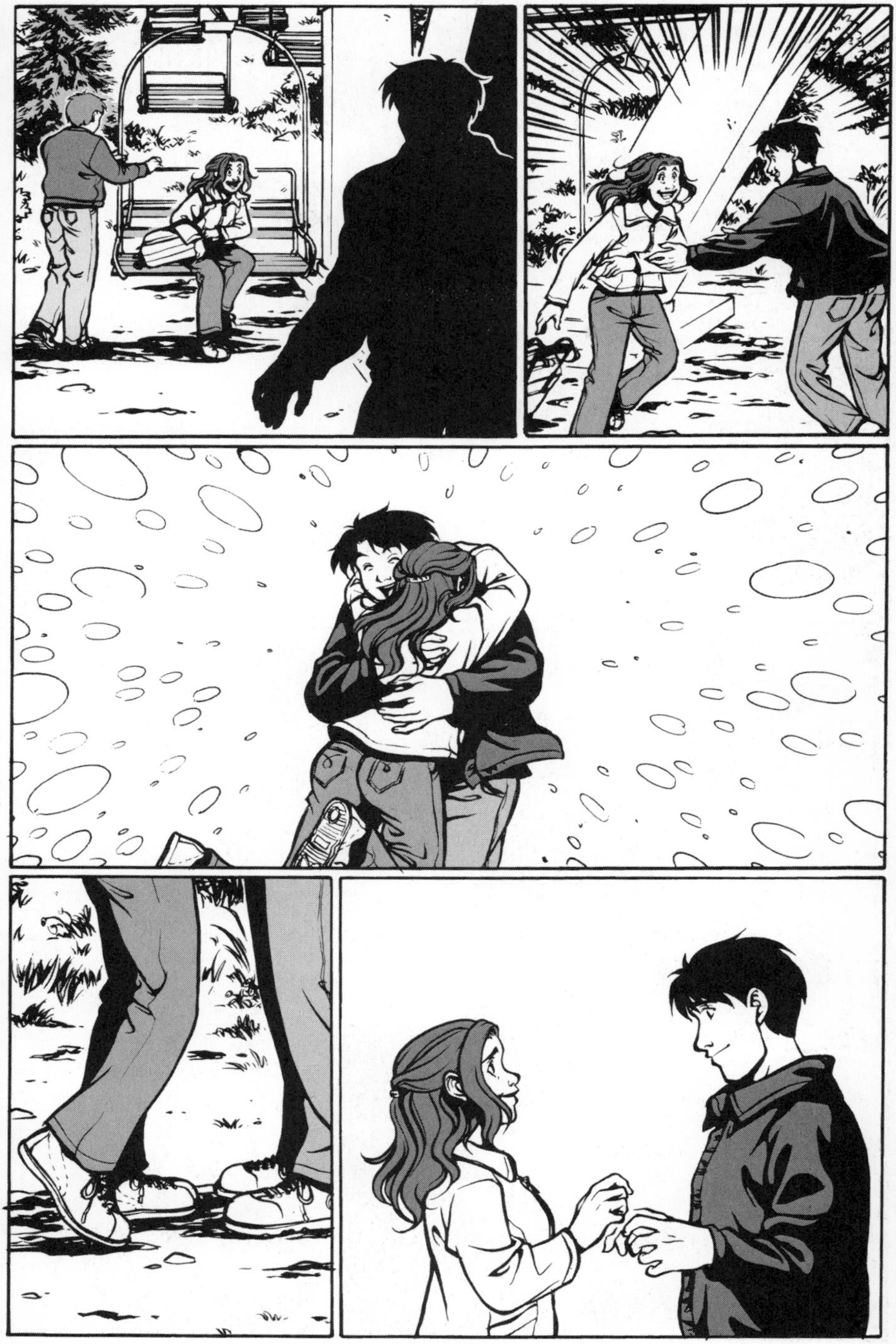

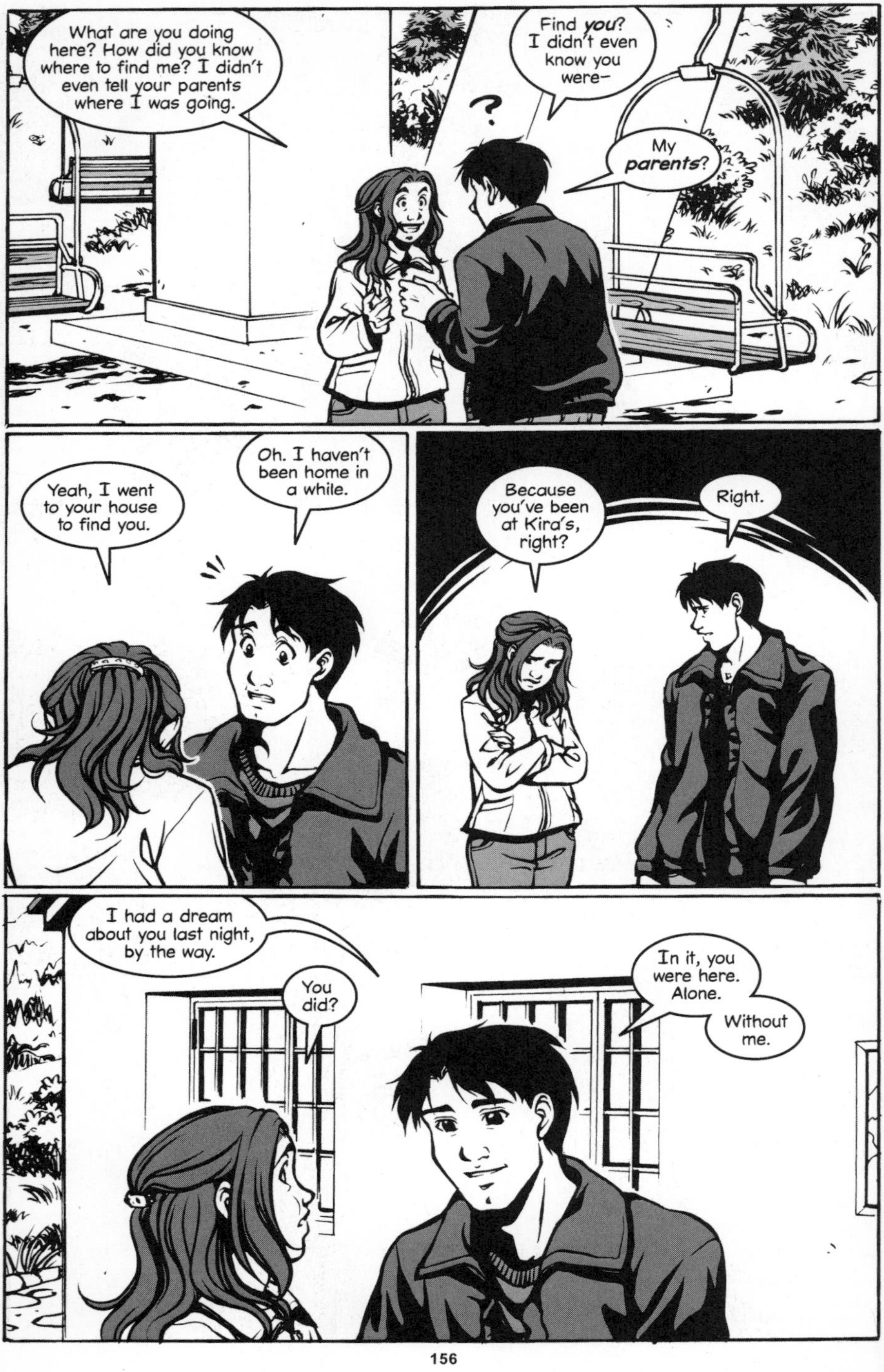
What are you doing here? How did you know where to find me? I didn't even tell your parents where I was going.
Find *you*? I didn't even know you were–
?
My *parents*?
Yeah, I went to your house to find you.
Oh. I haven't been home in a while.
Because you've been at Kira's, right?
Right.
I had a dream about you last night, by the way.
You did?
In it, you were here. Alone.
Without me.

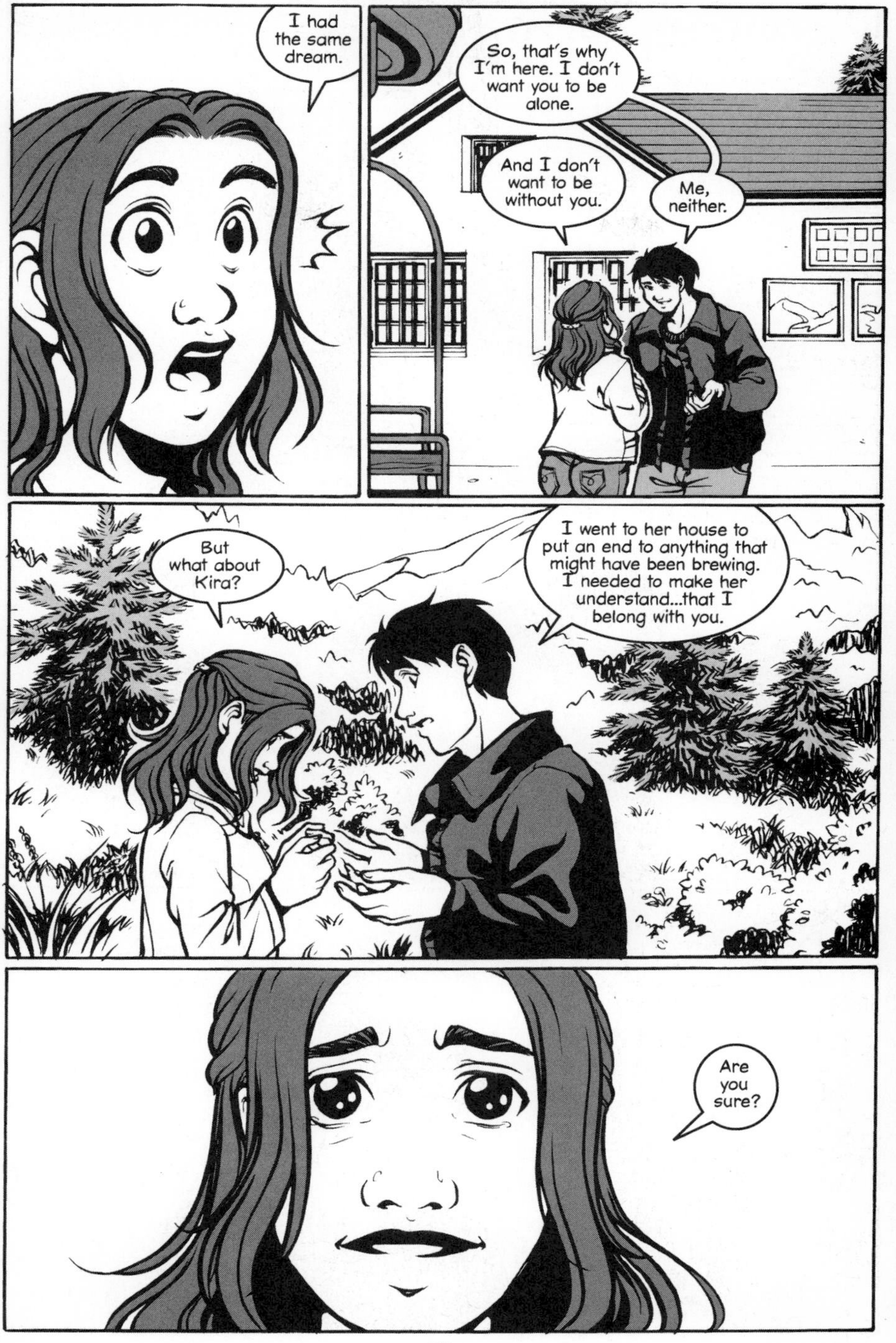
I had the same dream.
So, that's why I'm here. I don't want you to be alone.
And I don't want to be without you.
Me, neither.
But what about Kira?
I went to her house to put an end to anything that might have been brewing. I needed to make her understand...that I belong with you.
Are you sure?

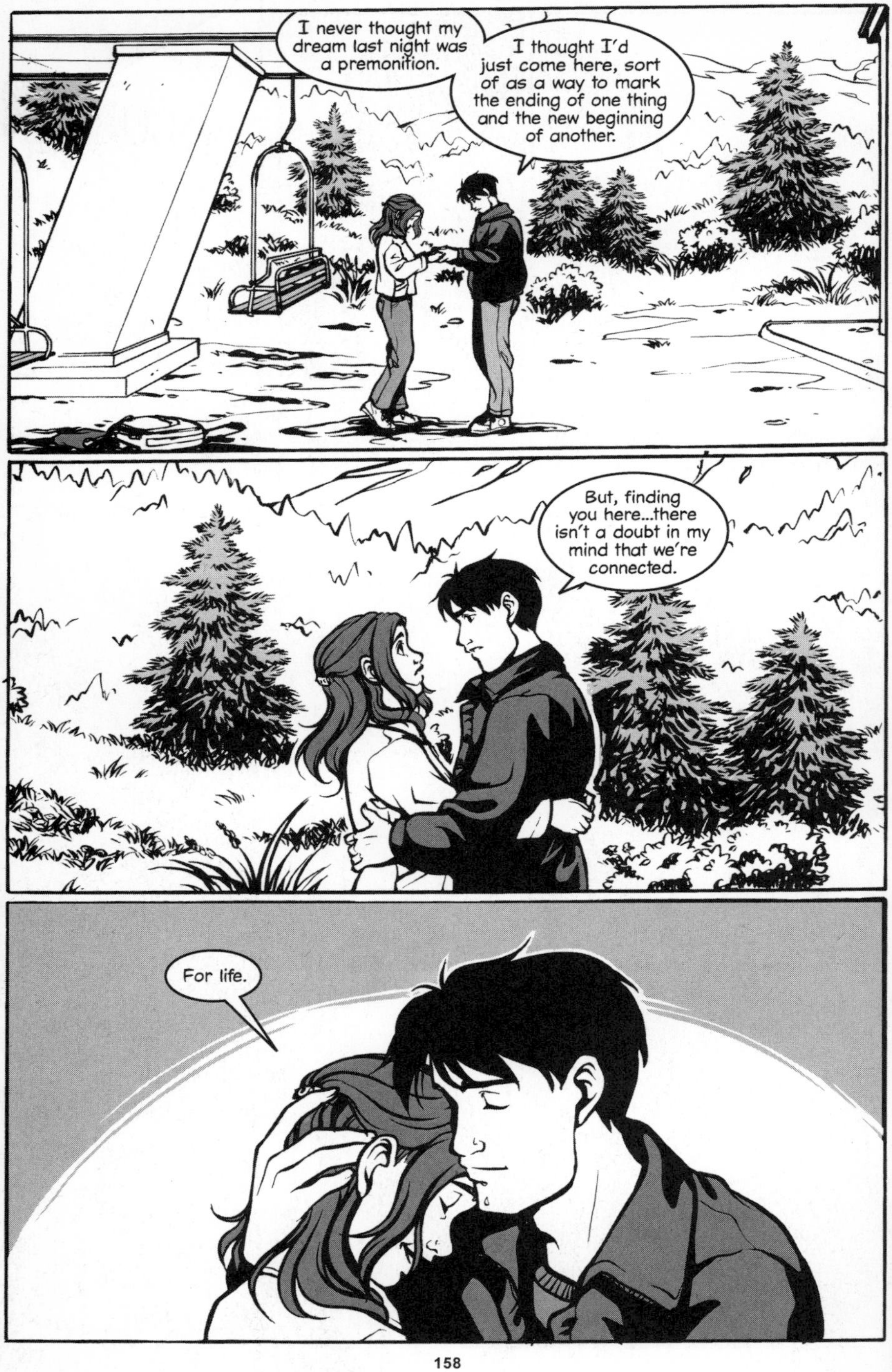
I never thought my dream last night was a premonition.
I thought I'd just come here, sort of as a way to mark the ending of one thing and the new beginning of another.
But, finding you here...there isn't a doubt in my mind that we're connected.
For life.

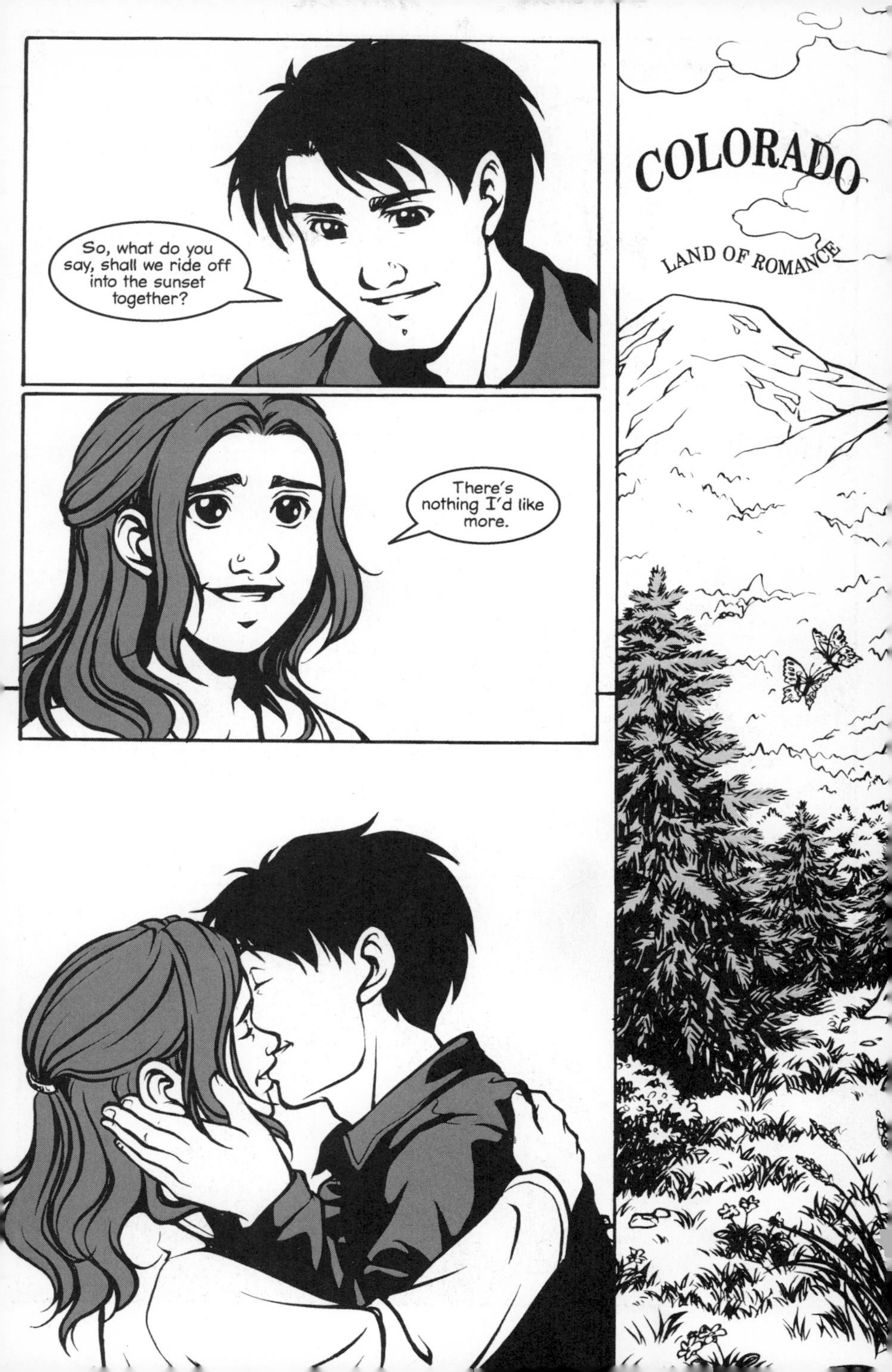
So, what do you say, shall we ride off into the sunset together?
There's nothing I'd like more.
COLORADO
LAND OF ROMANCE

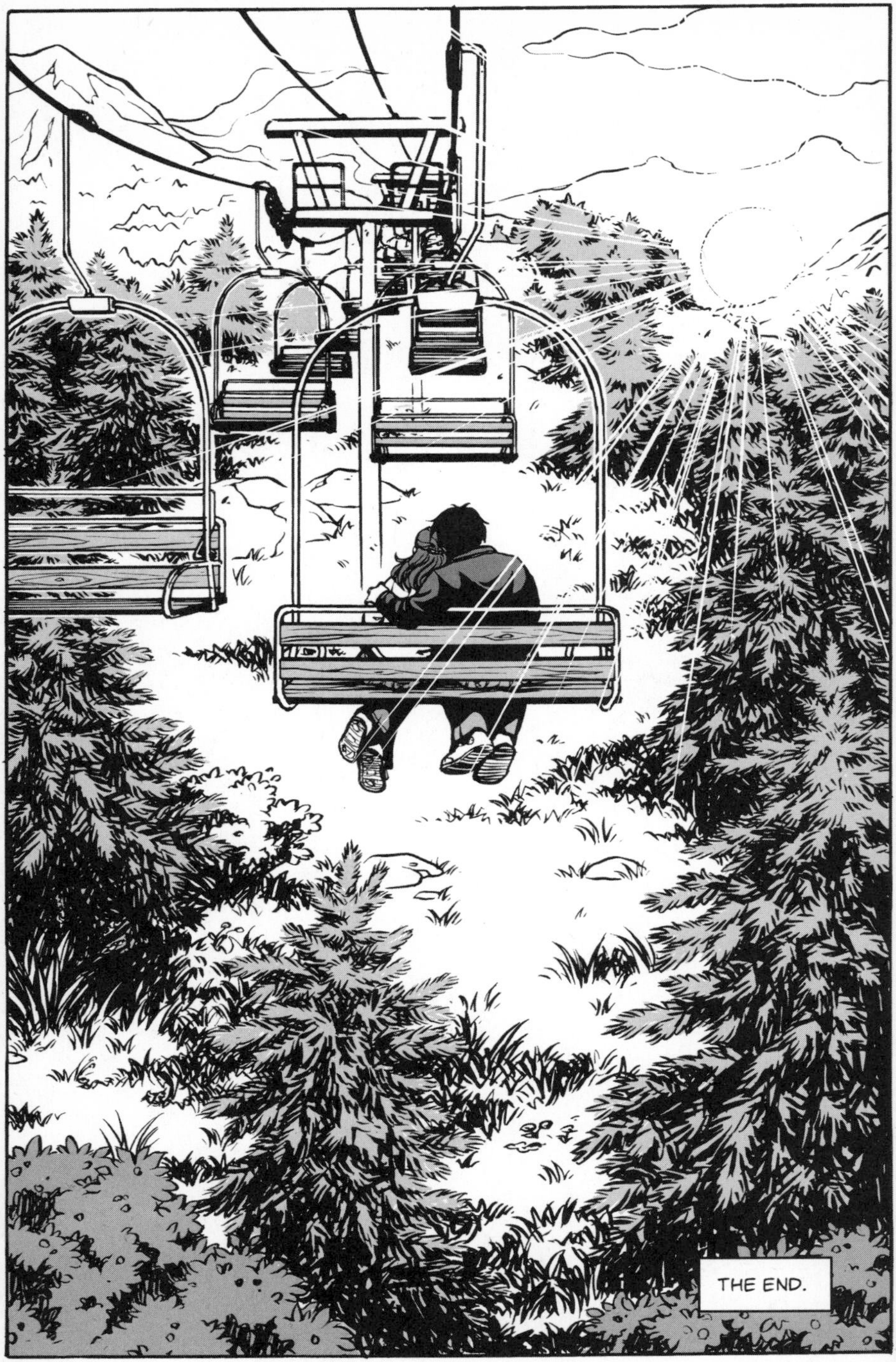
THE END.

Acknowledgments

First and foremost, I want to thank my former editor Megan Atwood, who, seven years ago, took a chance on my first novel, *Blue is for Nightmares*. I am forever indebted to your vision and enthusiasm for my work. Thanks also to Andrew Karre, who inspired me with the idea of writing a graphic novel.

Thanks to my editor Brian Farrey, my agent Kathryn Green, Lee Nordling and Barbara Randall Kesel at The Pack, the entire Llewellyn Publications family, and especially to my readers—all of whom have made this project possible. It has certainly been a pleasure, and I am so very, truly grateful.

THE CREATORS

Laurie Faria Stolarz's bestselling series started with *Blue is for Nightmares* and continued with *White is for Magic, Silver is for Secrets,* and *Red is for Remembrance.* She grew up in Salem, Massachusetts.

Script art director **Barbara Randall Kesel** is a comic book writer and editor who has worked on staff at DC Comics, Dark Horse Comics, and CrossGen Comics. Her editorial credits include *Hellboy, Star Wars,* and *Aliens.*

Artist **Janina Görrissen** studied the comic arts in Barcelona, Spain. Her work includes *Kairi,* a manga for French publisher Les Humanoïdes Associés (Humanoids). *Black is for Beginnings* is Janina's first published project in the United States.

First Edition
First Printing, 2009

Written by Laurie Faria Stolarz
Adaptation by Barbara Randall Kesel
Artwork by Janina Görrissen
Letters by Scott O. Brown
Cover design by Llewellyn art department
Produced by The Pack

Flux, an imprint of Llewellyn Publications

Library of Congress Cataloging-in-Publication Data
(Pending)

Flux
Llewellyn Publications
A Division of Llewellyn Worldwide, Ltd.
2143 Wooddale Drive, Dept. 978-0-7387-1438-7
Woodbury, MN 55125-2989, U.S.A.
www.fluxnow.com

Printed in the United States of America